THÉRÈSE

François Mauriac was born in Bordeaux on 11 October 1885. He was a brilliant pupil, studying first with the Mariantes at Caudéran, then at a lycée, and finally at the Faculté des Lettres in Bordeaux and the École des Chartes in Paris. He started writing early and his poems appeared in the *Revue de temps présent*; in 1907 his literary career began with a book of poetry, *L'Adieu à l'adolescence*, and a novel, *L'Enfant chargé de chaines*.

In 1914 he married and was then mobilized to serve in the First World War with the Auxiliary Medical Squad in Thessalonica.

In 1932 François Mauriac became President of the Society for 'Gens de Lettres'; in 1933 he was elected a Member of the French Academy; and in 1936 he was made a Commander of the Legion of Honour. He wrote plays, poetry, biographies, criticism and some articles for the press; his main achievement lay in the novel, and in recognition of this he was awarded the Grand Prix du Roman for *Le Désert de l'amour* (1925), and in 1952 received the Nobel Prize for Literature. He died in 1970.

Mauriac has been described as a master of plot and technique. In the words of one critic his work shows 'the true importance of love, charity and frailty even in the most arid of human situations'.

Penguin have also published *The Knot of Vipers*, *The Frontenac Mystery*, *The Desert of Love* and *A Woman of the Pharisees*.

François Mauriac

THÉRÈSE

*

containing

Thérèse Desqueyroux

Thérèse chez le docteur

Thérèse à l'hôtel

La Fin de la nuit

*

**Translated by
Gerard Hopkins**

PENGUIN BOOKS

PENGUIN BOOKS

Published by the Penguin Group
Penguin Books Ltd, 27 Wrights Lane, London W8 5TZ, England
Penguin Putnam Inc., 375 Hudson Street, New York, New York 10014, USA
Penguin Books Australia Ltd, Ringwood, Victoria, Australia
Penguin Books Canada Ltd, 10 Alcorn Avenue, Toronto, Ontario, Canada M4V 3B2
Penguin Books (NZ) Ltd, Private Bag 102902, NSMC, Auckland, New Zealand

Penguin Books Ltd, Registered Offices: Harmondsworth, Middlesex, England

Thérèse Desqueyroux was first published in 1927, the English translation in 1928
Thérèse chez le docteur and *Thérèse à l'hotel* were first published in *Plongées* in 1928, the English
translations in 1947
La Fin de la nuit was first published in 1935, the English translation in 1947
This collection first published by Eyre & Spottiswoode 1947
Published in Penguin Books 1959
15 17 19 20 18 16

Translations copyright © Eyre Methuen Ltd, 1972
All rights reserved

Printed in England by Clays Ltd, St Ives plc
Set in Monotype Garamond

CONTENTS

*

THÉRÈSE DESQUEYROUX

*

FOREWORD

Seigneur, ayez pitié, ayez pitié des fous et des
folles! Ô Créateur! peut-il exister des
monstres aux yeux de celui-là seul qui sait
pourquoi ils existent, *comment ils se sont faits,*
et comment ils auraient pu ne pas se faire. ...

CHARLES BAUDELAIRE

MANY, *Thérèse, will say that you do not exist. But I who for so
many years have watched you closely, have sometimes stopped you
in your walks, and now lay bare your secret, I know that you do.*

*I remember, as a young man, seeing you in a stuffy Court-room, at
the mercy of lawyers whose hearts were less hard than those of the over-
dressed women on the public benches. Your small face was white, your
lips scarcely visible.*

*Later still, I came on you again in a country drawing-room, a young
and ravaged woman plagued by the attentive care of aged relatives and a
foolish husband. 'What's wrong with her?' they said; 'haven't we
given her all that a girl could want?'*

*Often, since then, seeing that rather too large hand raised to your
high and lovely brow, I have been filled with wonder: often have
watched you prisoned behind that family barrier, prowling like a she-
wolf, and caught your sad, malevolent eye fixed full upon me.*

*Many will feel surprise that I should give imagined life to a creature
more odious than any character in my other books. Why, they will ask,
have I never anything to say of those who ooze with virtue and wear
their hearts upon their sleeves? People who 'wear their hearts upon
their sleeves' have no story for me to tell, but I know the secrets of the
hearts that are deep buried in, and mingled with, the filth of flesh.*

*I could have wished, Thérèse, that sorrow might have turned your
heart to God, and have long desired to see you worthy of the name of
Saint Locusta.* But had I shown you thus redeemed there would have*

* Locusta was a notorious woman poisoner who lived in Rome during
the reign of the Emperor Nero. Monsieur Mauriac's thought is here compressed and difficult. The implied argument would seem to run as follows:
Thérèse, like Locusta, was a poisoner. But great sinners may, with the gift
of Grace, become great saints. My wish was that Thérèse, by virtue of
repentance, should attain sanctity, and, had she done so, she might well
have been known as Saint Locusta. – TRANSLATOR

been no lack of readers to raise a cry of sacrilege, even though they may hold as an article of Faith the Fall and Ransom of our torn and twisted natures.

I take my leave of you upon a city's pavements, hoping, at least, that you will not for ever be utterly alone.

F. M.

Thérèse Desqueyroux

I

THE barrister opened a door. Thérèse Desqueyroux, in that out-of-the-way corridor of the Court-house, felt the fog upon her face and took deep breaths of it. She was afraid lest someone might be there to meet her, and held back. A man with his coat collar turned up moved out from the shadow of a plane-tree. She recognized her father.

'Case dismissed!' called the barrister; and then, turning to her:

'You can come out: there's no one here.'

She went down the damp steps. True, the small square seemed utterly deserted. Her father did not kiss her. He did not even look at her, but addressed a question to the barrister, Duros, who answered in a low voice, as though he were afraid of being overhead. The words they spoke came to her, but not plainly.

'Tomorrow I shall be officially notified that the case has been dismissed.'

'No danger of any last-minute surprises?'

'Not the least in the world. We've got it, as they say, served up on a plate.'

'After my son-in-law's evidence it was a foregone conclusion.'

'Hardly that – one can never be quite certain.'

'Once they'd got him to admit that he never counted his drops ...'

'But in cases of this kind, you know, Larroque, the evidence of the victim ...'

Thérèse spoke in a loud voice:

'There was no victim.'

'Victim of his own carelessness, I meant, Madame.'

For a brief instant the two men looked at the young woman standing there huddled in her coat. Her pale face was quite expressionless. She asked where the carriage was. Her father had told it to wait for them on the Budos road, outside the town, so as to avoid attracting attention.

They crossed the Square. Plane leaves were sticking to the damp benches. Fortunately, at this time of the year, the days were short, and their walk to the Budos road led them through some of the least frequented streets to be found thereabouts. Thérèse was between the two men. She was a head taller than either. They continued to discuss the case as though she had not been there. But her physical presence incommoded them, and they jostled her continually. She dropped back a few paces. She took off her left-hand glove and began picking at the moss which grew between the old stones of the walls they passed. Now and then a workman came by on a bicycle or a waggon. She had to flatten herself against the wall so as not to be spattered with mud. In the dim light nobody recognized her. The smell of fog and of baking bread was not merely the ordinary evening smell of an insignificant country town, it was the sweet savour of life given back to her at long last. She closed her eyes and breathed deeply of the perfume of the sleeping earth, of the wet, green grass. She tried not to listen to the little man with the short legs who never once addressed his daughter. She might have fallen into the ditch, and neither he nor Duros would have noticed it. They were no longer afraid to raise their voices.

'Monsieur Desqueyroux's evidence was first-rate. But the prescription might have made things difficult. The point was, had it, or had it not, been forged? ... Don't forget it was Dr Pédemay who laid the charge. ...'

'But he withdrew it. ...'

'All the same, her explanation ... that story of the prescription having been given her by a stranger ...'

Less because she was tired than in order to avoid hearing all this talk with which she had been deafened for weeks past, Thérèse began to walk more and more slowly. But it was useless. She could not help hearing her father's falsetto tones.

'I kept on telling her that she must cook up something better than that. Any story, I said, would be an improvement on the one she had. ...'

All that, of course, was perfectly true, and he could claim full credit for the part he had played. But why must he still harp on the subject? What he was so fond of calling the 'family honour' was safe. By the time the elections for the Senate came round the whole business would have been forgotten.

So ran Thérèse's thoughts. All she wanted was to keep well away from the two men. But so hot was their argument that they stopped dead in the middle of the road, gesticulating.

'The best thing you can do, Larroque, is to come out into the open. Take the offensive in the Sunday edition of *Le Semeur*. Or, I'll do it for you, if you'd rather. You want a good headline – "A Scandalous Rumour" – something like that ...'

'My dear chap, what's the point? It's perfectly obvious that the whole thing's been dropped. They didn't even bother to call a handwriting expert. Much better say nothing, and let it die of inanition. There's nothing I'd like better than to hit back ... but for the family's sake we've got to hush the whole business up. ...'

They were walking more quickly now, and Thérèse did not hear Duros's answer. Once more she breathed in the damp night air like someone threatened with suffocation. Suddenly there rose before her inner eye the face of Julie Bellade, the maternal grandmother whom she had never seen: never seen even in representation, for she might have sought in vain among the family possessions of the Larroques or the Desqueyroux for a portrait, a daguerreotype, a photograph of the woman about whom she knew only that one day she had just vanished. It occurred to her that she too might have been blotted out from human memory, completely obliterated, so that her own daughter, her little Marie, might never, in days to come, have found so much as a picture of the woman who had brought her into the world. As like as not, at this very moment, the child was fast asleep in her room at Argelouse, the house which she would reach late that night. There, in the darkness, the young mother would hear the even breathing of her slumbering child, would lean above the bed and drink down, like a draught of cool, refreshing water, the small sleeping life.

A barouche with its hood closed was standing drawn in to the edge of the ditch. The flanks of the two horses showed skinny in the lamplight. Beyond, to right and left, a wall of forest trees shut in the road. The summits of the nearer pines met above the twin strips of grassy verge, and beneath the arch thus formed the highway drove mysteriously on. Amid the tangle of high branches the sky had cleared for itself a twig-encumbered couch. The coachman stared at Thérèse with an expression of greedy curiosity. When she asked him whether they would get to Nizan station in time to catch the last train, he reassured her, but added that they had better get going.

'It's the last time I shall put you to all this trouble, Gardère.'

'They've finished with you, then, ma'am?'

She nodded her head. The man's eyes were still devouring her. Must she be stared at like this all the rest of her life?

'You must be very pleased, ma'am?'

Her father seemed, at long last, to have become aware of her presence. She took a hurried glance at his grubby, bilious face, at the stiff little yellowish-white bristles that covered his cheeks and stood out startlingly in the lamplight. She said in a low voice: 'I've been through so much. ... I'm at the end of my tether ...' then stopped. What was the use of talking? He wasn't listening, wasn't even looking at her. Much *he* cared about what she might be feeling. The only thing that mattered to him was his progress along the road that was to lead eventually to the Senate. Because of *her* he had met with a check, had seen his chance imperilled (all women are either fools or hysterical). Luckily, her name was no longer Larroque. She was a Desqueyroux now. At least she wouldn't have to face the Assizes. Thinking of that, he breathed more freely. His enemies, of course, would do their best to keep the wound from healing. What steps could he take about that? He must have a word with the Prefect tomorrow. It was fortunate that he'd got such a hold on the editor of *La Lande Conservatrice* ... the man had been playing about with girls once too often. ...

He took Thérèse by the arm: 'In with you, now: we mustn't dawdle.'

The barrister, in response, perhaps, to the sudden prompt-ings of malice, or perhaps simply because he did not want to see her go off without his having exchanged a word with her, chose this moment to ask whether she would be seeing Mon-sieur Bernard Desqueyroux that evening.

'Naturally,' she said – 'my husband is expecting me.'

As she uttered the words she realized for the first time since leaving the Court that in a few hours from now she would be actually entering the room where her husband lay, still far from well: that there was an indefinite vista of days opening before her, and of nights that she must spend with him for ever at her side.

Since the trial began she had been living with her father on the outskirts of the little town. More than once she had made the same trip as that on which she was now embarked. But on previous occasions she had been concerned only to give her husband precise instructions, only to understand exactly what it was that Duros was saying, as she got into the carriage, about the answers that Monsieur Desqueyroux must have ready when next he was called to give evidence. She had felt no pain, no sense of embarrassment at the thought of seeing the sick man. What then had been at issue between them was not what had happened in the past, but only what should now be said or left unsaid. This need for concocting a defence had brought husband and wife closer together than they had ever been before. They were of one flesh – the flesh of their little daughter Marie. Over and over again they had rehearsed together the story they had built up for the Judge's benefit. It was simple, well-knit, proof against all subtle attacks of logic. It had been the same carriage then as now. But how im-patient she had been on those occasions, how eager to finish a journey which now she wished would go on for ever! Hardly she remembered, had she taken her seat than she had longed to be already in that room at Argelouse. Again and again she would go over in her mind the instructions for which Bernard was waiting (how, for instance, he was not to be nervous about admitting that she had told him one evening of the stranger who had asked her to get a prescription made up for him, giving as an excuse the explanation that he owed the chemist money, and dared not go himself ... though Duros had been of the opinion that he had better not go so far as to say that he had blamed his wife for being imprudent). ...

But what would there be to talk about now that the nightmare was over? She could see in imagination the house in which he lay waiting – a lost and hidden place buried in a wild countryside. She had a vision of the bed standing in the middle of the stone-flagged room, of the lamp burning low amid the litter of newspapers and medicine-bottles on the table. The watchdogs, roused by the sound of the carriage, would bark awhile and then fall silent. ... All round them would be the solemn country stillness, as on those other nights when she had sat there gazing at Bernard as he struggled with his spasms of nausea. She forced herself to contemplate the immediate future, the way in which they would look at one another when they met – and then the prospect of the night ahead, the morrow, and all the days and weeks which lay before them in that house at Argelouse, with the need removed to build up a plausible version of the drama of their lives. Between them, from now on, would lie not fiction but reality. ... She was seized with sudden panic. Her face turned to the lawyer; but, addressing her words to the older man, she began to stammer:

'I expect to spend a few days with my husband, after which, if the improvement in his health is maintained, I shall come back here to my father. ...'

'You'll do nothing of the sort, my girl!' Gardère began to fidget on his box, and Monsieur Larroque lowered his voice:

'Have you completely taken leave of your senses? Abandon your husband at a moment like this? You've got to stick together from now on, till death do you part. ...'

'You're perfectly right, Papa – I don't know what I could have been thinking of to talk like that. You'll come to Argelouse, then, I take it?'

'I shall expect you as usual, Thérèse, on market days. You

will come and see me then, as you always have done in the past.'

It was extraordinary that she could not see how the least breach in the accustomed routine would blow everything sky-high. It must be clearly understood. He trusted that he could rely upon her. She had brought enough trouble on the family already. ...

'You will obey your husband. That is the best advice I can give you.'

And with these words he pushed her into the carriage.

Thérèse saw the lawyer's hand, with its coarse black nails, extended towards her.

'All's well that ends well,' he said: and he meant it. If the trial had been carried to a higher Court it would have done *him* no good. The family would have briefed Maître Peyrecave of the Bordeaux Bar. Yes, all's well ...

2

THÉRÈSE dearly loved the musty smell of worn leather in old carriages. ... She had forgotten her cigarettes, but found comfort in the knowledge that she never enjoyed smoking in the dark. The lamps revealed the grassy verges of the road, a fringe of bracken, the bottom part of the trunks of monster pines. Heaps of stones broke the shadow of the moving vehicle. Sometimes a country waggon passed, the mules automatically keeping to the right without any movement of their dozing driver. It seemed to her that she would never get to Argelouse. She hoped that she would not. More than an hour's drive to Nizan station, then the little local train with its endless stops at every intermediate Halt. Even when they got to Saint-Clair there would be six more miles to cover in the trap (the road was so bad that no car would face it in the darkness) before Argelouse was reached. At any or all of these stages on her journey destiny might intervene to save her. The day before the verdict was to be given she had been obsessed by the thought of what would happen should the

case go against her, had felt as one alert to an impending
earthquake; and now she let her mind play about the selfsame fantasy. She took off her hat, let her small, pale head
bump against the smelly leather cushion, and surrendered her
body to their jolting progress. Until this evening she had been
living the life of a hunted creature. Now that her safety was
assured she realized the degree of her exhaustion. With her
hollow cheeks and prominent cheek-bones, with her lips
parted as though for breath, and her high, magnificent forehead, she looked like a woman condemned – even though her
fellow-men had found her guiltless – condemned to an eternity
of loneliness. Her charm – so the world had said once – was
irresistible. Yet it was no more than all possess whose faces
would betray a secret torment, the throbbing of an inner
wound, did they not wear themselves out in a constant effort
to deceive. Deep in the recesses of this bumping carriage,
moving along a road sliced through the dense darkness of the
pines, sat a young woman, all defences down, gently stroking
with her right hand her scorched and scalded face. Bernard's
lying evidence had saved her. What would be his first words
to her now? Tonight, naturally, he would ask no questions ...
but tomorrow? Thérèse closed her eyes, then opened them
again as the horses slowed to a walk. She tried to recognize
this lift in the road. Much better not try to anticipate events,
and easier, perhaps, than she had thought. Let the future look
after itself. Sleep. ... Why was she no longer in the carriage?
Who was that man seated at a green-baize desk? ... The
examining magistrate ... that ever recurring face. ... He knew
well enough that the whole defence was a put-up affair. His
head moved from right to left. She was not to be discharged
after all. A new fact had come to light. A new fact? She turned
away lest the enemy see her ravaged countenance. 'Cast your
mind back, Madame. You mentioned an old cape which you
never use except when you go duck-shooting in October.
Are you sure there was nothing in the inside pocket? – nothing
you had forgotten? Nothing you had concealed?' Useless to
protest her innocence. She felt as though she were suffocating.
Without, for a single moment, taking his eyes from his prey,

the magistrate laid upon the desk a tiny package closed with a red seal. In harsh, incisive tones he began to read the formula written on the label. She knew it already by heart:

Chloroform	..	..	..	.. 30 grams
Aconite drops	..	..	..	.. 20
Digitalin sol.	..	..	..	.. 20 grams

The magistrate burst into a cackle of laughter ... the brake began to grate against the wheel: Thérèse woke up. Her lungs drew in great gulps of the misty air (they must be on the slope leading down to the stream). She used to have just such dreams when she was a girl, only then they had been about some mistake she had made in her examination, a mistake which meant that she would have to take School Certificate all over again. Tonight she felt the same relief from oppression as when, long years ago, she had woken from that particular nightmare, though she was conscious still of a faint uneasiness at the thought that her discharge had not yet been given its official form. 'Don't be silly. You know perfectly well that it will have to be notified first to your Counsel. ...'

Free ... what more could she want? It would be mere child's play to reach a *modus vivendi* with Bernard. She must be absolutely frank with him. Nothing must be left unsaid: that way, and that way only, lay salvation. All that was hidden must be brought into the light of day – and at once, tonight. Having made up her mind on this point, she was conscious of a flood of happiness. There would be time, before they reached Argelouse, for her to 'prepare her confession', as her pious friend Anne de la Trave used to say each Saturday at the time when they spent such happy holidays together. Little sister Anne, dear innocent, what an important part yours is in all this story! The really pure in heart know nothing of what goes on around them each day, each night; never realize what poisonous weeds spring up beneath their childish feet.

The dear little thing had been right when she said to Thérèse – at that time a mocking, argumentative schoolgirl: 'You've no idea how *light* one feels after telling everything and getting absolution – how lovely it is to know that the past has been wiped out, and that one can begin all over again with a clean slate.' Merely to have decided to make a clean breast of everything was enough now to give Thérèse a sense of bonds relaxed. It was a delicious sensation. 'Bernard shall know all: I'll tell him.'

What should she tell him? What should be her first confession? Could mere words ever make comprehensible that confused, inevitable conglomeration of desires, determinations, and actions unforeseen? How do those act who *know* the crimes they are committing? ... 'I *didn't* know. I never wanted to do that with which I am charged. I don't know what I *did* want. I never had the slightest idea to what that frantic urge inside me, yet outside too, was working, what destruction it would sow in its frantic progress. No one was more terrified of it than I was. ...'

A smoky paraffin lamp cast a light on the roughcast wall of the station at Nizan, and on the stationary cab. (How quickly the darkness flowed back and filled the world beyond the range of its beams!)

From a train standing at the platform came the melancholy sound of lowing, bleating animals. Gardère took Thérèse's bag and, once again, his eyes ate up her face. His wife must have given him a strict injunction to see 'how she takes it, and what she looks like'. ... Instinctively, Thérèse produced for Monsieur Larroque's coachman that famous smile of hers which led people to say: 'It never occurs to one to consider whether she's pretty or ugly. One just surrenders to her charm.' She asked him to take a ticket for her, because she felt nervous about walking through the waiting-room where two farmers' wives were seated, their baskets on their knees, their heads nodding, busy with their knitting. When he brought the ticket back she told him he could keep the change. He touched his hat, and then, gathering up the reins, turned for one last stare at his master's daughter.

The train was not yet made up. In the old days, Thérèse Larroque and Anne de la Trave, going off for the holidays, or returning at the beginning of term, had always thoroughly

enjoyed this stop at Nizan. They used to eat fried eggs and
bacon at the inn, and then, their arms round one another's
waist, walk along the road which tonight looked so dark and
threatening, though in that long dead time it had always, in
Thérèse's memory, been white beneath the moon. They had
laughed to see the mingling of their long black shadows, and
talked, no doubt, the while about their schools, their friends,
their mistresses – the one all eagerness in defence of her
Convent, the other of her College. ... 'Anne!' Thérèse cried
the name aloud into the darkness. It was of her that she must
first tell Bernard ... Bernard, that most precise of men, who
was never satisfied until he had labelled, ranged, and set aside
each separate emotion, ignoring their gradations, the subtle
nexus of their interchange. How make him see with his own
eyes that world of shifting forms in which Thérèse had lived
and suffered? It had got to be done somehow. The only
possible way would be to go straight to his room, to sit down
on his bed, to lead him gently on from stage to stage, until
at last she reached the point at which he would stop her with a
'*Now I* understand. Get up: you are forgiven.'

She tiptoed across the station-master's garden, smelling the
chrysanthemums although she could not see them. There was
no one in the first-class compartment which she entered, and,
in any case, the light from the lamp would have been too dim
to show her face. Impossible to read. But compared with her
own terrible existence all inventions of the novelist would
have seemed thin and colourless. She might die of shame, of
anguish, of remorse, of weariness but certainly she would
not die of boredom. She withdrew into one corner of the
carriage and closed her eyes. Surely a woman of her intelligence must be able to make the drama of her life intelligible to
another? Of course she could. Once let her pursue her confession to its end, and Bernard would raise her to her feet and
say: 'Let it be, Thérèse; leave worrying now. In this house of
Argelouse we will wait for death together, without trying
to unravel what is over and done. I am thirsty. Please go down
to the kitchen and make me some orangeade – with your own
hands. I will drink it at a draught, no matter how thick it

may look. What matter if its taste remind me of that morning cup of chocolate? Do you remember how sick I was, beloved? Your dear hand held my head. When I brought up all that green vomit, you did not turn away your eyes. My retchings did not frighten you. Yet how pale you looked that night when my legs went dead and lost all feeling. I shivered, do you remember? – and how staggered that fool Dr Pédemay was when he found my temperature so low, my pulse so irregular. ...'

'Ah!' thought Thérèse: 'he won't have understood. I shall have to begin again from the beginning ...' But what is the beginning where our actions are concerned? Our destiny, once we begin to try to isolate it, is like those plants which we can never dig up with all their roots intact. Would she find it necessary to go back to her childhood? But even our childhood is, in a sense, an end, a completion.

Thérèse's childhood. However sullied the stream, there is snow at its source. At school she had seemed withdrawn, a stranger to the trivial tragedies which played such havoc with her friends. The mistresses often held her up as an example. 'Thérèse asks no reward other than the joy which comes of knowing that one has achieved superior virtue. Her conscience is the light by which she lives, and it is enough. Her pride in belonging to an élite has more power to control her conduct than any fear of punishment. ...' In some such words had one of her teachers expressed herself. But Thérèse wondered, now: 'Was I really so happy, so innocent of guile? Everything which dates from before my marriage I see now as bathed in a light of purity – doubtless because that time stands out in such vivid contrast to the indelible filth of my wedded life. Looked at from the point where I now stand as wife and mother, College has all the glamour of a paradise. But at the time I did not see it so. How could I possibly have known that during those years before life had properly begun for me I was, in fact, living my true life? Pure? – Yes, I certainly was that; an angel? – perhaps, but an angel torn by passions. No matter what my mistresses might say, I suffered and made others suffer too. I delighted in the pain I caused – and knew at the hands of my friends. What then I experienced was undiluted suffering, unsoftened by remorse. Joys and agonies came to me from even the most innocent of pleasures.'

Her reward had been, when the dog days came, to feel herself worthy of Anne with whom she walked beneath the oaks at Argelouse. She had felt she must be able to say to the young pupil of the Sacred Heart: 'I can be as pure as you without all those good-conduct ribbons and all the hackneyed vocabulary of virtue. ...' Anne de la Trave was pure mainly because she was ignorant. The Ladies of the Sacred Heart hung a thousand veils between their little charges and reality. Thérèse despised them for confounding virtue with ignorance. 'You know nothing of life, darling ...' she had been wont to say in those summer days at Argelouse so long ago.

Such lovely summer days! ... Seated in the little train which now at last had started to move, she admitted to herself that she must go back in thought to them, if she was ever to see clearly what had happened. It might be incredible, but it was true, all the same, that the storms of life were already gathering above the innocent beauty of those dawn days. The morning air, too limpid and too blue – bad omen for the afternoon and evening, a warning of ravaged garden beds, of branches torn and broken of mud and filth. Never at any moment of her life had she planned her road or looked ahead. Not once had she made a sudden change of direction. The slow descent had been barely noticeable: only gradually had the pace increased. The lost woman that now she was could be seen as no different from the radiant girl who had lived those happy summers in that very Argelouse to which, at the end of all, she was creeping back, glad of the dark, concealing night.

What weariness! Could there be any point in searching out the secret springs of actions now fulfilled? Through the glass of the window she could see nothing but the reflection of her lifeless face. The rhythm of the wheels checked suddenly: there was a prolonged whistle from the engine as it nosed its way with care into a station. A lantern dangling from an outstretched arm, thick local voices, the squeal of young

pigs being unloaded. Uzeste already! One more station, and
they would be at Saint-Clair, and then there would be nothing
between her and Argelouse but the last stage in the trap.
How little time Thérèse had left in which to prepare her
defence!

3

ARGELOUSE is, quite literally, a 'land's end', a place beyond
which it is impossible to go, the sort of settlement which, in
this part of the world, is called a 'holding' – just a few farmsteads, without church, administrative centre, or graveyard,
scattered loosely round an acre or so of rye, and joined by a
single ill-kept road to the market-town of Saint-Clair, six
miles away. This road, with its ruts and potholes, peters out
beyond Argelouse into a number of sandy tracks. From there,
right on to the coast, is nothing but marshland – fifty miles of
it – brackish ponds, sickly pines, and stretches of heath where
the sheep, at the winter's end, are the colour of dead ash. The
best families of Saint-Clair derived originally from this remote
and arid corner. Towards the middle of the last century, when
the grandfathers of men now living started to draw a certain
amount of revenue from timber and resin as well as from
livestock, the families began to establish themselves in Saint-
Clair, leaving their mansion-houses at Argelouse to deterior-
ate into working farms. Carved beam-ends and an occasional
marble chimney-piece bear witness to an ancient splendour.
Each year the buildings sag more and more beneath their
weight, and here and there can be seen one of the great roofs
drooping like the huge wing of an exhausted bird until it
looks almost as though it were resting on the ground.

But two of these decaying dwellings still house gentlefolk.
The Larroques and the Desqueyroux have left their homes at
Argelouse much as they took them over from their ancestors.
Jérôme Larroque, Mayor and member of the Town Council of
B— , close to which stands the house where he mostly lives,
would never consent to change anything on the Argelouse

property which he inherited from his wife (who died in child-bed while Thérèse was still a baby). It did not in the least surprise him that she should elect, as she grew older, to spend her holidays there. Each summer, at the beginning of July, she went to live in the house watched over by her father's eldest sister, Aunt Clara, a deaf old spinster who loved the solitude of this remote corner of the earth because, as she said, she was spared the sight of other people's lips silently moving, and knew that there was nothing to be heard but the sound of the wind in the pines. Monsieur Larroque was delighted to think that, in this way, he not only got rid of his daughter, but threw her into the company of Bernard Desqueyroux, whom, it had been arranged, she should some day marry, though as yet there had been no official betrothal.

Bernard Desqueyroux had inherited at Argelouse, from his father, a house which stood at no great distance from that of the Larroques. He never went there before the beginning of the shooting season, taking up residence only in October, when his whole occupation was stalking duck. In the winter this solid, level-headed young man went to Paris to pursue his law studies. In the summer he gave the minimum of time possible to his family. Victor de la Trave, whom his mother had taken as her second husband, got badly on his nerves. The man had not had 'a shilling to bless himself with', and his extravagances were the talk of Saint-Clair. Bernard found his half-sister, Anne, too young to be interesting, and it is doubtful whether he paid very much more attention to Thérèse. The neighbours looked on their marriage as a foregone con-clusion, because the two properties seemed made for fusion, and on this point the extremely commonsensical young man was of one mind with the neighbours. But he left nothing to chance and took considerable pride in the neat planning of his life. 'No one's unhappy unless he deserves to be ...' was a phrase constantly on the lips of this rather flabby youth. Up till the time of his marriage he divided his existence equally between work and pleasure. He enjoyed food, drink, and, especially, shooting, but he also, in his mother's words, 'worked like a slave'. For it was the duty of a husband to be better educated than his wife, and Thérèse had the reputation, even at an early age, of being remarkably intelligent. The general view was that she was an emancipated young woman. But Bernard knew how women can be brought to heel, and it would be no bad thing, as his mother constantly reminded him, 'to have a foot in both camps'. Old Larroque might be very useful to him. At twenty-six Bernard Desqueyroux, after travelling extensively, and with much preliminary planning, in Italy, Spain, and the Low Countries would marry the richest and the most intelligent, if not the prettiest, girl in the district: 'It never occurs to one to think whether she is pretty or ugly. One just surrenders to her charm.'

Thérèse smiled to herself as she conjured up this caricature of Bernard. 'If it comes to that, he was a good deal more refined than many of the young men I might have married.' The women of that part of France are markedly superior to the men, who, from their schooldays onwards, live in an almost exclusively male society, and never cultivate their minds. The heathland has their hearts, and their imaginations never range beyond it. They have no thought for anything but the pleasures it can give. It would, they feel, be a base betrayal on their parts to be different from the men who work their land, to speak anything but the local patois, or abandon the crude, rough manners of their neighbours. But beneath Bernard's coarse exterior there was, perhaps, something of a natural kindliness. When he was on his death-bed his tenant-farmers said: 'There won't be no more gentlemen hereabouts when he's gone.' Yes, kindliness and a certain fairness of mind – more than his share of good faith. He rarely spoke of what he did not know: he accepted his own limitations. As a young man he was not bad looking, and gave the impression of a sort of ill-conditioned Hippolytus who was less interested in young women than in the hares he coursed upon the heath. ...

But Thérèse, sitting there with her eyes closed and her face pressed against the carriage window, was conjuring up a past in which he scarcely figured. It was not the young man to whom she was engaged but who meant so little to her that now she saw in imagination bicycling through those mornings of the long ago upon the road that led from Saint-Clair to Argelouse, about nine o'clock, before the heat of the day had grown intolerable: not him, but his sister Anne. She had a vision of the girl with her face aglow, while all around the cicadas were kindling into little flickers of flame on each successive pine, and the great furnace of the heath was beginning to roar beneath the sky. Millions of flies rose in a cloud above the blazing ling. 'Put on your coat before you come indoors; it's like an ice-house ...' Aunt Clara would say, adding, 'Wait till you've cooled down before you have a drink.' To the deaf old lady Anne shouted useless words of greeting: 'Don't yell yourself hoarse, darling; she can understand all you say by lip-reading. ...' But in vain would the young girl try to articulate each word, twisting her tiny mouth into the most agonizing grimaces. The aunt merely guessed and answered at random, so that the two friends had to take refuge in flight so as to be free to laugh in privacy.

From the darkness of the railway carriage she gazed at that unsullied season of her past – unsullied, but lit by a vague and flickering happiness. Fitful and unsure that happy time had been, while as yet she knew nothing of the part she would be called upon to play upon the world's stage. As she sat with Anne on a red rep sofa with a photograph album propped against her knees, no hint had come to warn her that the portion reserved for her in life's lottery would be a darkened drawing-room set in the merciless glare of summer heat. Whence had come all that happiness? Anne did not share a single one of Thérèse's preferences. She hated reading, loved only sewing, chattering, and laughing. She had not one idea in her head, while Thérèse devoured with indiscriminate avidity the novels of Paul de Kock, the *Causeries de Lundi*, *L'Histoire du Consulat*, and anything else that she could find lying about in the cupboards of an old country house. They had not a taste in common except that of being together through those afternoons when the blazing sky laid siege to human beings barricaded in the half-light of their shrouded rooms. Now and again Anne would get up and go to see

whether the heat had abated. But through the half-opened
shutters the blinding glare would pounce like a great stream
of molten metal, till it almost burned the carpet, and all must
be again shut tight while human beings went once more to
earth.

Even at dusk, when the sun had come so near its setting
that only the very lowest sections of the pine trunks were
reddened with its light, and a belated cicada was still scraping
away for dear life almost at ground-level, there was still an
airless heat beneath the oaks. The two girls would lie at full
length on the ground as though on the shores of a lake.
Great storm clouds hinted at shapes which formed only to
change almost at once and vanish. No sooner had Thérèse
caught a glimpse of the winged woman whom Anne had seen
pictured in the sky than she was gone again, and nothing was
left but what the younger girl described as 'a funny sort of
sprawling animal'.

When September came they could venture out after luncheon and wander through the parched land. No tiniest stream
of water flowed at Argelouse. Only by walking a long way
over the sandy heath could they hope to reach the head-waters
of the rivulet which went by the name of La Hure. It carved
a myriad courses through low-lying meadows laced with
alder-roots. Their feet turned numb in the ice-cold current,
and then, no sooner dry, were burning hot again. They would
seek the shelter of one of the huts set up in October for the
guns who went out after duck. It served them as the shuttered
drawing-room had done earlier in the year. They had nothing
to say to one another. No word passed. The minutes flew as
they lay there innocently resting. They were as still and motionless as the sportsman who, spying a flight of birds, imposes
silence with a movement of the hand. To have stirred so
much as a finger, so it seemed to them, would have set
scurrying in fright their chaste, their formless happiness.
It was Anne, always, who moved first – eager to be at the
business of killing larks at sundown, and Thérèse, though she
hated the sport, would follow, so hungry was she for the
other's company. In the hall Anne would take down the rook-

rifle which fired so light a charge that there was no recoil. Her friend, standing on a bank, would watch her in the field of rye, aiming at the sun as though in readiness to shoot it from the sky. At such moments she had always put her fingers in her ears. High in the blue, the bird's shrill song of rapture broke and dropped to silence, and the girl with the gun would pick up the wounded body, tenderly pressing it in her hand, kissing the still warm feathers, before she strangled it.

'Coming tomorrow?'

'Oh no – not every day.'

She did not want to see her every day – a sensible resolve which called for no argument. It would have seemed pointless to Thérèse to make a protest. Anne preferred not to come. There was no particular reason why she should not, but what was the point in their seeing one another every day? If they did, she had said, they would end by getting bored. To which Thérèse replied: 'Of course we should – you mustn't make a duty of it. Come when you feel like it, when you have nothing better to do. ...' And her schoolgirl friend would bicycle away down the darkening road, ringing her bell.

Then Thérèse would go back to the house – the farm labourers greeting her from afar, the children shyly keeping their distance. It was the hour at which the sheep lay dotted in the oak-trees' shade. Suddenly at the shepherd's call, they would huddle into a group. Her aunt would be waiting for her at the front-door, talking unceasingly, as deaf folk do, to keep the girl from speaking to her. Why so restless? She had no wish to read, no wish to do anything in particular, only to resume her aimless wandering. 'Don't go far; dinner's just ready.' She would find her way back to the road – empty now as far as the eyes could reach. She would hear the gong sound from the kitchen entrance. Perhaps, this evening, they would have to light the lamp. The silence was no deeper for the deaf woman sitting motionless with her hands folded in her lap than for the girl with the faintly hollowed cheeks.

Oh, Bernard, Bernard, how shall I fit *you* into this tumbled world, you of the blind, implacable race of simple souls? 'But', thought Thérèse, 'as soon as I start speaking he will interrupt. "Why did you marry me?" he will ask. "I never ran after you." ...' Why *had* she married him? It was true that he had shown no eagerness. She remembered how his mother, Madame Victor de la Trave, used to say to anyone who would listen: 'He would have been only too ready to wait, it was she who made the running – she, she, she! Her code is different from ours. She smokes, for instance, like a chimney. It is a sort of pose. But she's sound at heart, as good as gold. We'll soon teach her sense. ... We're not altogether happy about the marriage. ... Oh yes ... I know all about the Bellade grandmother ... but that's all over and done with. There was never anything that could really be called a scandal – they hushed up everything very successfully. Do you believe in heredity? Of course, the father has the *most* undesirable ideas, but it's only fair to say that he's never set her any but the best example. He may not be religious, but, for all that, he really is a saint – and very influential. It takes all sorts to make a world, and one has to make allowances. Besides, though you might not believe it, she's richer than we are. It's hard to credit, but it is so. And she simply adores Bernard – which is no bad thing. ...'

Yes, it was true she had adored him. Her feeling had been perfectly natural, and there had been no need for her to put constraint upon herself. Each time she looked at him in the drawing-room at Argelouse, or beneath the trees at the far end of the field, her eyes had been eloquent of simple love. So easy a conquest had flattered the young man, though it would be scarcely true to say that it surprised him. 'Don't play with her feelings,' his mother had kept on saying: 'she's eating her heart out for you.'

'I married him because ...' Frowning in deep thought, one hand shielding her eyes. Thérèse tried to remember.

There had, of course, been the childish delight with which she had looked forward to becoming Anne's sister-in-law as a result of that marriage, though it had been Anne, really, who had found the prospect so peculiarly 'amusing'. To

Thérèse it did not mean a great deal. The acres which Bernard stood to inherit had not left her indifferent – why should she be ashamed to admit it? She had always had 'the sense of property in her blood'. Often when, at the end of interminable meals, the cloth had been removed, and the drinks began to circulate, she had stayed behind with the men, held there by the talk of farm matters and pit-props, of mineral deposits and turpentine. She took a passionate delight in estimating the value of land. There could be little doubt that the idea of controlling so great a stretch of forest territory had exercised over her an irresistible fascination. 'He, too, was in love with my trees. ...' Perhaps, though, she had yielded to a deeper and less obvious feeling which now she was striving to set in the clear light of day; had hoped to find in marriage not pride of possession and the opportunity to dominate so much as a refuge. Might it not be argued that what had precipitated her into Bernard's arms had been, in some sort, a movement of panic? As a child she had been eminently practical, instructed in economies and household management. She was eager to assume her rightful position, to occupy the place that she was destined to fill. She wanted to be re-assured, to feel that she was protected against some danger the precise nature of which she did not understand. Never had she seemed so sensible as during the months of her engagement. She embedded herself in the substance of her new family, made it her object to 'settle down'. She had entered, as it were, into an Order. She had sought safety, and found it.

She remembered how, during the spring which preceded their marriage, they had once walked together down the sandy track which led from Argelouse to Vilméja. The shrivelled oak-leaves were still showing as dirty patches against the blue. The dried tangle of last year's bracken was thick upon the ground, the tender stalks of new growth striking a note of bright and acid green. Bernard said: 'Be careful of your cigarette. Even at this time of year it might start a fire. The heath is already without water.'

'Is it true,' she asked, 'that you can get prussic acid from

bracken?' Bernard did not know whether it would be enough
to provide a potent dose of poison. With tender concern he
had questioned her on the subject. 'Are you so anxious to
die?' At that she laughed, and he had said that really she was
becoming more like a child every day. She remembered how
she had closed her eyes, while he took her little head between
his great hands and whispered in her ear: 'There's still a lot
of foolishness in there.' And she had replied: 'Then, Bernard,
it's for you to get rid of it.' They had watched the bricklayers
at work adding a room to the farmhouse at Vilméja. The
owners – people from Bordeaux – were planning to have the
last of their sons, the one who 'suffered with his chest', live
there. His sister had died of the same complaint. Azévédo was
their name, and Bernard expressed considerable contempt for
them. 'They swear by all that's holy that they've got no
Jewish blood, but just look at them – and consumptive into
the bargain. They seem to be generously afflicted with every
ailment.'

Thérèse, at that time, was in a placid state of mind. Anne
was coming home from her Convent at Saint-Sebastian for the
wedding. She would pair off with the Deguilheim boy as best
man. She had asked Thérèse to describe, 'by return of post,'
what the other bridesmaids were going to wear. Couldn't she
get her a few cuttings of the material? It would be better all
round if they chose colours that would go together. ... Never
had Thérèse known such peace – or what seemed to her like
peace, though it was but a half-sleep, the torpor of the snake
within her breast.

4

THE day of their wedding had been stiflingly hot. In the
poky little church of Saint-Clair the women's chatter had
drowned the wheezy harmonium, and the incense had waged
a losing battle with the smell of human bodies. It was then
that the sense of being utterly abandoned had come over
Thérèse. She had entered this cage like a sleep-walker, to wake

with a feeling of miserable and defenceless youth at the sound of the heavy gate clanging to behind her. Nothing had changed, but she felt somehow that the feeling of abandonment involved more people than herself alone. She was fated to smoulder there, deep in the very substance of this family, like a damped-down fire worming its way beneath the heather, getting a hold first on one pine-tree, then on another, till finally the whole forest would blaze like a wilderness of torches. In all that crowd there was no face save Anne's on which her eyes could rest with a sense of finding peace. But the childish happiness of the younger girl kept her isolated from Thérèse. Oh, that happiness! It was as though she had no realization that they were to be separated that very evening, not only in space, but by reason of what Thérèse was about to suffer – of that irremediable outrage to which her innocent body would have to submit. Anne would remain upon the bank among the still untouched. Thérèse, very soon, would be one of the herd of those who have served their purpose. She remembered how, in the vestry, she had bent to kiss the laughing little face lifted to her own, and how she had realized suddenly the nothingness of everything round which she had built a universe of vague joys and sorrows no less vague. In the space of a few seconds she had seen the infinite disproportion between the mysterious promptings of her heart and the charming young countenance with its blotches of powder.

Long afterwards, at Saint-Clair and at B—, people talking of the wedding at Gamache (where more than a hundred tenant-farmers had eaten and drunk beneath the oaks) recalled that the bride – 'who isn't what you'd call really pretty, though she's the very embodiment of charm' – had looked quite ugly, almost hideous – 'so unlike herself, as though she had been somebody quite different. ...' What they meant was that her appearance had not been as it usually was. They blamed her white dress, the heat. Her real face they did not see.

When evening put an end to this half countryfied, half middle-class wedding, the car in which the newly married couple were driving away was forced to slow down because of the cheering crowd of guests, bright with the dresses of the girls. On the road, littered with acacia blooms, they passed zigzagging waggons driven by oafs who had drunk too much. Thérèse, brooding on the night that had followed, murmured, 'It was horrible! ...' then checked herself: 'No, it wasn't, not so horrible as all that. ...' Had she truly suffered on their trip to the Italian Lakes? No. She had been playing a desperate game, had been intent only on not giving herself away. A young man engaged can easily be taken in: not so a husband. No matter what lies the tongue may utter, the dissimulations of the body demand a different skill. Not everyone can ape desire and joy and happy languor. Thérèse learned how to accommodate her flesh to these new deceptions, and found a bitter pleasure in the task. Helped by her imagination, she made herself believe that for her too there might be pleasure of a sort within that world of the senses across whose threshold she had, under a man's compulsion, stepped. Of a sort, but of what sort? Much as when looking at a landscape shrouded in mist we fancy what it must be like in sunshine, so did Thérèse contemplate the delights of the flesh.

How easy it had been to take Bernard in! – Bernard of the vacant gaze, Bernard for ever worried lest the numbers on the pictures did not correspond with those in his Baedeker; satisfied if he could see, in the shortest possible time, all that there was to be seen. He remained imprisoned in his own pleasure like one of those charming little pigs whom it is so amusing to watch through the railings rooting about delightedly in their stye. ('And I was the stye,' thought Thérèse.) He always looked so much in a hurry, so busy, so serious. He was a man of method. 'Do you think it's altogether wise?' Thérèse would sometimes ask, appalled by the extent of his virility. Laughingly he reassured her. Where had he learned to draw such fine shades of discrimination in all matters pertaining to the flesh, to distinguish between what a decent man may or may not permit himself in the matter of sadistic self-indulgence? He was never for a moment in doubt. Once, when they stopped for a night in Paris on their way back, he pointedly left a music-hall where the performance had shocked him. 'To think that *foreigners* should see that! It's a disgrace. That's the sort of thing they judge us by! ...' It amazed Thérèse to think that this Puritan should be one and the same as the man whose sensual ingenuities would be forced upon her in less than an hour's time. 'Poor Bernard! – no worse than anybody else! The truth is that desire transforms a man into a monster, so that he becomes utterly unlike himself. Nothing is so severing as the frenzy that seizes upon our partner in the act. I always saw Bernard as a man who charged head-down at pleasure, while I lay like a corpse, motionless, as though fearing that, at the slightest gesture on my part, this madman, this epileptic, might strangle me. As often as not, balanced on the very edge of the ultimate excruciation, he would discover suddenly that he was alone. The gloomy battle would be broken off, and Bernard, retracing his steps, would, as it were, stand back and see me there, like a dead body thrown up on the shore, my teeth clenched, my body cold to his touch.'

There had been but one letter from Anne – who disliked writing – but, by some miracle, it contained not a single line which Thérèse could find displeasing. A letter expresses not so much what we really feel as what we know we ought to feel if it is to bring pleasure to the recipient. Anne complained that since the Azévédo's son had come to Vilméja she could no longer take her walks in that direction. She had seen, from a distance, his invalid chair standing among the bracken. She had a horror of consumptives.

Thérèse read the pages over and over again, and expected to hear no more from her friend. What, then, was her surprise, when the post arrived (on the morning following the interrupted visit to the music-hall), to see Anne de Trave's handwriting on three separate envelopes. They had been travelling fast, and the bundle of letters had followed them from one poste-restante to another, until finally it had caught up with them in Paris. They 'were in a hurry', Bernard had said, 'to get back to their nest'. The real reason was that their being together no longer gave him any happiness. He was bored to death away from his guns, his dogs, and the inn where the Picon grenadine had a different taste from anywhere else. His wife was so cold, so mocking. She never showed pleasure even if she felt any, would never talk about what really interested him. ... As to Thérèse, she longed to be back in Saint-Clair. She was like a transported criminal, sick to her soul of transit prisons, and anxious only to see the Convict Island where she would have to spend the rest of her life.

Very carefully she deciphered the date on each of the three envelopes, and was already opening the earliest of the series, when Bernard uttered an exclamation. She could not hear his words, because the window was open and the motor-buses were changing gear at the crossing beneath. He had stopped in the middle of shaving to read a letter from his mother. Thérèse could still see in imagination the cellular undervest, the strong, bare arms, the pale skin, and the sudden flood of raw scarlet which suffused his neck and face. The July morning was already stifling. The smoke-grimed sunlight made the dreary house-fronts beyond their balcony look dirtier even than usual. He came close to her. 'This really is a bit much!' he exclaimed. 'I must say, your friend, Anne's, going too far! Who would ever have thought that my young sister ...'

Thérèse looked at him inquiringly, and he went on:

'She's gone and fallen in love with young Azévédo – have you ever heard of such a thing? ... No, I'm not joking ... with that wretched consumptive they've been enlarging Vilméja for! ... Looks pretty serious, too. She says she'll wait until she's of age. ... Mother writes that she's carrying on like a lunatic. I only hope the Deguilheims don't get wind of it. ... I wouldn't put it beyond young Deguilheim to sheer off altogether. Are those letters from her? ... Go on, open them ... they may tell us something more.'

'I want to read them in their proper order. Besides, I'm not sure that I've any right to let you see them.'

How typical of her! ... always making things more complicated. Well, all that mattered was that she should force the girl to see sense.

'My parents rely on you. ... You've got so much influence over her ... oh yes, you have. ... They regard you as their only hope of salvation.'

While she dressed, he rushed off to send a telegram and to reserve two seats in the southern express. It was time she started packing.

'What are you waiting for? Why don't you read the letters?'

'I'm waiting until you've gone out.'

For a long time after the door had slammed behind him she lay there smoking cigarette after cigarette and staring at the dirty gold lettering on the opposite balcony. Then she opened the first of the envelopes. Surely these burning words could never have been written by the dear little simpleton, the Convent-bred child, of her memories? How could this song of songs have burst from the dry little heart she had known? – for it *was* dry, as she knew only too well ... this long, this happy wail as of a woman possessed, this cry torn from a body almost dead with joy at the first onset of love?

... When I met him, I couldn't believe it was he. He was playing with the dog, running about and shouting. How could he have been behaving so if he was a sick man? But he's not a sick man. It's only that they are being careful because of the family history. He's not even delicate – just rather thin, and used to being spoiled and cosseted. ... You wouldn't know me. I go and fetch his coat for him when it gets cool. ...

Had Bernard come back into the room at that moment he would have realized that the woman seated on the bed was not his wife at all, but someone completely unknown to him, some strange, nameless creature. She threw away her cigarette and opened the second envelope.

... I'll wait just as long as I have to. I'm not afraid of anything they can do to stop me. My love takes no account of obstacles. They are keeping me at Saint-Clair, but Argelouse is near enough for Jean and me to meet. Do you remember the duck-shooting hut? It was you, darling, who chose the very places where I was later to know supreme happiness. ... Please don't jump to conclusions and start thinking that we do anything wrong. He's so fastidious! you can't have any idea what he's like. He's done a terrible lot of studying and reading, just like you, but I don't mind it in a young man, and I never feel that I want to tease him about it. What wouldn't I give to know as much as you do! You've got your happiness already, darling, and I don't know anything about it yet. But it must be very wonderful if just the promise of it can be so heavenly! When I sit with him in the little hut where you used to enjoy our picnics so much, my happiness is like something solid. I feel that I can almost touch it. But I keep on telling myself that there is a still greater happiness to come, something bigger and lovelier than this. And then, when Jean goes away looking so pale, the memory of the kisses I have had, and the thought of the ones I'm going to have next day, make me deaf to the complaints, the prayers, and the reproaches of the poor fools who don't *know* ... who never have known ... Darling, forgive me. I'm talking about this happiness of mine as though you too were one of those who don't know, whereas I'm only a novice compared with you. ... I'm quite sure that you'll take our part against the people who are making us miserable. ...

Thérèse opened the third envelope. It contained only a few scribbled words:

... Come to me, darling. They've separated us. They never let me out of their sight. They think you'll be on their side. I've said that I will abide by your judgement. ... I'll explain it all to you when we meet. He's not sick. ... I am happy and terribly unhappy at the same time. I am happy at the idea of suffering for his sake, and I adore his misery because it is a sign that he truly loves me. ...

She read no further. As she slipped the sheet back into its envelope, she noticed a photograph which at first she had not seen. Standing close to the window, she studied the pictured face. It was that of a young man whose head seemed too large because the hair was so thick. She recognized the spot where the snapshot had been taken, the bank on which Jean Azévédo was standing, looking like the young David (behind him was an open heath on which sheep were browsing). He had his coat over his arm, and his shirt was partly open. ... 'He calls it the extreme point to which we can decently allow ourselves to go. ...' Thérèse raised her eyes, and was surprised at her own appearance in the glass. Only with a great effort could she have unclenched her teeth or swallowed her saliva. She dabbed her forehead and temples with eau-de-Cologne. 'She has found the secret of happiness ... and what about me? ... Why shouldn't I find it too?' The photograph was still lying on the table. Beside it glinted a pin.

'I did it – yes, I ...' In the bumpy train which was gathering speed as it took the downward slope she said again and again to herself: '... Two years ago, in that hotel bedroom, I took the pin, and I pierced the photograph of that young man just where the heart should be – not in a fit of temper, but quite calmly, as though I were doing a perfectly ordinary thing. Then I went to the lavatory, threw the photograph with the hole in it into the pan, and pulled the plug. ...'

When Bernard came back, he was surprised to find her looking solemn – looking as though she had been thinking hard, had already decided what was best to do. But it was wrong of her to smoke so much ... she was poisoning herself. ... One shouldn't, she said, pay too much attention to the whims of a young girl. She felt sure that she could make her see sense. ... Bernard longed for reassurance. The feel of their return tickets in his coat pocket gave him a little thrill of pleasure. Especially did it flatter his pride to think that his relations should turn to his wife for counsel. He told her that, extravagance or no extravagance, they would have their last luncheon at one of the restaurants in the Bois. In the taxi he talked to her of his plans for the shooting season. He couldn't wait to try out the dog that Balion was training for him. His mother wrote that the mare had been treated with hot needles and was no longer lame. ... When they got to the restaurant they found very few people there. The long row of waiters made them feel nervous. Thérèse remembered the mingled smell of geraniums and pickles that had hung about the place. Bernard had never before tasted Rhine wine. 'It costs a pretty penny, but we don't celebrate every day.' His body hid the room from her. Beyond the great windows silent cars kept gliding up and stopping. She noticed a faint movement in the region of his ears, and knew that it came from the muscles of his scalp. After the first few glasses of wine he turned excessively red. He looked like a fine, handsome, country-bred fellow. The only thing wrong with him was that for the last few weeks he had not had enough fresh air and exercise to absorb his daily ration of food and drink. She felt no hatred of him, but simply a wild desire to be alone with her pain, to discover where it was that the blow had struck her! If only he were not with her there: if only she had not got to make such an effort to eat her lunch and smile, to compose her features and to keep her eyes from blazing. If only she could fix her mind freely upon the mysterious despair which seemed to have seized upon her. ... A fellow-creature had managed to escape from the desert island where by rights they should have been together till the end, had crossed the chasm which kept her from the rest of the world, and gone back to it – had moved from one universe to another. ... No, it wasn't that. No one ever goes from one universe to another. Anne had always belonged to the race of simple souls who are content merely to be alive. Thérèse, looking at her in the old days of their lonely outings, lying asleep with her head against her friend's knees, had seen only a wraith. The real Anne de la Trave had been hidden from her, the girl who now ran to meet Jean Azévédo in a lonely shooting hut between Saint-Clair and Argelouse.

'What's the matter with you? You're eating nothing. Pity to leave food on your plate, considering what we're paying. Is it the heat? Not going to faint, are you? ... Can't, surely, be the first signs, already?'

She smiled, but only with her lips. She said that she was thinking about this adventure of Anne's (she had got to talk about Anne). When Bernard announced that he was perfectly easy in his mind now that she had taken the affair in hand, she asked him why his parents were so set against the marriage. He thought she was laughing at him, and begged her not to begin playing at paradoxes.

'To begin with, you know as well as I do that they're Jews. Mamma knew old Azévédo – the one who refused to be baptized.'

But Thérèse maintained that some of the oldest families in Bordeaux were Portuguese Jews.

'The Azévédos were somebody when *our* ancestors were a miserable lot of shepherds shaking with fever in the marshes.'

'Oh, for Heaven's sake, Thérèse, don't argue for the sake of arguing. Jews are Jews all the world over; besides, this particular family is thoroughly degenerate – eaten up with tuberculosis. Everyone knows that.'

The gesture with which she lit her cigarette had always shocked Bernard.

'What did your own grandfather die of, and his father? When you married me did it ever occur to you to inquire into the nature of my mother's last illness? Don't you think that we could find a sufficient number of consumptives and syphilitics in our own family tree to poison the whole world?'

'That's going beyond a joke, Thérèse, even if you are saying it only in fun and to get a rise out of me. I won't have you talking like that about the family!'

He was thoroughly annoyed and on his dignity – wanting to take a high line, yet, at the same time, anxious not to look a fool in her eyes. But she wouldn't give up her point.

'I can't help laughing when I see our precious families burrowing away in their dignity like a lot of blind moles! Their horror of the more obvious blemishes is only equalled by their indifference to those that don't happen to be generally known – and there are plenty of *them* in all conscience! Take yourself, for instance: aren't you always talking about "secret diseases", as though all mortal ailments weren't, by definition, secret? Our families never give them a thought, though they're careful enough not to wash their dirty linen in public. If it wasn't for the servants, one would never know a thing. Fortunately, there always *are* the servants. ...'

'I'm not going to discuss the matter with you. When you're in one of these moods the only thing to do is to wait until it's over. With me it doesn't matter. I realize that you say these things just to pull my leg: but they wouldn't be very well received at home. We're not in the habit of treating family matters as a joke.'

Always the family! Thérèse let her cigarette go out. She stared before her, seeing in imagination the cage with its innumerable bars, each of which was a living person, a cage full of eyes and ears, in which she would have to spend the whole of her life, squatting motionless, her chin on her knees, her arms clasped about her legs, waiting for death.

'Oh, don't look like that, Thérèse! If only you could see yourself! ...'

She smiled, readjusting the mask.

'It was just my fun. ... What an old silly you are, my dear!'

But when, in the taxi, Bernard crept close to her, she pushed him away, setting a distance between them.

On that last evening before their return to the country they went to bed at nine o'clock. Thérèse took something to make her sleep, but unconsciousness, too eagerly sought, evaded her. For a moment, indeed, she sank into oblivion, but Bernard, with a mutter of incomprehensible words, turned towards her, and she felt the heat of his great body against her own. She avoided him, seeking the extreme edge of the mattress in an effort to avoid the burning contact. But a few minutes later he lumbered towards her again, as though his flesh sought blindly its accustomed prey even in the insensibility of sleep. Roughly she pushed him from her once more, though without waking him. ... If only she could get free of him once and for all – could thrust him from the bed into the outer darkness!

Across the length and breadth of the shadowed city the motor horns were answering one another like the dogs and the fowls at Argelouse when the moon rose. No breath of freshness mounted from the street. She turned on the lamp, and, propped upon her elbow, gazed at the motionless male beside her – a male in his twenty-seventh year. He had thrown back the blankets; his breathing was inaudible, and the ruffled hair fell in a mass over his still unwrinkled forehead, over the as yet unscored temples. He lay sleeping there, a vulnerable and naked Adam, deep in a slumber that seemed eternal. She pulled a sheet over him, got up, found one of the letters in the middle of reading which she had been disturbed, and took it to the lamp.

... If he told me to follow him, I should leave everything, and never once turn back. We kiss, but on the verge of the ultimate surrender hold back, checked not by my resistance but by his power of restraint. It is truer to say that it is he who resists me, because I long for the extreme of passion, the mere approach of which, he says, surpasses all other pleasures. To hear him talk, one would think that last decisive step was never to be taken. He makes it a matter of pride to hold back on the precipitous slope. Once one lets oneself go, he says, it is impossible to stop. ...

She opened the window and tore the letter into tiny fragments. She hung there, leaning out over the deep gulf of stone which, in this hour before the dawn, echoed to the sound of a passing cart. The scraps of paper fluttered down to perch on the balconies of the lower floors. She caught a smell of growing things. From what countryside had it come to invade this wilderness of asphalt? She saw in imagination the stain made by her body lying crushed and mangled on the pavement – and all around a milling crowd of loiterers and policemen. ... You'll never kill yourself, Thérèse, your imagination is far too vivid! As a matter of fact, she had no wish to die. An urgent task awaited her – not of vengeance nor of hate. The little fool, far away at Saint-Clair, who was so sure that happiness was possible, must be made to see with *her* eyes, be made to understand that no such thing as happiness existed. That at least, if nothing else, they must have in common – boredom, the sense that no high destiny awaited them, or overriding duty. They must learn that there was nothing worth the winning save the squalid humdrum of the daily round – a loneliness without hope of consolation.

The first light was touching the roof-tops. She went back to the man lying there, motionless, upon the bed. But no sooner had she slipped between the sheets than he moved towards her.

When she awoke she was clear-headed and sensible. Why had she made such a to-do about what was really quite simple?

The family was calling on her for help. She would do what the family wanted. In that way only could she keep to the beaten track. When Bernard began to argue again that it would be disastrous if anything happened to prevent Anne's marriage to the Deguilheim boy, she agreed. The Deguilheims were not of their world. The grandfather might have tended sheep, but they owned the best forest land for miles around, and Anne, after all, was no heiress. All she could hope for from her father was a few acres of vineyard in the fens round Langon – and they were flooded out every other year. Nothing must be allowed to get in the way of that marriage.

The smell of chocolate made Thérèse feel sick. This vague bodily discomfort served to confirm her other symptons: she was already pregnant. 'Better get it over early,' said Bernard; 'and then one needn't bother any more about it.' He gazed with respect at the woman who bore within her the future master of unnumbered trees.

5

SAINT-CLAIR – already! Thérèse took the measure of the road her thoughts had come. Could she ever get Bernard to follow her so far? It was scarcely to be hoped that he would be willing to share her slow progress along that tortuous way. Yet, all the really important things still remained to be said. 'Even if I do manage to get him to the point which I've reached so far, what a lot will still have to be explained.' She brooded over the puzzle of her own existence. Silently she questioned the young middle-class married woman whom everyone had praised for her level-headedness when first she settled down with her husband in Saint-Clair. She revived the memory of those first weeks of the new life in the cool, dark house belonging to her parents-in-law. The shutters on the windows which looked into the Square were kept always closed, but in the left-hand wall a barred grille gave a glimpse of the garden aflame with heliotrope, geraniums, and petunias.

Between the old couple tucked away in the shadowed drawing-room on the ground-floor, and Anne wandering in the garden which she was forbidden to leave, Thérèse came and went, privy to all that was going on. To her mother-in-law she said: 'Give her her head a bit, suggest that she should travel for a while before making up her mind. I think I can promise that she'll agree: and then, while you're away, I'll act.' But how? The parents had a vague idea that she meant to scrape acquaintance with young Azévédo. 'A frontal attack won't do you any good, mother.' From Madame de la Trave she gathered that nothing definite had occurred as yet. Heaven be thanked for that! Mademoiselle Monod, the postmistress, was the only other person in the secret. She had held up several of Anne's letters. 'But she's as secret as the grave. Besides, we've got a hold on her. *She* won't gossip!'

'We must do our best,' Victor de la Trave kept on saying, 'to spare her as much pain as possible.' In the old days he had given in to all Anne's whims, no matter how fantastic. But now he had to admit that his wife was right. 'One can't,' he said, 'make an omelet without breaking eggs'; and, 'She'll live to thank us.' Perhaps, but meanwhile, wasn't she making herself ill? Husband and wife fell silent, gazing vaguely about them. In their hearts, no doubt, they felt for the poor child drooping in the summer heat. She turned in disgust from all food. She trod the flowers underfoot without noticing them, padding up and down behind the garden railing like a bitch in heat looking for some way of escape. ... Madame de la Trave shook her head: 'I can't eat for her, can I? She stuffs herself with fruit and leaves her plate untouched at meals.' And Victor: 'She'd live to blame us if we gave our consent – if only because of the miserable, sickly brats she'd bring into the world. ...' His wife was angry because he seemed to be trying to find excuses for their attitude. 'Fortunately, the Deguilheims are not back yet. It's a good thing for us that they've set their hearts on a marriage with their son ...' Only when Thérèse had left the room did they put into words the question which was stirring in both their minds: 'What ideas can they have been stuffing her with at the Convent?

Here, at home, she's had nothing but good examples, and we've been so careful about the books she reads. ... Thérèse says there is nothing more calculated to turn a young girl's head than the sort of love-stories that are recommended for family reading ... but, of course, she adores being paradoxical. ... Besides, Anne has never had a passion for books, which is *such* a blessing. We've never had to pull her up on that account. In the matter of reading she's her parents' daughter all right. It probably *would* be a good thing if she could have a change of air. ... Don't you remember how quickly she picked up when we took her to Salies after she'd had the measles and a touch of bronchitis at the same time? We'd go anywhere she liked – one can't say more than that. She has, really, very little to complain about.' Monsieur de la Trave gave a low sigh. 'A trip with us? – that wouldn't do any good,' he answered. 'What's that?' inquired his wife, who was slightly deaf. What memory of some former lovers' journey had come back suddenly into the old man's mind? For so long now he had been comfortably settled into the smooth existence of every day that it seemed strange he should be moved by a recollection from the golden time of his passionate youth.

Thérèse went into the garden to talk to the young girl. Anne was wearing a last-year's frock which had now grown too large for her.

'Well?' she cried, as her friend joined her. Thérèse could see again every detail of the scene – the burned-up paths, the dry, brittle meadow-grass; could smell in memory the hot geraniums. The girl had looked, that August afternoon, as though she were more utterly consumed than any growing thing. Now and again a thunder shower drove them for shelter to the greenhouse where they waited while the hailstones rattled on the glass roof.

'Why should you mind going away, since you never see him?'

'I may not see him, but I know that he is there, living and breathing, only six miles away. When the wind blows from the east, I realize that he and I can hear the church bells at the very same moment. Would it make no difference to you whether Bernard were in Argelouse or Paris? I don't *see* Jean, but I have the certainty that he is not far off. At Sunday Mass I don't even bother to turn round because from where we sit we can see only the altar, and there's a pillar between us and the rest of the congregation: but on the way out ...'

'He wasn't there last Sunday, was he?'

Thérèse had been accurately informed. She knew that Anne, following dutifully in her mother's wake, had sought in vain among the crowd for the face that was not there.

'He may have been ill. ... They stop his letters: there's no way I can get news of him.'

'All the same, it seems odd that he shouldn't have found some way of sending a message to you.'

'Oh, Thérèse, if only *you*! ... Of course, I know how difficult your position is, but ...'

'Agree to take this trip, and perhaps, while you're away ...'

'I can't leave him.'

'But in any case *he'll* be going away. In a few weeks now he'll leave Argelouse.'

'Don't talk like that ... I can't bear even to think of it! Not a word from him to help me go on living! I'm more than half dead already as a result of the long silence. I have to remind myself, every moment, of all the things he said which made me really happy. I repeat them over and over to myself – so often, indeed, that I end by wondering whether he ever actually said them at all. I can hear his voice now, the way it sounded the last time we met. "You're the only person in my life I care two hoots about," he said – at least, I think that was it, though it may have been "You're the most precious thing I have in life. ..." I don't remember the exact words.'

She stood there frowning, striving to catch the echo of that spoken consolation, endlessly elaborating its meaning.

'What is he really like?'

'You can have no idea ...'

'So unlike everybody else?'

'I wish I could describe him, but no words of mine could ever paint his portrait. ... He might, I suppose, seem quite ordinary to you ... though I'm almost sure he wouldn't.'

It was quite beyond her power to get a clear view of the young man who shone resplendent in the bright radiance of her love. 'Passion,' thought Thérèse, 'would made me clearer-sighted. I should take note of every detail in the man whom I desired.'

'If I agree to go on this trip, Thérèse, will you see him? Will you tell me what he says? Will you give him my letters? If I go away, if I pluck up courage enough to go away ...'

Making her way from that kingdom of light and fire, Thérèse plunged again, like a dark wasp, into the room where mother and father were waiting for the heat to abate and their daughter to surrender. Only after many of these comings and goings did Anne finally make up her mind to agree. It was not so much the efforts of Thérèse as the imminent return of the Deguilheims that finally prevailed. She trembled at the thought of this new danger. Thérèse had kept on saying that, for a tremendously rich young man, the Deguilheim boy wasn't 'really half bad'.

'I've hardly ever looked at him properly, Thérèse. All I know is that he wears spectacles, is going bald, and is an old man.'

'He is twenty-nine. ...'

'That's what I mean – an old man. But old or not ...'

At dinner that evening the de la Traves mentioned Biarritz, and began fussing about hotels. Thérèse kept her eyes fixed on Anne. The girl sat perfectly still: she seemed emptied of all vitality.

'Do make just a tiny effort ... one can always eat if only one tries,' Madame de la Trave kept on saying. Anne lifted the spoon to her mouth. Her eyes looked quite dead. The one person who was not there, alone had any existence for her. There was nothing, nobody, in her life save only he. At moments a smile flickered on her lips as she remembered something he had said, some kiss he had given her in those distant days when, in a hut of turves, his clumsy hands had undone the first few buttons of her blouse. Thérèse looked away, concentrating her eyes on Bernard leaning over his plate. He was seated against the light, and she could not see his face. But she could hear the sound he made as he chewed the food by which he set such store, like some ruminant cow. She got up and left the table. Her mother-in-law said:

'She'd rather one didn't notice her. I'd cosset her if she'd let me, but she hates being fussed over. Considering her condition, she's not having too bad a time. She smokes too much, but it's no use telling her.' The old lady fell into a series of reminiscences to do with child-bearing. 'I remember when I was expecting you I had to sniff at a rubber ball. It was the only thing that kept me from being sick.'

'Thérèse, where are you?'

'Here, on the bench.'

'So you are; I can see your cigarette.'

Anne sat down, rested her head against an unyielding shoulder, looked at the sky, and remarked:

'He is gazing at those same stars, hearing the same Angelus bell. ...' Then, after a pause: 'Give me a kiss, Thérèse.' But Thérèse made no effort to bend down to the trusting face beside her. She merely said:

'Are you miserable?'

'No, not this evening. I realize that somehow, somewhere, we shall be together again. I feel quite calm now. The only really important thing is that he should know – and you'll see to that. I have made up my mind to go on this trip. But when I get back walls shall not keep me from him. Sooner or later I shall lie against his heart. I am as sure of that as I am of my own existence. No, Thérèse, don't *you* start preaching and talking about the family. ...'

'I wasn't thinking about the family, darling: I was thinking about him. It's not so easy to worm one's way into a man's life. He, too, has a family, work, interests – there may even be another woman. ...'

'There isn't. He said, "You're the only person in my life"; and, another time, "Our love is the only thing that means anything at all now. ..."'

'Now?'

'What are you hinting? Do you think that by "now" he meant just at this particular moment?'

49

There was no need for Thérèse to ask again whether she were miserable. She could hear the sounds of her misery in the darkness. But she felt no pity. How sweet it must be to say a name over and over, the pet name of the man to whom one's heart is tightly bound! – merely to think he is alive and breathing; that he sleeps at night with his head upon his arm, and wakes at dawn; that his young body plunges through the morning mist ...

'You're crying, Thérèse! Is it because of me? Do you love me?'

The girl had slipped to her knees. For a while she stayed so, her head pressed against Thérèse's side. Suddenly she got up.

'I felt something moving against my forehead: something, I don't know what. ...'

'He started moving some days ago.'

'The baby?'

'Yes; he's alive already.'

They went back to the house, their arms round one another's waist, as in the old days on the road to Nizan, on the road to Argelouse. Thérèse remembered how frightened she had been of this twittering burden. What passions might not force an entry into the still unformed flesh within her womb! She could see herself now as she had sat that evening in her room, before the open window. (Bernard had called up to her from the garden, 'Don't put on the light: it will attract the mosquitoes.') She had reckoned the months that remained before the child would be born. She longed to have knowledge of some God. She wanted to pray that this unknown life which was still an undistinguishable part of herself might never see the light of day.

6

IT is strange that Thérèse remembered the days which followed the departure of Anne and her parents only as a time of torpor. At Argelouse, where it had been agreed that she should seek the joint in young Azévédo's armour and force him to relinquish his hold, she longed only for rest and sleep. Bernard had agreed that they should live, not in his house, but in hers, which was more comfortable, and where Aunt Clara could take over all the cares of housekeeping. Other people meant nothing now to Thérèse. They could look after themselves. Until the child should come she wanted nothing but to be left in her state of dull, animal languor. Each morning, Bernard irritated her by recalling her promise that she would arrange a meeting with the young man. She snubbed him for his pains. She was beginning to find it increasingly difficult to put up with him. It may have been, as Bernard thought, that her condition had something to do with her mood. He himself was already showing signs of an obsession which frequently afflicts the men of his race, though it rarely shows itself in persons under thirty. It was curious to find the fear of death so strongly developed in anyone who was, to all seeming, as strong as a horse. But what answer could she make when he said: 'Can't you realize what I'm suffering? ...' The bodies of these heavy eaters, bred of a lazy, over-nourished race, have only the appearance of sturdiness. A pine-tree planted in the rich soil of a field grows quickly: but its heart rots quickly too, and in its prime it has to be cut down. 'It's just nerves,' she told him; but was conscious of the weak spot, of the flaw, in the metal. And then the most extraordinary, the most inconceivable thing happened – he gave up eating, lost his appetite. 'Why don't you see a doctor?' He shrugged his shoulders at that and assumed an air of indifference. The truth was, he preferred his present state of uncertainty to a possible sentence of death. At night, Thérèse, would sometimes be jerked awake by a rattling sound in his throat. His hand would seek hers and press it to his left side that she might feel how irregularly his heart was beating. Then she would light a candle, get up and pour a few drops of tincture of valerian into a glass of water. What bad luck it was, she thought, that this draught should have the effect of relieving him. How much better if it turned out to be a mortal dose. Eternity is your only genuine guarantee of peace and quiet. Why should this whining creature at her side be so frightened of what would set his fears at rest for ever? He fell asleep before she did. How could she expect to drop off into unconsciousness with that great body in the bed beside her, its heavy breathing turning at times to a choking struggle? Thank God, though, he left her alone now – having come to the conclusion that love-making was the worst possible thing for his heart.

The cocks of dawn wakened the farmsteads. The sound of the Angelus came to her on the east wind from Saint-Clair, and then, at long last, sleep closed her eyes, just as he was struggling back to life. He dressed quickly, putting on old country clothes (his washing consisted in no more than wetting his face with cold water). Then he crept like a dog into the kitchen, greedy for the larder scraps. He breakfasted off what remained of last night's meat, or perhaps a hunk of cold paté, or grapes and a piece of bread rubbed with garlic – his only solid meal of the day. What was left over he threw to Flambeau and Diane, who snapped at the food. The mist had in it the smell of autumn. At that hour he no longer felt like a sick man, but was conscious once again of his old youthful vigour. Soon the duck would be on the wing. He must see to the decoy birds, put out their eyes.

When he returned at eleven o'clock he found Thérèse still in bed.

'What about young Azévédo? You know that mother is waiting for news of him – poste restante, Biarritz?'

'How's your heart?'

'Please leave my heart alone! Talking about my symptoms makes me conscious of them ... which only goes to show that it's nerves, really ... You think it is just nerves, don't you?'

She never gave him the answer he wanted.

'One can never be altogether sure. You're the only person who can know how you feel. ... But just because your father died of angina pectoris, that's no reason ... especially at your age ... Obviously, the heart is the Achilles heel of the Desqueyroux family. What an odd creature you are, Bernard, with your constant fear of death! Do you never have a feeling, as I do, of utter futility? No? Doesn't it occur to you that the sort of life people like us lead is remarkably like death?'

He shrugged his shoulders. Her paradoxes bored him. It is not particularly clever to be witty. All one has got to do is to take the ordinary, sensible person's point of view and turn it upside down. Why waste her gifts on him? he said. Much better keep them for young Azévédo when she saw him.

'You know that he's leaving Vilméja about the middle of October?'

At Villandraut, the station before Saint-Clair, Thérèse thought: 'How can I ever get Bernard to believe that I wasn't in love with that young man? I'm sure he thinks that I adored him. Like all those who really know nothing whatever about love, he imagines that a crime of the sort with which I was charged could have had its motive only in sexual passion.' Bernard must be made to see that at the period in question she was still far from hating him, tiresome though she often found his importunity. No other man would have been of the slightest use to her. When all was said, Bernard wasn't so bad. There was nothing she detested more in novels than the delineation of extraordinary people who had no resemblance to anyone whom one met in normal life.

Her father had been the only truly remarkable man she had ever known. She must give that headstrong, suspicious radical the credit of being built on heroic lines. His activities were numberless. He combined the functions of a landed proprietor and industrialist (in addition to his sawmills at B— , he handled the resin from his own trees and from those of his innumerable relations in a factory at Saint-Clair). But above all else, he was a man of politics. Though his cavalier way of dealing with others had done him no little harm, he still had the ear of the authorities. And how contemptuous he was of women! – even of Thérèse, at a time when everyone was praising her intelligence. The recent dramatic happenings had strengthened him in his opinion. 'Hysterical, all of 'em, when they're not fools!' he had said to her Counsel. For all his anti-clericalism, he was a thorough-paced Puritan. He might occasionally hum a song of Béranger's, but he would blush like a boy if certain subjects were so much as mentioned in his hearing. Bernard had been told by Monsieur de la Trave that Larroque had been completely innocent when he married: 'and it's common knowledge that he's never had a mistress since his wife died. Your father's a character if ever there was one!' Yes, he certainly was that. But though Thérèse, away from him, was inclined to touch up his portrait a bit, she had only to see him again to realize what a mean, vulgar creature he was. He came seldom to Saint-Clair, though more frequently to Argelouse, because he disliked meeting the de la Traves. Whenever they were present, though politics were barred, the same idiotic old quarrel inevitably began with the soup, and rapidly became embittered. Thérèse would have been ashamed to join in it. She felt it a matter of pride not to open her lips on those occasions, unless the talk turned to religion. Whenever that happened, she flung herself into the fray in her father's support. Everyone talked at the tops of their voices, making so much noise that even Aunt Clara managed to catch an occasional word and proceeded to join in the altercation. In her terrible deaf old voice she gave free rein to her radical fanaticism. *She* knew, she said, what went on in Convents, though at heart (thought Thérèse) she was a more sincere believer than any of the de la Trave clan. It was only that she waged incessant warfare against the Eternal Being who had let her become deaf and ugly, who had decreed that she should die without ever having been loved or possessed by a man. But ever since the day when Madame de la Trave had left the table they had entered into a tacit agreement to avoid all metaphysical discussion. But politics were quite enough to set them all by the ears, though fundamentally, whether their sympathies were of the Right or the Left, they were all in complete agreement on one point – that property is the most solid good this life can show, and that the only true value of existence is in earthly possessions. The sole question at issue was, should one or should one not set some limit to the acquisitive instincts, and, if so, where was it to be? Thérèse, who had the 'sense of property in her blood', would have preferred that they should face the question in a spirit of cynicism. What she hated was the sham air of righteousness with which the Larroques and the de la Traves attempted to disguise this shared passion. When her father announced that he was 'unshakably loyal to the principles of democracy,' she would interrupt him with, 'You needn't bother to talk like that here: we're quite alone, you know.' She said that all this highfalutin political posturing made her feel positively sick. The tragedy of the class-war was never really forced on her attention in a countryside where even the poorest have *some* property, and are for ever striving to amass more; where a common love of the soil, of shooting, of food, and of drink, creates between all – middle and labouring class alike – a close bond of brotherhood. But Bernard had, in addition, some degree of education. The neighbours said of him that he had got out of his rut, and even Thérèse took pleasure in the thought that he was the kind of man with whom it was possible to carry on some sort of rational conversation, a man who had 'risen superior to his environment ...' or so she regarded him until she met Jean Azévédo.

It was that time of year when the freshness of the night hours persists all through the morning: when, from luncheon on, no matter how hot the sun has been, a hint of mist announces the oncoming of darkness. The first of the duck were already flying, and Bernard scarcely ever came home before nightfall. On the particular day in question, however, he had decided, after sleeping badly, to go straight into Bordeaux and get himself examined by a doctor.

'I had no conscious wish at all,' thought Thérèse, looking back on the event. 'I used to take an hour's stroll every day up the road, because exercise is good for a woman when she's breeding. I avoided the woods because the shooting season had begun, which meant constantly stopping and whistling to announce one's presence, and waiting until one of the guns gave a shout to show that the coast was clear. But sometimes there would come an answering whistle which meant that a covey had settled in the trees. When that happened one had to lie low. Later, I would go back home and doze in front of the fire, either in the drawing-room or the kitchen, and let Aunt

Clara busy herself with doing little odds and ends for me. She was for ever droning on about household or farm matters, but I took no more notice of her than God does of his servants. She never stopped talking, because she didn't want to make the effort needed to hear other people. Almost always her soliloquies took the form of squalid stories about the country folk whom she looked after and watched over with a devotion which was completely disillusioned – stories of old men slowly starving to death, condemned to work until they could work no longer, abandoned by their relations and left to die, or of women forced to undertake the most exhausting labours. They would say the most frightful things, and these Aunt Clara would repeat almost gaily, just like a child. The one person she really loved was me, and yet I scarcely even noticed her when she got down on her knees to unlace my boots, take off my stockings, and warm my feet in her old hands.

'Balion used to come for orders the evening before he was due to go into Saint-Clair. Aunt Clara would make out a list of errands for him, entrusting him with the various prescriptions needed for the sick of Argelouse. "I want you to go first of all to the chemist. It'll take Darquey a long time to make up all these. ..."

'My first meeting with Jean. ... I want to get each detail clear in my mind. I had decided to go to the lonely hut where Anne and I used to eat our little snacks, and where I knew she had later loved to meet young Azévédo. I didn't regard it in the light of a sentimental pilgrimage. What took me there was the knowledge that the trees had grown too big to make bird-watching easy, and that, consequently, I ran little risk of disturbing the guns. The hut was no longer used for shooting because the forest all around blotted out the horizon. There were no long, open drives in which it was possible to follow the movement of the coveys. The October sun was still hot. The sandy path hurt my feet, the flies plagued me. How heavy my body felt! I longed to sit down on the rotting bench in the hut. I opened the door, and a young man came out. He was bareheaded. I recognized him at first sight. It was Jean Azévédo, and he looked so confused that I thought I might have interrupted some amorous tryst. I tried to get away, but in vain. Oddly enough, he seemed intent on keeping me there. "Please come in," he said. "You're not disturbing me at all; truly you're not."

'He was so insistent that I went into the hut, and was surprised to find nobody there. Perhaps the country girl whose presence I suspected had made good her escape by another exit. But no twig had snapped. He, too, had recognized me and began to talk of Anne de la Trave. I had sat down, but he remained standing just as I had seen him in the snapshot. My eyes sought, through the silk shirt, the spot where I had pierced him with my pin. There was no touch of passion in my glance, only a cold curiosity. Was he good-looking? He had a high forehead and the eyes of his race. His cheeks were too full, and he was afflicted with what I most dislike in young men, pimples, those signs of the sappy movement of the blood that speak of unwholesomeness. Worst of all, he had moist palms which he dried with his handkerchief before shaking my hand. But there was fire in the depths of his fine eyes, and I liked the wide mouth, which was never quite shut, and the sharp teeth. It reminded me of the muzzle of a young dog suffering from the heat. And how did I behave? I was very family-conscious, I remember, and took a high line with him from the first, accusing him, rather solemnly, of "bringing discord into a respectable home". There was nothing assumed about his amazement. He laughed in my face. "Do you really believe that I want to marry her? that I aspire to such a prize as that?" I was dumbfounded when I realized, as I did at once, the gulf which existed between Anne's passionate adoration and this young man's complete indifference. He defended himself hotly. How could he help, he said, yielding to the charms of so delightful a child? Where was the harm in having a bit of fun? Just because there never had been any question of marriage between them, it had all seemed to him perfectly legitimate. Of course he had pretended to fall in with her views. By this time I was mounted on my high horse,

but when I interrupted him he started off again more urgently
than ever. Anne would tell me herself that he had never gone
too far. Of one thing he was quite certain, that he had probably given Mademoiselle de la Trave the only chance she
would ever have in her whole gloomy existence of tasting real
passion. "You say she's miserable. But tell me honestly, do
you think she can look forward to anything better than such
misery? I know you by reputation. I know that one can speak
frankly to you, that you're not like most of the people round
here. She's all set for a dull life in some old house in Saint-
Clair. At least I have given her feeling and dreams to hoard
up against her old age – something to save her from despair,
perhaps, and certainly from becoming stupid and unimagina-
tive." I can't remember whether I was exasperated by this
monstrous piece of affectation, or whether I even noticed it.
Truth to tell, he spoke so fast that at first I had considerable
difficulty in following him, though after a while my mind
adjusted itself to his spate of words. "Was it likely that I
should contemplate such a marriage, should drop anchor in
such shifting sands, or saddle myself in Paris with a little girl
like that? I shall always remember Anne as a delightful
incident in my life – as a matter of fact, I was thinking of her
when you came on me so suddenly. But how can anyone dream
of tying himself up for good? One should be in a position to
suck the last drop of pleasure from each fleeting moment –
and every pleasure is different from those that have gone
before." This greediness, as of a young animal, this sudden
discovery of *one* intelligent person, seemed to me so strange
that I listened to what he had to say without making any
attempt to interrupt him. I was completely dazzled – pretty
easily, I admit: but the fact remains that I was. I remember
the pattering of hooves, the tinkling of bells, the wild cries
of shepherds in the distance, which told of an approaching
flock. I told the young man that it might seem rather strange
if we were found alone together in the hut. I should have
liked him to reply that we had better not make a sound until
the flock had passed. I should have enjoyed staying there with
him in complete silence, should have relished the sense of

guilty complicity (for I, too, was becoming exigent, was beginning to demand that each minute bring something to live for), but Jean Azévédo opened the door without a word of protest and, after ceremoniously taking leave, stood back for me to pass. He followed me to Argelouse only after making quite certain that I had no objection to his doing so. How quickly the time passed, though my companion managed to touch on a thousand different subjects. In an odd sort of way he gave a new freshness to things with which I had long been familiar – to the question of religion, for instance. When I repeated the kind of thing I was used to saying in the family circle, he broke in with: "No doubt that's true enough, but it's all really a great deal more complicated. ..." He brought to the argument a clearness of vision which I could not help admiring. ... But was it so admirable, after all? ... I feel pretty sure that today my stomach would reject such a mixed dish. He told me he had long believed that the only really important thing was to seek God and strive after Him. "All that matters is to hoist one's sails and make for the open sea, avoiding like the plague all those who persuade themselves that they have found what they sought, who cease to move forward, but build their little shelters and compose themselves to slumber. I have long mistrusted all such people. ..."

'He asked whether I had read René Bazin's *La Vie du Père de Foucauld*, and when I gave him a mocking answer assured me that the book had completely knocked him sideways. "To live dangerously, in the fullest sense of the word, that's what ought to be one's object. It's not so much seeking God that matters, as, having once found him, to remain within his orbit." He described to me the "great adventure of the mystics," and bewailed the fact that he was not temperamentally suited to follow in their steps. As far back as he could remember, he said, he had never been pure. How different was such immodesty, such facile self-confession, from the scrupulous wariness of my country neighbours, from the silence with which, at home, we surrounded the secrets of our personal lives! The gossips of Saint-Clair move only on the surface of things: one never sees into their hearts. What do

I really know of Bernard? Surely there must be a lot more to him than the caricature of a man with which I have to rest content whenever I feel tempted to conjure up his image? Jean did all the talking and I remained silent. Nothing came to my lips but the habitual phrases of which I made use in our family arguments. Just as in this part of the country all carriages are precisely "fitted to the road", or, in other words, just wide enough to ensure that the wheels will fit neatly into the ruts made by the passing waggons, so all my thoughts, till that moment, had been equally "fitted to the road" which my father and my parents-in-law had traced. Jean Azévédo walked bareheaded. I can see again his open shirt and the glimpse it gave of a chest which might have been that of a child, and of his rather over-developed neck. Had I fallen a victim to his physical charms? Good heavens, no! But he was the first man I had met for whom the life of the mind meant everything. His masters, his Paris friends – whose sayings and whose books he constantly quoted to me – made it impossible to regard him as in any way exceptional. He was just one of a numerous *élite* – "the people who are really alive", he called them. He mentioned names. It did not occur to him for a single moment that I might never have heard of them – and I pretended that I was not now making their acquaintance for the first time.

'When, at a turn in the road, we saw before us the Argelouse paddock, I exclaimed, "Back already!" Smoke from the scorched grass hung low over the poor soil from which the rye crop had already been lifted. Through a gap in the bank a flock of sheep was winding its way, looking like dirty milk, and apparently browsing on the sand. Jean had to cross the paddock in order to reach Vilméja. I said: "I'm coming with you: I'm wildly interested in all these questions." But we found no more to say. The rye stubble hurt my feet through the thin soles of my shoes. I had a feeling that he wanted to be alone, no doubt in order to pursue at leisure some line of thought which had presented itself to his mind. I pointed out to him that we had not spoken of Anne. He answered that we were not free to choose the subject of our conversation, or even of our thoughts. "One can do that," he added with a little show of arrogance, "only if one submits to the discipline invented by the mystics. ... People like us always float with the current, go where the slope leads. ..." In this way he brought back our talk to the books he was reading at the moment. We arranged to meet again in order to draw up a plan of campaign about Anne. He spoke absent-mindedly, and, without answering some question I had put to him, suddenly bent down. With a childlike gesture he pointed to a mushroom growing there, sniffed at it, and put it to his lips.'

7

WHEN she got back she had found Bernard waiting for her on the doorstep. 'There's nothing wrong with me!' he had cried, as soon as he caught a glimpse of her dress in the half-light; 'nothing at all – except, believe it or not, that I'm anaemic, a big, hulking fellow like me. Appearances, it seems, are deceptive. I've got to have a course of treatment – Fowler ... it's got arsenic in it, you know. The important thing is that I should get back my appetite. ...'

Thérèse remembered that at first she had felt no irritation. Bernard's affairs seemed to make less impression on her than usual (it was as though someone had fired at long range, and missed her). She barely heard him. She seemed caught up, body and mind, into an entirely different world, a place of eager beings whose sole desire was to know and understand; to be 'themselves', as Jean had said more than once with an air of deep satisfaction. Later, as they sat at their meal, and she brought herself to mention the afternoon's meeting, Bernard exclaimed: 'You *are* an odd creature! And what have you decided?'

She proceeded, there and then, to improvise the plan which was, in fact, the one they carried out. Jean Azévédo had agreed to write a letter to Anne in which, as gently as possible, he would kill any hope that she might have entertained. Bernard laughed sceptically when she insisted that the young man set no store whatever by such a marriage. What! an Azévédo not care whether he married an Anne de la Trave or not? 'You must be mad! The truth of the matter is that he knows there's nothing doing. Chaps of his kidney won't take risks when they know that they are bound to lose. You're still very innocent, my dear!'

Because of the mosquitoes, he had been unwilling to have the lamp lighted. Consequently, he could not see the expression of her face. He had 'recovered his appetite', as he put it. Already the Bordeaux doctor had given him a new lease of life.

'Did I see much more of Jean Azévédo? ... He left Argelouse towards the end of October. We may have gone walking together five or six times. The only occasion of which I have any clear recollection is the one on which we composed the letter he was to send to Anne. He was not a very experienced young man, and used expressions which he thought would allay her fears, though I knew perfectly well how horrible she would find them. Our last expeditions are all mixed up in a single memory. Jean Azévédo described Paris to me, and the friends he had there. I imagined a sort of a realm in which the only law was "be thyself".

' "Here you are condemned to a life of deceit until you die." Did he say that deliberately? What did he suspect? I should find it impossible, according to him, to breathe so stifling an atmosphere. "Look," he said, "at the vast, smooth surface of ice beneath which the minds of all here are frozen. Through an occasional hole the water shows black. That means that someone has disappeared after a violent struggle. But the crust re-forms above it. ... For each man, here as elsewhere, is born subject to the law of his nature : here, as elsewhere, individual destiny rules each single life. It is no good kicking against the pricks. But some do, and that accounts for those petty dramas which the various families agree to keep shrouded in silence. As they say hereabouts, 'Not a word ...' "

' "How right you are!" I exclaimed. "There have been times when I have asked about some great-uncle, or about some woman of an older generation, whose photographs have been removed from the family album: but the only answer I have ever got is: 'He took himself off ... it was arranged that he should. ...' "

'Did Jean Azévédo fear some such fate for me? He said that it would never occur to him to talk of these matters to Anne because, in spite of her passionate nature, she was really a very simple little soul. There was not much fight in her. She would quickly toe the line. "But you're different! In your every word I can detect a hunger and thirst after sincerity. ..." Need I tell Bernard all the things he said? It was madness to hope that my husband would be capable of even understanding them! But I must make him see that I did not surrender without a struggle. I remember arguing with Jean, telling him that he was merely dressing up the worst kind of moral depravity in high-sounding phrases. I even had recourse to the copybook maxim which lingered on in my memory from schooldays. "Be thyself," I said. "But we are what we are only in so far as we make our own characters." (Unnecessary to develop the thought now, though I might have to do so later for Bernard's benefit.) Jean Azévédo denied that there could be any depravity worse than the denial of self. He maintained that heroes and saints habitually struck a balance-sheet of their natures, that they became what they were only because they realized their limitations. "If one is to find God one must transcend one's limitations," he kept on saying. And, on another occasion: "Accepting ourselves for what we are forces each one of us to come to grips with his real nature, to see it clearly and engage it in mortal combat. That is why so many emancipated minds become converted to religion in its narrowest forms."

'I shall not discuss with Bernard the rights and wrongs of such a moral doctrine: I'm even prepared to subscribe to his view that it doubtless contains much wretched sophistry. But he must understand, must make himself understand, just how a woman of my sort could be irritated by the life we led, just what she felt on those evenings in the dining-room at Argelouse when he was taking off his boots in the kitchen next door, and regaling me the while, in a rich local dialect, with talk of the day's happenings. I can see it all now: the captive birds struggling in the bag on the table, distending it with their movements, and Bernard eating slowly, relishing his recovered appetite, counting with loving care the "Fowler" drops, and saying, while he did so, "This is what is making me well." A great fire used to be burning on the hearth, and he had only to turn his chair to be able to stretch his slippered feet to the blaze. He would nod over *la Petite Gironde*. Sometimes he snored, but there were times too, when I scarcely heard him breathe. Old Madame Balion's clogs would sound on the kitchen flags, and she would appear with the candles. All around us was the silence: the silence of Argelouse! People who have never lived in that lost corner of the heath-country can have no idea what silence means. It stands like a wall about the house, and the house itself seems as though it were set solid in the dense mass of the forest, whence comes no sign of life, save occasionally the hooting of an owl. (At night I could almost believe that I heard the sob I was at such pains to stifle.)

'It was after Azévédo had gone that I got to know that silence. So long as I was sure that he would come to me with the new day the thought of his presence robbed the smothering dark of all its terrors. The fact that he was lying asleep near by gave me a feeling that the night and all the sweep of moorland was rich with life. But when he left Argelouse after that last meeting at which he arranged that we should meet in a year's time, and was full of hope (he said) that when the day came I should have found some way of freeing myself (I still don't know whether he threw that out lightheartedly or whether there was some idea at the back of his mind. I have an impression that, being a bred-in-the-bone Parisian, he could not bear the silence, the particular silence of Argelouse, any longer, and that he adored me simply and solely because I was his one and only audience) – when I saw the last of him, I felt as though I had plunged into an endless tunnel, that I was driving ahead into a darkness which grew more dense the farther I advanced, so that I sometimes wondered whether I should suffocate before I reached the open air again.

'But until my labours began in January nothing happened...'

At this point Thérèse began to hesitate, forcing her mind from brooding on what had occurred in the house at Argelouse on the day after Jean's departure. 'No,' she thought, 'that has nothing whatever to do with what I've got to explain to Bernard when we meet. I have no time to waste wandering up blind alleys.' But the mind is impatient of discipline. We cannot prevent it from roaming at will. She completely failed to blot that October evening from her memory. Upstairs, on the first floor, Bernard was undressing. She was waiting until the last of the fire should have died down before joining him, happy to be left alone even for a minute. What was Jean Azévédo doing? Perhaps he was drinking in the little bar of which he had told her: perhaps (for the night was mild) he was driving in his car with a friend through the deserted Bois de Boulogne; perhaps he was sitting at his table, working, with the Paris traffic rumbling a distant accompaniment. If there was silence about him, it was of his own creation, a little niche of peace hollowed out of the hubbub of the world: not forced on him from without, like the silence in which Thérèse sat suffocating. His was the achievement of a determined will, though it reached no farther than the circle of lamplight and the packed bookshelves.

... So her mind worked, and then the dog barked, and followed the bark with a whimper, as a well-known voice, speaking in tones of utter exhaustion from somewhere in the hall, quieted him.

Anne de la Trave opened the door. She had walked all the way from Saint-Clair in the dark and her shoes were clotted with mud. In her face – which had grown much older – the eyes shone bright. She flung her hat into an arm-chair. 'Where is he?' she said.

Once the famous letter had been written and posted, Thérèse and Jean had regarded the whole affair as being over and done with. It never occurred to them that Anne might find it impossible to let go her hold: How could anyone be expected to yield to the promptings of reason or the force of logic when her whole life was at stake? She had managed to escape her mother's vigilance, and to take a train. On the dark road to Argelouse she had been guided by the strips of clear sky which showed between the trees. The only thing that mattered was that she should see him again. If only she could be at his side he *must* yield once more to her charm. She had *got* to see him. She stumbled in her haste to reach Argelouse. Her feet caught in the ruts. And now, here was Thérèse telling her that he had gone, that he was back in Paris. She shook her head in denial, refusing to believe it. If she did not refuse to believe it she would faint from weariness and despair.

'You're lying to me: you've always lied to me.'

Thérèse protested, but the girl went on:

'You're just like all the rest of the family ... for all your emancipated airs. ... As soon as you married you became just another woman of the same old lot. I know you meant well. You betrayed me for my own good, didn't you? Don't bother to explain; I know exactly what you're going to say.'

She opened the door again. Thérèse asked where she was going.

'To Vilméja, to his home.'

'But he hasn't been there for the past two days. I've told you that already.'

'I don't believe you.'

She left the room. Thérèse lit the lantern which hung in the hall, and followed her.

'You're going wrong, Anne dear. That's the way to Biourge; Vilméja's in the other direction.'

They walked on through the mist which was drifting up from the fields. Dogs woke as they passed. At length they saw the oaks of Vilméja, and the house itself, not sleeping now but dead. Anne wandered round the empty sepulchre. She beat on the door with her two fists. Thérèse stood there motionless. She had set the lantern on the grass. She saw the faint outline of her friend as she flattened herself against each ground-floor window. No doubt she was saying that one name over and over again, though not aloud, for what good would that have done? For a moment or two the house hid her. Then she reappeared, reached the door once more, and sank down on the threshold, clasping her arms about her knees, hiding her face. Thérèse raised her up and led her away. The girl, stumbling as she went, kept on saying: 'Tomorrow morning I shall go to Paris. Paris is large, but I shall find him all right. ...' She spoke like a child at the end of its tether, and as though she were already emptied of all hope.

Bernard, who had been awakened by the sound of their voices, was waiting for them in the drawing-room, wrapped in a dressing-gown. It was a mistake on Thérèse's part to turn her mind from the memory of the scene which flared up between brother and sister. This man, who could seize an exhausted young girl by the wrists, drag her upstairs, and lock her in her room, is your husband, that same Bernard who, in two hours' time, will be your judge. The spirit of the family inspires his every action, making it impossible for him to hesitate even for a moment. Always, in every circumstance, he knows what must be done in the interests of the family. You dread the meeting: you are busy preparing a detailed defence. But only men without strong principles can yield to the unexpected argument. Bernard will laugh at your carefully reasoned defence. 'I know what's got to be done.' He always knows what's got to be done. If, at times, he finds himself hesitating, he says: 'We discussed all that at a family council, and we've made up our minds. ...' Sentence has already been pronounced upon you: how can you doubt it? Your fate has been irremediably determined. You might just as well go to sleep.

8

WHEN the de la Traves had overcome Anne's resistance and taken her back to Saint-Clair, Thérèse remained at Argelouse until her child was due to be born. She learned to know every feature of its silence during those endless November nights. She had written a letter to Jean Azévédo, but it remained unanswered. Clearly, he thought it not worth his while to embark on the tedium of a correspondence with a country girl. Besides, an expectant mother is never a very pleasant object to remember. Perhaps, now that he was away from her, he thought of her only as a drab little nonentity. The fool! Had she cared to indulge in trumped-up subtleties and scenes of melodrama, she could have held him easily enough! How could a man of his kind understand such deceptive simplicity as hers? How interpret her honest gaze and clear-cut certainty of gesture? Better face the truth. He believed that she, just as he had believed that the poor child Anne, was quite capable of taking him at his word, of leaving all and following him. Jean Azévédo was distrustful of women who throw down their arms before the enemy has even had the time to lay siege to them. He dreaded nothing so much as victory and the fruits of victory. Nevertheless, Thérèse forced herself to live in his mental world, though the books he admired (she had ordered them from Bordeaux) seemed to her utterly incomprehensible. How bored she was! There was no question of her filling the hours with making and sewing for the expected baby. That, said Madame de la Trave, 'was not her responsibility.' Many women living in the country die in childbirth. Thérèse made Aunt Clara cry by insisting that she would, as her mother had done before her: that she was sure she would not escape the fate hanging over her. Whenever she spoke like that, she was careful to add that she did not much care whether she lived or whether she didn't. But that was a lie. Never had she been so hungry for life, and never had Bernard shown himself more attentive. 'He wasn't concerned so much for me as for what I was carrying *in* me. He might drool on in that appalling brogue of his, "Now do eat up your mince ... you mustn't have any fish ... you've done quite enough walking for one day. ..." It no more affected me than a complaint about the quality of her milk affects a wet-nurse who has no particular interest in her employer's family. The de la Traves bestowed on me the same sort of regard as they would have done on a sacred vessel. I was just the container of their young. Had the necessity arisen, I am quite sure that they would have sacrificed me to my unborn child without a qualm. I lost all sense of being an individual person. In the eyes of the family I was merely a species of vine-shoot. All that mattered to them was the fruit of my womb.

'I had to go on living in that gloomy world until the end of December. As though there weren't enough pines already, the ceaseless rain built a million moving barriers about the darkened house. When it seemed likely that the single road to Saint-Clair would soon be impracticable, I was taken into the local town and settled into a house which was scarcely less overgrown and dark than Argelouse. The old plane-trees in the public Square were fighting with the rainy wind in an effort to keep their last few leaves. Aunt Clara, who could live nowhere but at Argelouse, refused to keep me company. But she braved the journey in all weathers, driving over to see me in her "just wide enough" gig. She brought me the little treats I had loved as a child, thinking that I loved them still – greyish lumps of honey and rye called "miques", the sort of cake known locally as "fougasse" or "roumadjade". I saw Anne only at meals, and she no longer spoke to me. She seemed to be cowed and resigned. Quite suddenly she had lost all her former freshness, and wore her hair drawn back so tightly that it left her rather ugly and anaemic ears plainly visible. Young Deguilheim's name was never mentioned, but Madame de la Trave asserted that if Anne had not yet said "yes" she at least was no longer saying "no". How right Jean had been about her. It had not taken long to break her in to harness. Bernard was less well than he had been, because he had started tippling again. What did all these people among whom I lived talk about? They discussed the Curé a good deal, I remember (the Presbytery was just opposite). There was much curiosity expressed, for instance, about why he had crossed the Square four times in one day, returning on each occasion by a different route. ...'

On account of something that Jean Azévédo had said,

Thérèse paid a good deal more attention to this young priest than she would otherwise have done. He had few points of contact with his parishioners. They thought him 'arrogant' – 'He's not the sort of man we need here.' On the rare occasions of his visits to the de la Trave household, Thérèse studied his greying temples and high forehead. How did he spend his evenings? He had no friends. Why had he chosen the religious life? 'He is very scrupulous,' said Madame de la Trave. 'He makes his act of adoration every evening, but he lacks unction. He is not what *I* call pious, and he does nothing whatever about social work.' She deplored the fact that he had done away with all ostentation of charity. The local parents, too, complained that he did not play football with the children. 'It's all very well to bury one's nose in books all day long; but a man can very soon lose his hold on a parish.' Thérèse went regularly to church in order to hear him preach. 'You've chosen just the moment, my dear, when you might well be excused from all such duties by reason of your condition.'

The Curé's sermons on points of dogma and morals were completely impersonal. But Thérèse was interested in the inflexions of his voice, in his gestures. At times he would lay particular stress on some one word. ... Ah! he, perhaps, might help her to come to terms with the confusion of her spirit. He was not like the people round her. He, too, had chosen the way of tragedy. To the solitude within he had added that desert which the soutane creates round those who wear it. What comfort did he find in the daily rites? She would have liked to be present at his weekday Masses, when, with only a single choirboy for congregation, he bent, murmuring, above a scrap of bread. But for her to have done so would have seemed odd to the members of her family and to the good people of the town. There would have been gossip about 'conversion'.

Though Thérèse's sufferings at that time may have been severe, it was only after the birth of her child that she really began to find life unendurable. Not that anything much happened. There were no scenes between her and Bernard.

She was more deferential to the parents even than he was. That there was no apparent reason for a break made the whole business more tragic. It seemed that nothing could possibly occur to disturb the flat routine of their days. They would go on just like this till they died. Disagreement presupposes the existence of a common ground on which the struggle can be waged. But Thérèse had no ground in common with Bernard, and still less with her mother- and father-in-law. Their words made no impression on her. It never occurred to her that she might be expected to answer when they spoke to her. They did not even share the same language, but attached totally different meanings to every essential word. Occasionally Thérèse might be goaded into an expression of sincerity. But it had no effect. The family had long ago agreed that she loved talking for talking's sake. 'I just pretend not to listen,' said Madame de la Trave; 'and, if she goes on, I look as though I didn't attach any importance to what she says. She knows that all that talk of hers does not impress *us*. ...'

All the same, Madame de la Trave found it hard to put up with Thérèse's affectation of annoyance when people said how like her little Marie was. The ordinary chatter customary on such occasions ('You'd know at once whose child *she* is!') threw the young mother into transports of irritability, and these she could not always conceal. 'There's nothing of me in the little creature!' she would insist. 'Look at her brown skin and jet-black eyes. Compare her with one of *my* early photographs. I was a pasty little girl.'

She had no wish for Marie to be like her, she wanted to have as little as possible in common with the scrap of flesh and blood which had issued from her body. It began to be said that the maternal instinct did not trouble her unduly. But Madame de la Trave maintained that she was fond of the child in her own funny way. 'It's no good expecting her to give her her bath or to change her nappies. She's not that sort of woman. But I've seen her sitting a whole evening by the child's cradle, and not smoking at all, just so as she could watch her sleeping. ... We have an excellent nurse, and then, you see, there's always Anne. Now, *she's* utterly different!

She'll make a wonderful mother, no doubt about that. ...'
It was true that, with a child in the house, Anne had begun to
live again. Women are always attracted by a cradle, but Anne
seemed to find some peculiarly profound happiness in dandling
the baby. In order to have free access to it, she had made her
peace with Thérèse, though nothing of their old affection
remained apart from their use of pet names and familiar
gestures. The girl dreaded especially lest Thérèse's maternal
jealousy might be aroused. 'The little darling is much more at
ease with me than with her. Whenever she sees me she gurgles.
The other day I was holding her in my arms, and she started
to howl when Thérèse tried to take her from me. She is so
much fonder of me that it sometimes makes me feel quite
embarrassed. ...'

But she need not have been. All through this period of her
life Thérèse felt as though she were completely detached from
everyone, the child included. She saw people and things, her
own body and even her own mind, in the form of a mirage,
as a sort of cloud suspended outside herself. In all this emptiness Bernard alone had a horrible, a frightening, reality, with
his fat paunch, his nasal drawl, his peremptory way of talking,
his self-complacency. Escape from her world? – but how and
whither? The beginning of the hot weather completely
exhausted her. No premonition came to warn her of what she
was about to do. What happened that year? She could remember no single incident, no quarrel, only that she had felt more
detestation of her husband than usual on the occasion of the
Corpus Christi procession which she had watched from behind
half-closed shutters. Bernard was almost the only man walking
behind the Canopy. Within a few moments the village street
became as completely deserted as though a lion and not a
lamb had been let loose. ... The inhabitants ran for shelter
so as to avoid the necessity of uncovering or kneeling. Once
the danger had passed, doors began to open one by one.
Thérèse stared at the Curé, who was walking with eyes almost
completely shut, bearing in his two hands the strange,
mysterious object. His lips were moving. To whom was he

talking with that look of suffering on his face? And then, suddenly, she saw behind him Bernard 'doing his duty'.

Week followed week without so much as a drop of rain. Bernard lived in constant terror of fire. He was suffering from his heart again. More than a thousand acres had been burned over at Louchats. 'If the wind had been from the north I should have lost my Balisac pines.' Thérèse was in a state of waiting for she knew not what to fall from the immutable sky. It would never rain again. One day the whole surrounding forest would crackle into flame, even the town itself would not be spared. Why was it that the heath villages never caught fire? It seemed to her unjust that it should always be the trees that the flames chose, never the human beings. In the family circle there was a never-ending discussion about what caused these disasters. Was it a discarded cigarette, or was it deliberate mischief? Thérèse liked to imagine that one of these nights she would get up, leave the house, reach the most inflammable part of the forest, throw away her cigarette, and watch the great column of smoke stain the dawn sky. ... But she drove the thought from her, for the love of pine-trees was in her blood. It was not them that she hated.

And now the moment had been reached at which she must look her act straight in the face. How could she explain it to Bernard? All she could do would be to take him, step by step, over the road she had travelled to it. It was the day on which a big fire had broken out towards Mano. Some men from the estate had come into the dining-room where the members of the family were eating a hurried luncheon. Some of them said that the blaze was a long way from Saint-Clair, others that the tocsin ought to be sounded. The smell of burning resin filled the stifling air, and the sun looked dirty. Thinking back, Thérèse could see Bernard sitting there with his head turned, listening to Balion's report on the situation, and quite forgetful of the fact that his great hairy hand was holding his bottle of 'Fowler' over a glass of water, into which the drops were falling all unnoticed. He swallowed the medicine at a single gulp, before Thérèse, over-powered by the heat, could warn him that he had taken twice his usual dose. Everyone except herself had left the table. She sat there cracking fresh almonds, indifferent to what was going on, wholly detached from the drama of the fire as from every drama except her own. The tocsin did not sound, and Bernard came back into the room. 'For once you were right not to get excited. The fire's way over at Mano.' Then: 'Did I take my drops?' he asked. Without waiting for her answer, he began shaking some more into his glass. She said nothing, partly because she was too lazy to speak, partly, too, no doubt, because she was tired. For what was she hoping at that moment? 'I just can't believe that I deliberately *planned* to say nothing.'

But when, that night, Bernard lay vomiting and moaning in his bed, and Dr Pédemay asked her what had happened, she told him nothing about what she had seen in the dining-room, though it would have been so easy, without in any way compromising herself, to have drawn the doctor's attention to the arsenic which Bernard was taking. She could have said something like 'I didn't really notice it at the time ... we were all so much distracted by the fire ... but I'm prepared to swear now that he took twice his usual dose. ...' But she remained silent. Had she even felt tempted to say anything? The act which, at luncheon, had already though she did not know it, started to germinate in her mind began then to emerge from the depths of her being into the light ... formless still, but struggling into consciousness.

When the doctor had gone she stood there looking at Bernard, who had at last dropped off to sleep. She thought: 'There is nothing to prove it was *that*. It might be an attack of appendicitis, though there are no other symptoms ... or a case of virulent influenza.' But two days later Bernard was up and about again. 'It looks as though it *was* that.' Thérèse could not have sworn it was, and she wanted to be sure. 'I did not feel that I had been the prey of a horrible temptation. It was simply that I was curious, and, if I was to satisfy my curiosity, there were certain risks that I had to take. The first occasion on which I put some Fowler drops into his glass before he came into the room I remember saying to myself, "Just once, to clear my mind of uncertainty. I shall know now whether it really *was* that. Just this once – I won't ever do it again. ..." '

The train came to a halt, uttered a long whistle, and started to move again. Two or three lights showed in the darkness. Saint-Clair station. But there was nothing more at which Thérèse need peer and puzzle. The maw of her crime had swallowed her, had sucked her in, sucked her down. Bernard knew, just as well as she did, what had followed: the sudden return of his weakness, with Thérèse watching by him night and day, though she seemed to have no strength left, and was incapable of swallowing even a mouthful of food (she was so exhausted, indeed, that he had persuaded her to try the Fowler treatment herself, and she had actually got Dr Pédemay to give her the necessary prescription). Poor doctor! – so surprised at the greenish colour of Bernard's vomitings, finding it hard to believe that so great a discrepancy could exist between a sick man's pulse and his temperature. He had often, in cases of paratyphoid, met with a slow pulse combined with a high temperature, but what could it mean when a racing pulse went with a subnormal temperature? Toxic influenza, no doubt. That magic word 'influenza' was held to explain everything. Madame de la Trave played with the idea of calling in a well-known consultant, but did not wish to affront the doctor, who was an old friend. Besides, Thérèse feared the effect of such a step on Bernard. About the middle of August, however, after a more than usually alarming crisis, Pédemay himself suggested a second opinion. Fortunately, however, next day Bernard began to show signs of improvement, and three weeks later he was said to be well on the way to convalescence. 'That was a narrow escape for me,' said Pédemay. 'If the great man had got here in time all the credit for the cure would have gone to him.'

Bernard had himself moved to Argelouse, counting on the duck-shooting to set him to rights again. It was an exhausting time for Thérèse. A sharp attack of rheumatism had confined

Aunt Clara to her bed, and all the work of the house fell on the younger woman. She had two invalids to look after, as well as the child, and all the chores that were usually shouldered by Aunt Clara. She was only too glad to do what she could to take the sick woman's place with the poor of Argelouse. She went round the farms, saw that the doctor's instructions were obeyed, and bought the necessary medicines out of her own pocket. It never occurred to her that the empty house at Vilméja might be a cause of sorrow. She was no longer thinking about Jean Azévédo, nor, for that matter, about anybody else. She seemed tearing through a tunnel in utter loneliness. She had reached its darkest point. Like some panic-stricken animal, she felt only that she had got to get out of the blackness, out of the smoke, into the fresh air, as quickly as she possibly could.

At the beginning of September Bernard had had a bad relapse. He awoke one morning shivering, his legs useless and without feeling. What a nightmare the following days had been! A consultant had been brought from Bordeaux one evening by Monsieur de la Trave. He had examined the patient and then, for a while, said nothing. (Thérèse had held the lamp, and Madame Balion still remembers that she looked whiter than the sheets.) On the badly-lit landing, Pédemay, keeping his voice low lest Thérèse should overhear him, had explained to his colleague that Darquey, the chemist, had shown him two forged prescriptions. To one of them a criminal hand had added the words *Fowler Mixture*: the other contained pretty powerful doses of chloroform, digitalis, and aconite. Balion had given them to the chemist together with several others. Darquey, worried to death by the thought that he had supplied these dangerous drugs, had rushed off next morning to Pédemay. ... Yes, all these details were as familiar to Bernard as they were to Thérèse. An ambulance, hastily summoned, had taken him off to a hospital in Bordeaux, and from that moment he had begun to improve. Thérèse had remained alone at Argelouse. Despite her solitude, she had been conscious of the sound of many voices. She was like a trapped animal that hears the pack drawing close and lies exhausted after a gruelling chase. It was as though, within reach of her goal, her hand already stretched to touch it, she had been suddenly flung to the earth. Her legs had buckled beneath her. She could no longer keep her feet. One evening, towards the end of the winter, her father had come over. He begged her to clear herself of suspicion. There was still time to put everything to rights. Pédemay had agreed not to proceed with the charge: had pretended that he could not be sure that one of the prescriptions was not wholly in his own handwriting. He couldn't, he said, have ordered such strong doses of chloroform and digitalis, but then no traces of them had been found in the sick man's blood, and ...

Thérèse remembered that scene with her father. It had taken place at Aunt Clara's bedside. The room was lit by the flickering of a wood fire. Neither of them had wanted a lamp. She had explained, in the dull, flat voice of a child reciting a lesson (the lesson which she had rehearsed over and over again as she lay sleepless in her bed): 'I met a stranger on the road. He said that since I was sending someone in to Darquey's, he hoped I would consent to have a prescription made up for him. He owed money to Darquey, and didn't want to show his face in the man's shop. He promised to come and fetch the drugs from the house, but gave me neither his name nor his address....'

'You'll have to find a better story than that, Thérèse. I beg you, for the sake of the family, to do so. Wretched woman! you *must* do something!'

Over and over again old Larroque had upbraided her. The deaf old spinster, lying propped up on her pillows, and feeling that some mortal threat was hanging over Thérèse, had groaned: 'What's he saying? What does he want? Why is he being so horrible to you?'

She had summoned up sufficient strength to smile at her aunt. She had held her hand, and said again, like a small child reciting her catechism: 'It was a man I met on the road. It was too dark to see his face. He didn't tell me which of the farms he lived at.' Later, he had come one evening to fetch his medicines. Unfortunately, no one in the house had seen him.

9

SAINT-CLAIR at last. Thérèse was not recognized as she left
the train. While Balion was giving up her ticket she walked
round to the other side of the station and made her way between the wood-stacks to the road, where the trap was
waiting.

It had become, for her, a refuge. There was small risk that
anyone would meet them in the unmetalled lane. The whole
story of her past, so painfully reassembled, fell in ruins about
her. No jot nor tittle of her carefully rehearsed confession
remained. There was nothing that she could say in her defence, not so much as an explanation that she could give. The
easiest thing would be to say nothing, or, at least, to speak only
when she was questioned. What was there to fear? This night
would pass like other nights; tomorrow's sun would rise.
Whatever happened, she would come through. There could
be nothing worse in store for her than this feeling of utter
indifference, this sense of complete detachment which seemed
to have cut her off from the rest of the world, and even from
herself. Death in life. She was tasting death now as surely as
the living can ever do.

Her eyes grew accustomed to the darkness. At a turn in the
road she recognized a farm where the low outbuildings looked
like sleeping, crouching animals. It was here that, in the old
days, Anne had always been frightened of a dog which had a
way of jumping out at her bicycle wheel. A little farther on a
slight dip in the ground was screened by alders. No matter
how hot the day, a tremulous breath of coolness had always
touched their faces as they passed it. ... A child on a bicycle,
her teeth gleaming beneath a sun-hat – the sound of a bicycle
bell – a voice crying 'Look! I've taken my hands off!' ... In
those muddled memories was summed up all to which Thérèse
could cling. Mechanically, matching the words to the rhythm
of the horse's trot, she said over and over again to herself:
'The uselessness of my life: the emptiness of my life: unending

loneliness: no way out.' One gesture, and one only, would solve everything, but Bernard would never make it. If only he would take her in his arms and ask no questions! If only she could rest her head on a human shoulder, could weep knowing the comfort of a warm and human presence!

She saw the bank in the field on which, one blazing day, Jean Azévédo had sat. What a fool she was ever to have imagined that there might be some place in the world where she could sink to the earth with the knowledge that there were people round her who understood, who perhaps even admired and loved her! She was fated to carry loneliness about with her as a leper carries his scabs. 'No one can do anything for me: no one can do anything against me.'

'There's the Master and Miss Clara.'

Balion pulled on the reins. Two shadowy figures came forward. Bernard, though still very weak, was there to meet her – eager for reassurance. She half rose and, while they were still some distance off, cried out, 'Case dismissed!' All Bernard said was, 'I expected as much.' Then he helped his aunt into the trap and took the reins. Balion was left to walk back to the house. Aunt Clara sat between husband and wife. Thérèse had to shout in her ear that everything was settled (the poor old thing had only a very confused idea of what all the fuss had been about). As usual, she began to talk at breakneck speed. She said that *they* always did things in the same way: that it was the Dreyfus case all over again. 'Throw enough mud and some of it is bound to stick.' *They* were very powerful. The Republicans had been fools. They ought to have watched their step more closely. Give the beasts half a chance and they'd be on top of you. ... Her prattle made it unnecessary for the man and woman beside her to exchange a single word.

Aunt Clara, breathing heavily, climbed the stairs, a candle in her hand.

'Aren't you going to bed? Thérèse must be absolutely dead. You'll find a cup of soup in your room, and some cold chicken.'

But they remained standing in the hall. The old woman saw

Bernard open the drawing-room door, stand back to let Thérèse pass, and then follow her. If she had not been deaf she would have listened ... but they didn't have to worry their heads about people like her who were buried alive. Nevertheless, she blew out her candle, crept downstairs again, and put her eye to the keyhole. Bernard was moving the lamp. His brightly lit face looked at once solemn and intimidated. She saw Thérèse's seated back. The young woman had thrown her coat and hat on to an arm-chair. Her wet shoes were steaming in front of the fire. For a moment she turned her face towards her husband, and the old woman rejoiced to see that she was smiling.

Thérèse was smiling. In the brief moment of time which had elapsed, the few yards of space which had intervened between house and stable, she, walking there at Bernard's side, had realized suddenly – or thought that she had realized – what it was that she must do. His mere approach had reduced to nothing any hope she might have had of explaining herself, of throwing herself on his mercy. How distorted in our minds the people we know best become when we are not actually with them! All through the journey she had been busy, quite unconsciously, creating a Bernard who might be capable of understanding, of trying to understand. But she had only to see him, even for a moment, to remember what he was really like – a man who had never once in his life put himself in another person's shoes, to whom the effort to get outside himself, to see himself as others saw him, was inconceivable. Would he, if it came to that, even listen? He strode up and down the damp, low-ceiled room. Here and there the woodwork of the floor was rotting. It creaked beneath his tread. Not once did he look at his wife. He was bursting with a desire to say all the things that he had long premeditated. She, too, knew what she was going to say. The simplest solution is always the one we never think of. She would say: 'I am going to vanish out of your life, Bernard. Don't bother your head any more about me. I will go into the night – now, at once, if you want me to. I am not frightened of the forest,

nor yet of the darkness. They know me: we know one another.
I was created in the image of this barren land, where nothing
lives but passing birds and the roaming wild boar. I accept
your rejection of me. Burn all my photographs. Let my
child grow up in ignorance even of my name. Let it be to the
family as though I had never been.'

Already her lips were parted. She said:

'Let me just disappear, Bernard.'

At the sound of her voice he turned his head. He strode
towards her out of the shadows. The veins of his forehead
were swollen.

'What!' he sputtered, 'do you dare have an opinion? Are
you brazen enough to express a wish? Don't say another
word! Your business is to listen, to receive my orders – to
abide by my irrevocable decision!'

He had got control of his voice now. He had carefully
thought out what he was going to say, and now he was saying
it. Leaning on the mantelpiece, he proceeded to express himself with portentous solemnity. He took a paper from his
pocket and consulted it. Thérèse was no longer frightened:
she wanted to laugh. He was just comic – a figure of fun. It
did not matter what he said in that awful accent of his which
everywhere but in Saint-Clair made him a laughing-stock –
she was going away. Why all this fuss? It would not have
made the slightest difference to anyone if this fool had disappeared from the face of the earth! The paper trembled in his
hand, and she noticed his badly kept finger-nails. He was
wearing no cuffs. He was just a country oaf who looked merely
comic anywhere but in his accustomed rut, the kind of man
who, from any intellectual, or even personal, point of view,
is completely null and void. Only habit makes us attach importance to the life of the individual. Robespierre had been
right – and Napoleon and Lenin. He noticed that she was
smiling. The sight set him beside himself. He raised his voice.
She *should* listen.

'I've got you where I want you – understand that! You will
obey the decisions made by the family. If you don't ...'

'Well, if I don't – what?'

She no longer pretended to be indifferent. She faced him now with an air of mockery.

'Too late!' she cried: 'You gave evidence in my favour. You can't go back on what you said. If you do you will be guilty of perjury.'

'It is always possible to discover new facts. I've got one carefully locked away in my desk – proof positive that so far has not been made public. The law can't prevent me from producing *that*!'

She gave a start.

'What do you want me to do?' she asked.

He consulted his notes. For several seconds she was profoundly aware of the silence of Argelouse. Cockcrow was still far off. There was no sound of running water in this arid waste: no breeze stirred among the innumerable trees.

'I am not considering myself in this matter. For the moment I am out of the picture. The only thing I am worrying about is the family. Every decision of my life has been dictated by the interests of the family. For the honour of the family I consented to cheat justice. Let God be my Judge.'

His pomposity made Thérèse feel sick. She would have liked to tell him to say what he had to say more simply.

'For the sake of the family the world must suppose that we are in complete harmony. I shall make it quite clear that I believe in your innocence. On the other hand, I shall do everything in my power to protect myself. ...'

'Are you frightened of me, Bernard?'

In a low voice he said: 'Frightened? No: merely disgusted.' Then: 'I will come to the point and say what I have to say once and for all. Tomorrow we shall leave this place and move into the Desqueyroux house. It is not my wish that your aunt should live with us. Madame Balion will give you your meals in your room. You will be forbidden to enter any other, though you will be free to walk in the woods. On Sundays we shall attend High Mass at Saint-Clair together. You must be seen on my arm. On the first Thursday of each month we shall drive in an open carriage to the market at B—, and pay a visit to your father, as we have always done.'

'And Marie?'

'Marie will leave tomorrow with her nurse for Saint-Clair. Mother is going to take her to the South. We shall put it about that the state of her health has made change of air necessary. You didn't think, surely, that she was going to be left to *your* tender care? She, too, has got to be protected. Once I am dead and she has turned twenty-one, the property will go to her. First the husband, then the child. ... Why not?'

Thérèse got up. She wanted to scream.

'So you thought it was for the sake of your miserable trees that I ...'

Among all the myriad causes which had prompted her act this fool had not been able to understand a single one. He had had to invent the most squalid reason imaginable.

'Naturally – what other reason could there be? In matters like this one has to proceed by the method of elimination. I defy you to give me any other motive ... not that it is of the slightest importance. I am no longer interested in motives. You have ceased to have any meaning for me. The name you bear is the only thing that matters. In a few months' time, as soon as the fact of our reconciliation has been fully established, and Anne has married young Deguilheim ... you know, of course, that his parents have insisted on a delay ? they want to think things over ... in a few months' time, I say, I shall take up residence at Saint-Clair, and you will settle down here. We'll think up some plausible story – that you are suffering from neurasthenia, perhaps: something of that sort. ...'

'Wouldn't it do just to say that I am mad?'

'No, that would reflect on Marie. Don't worry; we'll find something.'

Thérèse murmured: 'Argelouse ... until I die. ...' She went over to the window and opened it. At this moment Bernard knew real happiness. Till now his wife had intimidated him, had made him feel small: but now *he* was on top! How conscious she must be of his contempt! His very moderation gave him a sense of pride. Madame de la Trave was never tired of telling him that he was a saint. The whole family

was loud in praise of his generous mind. For the first time he
really felt that he was a great man. When, at the hospital,
they had told him – oh, how tactfully! – of his wife's attempt
upon his life, the calm way in which he had responded had
earned him unstinted admiration – though it had cost him
remarkably little effort. Nothing is ever wholly serious for
those who are incapable of love. Because he was without
love Bernard had felt only that flicker of joy which comes to a
man when some great danger has been safely surmounted.
He felt like a man who has just been told that for years, and in
blissful ignorance, he has been living cheek by jowl with a
dangerous lunatic. But this evening he was conscious of a new
forcefulness. He felt that he was master of his fate. He realized,
not without surprise, that nothing can resist the man of upright character who has a mind which can reason logically.
Even though he had just come through a terrible ordeal, he
was ready to maintain that no one is ever really unhappy save
by his own fault. Nothing could be much worse than what he
had experienced, yet he had settled it as he might have settled
any other problem submitted to him for solution. Not that
he would ever let it be generally known. He would save his
self-respect. No one should pity him. He did not want pity.
What was there so particularly humiliating in having married a
monster? Nothing mattered so long as one had the last word.
After all, there was a good deal to be said for the life of the
unattached male. The close approach of death had put a
marvellous edge on his appetite for possessions – on his taste
for shooting, for driving his car, for eating and drinking – in
short, for life!

Thérèse was still standing by the window. She could see a
patch of white gravel, could smell the chrysanthemums
growing there behind the fence which gave protection from
the wandering cattle. Beyond the garden a dark mass of oaks
hid the pines from view, but the scent of resin filled the darkness. They stood ranked there, like a hostile army, unseen
but close at hand. She knew that the house was surrounded
by them. Like muffled warders, moaning in the wind, they
would watch her languish all the winter through, would hear

her gasp for breath in the stifling summer days. They would witness the slow process of her suffocation.

She closed the window, and turned back to Bernard.

'So you think you can keep me here by force?'

'I trust that you will make yourself quite at home. Only, please realize, once and for all, that if you leave this house it will be with handcuffs on your wrists.'

'Don't exaggerate! I know you too well to be bluffed, and there's no point in painting yourself blacker than you are. You would never expose the family to *that* disgrace. I'm not worrying.'

Like a man who has well weighed the pros and cons of a situation, he explained that by the very act of leaving she would tacitly admit her guilt. Should she choose to do so, then the family could avoid sharing in the general obloquy only by amputating the rotten limb, by casting her out, by publicly disclaiming her.

'That was what my mother, at first, wanted us to do. We were within an ace of letting justice take its course. Do you realize that? If it hadn't been for Anne and Marie ... But there is still time for us to change our minds. You needn't make your decision now. I give you until tomorrow.'

In a low voice Thérèse said:

'I've still got my father.'

'Your father sees eye to eye with us. He has his career to think about, his politics, the ideas for which he stands. He cares only about avoiding a scandal at all costs. You ought at least to show some gratitude for what he has done. If the prosecution broke down, it was entirely owing to him. ... I can scarcely believe that he has kept his decision from you.'

Bernard was no longer shouting. He had relapsed into a manner which was almost polite. It was not that he felt the slightest compassion. But this woman, whose breathing he could barely hear, was lying, at last, helpless at his feet. She was where she ought to be. The whole situation was getting itself very satisfactorily sorted out. Beneath such a blow any other man would have said good-bye to happiness. He took pride in the fact that he had managed to withstand the shattering shock. The world in general may be wrong: the world in general *had* been wrong about Thérèse – even Madame de la Trave, whose sharp eye for character had been bred of long practice. The trouble nowadays was that the world no longer set any value on moral principles, was no longer willing to admit that there may be great danger in the kind of education that Thérèse had received. No doubt she was a monster; still ... if only she had believed in God ... Fear is the beginning of wisdom.

So thought Bernard. He reflected that the small-town society, eager to taste the sweetness of the humiliation which had fallen on the Desqueyroux, would be nicely hoodwinked at the sight of so united a family each Sunday morning! He could hardly wait for Sunday to come round, so anxious was he to see his neighbours' faces! ... But Justice would not be cheated: he would see to that. ... He took the lamp and held it high so that the light fell on the back of Thérèse's neck.

'Are you coming up?'

She seemed not to hear him. He went out of the room, leaving her. Aunt Clara sat crouched on the bottom step of the stairs. She searched his face, and he smiled down at her with an effort. He took her arm, meaning to help her to her feet, but she resisted – like an old dog that will not stir from the bed-side of its dying master. Bernard set the lamp down on the tiled floor and shouted in her ear that Thérèse was already feeling better, but that she wanted to be left alone for a while before going to bed.

'You know that's one of her fads.'

Yes, her aunt knew it all right. It was always her misfortune to go into any room where Thérèse happened to be just when the young woman wanted to be alone. Often she had only to open a door the slightest little bit to realize that she was in the way.

She got up with an effort. Leaning on Bernard's arm, she reached her bedroom, which was immediately above the big drawing-room below. Bernard entered behind her in order to light the candle on her bed-table. Then he kissed her on the forehead and went out again. All this while her eyes had never left his face. She learned much from the features of those she could not hear. She waited until Bernard should have had time to reach his own room, then softly opened the door once more. But he was still on the landing, leaning against the banisters, rolling a cigarette. Hastily she withdrew, her knees trembling. So upset did she feel that she scarcely had sufficient strength left to undress.

She lay there on the bed, her eyes wide open.

10

DOWN in the drawing-room, Thérèse was sitting in the dark. A few embers still glowed red beneath the ashes. She did not move. From the depths of her memory, now that it was too late, rose scraps and fragments of the confession which she had prepared during her journey. But why reproach herself with having made no use of it? Truth to tell, the story which she had so carefully thought out, so neatly fitted together, had little connexion with reality. How stupid of her to have attached so much importance to what young Azévédo had said! No words of his had had the slightest influence on her. No; she had acted in obedience to some profound, some inexorable, law of her being. She had not brought destruction on this family: rather it was she who would be destroyed. They were right to look on her as a monster, but in her eyes they too were monstrous. They were planning slowly and surely to obliterate her, few thought the signs might be of their intention. 'From now on the whole powerful machinery of the family will be set in motion to crush me – unless, that is, I can either check its movement or slip, in time, from beneath its wheels. Useless to look for any other reason than that "they are they and I am I. ..." Less than two years ago I might have mustered strength enough to play the hypocrite, to save my face, to put them off the scent. There are others, I suppose (women in all respects like me), who could go on doing that until they died; women who might be saved by mere habit, drugged by custom, their senses deadened: women who might be content to sleep on in the bosom of the all-powerful family. But for me – for me, for me ...'

She got up, opened the window, and breathed in the chill dawn air. Why not escape? She had but to climb across the sill. Would they pursue her? Would they hand her over, once again, to justice? It was a chance worth taking. Anything would be better than this interminable agony. She dragged an arm-chair to the window, and set it firmly against the wall. But she had no money. Thousands of pine-trees might be hers in law, but without Bernard's agency she could not touch a single penny of her fortune. She would be no better off than Daguerre, the hunted murderer who had plunged at random into the heathy wastes. As a child she had been moved to pity for him (she remembered the policeman whom old Madame Balion had served with wine in the kitchen at Argelouse): it was the Desqueyroux dogs which had got on to the wretched man's scent. He had been found in the heather and brought back half dead with hunger. Thérèse had seen him lying trussed on a hay-cart. It was said that he had died on the boat before reaching Cayenne ... a boat, and then a prison cell. ... Weren't they perfectly capable of handing her over to the authorities as they had said they would do? What about the piece of evidence which Bernard pretended he had got up his sleeve? Probably it was all bluff ... unless, of course, he had found that packet of poison in the pocket of her old coat.

She *must* make certain. She began to feel her way up the stairs. The higher she climbed the more clearly could she see, because the dawn light was already paling the upper windows. On the attic landing stood a wardrobe which contained all the old clothes that were never given away because they came in useful during the shooting season. The faded old coat had a deep pocket. Aunt Clara used to stuff her knitting into it in those far-away days when she, too, had sat in a lonely cabin or 'jouquet', watching the flying duck.

Thérèse slipped her hand into it and brought out the little package sealed with wax:

Chloroform	..	..	..	.. 30 grams
Aconite drops	..	..	..	.. 20
Digitalin sol.	..	..	..	.. 20 grams

Once again she read the words, the figures. Death. She had always been terrified of dying. The important thing is not to look death squarely in the face – to see no farther than the immediately necessary actions – pouring out the water, dissolving the powder, gulping the stuff down, lying on the bed with her eyes closed. She mustn't try to look beyond those few simple motions. Why should she fear *that* sleep more than any other? She was shivering, but only because the early day struck cold. She went downstairs again and stopped outside the door of the room where Marie was sleeping. The nurse's snores were like the grunting of some animal. Thérèse pushed the door ajar. The waxing light was seeping through the shutters. The narrow iron bedstead showed white in the gloom. Two tiny fists lay on the coverlet. The still unformed profile lay sunk in the enfolding pillows. That over-large ear was *her* gift to the child. People were right. The form that lay unconscious there in sleep was a replica of herself. 'I am going away – but this part of myself will stay behind until it has fulfilled its destiny. Not a single iota will be omitted.' Tendencies, inclinations, laws of the blood – ineluctable laws. Somewhere Thérèse had seen accounts of desperate women who had taken their children with them to the grave. Decent folk, reading such things, would fling the paper from them. How could these things be? Being by nature a monster, Thérèse realized quite clearly that they very easily might be, and for next to no reason. ... Kneeling down, she touched one of the little hands very lightly with her lips. She was surprised to find that something from deep down in herself welled into her eyes and burned her cheeks: a few poor tears shed by one who never cried!

She got up, took one more look at the child, then went to her own room. She filled a glass with water, broke the wax

on the little package, and hesitated, not knowing which of
the boxes of poison she should choose.

The window was open. The cocks were tearing to shreds the
morning mist which draped the branches of the pines with
translucent tatters. The countryside lay soaked in dawn. How
could she bring herself to abandon so much light? What is
death? No one knows. Thérèse did not feel any certainty of
annihilation. She could not be absolutely sure that nothing
and Nobody awaited her. She loathed herself for feeling so
much terror. Without a moment's thought she would have
precipitated someone else into that nothingness, yet drew
back when she herself stood there upon its verge. How
humiliating cowardice can be! If that Being really did exist
(for a brief moment she saw again that Corpus Christi day of
blinding heat, a solitary man bowed down beneath a golden
cope, the Something that he bore between his hands, his
moving lips, his look of suffering) – since he *did* exist, let
him prevent the criminal act while there was still time. Or,
if it was his will that a poor blind soul should open for itself
a way to death, let him at least receive with love the monster
he had made. Thérèse poured the chloroform into the glass.
Its name was familiar. It conjured up a picture of sleep, and
so was the less terrifying. But she must hurry! The household
was astir. Old Madame Balion had already thrown wide the
shutters of Aunt Clara's room. What was it she was shouting
into the deaf ears? She had grown used to making herself
understood by the movement of her lips. There was a noise
of opening doors and running feet. Thérèse had just time to
throw a shawl over the table and so hide the poisons from
sight. Madame Balion entered without knocking.

'Mademoiselle is dead! I found her fully dressed upon the
bed – and already quite cold!'

Though the old lady had been an unbeliever, they put a
rosary between her fingers and a crucifix upon her breast.
Some of the local farmers came into the room, knelt, then
left again – not without staring long and fixedly at Thérèse,
who was standing at the bed's foot. ('For all we know, it may
be her as done it.') Bernard went into Saint-Clair to break

the news to the family and attend to the necessary business. He must have been thinking that this accident had fallen pat to the occasion, providing, as it did, diversion for the prying eyes.

Thérèse gazed at the body, the faithful old body which had lain down in front of her feet just as she was about to take her leap to death. Chance: coincidence. Had anyone spoken to her of a special intention, she would have shrugged her shoulders. People were saying to one another: 'Did you see her? – not even pretending to cry!' Deep in her heart Thérèse held colloquy with her who was no longer there. She would live on, but like a corpse at the mercy of those who hated her. She would try not to look beyond that fact.

At the funeral she occupied the place allotted to her. On the next Sunday she went to church with Bernard, who, instead of entering by a side-aisle as was his custom, made a point of walking down the nave for all to see. Thérèse kept her crape veil down until she had taken her seat between her husband and her mother-in-law. A pillar hid her from the congregation. There was nothing between her and the choir. On every other side she was hedged in. Behind her was the crowd of worshippers, on her right hand Bernard, Madame de la Trave on her left. Only in front of her was there a free and open space, empty as is the arena to the bull when he comes from the darkness into the light – space where, flanked by two small boys, a man in fancy dress was standing, his arms a little spread, whispering.

II

THAT same evening Bernard and Thérèse went back to Argelouse, to the Desqueyroux family house, which for years had hardly been lived in. The fires smoked, the windows were ill-fitting, and draughts came in under doors which the rats had gnawed. But so fine was the autumn this year that at first Thérèse did not suffer from these various inconveniences. Bernard was out with the guns until nightfall, and almost as soon as he got in he settled down in the kitchen, where he ate his evening meal with the Balions. Thérèse could hear the sound of forks, the drone of voices. In October it gets dark early. The small number of books which she had brought from the other house she knew from cover to cover. She asked Bernard to send an order to his bookseller in Bordeaux, but he did nothing about it, though he did allow her to renew her stock of cigarettes. ... There was little for her to do but poke the fire ... though the resinous smoke, blown down into the room, irritated her throat, which was already in a bad state from her over-indulgence in tobacco. Almost as soon as Madame Balion had cleared away the remains of her hasty meal she extinguished the lamp and went to bed. For hours she would lie, unvisited by sleep. The effect of the silence at Argelouse was to keep her awake. She liked best the nights when there was a high and gusty wind, for she seemed to find a hint of human tenderness in the monotonous soughing of the tree-tops. It lulled her, and when the equinox raged she slept better than in quiet and tranquil weather.

Interminable though the evenings were, she took to coming home before dusk – either because some farmer's wife, at sight of her, had caught her child by the hand and pulled it roughly within doors, or because a drover with whose name she had long been familiar had left her words of greeting unanswered. How lovely it would have been to lose, to drown, herself in a city crowd! At Argelouse every shepherd knew her story (even Aunt Clara's death was popularly laid to her charge). There was not a house that she dared enter. She had got into the way of leaving her home by a side-door, and she avoided the habitations of men. At the mere sound of an approaching cart she would hastily turn into a lane. She walked quickly, suffering in her heart the agonies of a hunted animal, and would lie in the heather to hide from a passing bicycle.

On Sundays, when she went into Saint-Clair for Mass, she was spared these terrors, and could enjoy a respite. The people of the little town seemed to be more kindly disposed. She did not know that her father and the de la Traves had represented her as a poor innocent, suffering under a mortal blow. 'We're terribly afraid that she'll never be herself again. She refuses to see anybody, and the doctor says that she must not be crossed. Bernard takes great care of her, but she seems to have lost the will to live. ...'

On the last night of October a wild wind from the Atlantic tossed the tormented tree-tops for hours together. In a half-sleep, Thérèse lay and listened to the thunder of the sea. But when she woke at dawn it was to a different sound. She opened the shutters, but the darkness of the room was unrelieved. A thin, dense rain was falling on the cobbles of the yard and pattering between the still thick foliage of the oaks. Bernard did not leave the house that day. Thérèse smoked, threw away her cigarette, went out on to the landing, and listened to him moving from room to room on the ground-floor. The smell of his pipe drifted up the stairs to her, overpowering the scent of her own much milder tobacco. The whole of her past life seemed to be concentrated in it. ... The first day of bad weather. ... What an endless vista of them lay before her, and through all that dreary time ahead she would just sit beside a dying fire doing nothing. The damp had loosened the paper in the corners of the room. She could see on the walls the marks left by the pictures which Bernard had taken for the drawing-room at Saint-Clair – and the rusty nails which no longer served any purpose at all. On the mantelpiece, in a triptych of artifical tortoiseshell, the photographs looked pale, as though the dead they pictured had died a second time: Bernard's father and grandmother, Bernard himself, dressed like one of the 'little Princes in the Tower'. Somehow or other she had got to get through the whole long day in that room, through weeks and months of such days. ...

When night came she could stand it no longer. Very quietly she opened the door, and went downstairs into the kitchen. She saw Bernard sitting in a low chair by the fire. At sight of her he jumped up. Balion stopped cleaning his gun. His wife let her knitting fall. So oddly did all three look at her that she said:

'Are you frightened of me?'

'You are forbidden to come into the kitchen – don't you know that?'

She made no answer, but backed towards the door. Bernard called her into the room.

'Since you're here, I may as well tell you that there is no longer any reason for my presence in this house. We have managed to create a sympathetic atmosphere in Saint-Clair. The people there believe, pretend to believe, that you are somewhat neurasthenic. It is generally understood that you prefer to live alone, and that I pay you frequent visits. From now on you need no longer go to Mass.'

She stammered back that she 'didn't at all mind going to Mass'. He replied that it wasn't a question of what she minded or didn't mind. The task they had set themselves had been accomplished.

'And since the Mass means nothing to you ...'

She opened her mouth, seemed about to say something, but remained silent. He saw to it that no word, no gesture, of hers should compromise this sudden and unexpected success. She asked how Marie was. He replied that she was in excellent health, and was leaving next day, with Anne and Madame de la Trave, for Beaulieu. He meant to join them there for a few weeks – a couple of months at most. He opened the door and stood back for her to pass.

In the darkness of the dawn she heard Balion putting in the horses, then the sound of Bernard's voice, the pawing of hooves, the bump and rattle of departing wheels, and, at last, when all was over, the pattering of rain upon the tiles and dirty windows, upon the empty fields and all the sixty miles of heath and bog, upon the shifting dunes and on the sea.

She lit another cigarette from the one she had just finished. About four o'clock she put on an oilskin and plunged into the rain. But the darkness frightened her and she went back to her room. The fire had gone out. She was shivering with cold, and went straight to bed. About seven Madame Balion brought her a fried egg on a rasher of ham, but she refused to eat it. The smell of fat made her feel sick. Never anything but *pâté* or ham. Madame Balion said that was the best she could do:

Monsieur Bernard had forbidden her to touch the poultry. She grumbled about being made to go up and down stairs to no purpose (she suffered from her heart, and had varicose veins). The work of the house was too much for her, she said. She had only consented to do it for Monsieur Bernard's sake.

That night Thérèse had a touch of fever. Her mind felt curiously clear, and in it she built up a complete picture of what life must be like in Paris. She saw again in imagination the restaurant in the Bois where she had once been in the old days – but now it was not Bernard who was with her, but Jean Azévédo and a crowd of young women. She put her tortoiseshell cigarette-case on the table and lit an Abdullah. She talked, baring her heart, while an orchestra played with muted strings. She held the circle of listening faces beneath her spell. Their owners were entranced, but not surprised. A woman said: 'Just like me – I've felt that way too.' A literary gentleman took her aside. 'You ought to write down your thoughts. We'll publish them in our magazine – the *Diary of a Modern Woman*.' A young man who was suffering torments for her sake drove her home in his car. They went up the Avenue du Bois. She was pleased rather than disturbed by the sense of all that unhappiness at her side. 'No,' she said; 'not to-night. I'm dining with a woman friend.' – 'What about to-morrow, then?' – 'No, not tomorrow, either.' – 'Are you never free in the evenings?' – 'Scarcely ever … I might almost say never. …'

Someone was in her life who made the rest of the world seem meaningless: someone completely unknown to the rest of her circle, someone very obscure and very humble. But her whole existence revolved about this sun which she alone could see, the heat of which she only could feel upon her flesh. Paris rumbled like the sound of the wind in the pines. The sensation of her companion's body pressed against her own, light though the contact was, hindered her breathing. But rather than push him away she would stop breathing altogether. (She made the gesture of pressing someone in her arms. She clasped her left shoulder with her right hand. The nails of her left hand dug into her right shoulder.)

She rose, barefooted, and opened the window. The night was far from cold, but somehow it was impossible to imagine that a day would ever come when it would not be raining. It would rain until the end of the world. If only she had money she would run away to Paris, would go straight to Jean Azévédo and throw herself on his mercy. He would manage to find her a job. How exquisite to be a woman alone in Paris, earning her own living, dependent on no one! ... To be without a family! ... to choose her friends as her heart dictated, prompted not by the tie of blood, but by the movement of the mind – and of the body too. How lovely to discover her own true kith and kin, no matter how widely scattered they might be. ... At last she went to sleep, leaving the window open. She awoke to a cold, wet dawn. Her teeth were chattering. She could not bring herself to get up and close the window. She was incapable even of stretching out her arm and pulling up the coverlet.

That day she did not get up at all, did not even tidy herself. She swallowed a few mouthfuls of *pâté* and some coffee, just in order that she might be able to smoke (tobacco on an empty stomach made her ill). She strove to recapture her fantasies of the previous night. There was scarcely more noise in Argelouse than there had been then, and the gloom of the afternoon was almost nocturnal. On these, the shortest days of the year, the solidly falling rain made all time seem as one. There was nothing to separate the hours. One dusk joined hands with another. It existed, as it were, in a motionless medium of silence. But she had no desire to sleep. Her dreams took on a sharper precision of outline. She sought deliberately in her past for facts long since forgotten, for lips that from afar she had adored, for bodies vaguely recognized which chance meetings and the random happenings of dream had brought into innocent contact with her own. She composed a symphony of happiness, invented a world of delights, built up from odds and ends a wholly impossible universe of love.

'She's not even bothering to get up now – leaves the *pâté* and the bread untasted,' said Madame Balion to her husband.

'But I'll take my oath she drinks the bottle dry. She'd get through as much liquor as one cared to give her, the slut! – and when she's had her fill, she burns the sheets with cigarette ends. She'll finish by setting the house on fire. She smokes so much that her fingers and nails are as yellow as though they'd been soaked in arnica. It's a wicked shame – them sheets as was woven on the place. ... Well, she won't get any clean ones out of me!'

It wasn't she – so the complaint went on – who refused to sweep the room or make the bed. But what could she do if that lazy-bones never got up? Why should she toil up and down stairs with jugs of hot water, and her with varicose veins and all? There they'd be at night, standing just where she'd put them in the morning.

Thérèse's mind drifted away from the unknown body of flesh and blood which she had conjured up for her delight. She grew weary of her happiness, felt the satiety of her imagined pleasures – and invented new methods of escape. People (she pretended) were kneeling round her truckle bed. A child from Argelouse (one of those who commonly fled at her approach) was brought dying to her room. She touched it with her hand – all yellowed with nicotine – and it got up, cured. Other, humbler, dreams, she improvised – seeing, in imagination, a house at the sea's edge, a garden, and a terrace. She set about arranging the rooms, choosing the furniture piece by piece, deciding where to put what she had brought from Saint-Clair, involving herself in long arguments about covers and materials. Then the scene would fade, losing its clearness of outline, until nothing remained but a beech-hedge and a bench overlooking the sea. Seated there, she rested her head on her companion's shoulder, rose at the sound of the dinner-gong, entered the gloom of the long pleached alley. Someone walking at her side put sudden arms about her, held her close. A kiss, she thought, can stay the wheel of time. The seconds of love can draw out to infinity. Or so she imagined, for she would never know. She saw the house, still gleaming white, the well. Somewhere a pump creaked. Freshly watered heliotrope scented the air. Dinner would be an interval of rest before the evening's happiness, before that night of which she could not think, so far did it exceed the power of human heart to contemplate. Thus did the love of which, more than any living creature, she had been deprived, possess and penetrate her utterly. She scarcely heard old Madame Balion's complaints. What was the woman saying? That Monsieur Bernard would come back from the south one of these days without warning. 'And what'll he say when he sees this room looking like a pigsty?' If Madame wouldn't get up of her own accord, she'd have to be made to. Seated upon the bed, Thérèse was horrified by the sight of her skinny legs. The feet looked, to her eyes, enormous. Madame Balion wrapped her in a dressing-gown and pushed her into a chair. She felt beside her for her cigarettes, but her hand met only emptiness. A cold shaft of sunlight entered through the window. Madame Balion fussed about with a broom, short of breath, wheezing and grumbling – yet, for all that, she was a good soul, for it was common knowledge that at Christmas-time she cried when her fattened pig was killed. She resented Thérèse's silence, regarding it as an insult, as a sign of contempt.

But it was not for Thérèse to decide whether she should speak or not. When her body felt the coolness of clean sheets she thought she had said 'Thank you,' when, in fact, no sound had issued from her lips.

Madame Balion, at the door, threw back at her: 'Well, you won't burn those!' Thérèse, terrified lest she had taken the cigarettes, stretched her hand to the table. The cigarettes were no longer there. How could she live without smoking? Her fingers *must* be able continually to know the feel of that tiny object, so dry, so warm. She must have the smell of tobacco in her nostrils: the room must be filled with the thin vapour which she inhaled and then breathed out. Madame Balion would not come near her till the evening. A whole afternoon without tobacco! She closed her eyes. Her stained fingers made the accustomed gesture of holding a cigarette.

At seven o'clock Madame Balion came into the room with a candle, and set a tray upon the table: milk, coffee, a scrap of bread. 'Anything else you want?' She waited malevolently for

Thérèse to ask for cigarettes. But Thérèse still lay with her face to the wall, and did not turn her head.

Madame Balion must have neglected to fasten the window. A gust of wind blew it open, and the chill night air filled the room. Thérèse could not muster sufficient energy to throw back the bedclothes, to get up and cross the room on bare feet to shut it. She lay curled in the bed, the sheet drawn half-way over her face, so that only on her eyes and forehead did she feel the icy blast. The deep murmur of the pines filled Arge- louse, but, despite this sound, as of a fretting sea, the silence of the place was there. If she were really in love with suffering (she thought) she would not lie huddled thus beneath the bedclothes. She tried to throw them off a little, but could not long endure the cold. She tried again, and this time succeeded in remaining a longer while uncovered. It was as though she were playing a game with herself. Almost without her willing it, her pain had become her sole preoccupation, the sole reason – why not? – of her existence.

12

'A LETTER from Monsieur.'

Because Thérèse did not take the envelope which Madame Balion held out the old servant began to nag her. Monsieur, no doubt, had written to say when he would be coming back. She must know, so as to have everything ready.

'Would Madame rather that I read it to her?' 'All right, read it!' Thérèse said: and then, as always, when Madame Balion was in the room, turned her face to the wall. But the words that the voice spelled out roused her from her apathy.

'I was glad to hear from Balion that all goes well at Argelouse. ...'

Bernard wrote that he was coming home by road. Since, however, he intended to stay at several towns on the way, he could not say exactly when he would arrive.

'... It certainly won't be later than 20 December. Don't be sur- prised when you see Anne and the Deguilheim boy with me. They got engaged at Beaulieu, but it's not yet official. He particularly wants to see you first. Merely a matter of good manners, he says, but I have a feeling that he wants to make up his mind about you know what. You are far too intelligent not to get through the ordeal with flying colours. Remember that you are a very sick woman, and a nervous wreck. I rely on you. Perhaps I may show my gratitude to you for not spoiling Anne's happiness or in any way compromising the successful issue of a scheme which, in every way, is so satisfactory for the family. But if anything goes wrong, if you try to sabotage the arrangement, I can make you pay dearly. I shouldn't have the slightest scruple about doing so. But I feel quite certain that nothing of the kind would occur to you.'

The day was fine and bright, though cold. Obedient to Madame Balion's instructions, Thérèse got up and went for a short walk in the garden, leaning on her arm. But she had great difficulty in finishing her wing of chicken. There were still ten days to go before 20 December. If only Madame would make a little effort. Ten days were more than enough time in which to get her up and about again.

'No one could say she's not trying,' said Madame Balion to her husband. 'She's doing what she can. Monsieur Bernard's a great hand at training vicious dogs. You've seen him at it, with that special collar of his. It didn't take him long to get our fine lady upstairs crouching and whimpering. But he'd be wise not to count his chickens ...'

Thérèse, in fact, was doing everything possible to free herself from her dream fantasies, to fight her way back from sleep and nothingness. She forced herself to walk and eat, but especially to recapture her clearness of vision, to see things and people with her bodily eyes. And since the waste land to which now she came had been fired by her own hand, since she must tread on still warm ashes, and find her way through burned and blackened trees, she would do her best to talk and smile in the bosom of the family – his family.

On the 18th, at about three o'clock of an overcast but rainless day, she was seated in front of the fire in her room, leaning back in her chair with her eyes closed. The purring of a motor-car awoke her. She heard Bernard's voice in the hall, and Madame de la Trave's as well. When Madame Balion, panting and breathless, opened the door without knocking, she was already on her feet before the glass, putting rouge upon her lips and cheeks. She said: 'I mustn't frighten the poor young man.' But Bernard, in not going straight up to see his wife, blundered. Young Deguilheim, who had promised his family to 'keep his eyes skinned', said to himself that 'at the very least it showed a lack of eagerness and made one think'. He moved a pace or two away from Anne and turned up the fur collar of his coat, remarking that 'it's never any good trying to warm these country rooms'. He addressed himself to Bernard: 'I suppose you've got no cellar? Without a cellar you're bound to get dry-rot in the floors, unless you have them laid on cement. ...'

Anne de la Trave was wearing an overcoat of light grey cloth and a felt hat without ribbon or trimming of any sort ('though,' said Madame de la Trave, 'it costs more like that than the hats we used to have with all those feathers and aigrettes. But, of course, it's the very finest quality felt from Lailhaca's – a Reboux model.') Madame de la Trave stretched her feet to the fire. Her face, at once imperious and puffy, was turned towards the door. She had promised Bernard not to let him down. But she had warned him that he must not ask her to kiss his wife. 'You wouldn't I'm sure, expect your mother to do any such thing. It'll be bad enough having to take her hand. God knows, she was sufficiently guilty, but that's not what I mind most. There have always been people capable of murder – we all know that ... it's her hypocrisy that I can't forgive! That's what really shocks me. Do you remember how she used to say, "Take this arm-chair, Mother, you'll be more comfortable"? ... And then, how nervous she always pretended to be about frightening you. ... "The poor darling is so terrified of dying: the very idea of going to see a doctor might be fatal. ..." God knows, I never had the faintest suspicion, but I confess that "poor darling" on her lips *did* somewhat surprise me.'

Now, in the Argelouse drawing-room, she was conscious

only of the general atmosphere of embarrassment. She noticed young Deguilheim's little bird-like eyes fixed on Bernard.

'Bernard, you really ought to go and see what Thérèse is doing. ... She may be feeling worse.'

Anne (indifferent, and seemingly not interested in what might happen next) was the first to recognize a familiar step. 'I can hear her coming downstairs.' Bernard, his hand pressed to his heart, was suffering from an attack of palpitations. He was a fool not to have arrived the previous night. He ought to have arranged with Thérèse all the details of this meeting. What was she going to say? He wouldn't put it beyond her to spoil everything, though without committing herself to anything sufficiently definite to be held against her. How slowly she was coming downstairs! When, at last, she opened the door, they were all on their feet, looking in her direction.

Bernard was to remember, many years later, that, as this woman with the wasted body and the small, white, painted face came into the room, his first thought had been 'The Dock'. But it was not because of her crime that the words had come into his mind. In a flash he saw again the coloured picture torn from the *Petit Parisien* which, with many others, had adorned the wooden outside lavatory in the garden at Argelouse; and how, on a blazing hot day, while the flies buzzed and the grasshoppers were noisy in the fields, his childish eyes had gazed at the red and green daub representing the *Woman Prisoner of Poitiers*. With just such eyes he gazed now at Thérèse, a bloodless figure, little more than skin and bone. He realized what a fool he had been not, at any cost, to have kept that terrible figure out of sight. He ought to have got rid of her, as one gets rid of an infernal machine – by throwing it into the water before it can explode. Whether intentionally or not, Thérèse had brought into the room an atmosphere of drama – worse still, of newspaper gossip. One of two things she must be – either criminal or victim. ... There broke from the family a murmur of astonishment and pity. So little feigned was it that young Deguilheim hesitated to draw any conclusion. He no longer knew what to think.

Thérèse said: 'There's nothing to worry about. The bad weather has been keeping me indoors, and I have lost my appetite. I've been eating hardly anything. But I'd rather get thin than fat. ... Anne, dear, let us talk of your affairs. I am so happy ...'

She took the girl's hands (she was seated, Anne still standing), and looked at her. In the face now worn to a skeleton thinness Anne recognized the old intense look which once she had found so irritating. She remembered how she used to say: 'When you've quite finished looking at me like that!'

'I rejoice in your happiness, Anne dear. ...' She directed a brief smile at the cause of 'Anne's happiness', at young Deguilheim, with his receding hair, his policeman's moustache, and his drooping shoulders. She took in the short coat he was wearing, the fat little legs in their grey and black striped trousers. (What was there so surprising about him – he was just another man, just a husband.) Then her eyes went back to Anne, and she said:

'Take off your hat. ... Ah! now I know it's you, darling!'

Anne saw close to her a faintly grimacing mouth and a pair of dry, tearless eyes. But she did not know what Thérèse was thinking. The Deguilheim boy was saying that winter in the country was not so bad for a woman who is fond of her home. 'There's always so much to do in a house.'

'Don't you want to hear about Marie?'

'Yes, yes, of course I do. ... Tell me about her.'

Anne seemed to have got back into her old mood of hostility and mistrust. For months she had been saying, in a voice that held just her mother's inflexions: 'I'd overlook almost anything, because, after all, she really is terribly ill, but I just can't bear the way she shows no interest whatever in her child. I think it's absolutely beastly of her!' Thérèse could read the girl's thoughts. 'She's holding it against me that I wasn't the one to start talking about Marie. How *can* I explain it all to her? She'd never understand that my mind is filled with my own concerns, that nobody interests me but myself. She lives for the day when she has children of her own in whom she can become completely lost and absorbed. In that way she's just like her mother – and all the other women of her family. But with me it's different. I've always got to be the centre of my own picture; I *must* get myself in focus. ... My little scrap of misery has only got to start whining, for Anne to forget all about the odd tension which was always between her and me when we were girls, all about Jean Azévédo's kisses ... she flies straight to the child without waiting even to take her coat off. The women of her family are all the same. They ask nothing better than to lose themselves in something or some-one else. Such complete surrender to the interests of the species, such utter self-effacement and annihilation, is very beautiful, of course ... but, somehow, it's not for me. ...'

She tried not to listen to what the others were saying, to concentrate her thoughts wholly on Marie. Very soon now the child would be beginning to talk. 'It'll amuse me to hear her for a moment or two, but I shall very soon get bored, and all impatient to be alone with myself again.'

Turning to Anne, she said: 'She's really beginning to talk quite well, isn't she?'

'She can repeat anything one says – it's really terribly funny. ...'

Thérèse thought: 'I *must* listen to what they're saying. My mind's a complete blank. What's the Deguilheim boy talking about?' She strained her ears, trying to catch the words.

'The men on my Balisac property don't do half the work on the trees that yours do. The chaps here get twice the yield of resin. ...'

'Yours must be bone-idle, then, with the stuff fetching the price it does. ...'

'Do you realize that at the present time a man cutting for resin can make as much as a hundred francs a day? ... But I'm afraid we're tiring your wife. ...'

Thérèse leaned back in her chair. Everyone got up. Bernard decided not to go back to Saint-Clair. Young Deguilheim fell in with the suggestion that he should drive the car. The chauffeur could bring it back next day with Bernard's things. Thérèse made an effort to get up, but her mother-in-law laid a restraining hand on her.

She closed her eyes. She heard Bernard say to Madame de la Trave: 'Really, that Balion couple! I'm going to give them a piece of my mind! ...' – 'Be careful what you say, it might be awkward if they gave notice. They know too much ... besides, I really don't see how you'd get on without them. ... No one knows the details of the estate as Balion does.'

Bernard said something which Thérèse did not catch, but she heard Madame de la Trave's reply: 'All the same, don't be rash ... and whatever happens, be sure not to trust *her*. You must watch her every movement, and never let her go into the kitchen or the dining-room alone. ... Don't worry; she's not fainted. She's asleep, or pretending to be.'

Thérèse opened her eyes. Bernard was standing in front of her. There was a glass in his hand. He said: 'Drink this – it's Spanish wine: it'll do you good.' And because he always did what he had a mind to do, he proceeded to work himself up into a fury, and stormed into the kitchen. Thérèse could hear voices raised in a babble of brogue. She thought: 'He was obviously afraid of something – but of what?' He came back.

'I think you'd eat with a better appetite in the dining-room than upstairs. I've given orders for your place to be laid as it always used to be.'

He was once more as he had been during the trial – her ally, intent, at all costs, on getting her out of a mess. He had made up his mind that she must get well again. It was plain that something had given him a fright. Thérèse watched him sitting opposite her, poking the fire. But she could not see into his mind, could not guess that what those large eyes saw in the flames was the red-and-green picture from the *Petit Parisien – The Woman Prisoner of Poitiers*.

In spite of all the rain that had fallen there were no puddles in the sandy soil of Argelouse. Even in the depths of winter one hour of sunshine was enough to dry the ground sufficiently to make it possible to walk without discomfort in rope-soled sandals over the dry, springy carpet of needles which overlay the roads. Bernard was out all day, shooting, but came home to meals. He was worried about Thérèse,

and looked after her as he had never done before. Relations
between them had become fairly easy. He made her weigh
herself every three days, and cut down her smoking to two
cigarettes after each meal. On his advice, she did a lot of
walking. 'Exercise is the best way of getting an appetite.'
She was no longer afraid of Argelouse. It seemed to her that
the wall of pine-trees had withdrawn and grown less dense:
as though they were pointing out to her a way of escape. One
evening Bernard said: 'All I ask is that you should wait until
Anne is safely married. The neighbours must see us, just once
more, together. As soon as the ceremony is over you can do
as you like.' That night she had been unable to sleep. An
uneasy happiness made it impossible for her to close her eyes.
At dawn she heard the clamour of innumerable cocks. She
got the impression that they were not so much answering
one another as all crowing at the same moment, filling earth
and sky with their noise. Bernard would turn her loose upon
the world as he had turned the old sow which he had never
succeeded in domesticating loose upon the heath. Once
Anne was married people could say what they liked. He would
drop Thérèse into the unplumbable depths of Paris and then
take to his heels. Everything was arranged between them.
There would be no divorce, no legal separation. Some excuse
about her health could be trumped up to satisfy the world at
large ('she's never really well unless she's travelling'). Each
November he would see that she got her fair share of the
profits from her resin.

He asked no questions about her plans: she could go hang
herself for all he cared – provided it wasn't at Argelouse. 'I
shan't know a quiet moment,' he said to his mother, 'until
she's out of the way.' – 'I suppose she'll resume her maiden
name, but that won't prevent people from putting two and
two together if she gets up to her old tricks again.' But
Thérèse, he insisted, kicked only when she was between
shafts. Left to herself, she might be more sensible. In any
case, that was a risk they'd got to take. In this opinion Monsieur Larroque fully concurred. All things considered, the
best thing would be for Thérèse to disappear altogether. Like

that, she would be soon forgotten. People would quickly get out of the way of talking about her. The important thing was that the whole wretched business should be buried in silence. This idea had taken such deep root in their minds that nothing could shift it. Thérèse must be got from between the shafts. How impatient they were to have it all over and done with!

She loved the way in which the tail-end of winter stripped the bare earth and made it barer still, though even then the dead leaves clung tenaciously to the oaks. She discovered that what she had always thought of as the silence of Argelouse had no real existence. On the quietest day there was a murmur in the forest, as though the trees were gently crying themselves to sleep, moaning a muted lullaby which turned the nights into a time of ceaseless whispering. In the days to come there were to be many hopeless dawns, though at present she could not imagine such a possibility – dawns so empty that they would make her look back with regret to those wakeful hours at Argelouse when only the clamour of the farmyard filled the silence. She was to remember, in those future summers, the grasshoppers by day and, at night, the crickets. In Paris, she was to know, not blasted and tormented pines, but the terror of men and women: a crowd of persons after a crowd of trees.

Husband and wife grew astonished to find so little awkwardness between them. We find our fellow-creatures tolerable, thought Thérèse, once we know that it is in our power to leave them. Bernard took a lively interest in her weight, but also in her words. She spoke to him now more freely than she had ever done before. 'In Paris – when I'm settled in Paris ...' She would live in an hotel and, perhaps, look round for a flat. She was planning to attend courses, lectures, concerts. She meant to start her education over again 'from the beginning'. It never occurred to Bernard to watch her movements. He ate his food and drank his wine without any sign of hesitation. Dr Pédemay, who often met them on the road to Argelouse, said to his wife: 'What makes it all so odd is that they don't seem to be shamming.'

13

At about ten o'clock of a warm March morning the human tide was already flowing strongly. It lapped at the terrace of the Café de la Paix in front of which Bernard and Thérèse were seated. She dropped her cigarette and – sign that she was a true daughter of the heathlands – carefully put her foot on it.

'Afraid of setting fire to the pavement, eh?' Bernard laughed, but it was only with something of an effort that he did so. He blamed himself for having come with her as far as Paris. He had done so partly because, with Anne's marriage only just past, he was anxious not to give the neighbours any cause for gossip, but also because she had wanted him to. She had, he told himself, a genius for putting one in a false position. So long as she remained part of his life there would always be the risk of his making these irrational gestures. Even on a nature as solid and as well-balanced as his own this wild creature still, to some extent, exercised an influence. Now, at the moment of parting, he could not but feel a pang of melancholy ill-suited though it was to his general mood. It was utterly unlike him to have any such feeling, to submit thus to the impact of another person (especially when that other person was Thérèse: he would never have imagined it to be possible). How impatient he was to cut free of the whole sorry business! He would not know a moment's peace until he was safely seated in the train which left at noon. The car would be waiting for him that evening at Langon. Very soon after leaving the station at Villandraut the pines begin. He looked at Thérèse's profile as she sat there beside him, staring at her as he would so often stare at some face seen in a crowd, watching it until it vanished.

Suddenly:

'Thérèse,' he said, 'there's just one thing I want to ask you …' He averted his eyes. He had never been able to endure her fixed gaze. Hastily he finished the sentence: 'Was it because you hated me – because you had a horror of me?'

His own words filled him with an emotion of astonishment and irritation. Thérèse smiled, but when she turned to look at him her face was serious again. Bernard had actually asked her a question – and the very question she herself would have asked had she been in his position. The confession so long pondered and prepared as she drove in the Victoria along the Nizan road, and, later, in the local train to Saint-Clair, on that night of queries and patient self-examination when she had tried so hard to trace the act back to its source, only to exhaust herself in a frenzy of introspection – that experience was at last, then, to have its reward. Unknown to herself she had troubled Bernard's peace of mind. She had tangled him in a maze of uncertainty, so that he had been forced to question her, like a man who cannot see his way clear before him, but gropes and hesitates. He was no longer the simple creature he had been: consequently, he was no longer implacable. Upon the stranger at her side Thérèse fixed a sympathetic, almost a maternal, gaze. But her answer, when it came, was mocking.

'Do you mean to say you don't realize that it was for the sake of your trees? ... I wanted, you see, to have sole possession of them.'

He shrugged his shoulders.

'I don't believe that now – if I ever did. What *was* your motive? You can be perfectly frank with me – now.'

She stared before her into space. On this pavement, this bank above a river of mud and humanity into which she was about to plunge, knowing that she must fight to keep her head above water if she were not to be sucked down into the depths, she saw a gleam of light, a hint of dawn. She played in imagination with the idea of going back to the sad and secret land – of spending a lifetime of meditation and self-discipline in the silence of Argelouse, there to set forth on the great adventure of the human soul, the search for God. ... A Moroccan with carpets and strings of beads for sale, thinking she was smiling at him, approached. On the same note of mockery she said:

'I was about to say that I don't really know why I did it. But now at last I believe that I do! I'm not sure that it wasn't simply to see that look of uncertainty, of curiosity – of unease which, a moment ago, I caught in your eyes!'

He started to rate her in a way that brought back memories of their honeymoon:

'Still talking for effect! – up to the very last moment! ... Do, for Heaven's sake, be serious. Why was it?'

She was no longer laughing, but, in her turn, asked a question:

'You're the kind of man, aren't you, Bernard, who always knows precisely why he does a thing?'

'Naturally ... at least, I think I do.'

'I should like nothing better than to make the whole thing crystal-clear to you. You've no idea how I have tortured myself in an effort to see straight. But if I did give you a reason it would seem untrue the moment I got it into words. ...'

He was becoming impatient:

'But there must have been some stage at which you made up your mind, at which you took the first step?'

'There was – it was on the day of the great fire at Mano.'

They had suddenly achieved intimacy, and were speaking now in low voices. Here, in this busy Paris street, with a mild sun shining and a rather chilly wind blowing, smelling of American tobacco and agitating the red and yellow awnings, she found it odd to conjure up the picture of that oppressive afternoon with its pall of smoke through which the blue looked dimmed and sooty, to smell again the acrid scent as of torches which comes from burning pines. In her drowsed and brooding mind she thought of a crime slowly taking shape.

'It really all began in the dining-room. There was not much light – there never was at midday. You had your head turned towards Balion, and were busy talking: so busy that you never thought to count the drops falling into your glass.'

So intent was she on not omitting a single detail of her story that she did not look at him. But she heard him laugh, and the sound brought back her eyes to his face. Yes, he was actually laughing, in the same stupid way with which she had once been so familiar. He said: 'Come now, what do you take me for?' Obviously, he didn't believe her. (Who would have, if it came to that?) He continued to chuckle, and she recognized the old Bernard, the Bernard who had always been sure of himself, who had never let anyone get the better of him. He was once more securely in the saddle. Suddenly she felt lost and helpless. He began to tease her.

'So the idea came to you quite on the spur of the moment, did it? – almost like a visitation of Grace?'

How he hated himself for ever having questioned her! By so doing he had lost the advantage of that attitude of contempt by which he had dominated her mad, unbalanced moods. She was actually getting the bit between her teeth again! Why had he ever given way to that sudden desire to understand? – as though with women of her irresponsible type there was ever anything *to* understand! But impulse had got the better of him. He had not stopped to think. ...

'I'm not telling you all this, Bernard, in order that you should think me innocent – quite the contrary!'

She went on to accuse herself with a strange urgency. She could only – she made it clear – have acted in that half-mechanical, that somnambulistic fashion, because for months past she had not attempted to resist, had, indeed, been encouraging, criminal thoughts. Once the first step had been taken, with what devilish clear-sightedness, with what tenacity, had she carried through her scheme!

'I never felt that I was being cruel – except when my hand hesitated. I detested myself for prolonging your sufferings. I felt that I must get the whole thing over and done with as quickly as possible. I was the victim of a terrible duty. Yes, honestly, I had the feeling that it was a duty.'

Bernard broke in on her:

'Talk, talk, talk! For Heaven's sake, do try, once and for all, to tell me what it was you wanted! The truth of the matter is, you can't!'

'What I wanted? It would be a great deal easier to tell you what I didn't want. I didn't want to be for ever playing a part, to go through a series of movements, to continue speaking words, that were not my own: in short, to deny at every moment of the day a Thérèse who ... Oh, Bernard, my one wish is to be absolutely truthful about all this. Why does every word I utter sound so *sham*?'

'Speak lower; the man in front just looked round.'

By this time he had only one desire – to put an end to their discussion. But he knew her wild moods only too well. Nothing would please her better than to go on splitting hairs. She, too, realized that the man beside her, with whom she had been caught up in a moment's intimacy, had once more become a stranger. But she forced herself to go on, tried on him the effect of her most charming smile, spoke in the low, hoarse tones that once he had loved.

'But I know now, Bernard, that the Thérèse who instinctively stamps out a cigarette because the tiniest spark will set heather on fire – the Thérèse who used to love counting over her tale of pines and reckoning her profits – the Thérèse who took pride in marrying a Desqueyroux and so becoming one of a good county family, in settling down, as they say – I know now that *that* Thérèse is just as real, just as much alive, as the other. There was no good reason why she should be sacrificed to the other.'

'What other do you mean?'

She did not know what answer to make. He looked at his watch. She said:

'I shall have to come down from time to time on business – and to see Marie.'

'What business? *I* look after our joint property: we've had all that out. Why bring it up again? You will, of course, be included in all official ceremonies at which it is important, for the honour of our name and in Marie's interest, that we be seen together. In a family as large as ours there is never, thank goodness, any lack of weddings – or of funerals either, if it comes to that. Which reminds me, I should be very much surprised if Uncle Martin lasted out the summer. ... That'll give you an opportunity, since, seemingly, you've already ...'

A mounted policeman put a whistle to his lips, swung open an invisible pair of lock-gates, and a flood of pedestrians

surged across the black roadway before it should be sub-
merged by the oncoming tide of taxis. 'I ought to have slipped
away one night and made for the southern part of the heath,
like Daguerre. I ought to have walked through the sickly
pine clumps of that barren land – walked until I could walk
no longer. I should never have had the courage to put my
head in a pond and keep it there (like that Argelouse shepherd
did last year because his daughter-in-law wouldn't give him
enough to eat). But I could, at least, have slept on the sandy
soil and closed my eyes – though there are crows, of course,
and ants, who don't wait until ...'

She looked at the human flood, the mass of living and
breathing humanity, which was about to open before her,
roll over her, envelop her. There was nothing more she could
do. Bernard took out his watch again.

'Quarter to eleven ... Just time to look in at the hotel. ...'

'Won't you be too hot on the journey?'

'I must have something extra to put on this evening in the
car.'

She saw in imagination the road along which he would
drive, could almost feel the cold wind on her face, the wind
smelling of marsh and pine-clad slopes, of mint and country
mists. She looked at him with that smile upon her lips which
once had made old countrywomen: say 'No one could say
she's pretty, but she's a bit of living charm.' Had Bernard
said, 'All is forgiven; come back with me,' she would have
got up there and then and followed him. But Bernard was
annoyed to think that he had given way to a moment's sentiment, was filled with distaste at the thought of going through
unaccustomed movements and using the words that were not
the words of every day. He 'fitted' the well-trodden roads of
life, as his carts fitted the lanes of their home country. He
needed the clearly marked ruts. Once let him get back into
them, as he would have done when he sat this evening in the
dining-room at Saint-Clair, and the peace and calm of habitual
things would be his again.

'For the last time, Bernard, I want to say how terribly sorry
I am. ...'

She made the words sound a little too solemn, a little too hopeless – it was her final effort to keep their conversation going. But all she got from him was a protest: 'Oh, please don't let us go into all that again.'

'You'll feel very lonely. Even though I shan't be in the house I shall still be in your life. It would be much better for you if I were dead.'

He just perceptibly shrugged. In a tone that was almost gay, he begged her 'not to worry about him'.

'Every generation of Desqueyroux has had its old bachelor, and that is what I ought to have been. I have all the necessary qualities for the part (you can't deny that, can you?). My one regret is that our child was a girl, because it means that the name will die out. Though, of course, even if we had stayed together, we shouldn't have wanted another ... so, on the whole, all's well that ends well. ... Don't bother to come with me; just stay on here.'

He hailed a taxi, and turned his head as he was getting into it to tell her that he had paid for their drinks.

For a long time she sat staring at the drop of port in the bottom of Bernard's glass; then, once more, gave her whole attention to the passers-by. Some of them seemed to be waiting, walking up and down the pavement. There was a woman who twice turned and smiled at her (a working-girl, or someone got up to look like a working-girl?). It was the hour of the day at which the dressmakers' workrooms empty. Thérèse had no intention of leaving. She felt neither bored nor sad. She decided that she would not pay Jean Azévédo a visit that afternoon – and heaved a sigh of relief. She did not want to see him, to embark on another conversation, another endless effort to find the right words. She knew Jean Azévédo, but the kind of people she wanted to meet she did not know. Of one thing only was she certain, that they would not call on her for words. No longer did she feel afraid of loneliness. It was enough that she need not move. Had she been lying on the heathland to the south, her body would have been a magnet for ants and dogs. Here, too, she felt herself already at the heart of an obscure ebb and flow. She was hungry. She got up. In the window of the *Old England* tea-shop she saw herself reflected, and realized how young she was. The close-fitting travelling suit became her well. But those years at Argelouse had left their mark upon her face. She looked worn and haggard. She took note of her short nose and too promin-ent cheek-bones. 'I'm not an old woman yet', she thought. She lunched (as so often in her dreams) in the rue Royale. Why go back to the hotel? She had no wish to. The half-bottle of Pouilly she had drunk filled her with a warm sense of well-being. She asked for some cigarettes. A young man at the next table snapped his lighter and held it out to her. She smiled. Difficult to believe that only an hour ago she had been longing to drive with Bernard along the road to Villan-draut in the evening light between the ominous pines! What did it matter – the sort of country one was fond of, pines or maples, sea or plain? Life alone was interesting, people of flesh and blood. 'It is not the bricks and mortar that I love, nor even the lectures and museums, but the living human forest that fills the streets, the creatures torn by passions more violent than any storm. The moaning of the pines at Argelouse in the darkness of the night thrilled me only because it had an almost human sound!'

She had drunk a little and smoked much. She smiled to herself, as though she were happy. Very carefully she set about touching up her cheeks and her lips, and then walked casually out into the street.

THÉRÈSE AND THE DOCTOR
and
THÉRÈSE AT THE HOTEL

*

Readers who remember Thérèse Desqueyroux frequently ask me about her life as it developed between the moment when I left her on the threshold of a restaurant in the rue Royale, and the episode of her final illness which is described in The End of the Night. *In one single chapter of* That Which Was Lost *we catch a glimpse of her sitting in the darkness on a bench in the Champs Élysées, but thereafter she passes entirely from our ken. These two stories,* Thérèse and the Doctor *and* Thérèse at the Hotel, *both written in 1933, represent two attempts to 'sound' the obscure periods of her life. ...*

Thérèse and the Doctor

*

'I HAVE already told you that the doctor will not be doing any more work this evening. You can go as soon as you like.'

No sooner had Dr Élisée Schwartz heard Catherine's words through the wall than he opened the door of his consulting-room. Without so much as a glance at his wife, he said to his secretary:

'I will call you in a moment. Please remember that in this house it is I who give orders.'

Catherine Schwartz did not quail beneath Mademoiselle Parpin's insolent stare. Instead, she smiled, took up a book, and walked over to the french window. The shutters had not been closed. The rain was pelting down on the balcony of their sixth-floor flat. The ceiling-light in the doctor's consulting-room illuminated the gleaming flagstones. For a moment Catherine followed with her eyes the distant vista of a street in Grenelle dwindling away between the shadowed mass of sleeping factories. Élisée, she thought, had yielded, as so often before during the last twenty years, to the pleasure of contradicting and humiliating her. But already, no doubt he was paying the penalty. What was there, this evening, for him to dictate to Mademoiselle Parpin? ... Three or four pages, perhaps. ... His study of the *Sexual Life of Blaise Pascal* was making very slow progress. Ever since the great psychiatrist had indulged the whim of annotating a chapter in the history of literature he had become more and more bogged down in the difficulties of the undertaking.

The secretary had remained standing. Her eyes, fixed on the door of her employer's room, were those of a faithful dog. Catherine opened her book and tried to read. The lamp was set on a very low modern table, and, though the couch, too, was low, she had to sit on the floor in order to catch the light. The sound of the little girl upstairs practising her piano in no wise drowned the noise of the radio next door. The 'Death of

119

Isolde' was suddenly cut short. In its place came the strains of a French music-hall song. The young couple in the flat below were quarrelling. A door slammed.

Maybe Catherine was dreaming of the silence that used to envelop her parents' big house in the rue de Babylone, with its courtyard on one side and its garden on the other. By marrying, just before the war, a young, half-Jewish doctor from Alsace, Catherine de Borresch had not merely been yielding to the fascination of an intelligence in which, at that time, she could find no blemish, nor even to that physical appeal, that dominating force of character before which so many patients still felt themselves to be helpless. The truth of the matter was that between 1910 and 1913 the Baron de Borresch's daughter had reacted violently away from her family. She had hated her awful-looking father, whose ugliness was almost a crime against society, the clockwork figure whom Dr Élisée Schwartz came twice or three times a week to wind up. Her contempt for her mother's narrow existence was hardly less acute. In those days it was a pretty daring thing for a young woman of her social position to read for a degree and attend lectures at the Sorbonne. Her acquaintance with Schwartz had been limited to a few glances exchanged at hurried lunches, and to the sound of his voice booming away at the far end of the table when he was asked to formal dinner-parties. But in her eyes he stood for progress and the sacred integrity of science. She had built up their marriage into a sort of wall between herself and that world from which she had fought free. As a matter of fact, this man who had already attained some degree of eminence, and was Secretary to the League of the Rights of Man, was only too glad to have the freedom of the great front-door of the Borresch house. He would have dearly liked to make his peace with the family, and had almost succeeded in doing so. He had already placed his batteries in position for the final assault, and gave up the attempt only when he realized that his betrothed had fathomed his intentions. Their life together had begun in insincerity. Beneath Catherine's eagle eye, Schwartz had had to swallow his snobbish instincts and resume his role of the advanced and emancipated man of science.

He had taken his revenge by treating her, especially when other people were present, with an extraordinary lack of consideration. His language, when he addressed her, was carefully designed to wound. After twenty years, he had got so much into the habit of humiliating her on every possible occasion that he did so now, as on the evening with which we are concerned, quite automatically and without any deliberate intention.

He was fifty, and there was a look of nobility about his head with its shock of grey hair. His dark, tanned face, in which the blood showed warm, was of the type that stands up well to the ravages of time. He still had the supple skin of a young man, and his mouth told of health unimpaired. This it was, thought the world, that kept Catherine faithful to him (for the people from whom she had set herself to escape had gradually drifted back, attracted now by those very same Left-Wing ideas which had once alienated them. It was said, too, that she enjoyed being 'knocked about'. But those who had known the Baroness were of the opinion that her daughter for all her airs of emancipation, and though she probably did not know it, was remarkably like her mother. She had the same absent-minded ways, alternating with periods of excessive friendliness, and, in spite of changing fashions, the same severe taste in clothes.

Nothing could have been less in the tone of her general 'style' than to sit on the floor as she was doing this evening. Her short hair, touched with grey, left the back of her neck uncovered. Her face was small, and the way in which she wrinkled her brow gave her the appearance of a pug-dog. Her lips lacked fullness and she suffered from a nervous tic which made people believe, quite wrongly, that she looked at the world with a mocking grin.

Mademoiselle Parpin, still on her feet, was turning over a pile of illustrated papers which lay on a side-table. Their pages showed the finger-marks of the doctor's patients. She was a shortish woman running to fat. She would have been well advised to wear stays. The telephone bell in the hall started to ring. She went to answer it, pointedly closing the door behind her as a hint to Madame Schwartz that she had no right to listen to what was being said. The precaution, however, was quite useless, because everything that happened in one room could be heard in the others, even when the piano upstairs and the radio next door were going full blast. Besides, the secretary's voice grew louder and louder as the conversation proceeded.

'Would you like me to make an appointment for you, Madame? ... You want to see the doctor now, at once? ... Quite out of the question. ... It's really no good insisting. ... I can't believe he ever promised any such thing. ... You must have made a mistake, Madame: Dr Élisée Schwartz is not in the habit of frequenting night-clubs. ... I can't stop you from coming, of course ... but I warn you, you'll merely be wasting your time. ...'

Mademoiselle Parpin entered the doctor's consulting-room by a door which gave direct on to the hall. Catherine could hear every word without having to strain her ears.

'It was some mad creature, sir, who says that you promised to see her at any hour of the day or night she might like to come ... She says she met you two years ago in some bar or other. ... it sounded like *Gerlis* or *Gernis* ... I couldn't quite hear.'

'And I suppose you put her off, eh?' fumed the doctor. 'Who gave you the right to make decisions for me? ... I wish to goodness you'd mind your own business.'

She stammered that it was after ten o'clock ... that it had never occured to her that he would consent to see a patient at that hour ... to all of which he replied in a loud voice that he didn't care a damn what she thought. He knew all about the patient in question – a remarkably interesting case. ... Another opportunity missed through her blundering idiocy. ...

'But she said she'd be here in less than half an hour, sir.'

'So she *is* coming, after all?'

He seemed to be both excited and put out. After a brief hesitation, he said:

'Show her in as soon as she turns up, and then you can go and catch your train.'

At this moment Catherine entered the room. The doctor, who had resumed his seat at the table, half rose, and asked her roughly what she wanted.

'Élis, you're *not* going to see this woman?' She remained standing there in front of him, her body encased in a dark-red stockinet dress, angular, narrow-hipped, holding her head high. Her eyes were devoid of lashes, and she blinked them in the glare that beat down from the ceiling. Her long, well-formed right hand was motionless at her throat, the fingers clutching at her coral necklace.

'So you've taken to listening at keyholes, have you?'

She smiled, as she might have done had he indulged in a joke.

'Short of having the door padded, the wall and the floor and the ceiling lined with felt ... I must say you've chosen the oddest sort of place in which to hear the intimate confessions of the poor wretches who come to see you. ...'

'All right ... all right ... and now let me get on with my work.'

A motor-bus came charging noisily down the rue de Boulain-villiers. Catherine, her hand on the latch, turned towards him.

'Mademoiselle Parpin will tell this woman, of course, that you can't see her?'

He took a few steps towards her, his hands stuffed in his pockets, swaying his heavy shoulders: a great, hulking figure of a man. Was she, he inquired often taken that way? Lighting a Caporal cigarette, he added:

'I don't suppose you've got the slightest idea what's at issue, have you?'

Catherine, leaning against the radiator, replied that she knew perfectly well.

'I remember the evening clearly. It was in February or March three years ago, at a time when you were going about a good deal. You told me all about it when you came home – about the woman with an obsession who had made you promise ...'

He was looking, now, at the floor. There was something slightly furtive in the expression of his face. Catherine sat down on the leather-covered couch which Élisée called his 'Confessional'. Stretched upon it, thousands of poor sufferers had stammered out the stories of their lives, lying, hesitating, and striving to reveal secrets which they pretended not to know. ... On the radio a juicy and aggressively stupid voice was recommending furniture bearing the hall-mark 'Levikhan'. There was an uninterrupted noise of cars sounding their horns at the street crossing below. Silence would set in only at midnight, and not even then if somebody in the block was giving a party. The doctor raised his eyes and saw Mademoiselle Parpin waiting by the little table on which the typewriter stood. He told her to go into the hall and stay there until the lady arrived. When she had left the room, Catherine said dryly:

'You won't let her come in?'

'We'll see about that.'

'You won't let her come in because she's dangerous. ...'

'It would be nearer the truth to say that you are jealous. ...'

There was an unexpected spontaneity about the laugh with which she greeted this statement.

'Oh, come now ... my poor dear ... *I*, jealous?' For a brief moment she seemed to be thinking nostalgically of the time when she might have been jealous. Then, suddenly:

'You're not, presumably, any more attracted than I am by the idea of stopping a revolver bullet. ... Such things don't happen, you say? ... How about Pozzi? ... You think I don't know her, have never set eyes on her? I could repeat, word for word, what you told me that evening. ... I've got a frighteningly good memory where you are concerned. Nothing that you say in my hearing is ever lost – not a syllable. I may not actually have seen her, but I'm pretty sure I should recognize her at once: a woman with a Tartar face, the only one among all your naked little friends who was wearing a tailor-made suit, the only one with a hat pulled down over her eyes. ... Later in the evening she took it off, revealing a superb forehead. ... You were a bit drunk, you know, when you told me all that. Do you remember how you kept on saying, "A marvellous forehead, like a tower". ... You can't have forgotten how you went on and on about it? And then you said, "One can't be too careful with women of that Kalmuck type." You're a bit frightened of her even now; you can't deny it. ... You're longing to show her the door. If you do see her, it'll be only because you're ashamed not to. ...'

Élisée made no attempt to abuse her. Since there was no stranger present, he did not see any point in feigning heroism. He contented himself with saying in a low voice, 'I gave her my word.'

They both fell silent, listening with strained attention to a rumbling sound in the belly of the building which indicated that someone had started the lift. The doctor muttered: 'That can't be her – she said half an hour. ...' Both husband and wife were busy with their secret thoughts, shut away from one another, remembering, perhaps, the time when he was trailing along after the notorious Zizi Bilaudel. It had been necessary to keep from the world what was really in the wind. Every day Catherine said, 'People are laughing at you.' Unknown to her, he had started taking private lessons in the Tango. At the various night-clubs haunted by Zizi and her faithful followers the youngsters laughed themselves sick at the sight of this great lump of a man dancing with a strained and concentrated look. He sweated like a pig, and was for ever going to the lavatory to change his collar. At that time the painter Bilaudel had not yet married Zizi, though she already bore his name. She was not exactly 'received', but had managed to pick up a number of acquaintances among the less fastidious members of the fashionable world. The plump, golden-haired creature, who passed for being so *terribly* Renoir', thoroughly deserved her reputation for intelligence. She was one of those women who can live a life of the wildest debauchery without showing the slightest sign of it, and had amassed an amount of varied experience which would have brought ruin to anyone less skilful in her technique of exploration. But from what particular gutter she had collected the rag, tag, and bobtail who trailed behind her no one knew. Catherine put it about that they furnished the doctor with admirable subjects for study, implying that he was getting a great deal of material out of this affair which would be useful to him in his scientific work. The lie was generally believed. As a matter of fact, it was perfectly true that one woman of the group *did* interest him to an exceptional degree. She alone could distract his attention when Zizi Bilaudel danced with younger men. This woman it was who had just telephoned: who, in a few minutes, would be actually in the flat.

The doctor was making a pretence of reading. Catherine went across and laid a hand on his shoulder.

'Listen to me. Do you remember what it was she told you that evening when you promised that you would see her whenever she liked to come? – that ever since she had tried to poison her husband she had been hag-ridden by the desire to commit murder ... that she had to fight tooth and nail against the temptation ...? That's the woman with whom you propose to shut yourself in a room at eleven o'clock at night!'

'If that had been the truth she would never have told it me. She was just putting on an act. But even supposing there *were* a risk, what do you take me for?'

Her eyes were as honest as the day. She spoke again in the same low, level tones;

'You're afraid, Élis: look at your hands.'

He thrust them into his pockets, hunched his shoulders, and made a short, sharp gesture with his head towards the right-hand side of the room.

'Off with you – quick march! – and don't let me set eyes on you again till tomorrow morning.'

Very calmly she opened the door which led into the hall. The secretary was sitting on a bench. He called to her to show the lady in as soon as she arrived, and then to clear off.

On the other side of the closed door Catherine and Mademoiselle Parpin remained for a moment or two in darkness. Then the secretary switched on the light.

'Madame!'

Catherine, already half-way up the stairs leading to the bedrooms, turned her head and noticed that the plump young woman's cheeks were wet with tears.

'Madame, you won't be far off, will you?' Her voice had lost all hint of insolence. She spoke as one asking a favour.

'It is important that this woman should realize that she's being watched. She must be made to feel that there's somebody next door. Hadn't I better stay? It would be better if there were two of us. ... But, no, I can't do that ... he's forbidden it.'

'He need never know.'

The secretary shook her head. 'I daren't do it!' she whispered. She suspected a trick to get her the sack. Madame Schwartz would give her away. The doctor would never forgive the least movement of disobedience. For a moment or two neither woman spoke. This time there could be no doubt about it: the lift really was coming up. In a low voice Catherine said:

'Show her in, and then go home. You can sleep in peace. I promise that nothing shall happen to the doctor tonight. I was his guardian angel for twenty years – long before you came on the scene, Mademoiselle.'

She vanished up the dark staircase. But no sooner had she reached the landing than she turned and came a little way down again. She stood leaning on the banisters.

The gate of the lift clanged. There was a quick ring at the bell. ... It was impossible to see the visitor's face as Mademoiselle Parpin stood aside to let her pass. A quiet voice asked whether this was where Dr Schwartz lived. The secretary took her dripping umbrella, and would have relieved her of her bag. But to that she clung fast.

Mademoiselle joined Catherine where she was sitting on the stairs. She whispered nervously that the stranger smelt of whisky. ... They strained their ears, but could hear nothing beyond the booming of the doctor's voice. Catherine asked how the woman was dressed. She had on a dark coat, said the other, with a rather shabby chinchilla collar.

'It's the bag that worries me, Madame. She kept it tight under her arm. ... We *must* try to get it from her. ... She may have a revolver in it. ...'

There was a burst of laughter from the stranger, followed

by the sound of the doctor speaking again. Catherine told Mademoiselle Parpin not to get rattled, but to keep her head. The secretary seized her hand with a sudden little display of emotion, and could not keep herself from murmuring 'Thank you' – though she realized how absurd the phrase must sound almost as soon as she had spoken it. From her post of vantage at the top of the stairs, Catherine, quite unmoved, watched the girl arranging her hat before the glass, and powdering her flushed cheeks. At last she went.

Once more Catherine squatted on the stairs. The sound of the two voices, her husband's and the woman's, reached her. They seemed to be talking quite quietly. There were no sudden bursts of louder words. How odd it seemed to be listening to Élis unseen by him! She could have sworn that it was another man he had in there with him, some good-natured friend whom she did not know. She realized why it was that his patients so often said: 'He's perfectly charming – so kind, so gentle.'

The woman's voice was too high-pitched for Catherine's taste. Maybe she had been drinking and was in an excited mood. Her rather unbalanced laugh reawakened the watching wife's anxiety. She tip-toed down the stairs, slipped into the drawing-room and, without switching on the light, sat down.

In front of her, through the muslin curtains, she could see the rain-drenched balcony shining like a lake. Beyond, the lights of Grenelle showed as scattered points of fire in the wet darkness. The doctor, in easy, conversational tones, was talking of Zizi Bilaudel, and asking what had happened to the 'gang'.

'Blown to the four winds, Doctor. ... I'm beginning to know something about "happy bands of brothers" ... they have a way of breaking up pretty quickly. I've seen a goodish few in my time. Bilaudel and I are the only two left of the particular one in which you were caught up for a few weeks, Doctor. Palaisy – you remember him? – a fine figure of a man who drank like a fish (and the stuff just made him gayer and gayer) – well, he broke up altogether, and went off to live with his parents in Languedoc. Then there was that fierce little surrealist, the one who tried to scare us, like children who try to frighten each other by tying handkerchiefs round their heads and pretending to be brigands (he had a way of scowling and never brushing his hair, and generally doing all he could to seem like an escaped convict – but somehow, whatever he did, he always looked like an angel). ... We used to ask him whether his suicide was timed for the next morning ... though personally I never treated it as a joke, because heroin's not like other drugs – it always ends up badly. ... Yes, it happened last month, over the telephone. ... Azévédo rang him up one night, just for fun – didn't let on who it was, but just said that Dora was playing fast and loose with Raymond ... he meant it as a leg-pull, because he knew perfectly well that it was a lie. ... He heard a quiet voice at the other end of the line saying, "You're sure of that?" ... and then a dull thud. ...'

The unknown visitor was talking fast and rather breathlessly. Catherine was so intent on listening to the doctor's grave, kindly tone (which he never used to her) that she did not fully grasp the purport of his reply. There, in the dark drawing-room, her face turned towards the streaming panes, the drowned roof-tops, the dwindling perspective of street-lights, she sat brooding over the thought that only to her did this man make a deliberate display of brutality ... only to her.

'Oh' – a note of insistence had crept into the woman's voice – 'please don't feel embarrassed. I don't in the least mind talking about Azévédo ... I can afford to laugh at all that now. ... No, that's not quite true. ... Love doesn't ever die altogether. I ought to hate him, but he still exercises a spell over my imagination, if for no other reason than that he hurt me so abominably. I know exactly what manner of man he is – the sort who can make money on the Stock Exchange on a rising market – but that doesn't alter the fact that he succeeded in dragging from my body every scrap of pain of which it was capable. No matter how petty a man may be, he can always attain a certain greatness by the sheer power of destruction. Because of his meanness I have sunk an inch or two deeper into the mud, have plunged farther into the mire, have reached the last door of all. ...'

In honeyed tones the doctor said:

'But, at least, dear lady, he has cured you of love, has he not?'

Catherine trembled. The peal of laughter with which the unknown greeted these words (it was like the sound of rending calico) must, she felt sure, have penetrated down through all seven floors of the building until it was audible even in the cellar.

'Should I be here at eleven o'clock at night? ... Haven't you noticed that ever since I entered this room I have been on fire? What's the use of all your fine knowledge?'

He replied, in high good humour, that he did not claim to be a wizard.

'I take no notice of what you tell me. I am just a pair of ears – nothing more. ... All I do is to help you straighten your own tangled skein. ...'

'One gives away only what one wants to. ...'

'That is where you are profoundly wrong, Madame. ... In this room people let the light in on what they most want to conceal. Let me correct what I said just now. I *do* take notice, but only of what they try to hide, of what leaks out in spite of themselves. It's my job to hold it out for their inspection. I give the little gnawing creature its true name ... and then they are no longer afraid of it. ...'

'The mistake you make is in believing what we say. ... Love can turn us into terrible liars. For instance, when I broke with Azévédo, he sent me back all my letters. I spent one whole evening just sitting with the bundle in front of me. It seemed so light! I had always fondly imagined that I should need a suitcase, that nothing less would suffice to hold that vast mass of correspondence. But here it all was, just a few sheets that would go comfortably into an envelope. I laid them out on the table. When I thought of all the pain those letters contained – you'll think me an awful fool – I was filled with a feeling of respect and terror (that's made you laugh; I knew it would!). ... So strong was the feeling that I couldn't pluck up courage

to read a single one of them. And then, at last, I forced myself
to open the most frightening of the whole collection. I remembered the agonies I had gone through when I wrote it,
one day in August, at Cap Ferrat. It was mere chance that I
had not killed myself then and there ... and now, three years
later, with all love dead in my heart, my hand still trembled
at the touch of that piece of paper. Yet, would you believe it?
when I did bring myself to look it over it seemed so mild,
so harmless, that for a moment I thought I must have picked
on the wrong one. ... But no, there couldn't be any doubt
about it. Those were the very lines I had scribbled within
touching distance of death. They revealed nothing but a
pitiful attempt at flippancy, nothing but my eagerness to hide
the appalling pain I was suffering, as I might have concealed a
physical wound – from a sense of shame, from a fear that the
sight of it might disgust the man I loved, or move him to a
show of pity. ... Don't you think there's something rather
comic, Doctor, about tricks like that which never, somehow,
come off? I had believed, poor fool, that if I assumed an
attitude of indifference, I might succeed in making Azévédo
jealous. ... The rest of the letters were all of the same kind.
Nothing can well be less natural, less spontaneous, than love's
double-dealing. ... But I'm not telling you anything you don't
know already. It's your job, and you know it better than anyone else. When I'm in love I'm for ever plotting, planning,
anticipating, but with a constant clumsiness which ought to
touch the heart of him I love, instead of irritating him, as it
always does. ...'

Catherine Schwartz sitting in the darkness, heard every
word. The woman was talking in an odd, jerky way. Her
phrases followed no ordinary speech rhythm. It was as though
her voice had suddenly got out of control. Why had she come
to Élis? – why chosen him, of all men, as the repository of her
confidences? Catherine felt a sudden desire to fling open the
door of the consulting-room, to cry to the unknown woman
within, 'He has nothing to give you: all he can do is to tread
you still deeper into the mud. I don't know to whom you

ought to go, but certainly not to him – no, certainly not to him!'

'I wouldn't mind betting, dear lady, that you couldn't talk so eloquently of love if you hadn't let yourself be caught a second time. ... I'm right, am I not?'

There was something paternal, gentle, calm, kindly, in the way he spoke. But the tone in which the visitor broke in upon his words was vulgar, almost coarse.

'Of course I have – any fool could see that. ... You don't have to work hard to make me talk – why else do you think I have come here? If you leave the room I shall still go on talking – to the leg of the table, if need be, or the wall.'

It was borne in sharply on Catherine how atrociously she was behaving – a doctor's wife listening at doors and overhearing the secrets confided to her husband. ... Her cheeks felt on fire. She got up, went into the hall and up the short flight of stairs to her own room, which was brilliantly illuminated by a single hanging light. She crossed to the mirror and looked long and hard at the unattractive face which must be her constant companion through life. The light, the familiar objects, all reassured her. Why had she been frightened? What danger was there? Besides, that woman down there was no casual stranger. ...

At that moment a sound of raised voices set her trembling. The door of the room was only half closed. She pushed it open and went part way down the stairs – though not far enough to enable her to hear what the visitor was shouting (for shouting she was). A few steps farther and she would hear everything. The secrets of the Confessional ... yes, but perhaps Élis's life was at stake. ... Once again she yielded to temptation, and sat down on the couch in the hall. For a moment the noise of the lift prevented her from hearing. Then:

'You do understand, don't you, Doctor? ... I had spent the whole summer away from Phili. I have never needed anyone, not even Azévédo, as I need Phili. When he's not there I feel as though I am suffocating. He had been avoiding me – oh, on all sorts of pretexts, business, visits. ... What was really happening was that he was hunting for a rich wife ... but that's not so easy to find these days ... besides, he's already been divorced once, even though he is only twenty-four. ... I just couldn't stay still anywhere. I can't begin to describe the kind of life I was leading. I wanted only one thing – letters. In every town I stopped in only one object held any interest for me – the counter of the poste restante. That's what travelling always means to me, the poste restante.'

Catherine knew perfectly well that she was not listening now merely from a sense of duty. She was no longer concerned to help her husband in case of attack. No, she was a prey to irresistible curiosity – she, who had always been so scrupulously discreet that discretion had become almost a mania with her. This unknown voice fascinated her. But even while she felt the lure of it, she could not bear to think of the disappointment lying in wait for its wretched owner. Élis was quite incapable of understanding her, even of feeling compassion for her. All he would do, as he had done with other victims, was to urge her to find relief – to free her emotions through the gratification of the body. That was what his method amounted to. The same filthy key served him whether it was heroism, crime, sanctity, or renunciation that he had to interpret. ... These thoughts passed confusedly through her mind, though they did not prevent her from hearing all that was going on in the consulting-room.

'... Imagine my surprise when I began to notice that Phili's letters were getting longer and longer, that he seemed to be writing them with considerable care, that he seemed to want to console me, to make me happy. They became increasingly frequent as the summer wore away, until at last they were coming daily.

'It all happened during the week I was spending, as I do every year, with my daughter. She's eleven now. Her governess takes her to some place that I have fixed on in advance, somewhere that must always be, at least, five hundred kilometres from Bordeaux – my husband insists on that. It's always a terrible time for me. You see, I don't know whether the child knows of the horrible charge hanging over me, and, in any case, she is frightened of me. The governess always arranges things so that I never pour out her drinking water. I'm the sort of woman, you see, who would stop at nothing – which is what my husband said the evening of the day on which my case was dismissed. (I can still hear that country drawl of his: "You don't really think I'd leave the child to your tender mercies. She, too, must be kept at a safe distance from your drugs. If I'm poisoned, the estate will go to her when she's twenty-one ... first the father, then the child! You wouldn't hesitate two seconds about liquidating her!") All the same, he lets me have her for one week in every year. I take her to restaurants, the circus ... but that's all by the way. ... As I've told you, Phili's letters had made me happy. I wasn't suffering any more. He couldn't wait to see me. He was more impatient even than I was. I was happy and at peace. It must have shown in my face. Marie was less frightened of me than usual. One evening at Versailles, on a bench near the Petit Trianon, I stroked her hair. ... Poor fool! – I was thinking, hoping ... I had reached a stage at which I even felt gratitude to God. I was ready to bless life ...'

Once more Catherine got up and started to climb the stairs that led to her room. Her cheeks were aflame. Listening there, behind the door, she had felt like a criminal engaged in a particularly low form of theft. What was Élis going to do with that poor creature emptying her heart of all its secrets at his feet? No sooner had she sat down than she got up again, and a moment later was at her post of observation on the stairs. The unknown was still talking:

'He was waiting for me at the station exit. It was seven o'clock in the morning. I was in Heaven, as you can imagine. I saw his poor, worn, hunted face. There always comes one brief moment, when one sees the man one loves for the first time after a long absence, in which he stands before us as he really is and not as our infatuation has painted him. Don't you agree, Doctor? – one tiny second in which we can take the squalid tricks of passion unaware. But we are too much in love with suffering to seize such opportunities to the full. He took me along to the Café d'Orsay. We chatted casually of this and that, joining up loose ends. ... He asked me about the resin, the trees, the pit-props (at that time I was still getting an income from my property). I laughed and told him that we should have to tighten our belts. The bottom had fallen out of the resin market. The Americans had found a substitute for turpentine. It was quite impossible to sell timber. The Argelouse saw-mills were working on imported lumber from Poland, and the pines growing at their very doors were left to rot where they stood. I was faced with ruin ... like everybody else. ... I rattled on, and Phili grew paler and paler. He kept on asking whether the trees couldn't be sold even at a loss, and when I protested that to take such a step would be to court disaster, I could feel that his attention was beginning to wander. Whatever value I had for him diminished in strict ratio with that of my Argelouse property. You do understand what I'm talking about, don't you, Doctor? I didn't cry. I actually laughed – laughed at myself, as no doubt you realize. And all the time he was utterly withdrawn from me: he might have been a thousand miles away. He no longer even saw me. Only those who have suffered as I did then can possibly know what such an experience is like. Not so much as to exist in the eyes of the man who is the only living creature in one's world. I would have done anything, no matter how mad, to recapture his attention. ... But you'll never guess what I did do.'

'The puzzle is not insoluble. ... You told him about your past, about the crime with which you had been charged. ...'

'How on earth did you know that? ... Yes, that is precisely what I did do. ... I didn't know then that there was someone who had a hold over Phili, someone who was blackmailing him and could have had him arrested (but I won't go into all that). I just told him about my own troubles. ...'

'And he was interested?'

'You'd never guess how much. He listened with a terrible sort of concentration. In a vague kind of way I was frightened. I began to feel that I had been a fool to give myself away so completely. Oh yes, he was interested now all right, much *too* interested, if you see what I mean. At first I thought that he was planning to use what I had said to get something out of me. But it wasn't that. ... Besides, he couldn't. ... That particular danger, so far as I was concerned, had long passed. My case had been shelved. No: his mind was working along quite different lines. ... He thought I might be able to help him.'

'Help him – but how?'

'Aren't you being a bit slow, Doctor? – help him, of course, to commit a deed from which his conscience recoiled. He swore that once it was all over he would marry me, that we should be irretrievably bound to one another, because I should have a hold on him and he on me. He had got a plan all worked out. He gave me his word that I should run no risk whatever. What I had done once I could do again. ... I must tell you that his enemy, the man who held his life in his hands, lived in the country. He was a small landowner, scarcely better than a peasant, somewhere in the south-west – a vine grower. I had been to see him once with the idea of buying some of his wine. Nowadays, you know, there is no job a woman can't take on, even to selling on commission. I had put through one or two deals for him, quite successfully. He showed me round his cellars; we sampled his vintages. ... Do you see what I'm getting at? We drank out of the same glass. He was known to be a tippler ... and had already had more than one stroke, though nothing very serious. ... It wouldn't cause the slightest surprise ... and, you know, they don't go in for post-mortems in the country. ... The chances of anything ever coming out were nil. ...'

She broke off. The doctor said nothing. Catherine, in the darkness of the staircase, felt her heart thumping. Then the woman's voice began again, but a change had come into it.

'Save me, Doctor! ... He gives me no peace. ... I shall end by doing what he wants. He looks as innocent as a child, I know, but there's something about him that terrifies me. ... What is this awful power that you sometimes find in people with angel faces? One feels it was only yesterday that they were schoolboys. ... Do you believe in a devil, Doctor? Do you think that Evil can take on human form?'

Catherine could not bear the sound of her husband's

laughter. She shut the door of her room behind her, sank to her knees beside the bed, put her fingers in her ears, and so remained for a long while, utterly prostrated, shattered, thinking of nothing. ... And then, suddenly, she heard her name cried aloud on a note of terror. She rushed downstairs and burst into the consulting-room. At first she could not see her husband and thought he must be dead. But a moment later she heard him.

'She's got nothing against *you* ... but be careful all the same. ... Quick! get it away from her! ... She's armed!' She realized then that he was crouching behind his desk. The stranger was leaning against the wall. Her right hand was concealed in her half-open bag, and she was staring fixedly in front of her. Quite calmly, Catherine took hold of her wrist. The woman made no attempt to resist. She let her bag fall to the ground. Her hand had closed about something, but it was not a revolver. The doctor had emerged now. He was pale, and took no trouble to conceal the fact that his hands, as he leaned forward on the desk, were trembling. Catherine, still holding the other's wrist, forced her to loosen her grasp. A packet wrapped in white paper dropped to the carpet.

The unknown looked at Catherine. She took off her close-fitting hat and revealed her forehead. It was much too massive. Her drab, sparse hair was going grey. There was neither rouge nor powder on her thin face, her roughened lips, her cheekbones. The yellow skin was marked with blotches of purple beneath the eyes.

She did nothing to prevent Catherine from picking up the packet and reading what was written on the label – an ordinary chemist's label. She opened the door, still holding her hat. In the hall she said that she had an umbrella. Catherine spoke gently to her.

'Would you like me to ring for a cab? It's raining hard.'

The woman shook her small head. Catherine led the way to the stairs, switching on the self-extinguishing light as she went.

'Aren't you going to put on your hat?'

Getting no answer, she herself put the hat upon the stranger's head, buttoned her coat for her, turned up the chinchilla collar. She wanted to smile, to lay a comforting hand on her shoulder. ... She watched her disappear down the staircase, hesitated a moment, and then went back into the flat.

The doctor was standing in the middle of the room, his hands in his pockets. He did not look at Catherine.

'You were quite right – the most dangerous kind of lunatic. In future I shall be more careful. She pretended she'd got a revolver. ... Anyone would have been taken in. ... Let me tell you what happened. It was like this. After she'd told me her wretched story she said I'd got to cure her. ... It was when I explained that I'd already done more than enough by letting her sort out her troubles that she lost her temper. I pointed out that she'd be able to see her way more clearly now, that she would be mistress of the situation, that she'd manage to get all she wanted from this man without falling in with his plans. ... Didn't you hear her scream? She said I was a thief. ... "You pretend you want to cure the soul," she shouted "and all the time you don't believe in the soul. Psychiatrist ... that means a Soul-Doctor, but you say there's no such thing as the soul. ..." The same old story, of course ... a familiar tendency to indulge in the crudest form of superstition. ... She'd been bad enough earlier on, but nothing to what she was then. ... Why are you laughing, Catherine? Have I said anything comic?'

He looked at his wife in amazement. Never before had he seen such a glow of happiness on her face. She stood there, her arms hanging at her sides, her hands held slightly away from her skirt.

'It's taken twenty years. ... But it's all over now ... I'm a free woman at last. You see, Élis, I realize now that I don't love you any more.'

Thérèse at the Hotel

*

IF there were, anywhere in the world, a single human creature in whom I could confide, should I ever be able to explain clearly what it was that happened between that boy and me in the hotel where I was this morning, and where yesterday, at this very hour, we sat in the garden invisible to one another, talking so intimately? My disinclination to embark on the labour of writing is less strong than the desire I feel to scrutinize my own story. No other woman would endure such monstrous loneliness as weighs upon me. What saves me is that I am never bored by my own company.

My acts are my prison. My acts? No, say, rather, that one, that single, 'act'. Even at night I am never quite certain that I lose altogether the consciousness of what, at one moment of my life, I actually did – when I *really* put a few drops into a cup, into a glass, so that death began to breed in the great body, so that I saw death opening within my husband like a plant which I had carefully watered.

For the last ten years this nightmare has been less obsessive. Bernard, saved from my attentions, is prosperous, and, though the death that will take him at last is, doubtless, already at work, stimulated by too much food and too much drink, I am no longer there to give it a helping hand. There is no one with him now who lives racked with impatience, no one who feels the need to wipe from the face of the earth that blob of self-satisfaction and self-sufficiency. ... It is I who am fated to live on in the prison of my useless act: I who have been cast into the outer darkness by my intended victim and by my family as well: I, the most rootless, the most utterly lost, creature in all the world.

I have been reading over what I wrote. No doubt about it, I get a certain satisfaction from my self-portrait. Isn't it the fact of the matter that I am the prisoner, really, of the part I have elected to play, of the 'character' I have assumed? But somewhere, surely, there must be a *real* Thérèse, the *only* real Thérèse – the woman from whom I have become separated as a result of that far-distant crime? Has it not, that crime, forced upon me a definite attitude, a set of gestures, a way of life, that do not, in very truth, belong to me at all?

No matter where I drag this worn-out body and this love-starved heart, my act lies all about me ... a living wall. ... No, not so much a wall as a quickset hedge which yearly grows more tangled.

... I am never bored by my own company. This in-turned curiosity is, perhaps, the most inhuman thing about me. Most people manage to live by deliberately turning away from memories. For them the skeins which they have woven into the texture of their lives cease to exist. Women, in particular, are of a race that knows nothing of memory. That is why, no matter how horrible their lives may have been, they can still look out at the world with the eyes of a child. They carry with them no reflection of their acts. But in this I am not like other women. For instance, any other woman would say, 'I went to earth in that hotel at Cap Ferrat, after Phili's suicide, in order that I might suffer in peace, might be alone with my pain.' But my mind works differently. While he was alive he dragged me through hell (I measured the love I had for him in terms of the misery he could cause me), but his suicide has saved me. As soon as I knew he was dead a great weight was lifted from me, and I knew happiness. Not only was I freed from the agony of a love which had been wholly one-sided, but also from a far more trivial cause of anxiety. When I knew that he might get into trouble with the police over that faked cheque I foresaw that inquiries would be set on foot to determine how he had been living all this while, and that I should very soon have been brought into the picture. In that sort of police-court gossip one always comes, sooner or later, on the figure of an older woman who never fails to elicit from the journalists the same dreary old ill-mannered gibes: the eternal figure of the woman who always pays, a squalid, pitiful, ageing figure – and this time it would have been I, I,

Thérèse, who would willingly give all my life for just fifteen minutes of genuine, disinterested affection – who has never, at bottom, wanted anything else of life but that.

My pride could not have borne the shame of it. But I was spared that ordeal by Phili's death. To be honest, that wasn't the only thing I dreaded. I couldn't have faced cross-examination in a magistrates' court – even though I should have been only a witness. ... The Bench would have ferreted into my past, would have nosed out the woman who had once stood in the dock. ... And even if I had succeeded in confusing the scent, it would have been intolerable merely to sit there, as I did ten years ago, facing a man whose every question concealed a trap. ... *That* I could never have endured. ...

... But what, then, was that love worth of which you were always so proud, Thérèse, seeing that you can welcome with delight the death of the very man who inspired it? Hypocrite! What you call love is nothing but a prowling demon who roams the waste places of the earth, seeking whom he may devour. And when she has been duly made away with he starts again on the old weary round. Such love, for all it glories in its sense of freedom, must ever be obedient to the law of its being – which is to seek out someone else whom it may kill for food. ...

Once Phili was buried (what an emblem of despair that poor wife of his was, the little woman from Bordeaux whom he had abandoned, and who came to claim his body. Why hadn't he gone to her for money? She would have given him all he needed. 'I'd rather see myself dead first,' he used to say), once Phili was buried, I came to this hotel, not in the guise of a mourning lover, but as a convalescent, revelling in the two-fold and delicious pain of knowing that my demon was at a loose end, yet feeling certain that he was already on the track of a new victim.

Being the sort of woman I am, what constantly amazes me is not the thought of what I have done, but of what I have refrained from doing. Rejected, as a result of my crime, more wholly than anyone was ever rejected before, and with such a heart and such a body, why didn't I, as the phrase is, go to the dogs altogether? I know perfectly well why. You are intelligent, Thérèse – why be shy about admitting it? – you are extremely intelligent, whereas the drink-sodden creatures with whom you used, occasionally, to get into conversation on benches in the Champs-Elysées or the Bois, or in front of cafés, were fools. We stand in greater need of intelligence than men. Stupid women sink to the level of animals once the ties of family and worldly convention are loosened. Yes, you were intelligent enough to escape that ultimate degradation, though not to save yourself from vice. ... Oh, I know that the women of your family would cross themselves in horror merely to think of what you have done. Had I ever yielded to the fantastic temptation which sometimes came over me when, completely exhausted, with my feet bruised and aching from my long trudging of the streets, I used sometimes to sit down in an unfamiliar church; had I really gone into one of the boxes where a man sits with his ear to a grille; had I surrendered to the need I felt to lay down the burden of my heaviest sins, I could never have confessed but a fraction of them, so numberless they are. How do people manage when they go to Confession after a long interval of years? How do they fish it all up out of the past? How can they be sure of omitting nothing? In their place I should feel that one single forgotten misdeed would invalidate the absolution, that one tiny scrap omitted from the mass would start to crystallize all my infamy about me.

There is a point, though, beyond which I have never gone ... but I should feel a fool if I put it into words. This damned heart of mine is at once my curse and my salvation – my curse because it gets me into trouble, my salvation because it always keeps me from seeking a purely physical satisfaction. ... Of what are you trying to persuade yourself, Thérèse? Are you not just as capable as any other woman of doing evil? Of course you are ... only, when you set about balancing accounts next morning, setting pleasure against shame and disgust, horror is always your prevailing emotion.

The result is that you can still count the total of your relapses. ... Almost always, the trap has got to be baited with a show of sentiment. Your heart was always involved even in your most sordid adventures. Only if that lure is present can you advance along the path of sin, can you commit yourself utterly: only if you can indulge a hope which, doubtless, you have always known to be condemned in advance to disappointment. That monstrous indifference of mine at the thought of Phili's suicide can, almost certainly, be explained by the fact that I *knew* from the start (it was that kind of adventure) that I was embarked upon a voyage of self-deception in which the man was merely an excuse. ... That is the truth of the matter. Men are just the excuse my heart demands, and it snatches at them almost casually. My love is a mole, a sightless animal. As though one should happen, accidentally, upon a tender heart! *Are* there any tender hearts in the world? I wonder. All of us, men and women alike, are tender only when we love; never when we are the object of love.

What *did* happen between that boy and me? ... Nothing happened. It is what I felt, what I still feel, that is new. ... The very first day I set eyes on him, I had gone into the hotel dining-room with a sense of calm and well-being. Most likely the various families brought together there by the Easter holidays felt sorry for the lonely woman who was reduced to reading a book while she ate her luncheon. They could not guess that in the desert of my experience the life of this hotel took on the semblance of a haven: that their very presence gave off a little human warmth: that even to know people by sight is something.

Yes, they gave me a feeling of warmth, but without exciting my envy. Just to see father, mother, and children seated round a table reminded me of a period of my life when Bernard, opposite, chewed his food, wiped his mouth, and drank in a way that used to fill me with horror: so much so that when, one day, he complained of the light in his eyes and moved round to sit beside me, I felt as though I had been freed from an ordeal. ... Who knows? Perhaps if I had stuck to the new arrangement, if I had never had to look at him across the table again, the idea would not have occurred to me. ... But why must I go over all that again, always and always?

The family at the next table, mother, grandmother, and young sister, had a stuffy, honest look. It was as though precisely the same qualities had been incarnated in three separate persons, beginning with grandmamma and descending intact and unmodified to the girl. ... But what about the boy? How old was he? Eighteen? Twenty? I couldn't be sure, but whatever it was, he was nothing much to look at. What kept my eyes fixed on him was something in the nature of a miracle. Youth without alloy, youth in its pure state. The light of dawn shone in his face, undimmed, untroubled. I saw him quite objectively – at least, I thought I did ... as though the ashes of my passion for Phili were not still glowing! It's always the same, always in these periods between tides that I let myself get caught. I persuade myself that my heart is dead, when really it is only getting its second breath. In the slack periods between successive bouts of passion, when there is no one there to put me in blinkers, I can see myself in the mirror, looking far older than my age; can see the reflection of a used-up woman who is no longer good for anything. And seeing myself so, I achieve a sort of repose. The knowledge of what I am comes as a consolation. The years of struggle are ended: that filthy business, love, no longer concerns me. I lean over and watch the lives of others, and my own past, as from some inaccessible balcony. I never remember that in the interval that separates one orgy of passion from another I always have this same sense of final and absolute security. Each experience of love that has come my way has, I have always told myself, been the last. What more logical than that? At the outset of every falling in love there is an act of will. I know the precise minute at which, deliberately and with full knowledge, I take the fatal step forward. But how comes it, then, that I, with the traces of burns still fresh on me, should imagine that I could ever be so mad as to go back, of my own free will, into the furnace? The thing is unbelievable. ... And I never do believe it.

And so it came about that I looked at this strange young man as I might have looked at some lovely, growing plant. The school examinations must have tired him, for I noticed that he was in the habit of taking pills, and that after every meal he was made to lie down. All this fussing seemed to irritate him. He showed signs of ill-temper with his mother and his grandmother, but however much he grumbled, there was a note of affection in his voice. He read a great deal, and had a special liking for the sort of magazines that one can't recognize at first sight from the colour of their wrappers. Even while he ate, he would take one from his pocket and bury himself in it. But whenever that happened he was quickly called to order. He would submit with a sigh, and jerk back a lock of hair which was for ever falling across his forehead.

All this amused me a good deal. I watched the whole process each time that it occurred, for I had developed considerable skill in observing my neighbours without seeming to do so. I, too, had a book, *Lady Chatterley's Lover*, which I pretended to read between courses, though I didn't, for a moment, let the young man out of my sight. He had shown not the least sign of interest in me, beyond turning the pages of Lawrence's novel when I left it, one morning, lying about on one of the tables in the lounge. I had caught him in the act. He had hastily put the book down at my approach, and the blood had rushed into his baby cheeks. He had hurried away, averting his eyes.

It was on the day following that I was struck down in the old familiar way, the way to which I should by that time, have grown accustomed, though I know perfectly well that when next that particular experience occurs it will still have the power to take me by surprise. ...

I noticed at luncheon that he was eating absent-mindedly, his eyes staring blankly in front of him. There is nothing lovelier than the remoteness which belongs to certain young people, the air they have of being somewhere else, with their minds intent on some mysterious dream. So distrait did he appear that I felt free to watch him without taking my usual precautions. But so absorbed did he seem to be that I couldn't, in spite of myself, help feeling somewhat surprised. I followed the direction of his gaze, and what was my amazement when

I discovered that by some trick of reflection (the dining-room was full of mirrors) it was me at whom he was looking! His expression was so intense that I felt quite dumbfounded. I lowered my eyes quickly so that he should not see that I had tumbled to what he was doing. He continued to stare at my reflection with an air of mingled passion and remoteness.

To what shall I compare my sensations at that moment? I felt as must the burnt-up grasses when the first shower brings them new life. ... Yes, that was it: I was experiencing a sudden, an utterly lunatic, spring. All that I thought was dead within me burgeoned and came to flower. That earlier realization of my physical deterioration was now a dead letter. In a flash I forgot entirely everything to do with my body. The interest which I had inspired in this stranger – if I could believe my eyes – brought back to me my youth and my faded charm. Perhaps a still small voice within me did utter a note of protest – 'You know it's impossible' – but I brushed it aside, remembering only that women a great deal older than I was had been able to rouse adoration. And it wasn't, either, that he saw me against the light, for the cruel glare of midday was full upon my face. No, something in me, in me as I actually was, had struck and enslaved him, something that had no name. Often, during the first years of my life in Paris, I had been made aware of my power. That one experience of being stared at did the trick. I was ready to start again on the old round! The thing would begin with a sensation of happiness, however brief. I knew that, very quickly, I should have to pay for it, but I refused to look at the inevitable sequel. Whatever happened later, I should have had this momentary joy, the first smile of mutual understanding, the first murmured words. The invasion of my whole being, which was beginning even now, was already making me catch my breath.

No one, looking at this boy who was little more than a child, would ever have believed that he could pay so much attention to a woman. It was easy to see that he was consumed by passion. His eyes, in their excessively deep sockets, were burning with a dark fire. His full, beautiful lips showed a flash of teeth when they parted in a smile. The lock of hair which kept falling across his forehead softened the asceticism of his young face.

On his way out of the dining-room he brushed against me, though he did not so much as give me a look. How tall he was! He belonged to that type of adolescent whose bodies develop more quickly than their features, so that they have the appearance of men with the faces of children.

I refrained from following him too obviously. When I reached the lounge he was having an argument with his grandmother, who wanted him to lie down (the other members of the family were going out in the car). How odd! Didn't he want to remain alone in the hotel? Wasn't he eager to get a chance of speaking to me? Already I was aware of a feeling of uneasiness. The old doubt, the old pain, was beginning once more! It hadn't wasted much time in getting on my trail! But, if it came to that, what reason had he for believing that I should stay in the lounge? I was not in the habit of doing so. Was it altogether a coincidence that he should suddenly yield to the representations of his family just as I settled down at the next table to theirs? Once again a feeling of happiness seized me by the throat. I sat there, slowly sipping my extremely hot coffee.

His heavy shoes, I could see, knew nothing of the refinement of trees. His socks hung loosely round his ankles. He wore a pair of cheap grey flannel trousers which were rather tight over the thighs. I pretended to read. There was no mirror here to help him, but I was careful not to disturb his manoeuvres. I did not have to raise my eyes: I could feel him staring at me. Time passed and nothing happened. I knew that he never rested for more than an hour. Each wasted minute became an agony. What excuse could I make to address him? I was utterly incapable of finding one. Was it a fine day or was it raining? I can't remember. The outer world had disintegrated about the hard core of my anxiety. The hour wore away without a single exchange of words between us.

At last he got up, stretching himself sleepily to his full height: he was so tall that I got the impression that his head was too small – it was rather like a snake's (the top slightly flattened). He moved towards the door. I threw away my cigarette.

'Excuse me ...'

He turned and smiled at me. There was something in his expression that was very gentle, though at the same time almost intolerably concentrated. I told him that I had seen him turning the pages of Lawrence's novel, and that if he wanted to read it I should be only too happy to lend it. The smile vanished from his lips, his features hardened. The way in which he looked at me might have betokened anger and certainly expressed sadness. I breathed: again I had spoken; he was there. The first difficult step had been taken: contact had been established. I had stepped into his life and he into mine, as a result of those preliminary words. That one look of his had given him right of entry. Not yet did he know how hard he would find it to get out again, to escape. I scarcely heard what he said, so obsessed was I by happiness, by that sense of slackened tension which followed my initial victory. No matter what happened now, the stage was irrevocably set. His eyes were still devouring my face with a sort of innocent impertinence. We were alone in the lounge. I remember now that it *was* a fine day, and that everyone had gone out. At last I so far recovered myself as to hear what he was saying. There was a harsh note in his voice.

'What is the point of reviews if they don't spare one the necessity of reading books like that? I don't need to look at it to know what it is about.'

Just so as to say something, I uttered the first words that came into my head, to the effect that it was an extremely good novel. ...

'Ah,' he said, with a sigh; 'I feared as much. ...'

His tone sounded to me not so much irritated as anxious. He looked fixedly at me. Already he was beginning to dislike me. I was grating on him. Already he had realized that I was not like the picture he had painted of me. How gladly I would have reassured him! I did not yet know what sort of a woman he wanted me to be, but I would soon, and it would be easy enough for me to adapt myself to his ideal. What was really difficult was this first fumbling interchange of words.

I tried hard to fix my attention on what he was saying. He spoke so quickly that his tongue almost stumbled over the words.

'An extremely good novel. ... So you weren't even shocked!'

I thought that he was the victim of some obscure kind of jealousy, that he was afraid lest I might turn out to be a second Lady Chatterley. Instinctively I took refuge in one of my 'effects'. It had never failed with the people among whom I habitually moved whenever a rather daring book was under discussion. I assured him that when I wanted to imagine delicious situations I didn't need any book to help me.

'That's a perfectly disgusting thing to say. ...'

I was a bit staggered by that, and he added: 'But I don't believe you really mean it!'

He flung back the lock of hair with a movement of his head and fixed on me a glance which was full of fire and (or so I thought) of tenderness. How terribly I was in love with him at that moment! Had not a number of waiters been in the room setting the tables for tea I am pretty sure that I should have given myself away. So disturbed was the state of my mind that I hardly knew what he was saying. But that wasn't the only reason, for what he *was* saying was very odd indeed. I had begun to pay more attention to him now. It was obvious, of course, from the way he looked, from the tone of his voice, that I had roused his interest: but his words in no way corresponded to the warmth with which they were uttered. When I remarked that I did not want him to have any illusions about me:

'No,' he countered; 'I don't imagine you to be any better than you are' (and the ardour of his gaze seemed to wrap me round). 'I have had a great deal more experience than you think, and I am not often taken in by faces. I doubt whether I have ever gone seriously wrong, especially when I've been dealing with people who are no longer young.'

This he said in the most natural way imaginable. I did not

really believe that he included me in this category, but, all the same, my heart grew heavy.

'I find it harder to be sure with my contemporaries. One has to be on one's guard with the baby-faced, whether men or women. But I think I've learned to read them pretty thoroughly. Angels of darkness are always beautiful, aren't they? The important thing is to know, to be able to distinguish. Those who have lived their lives. ...'

This time there could be no further doubt ... he *did* mean me.

'Old people, you mean,' I said, with rather a strained smile. I was fishing for some sort of denial, even if it were to be only a conventional one. But nothing came. Instead, slightly averting his eyes, he said:

'In their case, the book of their lives lies open for all to read.'

For a moment or two I remained speechless, completely disconcerted by this child with the eyes of an Inquisitor. But almost immediately I responded to the automatic reaction which takes control of me whenever I like anybody. I set about waking his curiosity, holding his attention with the promise of mystery and drama.

'You would find the book of *my* life pretty staggering. If I told you all that it contains you would be horrified. I don't know what you imagine, but ...'

I broke off almost roughly. It was clear that he desired no intimate confession. In the oddest way he hastened to assure me that he held no authority to listen to any such thing – still less to 'grant absolution', he added in a low voice.

It was at this moment that I fully realized how I had been taken in by the hard though passionate expression which showed upon his face: though even then I would not admit the fact even to myself. I drew comfort from the intense interest which he was showing on my account. He might think of me as of someone who was no longer young, but, though I might seem old in his eyes, no man had ever before stared at me quite like that, as if he wanted to 'eat me up'.

'Whatever you may have done,' he went on, still in little more than a whisper, 'I don't, with you, get the impression which, somehow, never deceives me. I don't quite know how to explain what I mean. With certain men and women whom I meet in the great world it's as though I have an almost physical sense of spiritual death. ... Do you realize what that means? It's as though their souls were already stiff and rigid. But with you – please forgive me for being so frank (and, of course, I may be wrong) – I wouldn't mind betting that your soul is very sick, terribly sick, but still alive ... yes, overflowing with life. Ever since I first noticed you I have been haunted by the contrast between what your life may have been up to now and the possibility of ... I'm not shocking you, am I? ... Are you making fun of me?'

He had stopped, disconcerted by my laughter. I was laughing not at the young fool before me but at myself at the absurd mistake I had made. Yet, at the same time, I was laughing with joy to think how I had escaped making an utter idiot of myself. I had been so near to the irrevocable gesture, had caught myself back on the verge of taking his hand. ... I breathed again. I saw myself with the eyes of this young Galahad* as an old woman. He had not the slightest idea of what was churning round in my mind. I looked at him – a young ass of twenty who was worried about women's souls. I hated him.

Again he said: 'Are you making fun of me?'

I had got up. I felt that, at all costs, I must have some fresh air, must walk off the furious anger that had laid hold of me. At the same time I was fearful lest I might utter the one word which would separate us for ever. I did not want to lose him – boy though he was. I had still to prove to him that I was indeed living, but not in the way that he imagined. I heard myself saying, without the least hint of ill-temper:

'You have thought very deeply for your age. Your views may be somewhat daring, but they are profound!'

---

* I have used the name Galahad as meaning more to English readers than Eliacin, the character from Racine to whom M. Mauriac actually refers. – TRANSLATOR.

He protested that it was not his intention to be profound. As to daring – he knew he was that. He wanted to drive straight ahead at full speed, not to get bogged down in the wary periphrases of convention. No matter how often he might be brought up short, nothing would ever alter that attitude of his. Once more he proffered his excuses, striving to read my thoughts. But I gave nothing away.

'Your zeal does you great honour,' I said.

I held out my hand and did not at once let go of his. It was rather damp, and I shrank now from its touch. Then I added, with that smile which once upon a time had made men love me:

'I should like to have some more conversation with you this evening.'

Without waiting for his reply, I fired my Parthian shot:

'You can do a great deal for me,' I said. I stressed the words, half closing my eyes. I knew so well what to say to men with exquisite consciences. He was not the first of the type whom I had met, though never before had I been so completely taken in. I was longing to be alone. I could not have controlled myself much longer.

I hurried off to Villefranche.

I have a clear memory of the café on the water-front of that tiny harbour. A number of bedraggled sluts were looking at some English sailors who were piling into the boat which was to take them back to their ship. Some late-comers were hurrying down to the quay. They had been playing football, and their 'shorts' left bare their huge knees covered with blood and earth. The girls were trying to pick out from the crowd the men with whom they had spent a casual hour. 'That's mine ... the one in front ... the big chap with red hair. ...' I thought of the young man who was so deeply concerned about the soul, who believed that these bitches were heirs of immortality! How I should have loved to throw that little Christian to those beasts ... better still, to have picked one out for him, the one-eyed girl for choice who was screaming and yelling because 'her boy' hadn't had time to finish his beer. Suddenly, urged on by the laughter of her companions, she took the glass in her two hands and, rushing down to the boat, held it out to the man in question, who drained it at a single gulp under the impersonal gaze of his officer, who looked as though he were little more than a schoolboy.

The evening was heavy and overcast. There was no moon. The smell of the invisible sea was less strong than that of the scented stock. He had followed me with his eyes as I left the lounge. I did not go far, for fear lest he lose me. I wandered about aimlessly in the light which streamed from the hotel windows; I could not help feeling how different my emotions would have been, as I waited there, had he been in love with me. For a moment I played with the idea that perhaps I might be able to rouse an answering flame in him. How difficult it is for us not to believe in our own power! Does such a being as a chaste man exist? Probably not – for beneath the apparent virtue of those who seem to be so there always lurks some secret. .. Again and again I told myself that, knowing it was not true. I remembered the young men who had been so naturally solemn that a great effort had been needed before they could debase themselves to my level. ...

He came down the steps of the terrace. His dinner-jacket fitted him badly, and his tie was anyhow. I waved my cigarette to show him where I was. He came towards me. I said no word, enjoying his embarrassment to the full. He apologized for this indiscretion, but, all the time, he was trying to read my face. My silence was obviously having an effect on him. He may, in a confused sort of fashion, have realized how much I hated him at that moment. Had he wanted to harm me, I should have detested him less wholeheartedly. But it had never for a moment occurred to him to think of me as a woman, or that I might be expecting him to do so. That was what was so horrible about it – the simple fact that the question did not even arise. To him I was just someone who had lived her life, someone for whom there was no future. It is not intention that makes the crime, but the absence of intention. Had he sought to harm or hurt me, I could have found consolation in the thought of his malevolence. A woman can always see room for hope when a man hates her. But against a certain kind of gentleness there is no appeal. He stood there, a living witness to the fact that, as a woman, I was dead. He may have been an involuntary witness, but for that very reason the evidence was irrefutable.

We sat down on a bench. Suddenly I asked how old he was. 'Twenty – almost twenty-one. ...'

The little horror! If only I could have managed to wake in him a sense of uneasiness, a feeling that time was fleeting, that he was suffering an irreparable loss. Wouldn't *that* have satisfied my lust for vengeance? No young man has ever crossed my path to whom I have not been able to impart the agonizing sensation that he is losing something of his youth with each passing moment. Torture me, abandon me, though he may, I have always managed to leave him embracing a corpse, the corpse of his youth, dying there before his eyes. From that moment nothing else is ever real to him again but that one supreme agony.

It was my turn to speak. I said the most ordinary things about the invisible sea, about the smell of the scented stock, about the sound of the hotel orchestra muted by distance. The perfect frame for happiness, I said: only – the happiness was absent.

'You can't see me ... try to imagine that I am a young woman. ...'

I broke off for a moment, but it never occurred to him to protest that he did not need the aid of darkness to believe in my youth. He answered that, to him, the setting of love as presented on the stage or the screen had no connexion with reality. He added something rather self-conscious about the love that 'comes spontaneously to birth, more often in a hospital ward or a leper settlement than on a terrace over-hanging the sea'. I replied that we were not talking about the same kind of love. He, however, maintained that all love is one. The love is the same though we may lavish it on different objects. All this meant nothing at all, expressed nothing of the real tension which lay between him and me. At last, I plucked up courage to ask him a definite question. Wouldn't he, I said, live to regret this refusal of human happiness? Wouldn't he be haunted by the memory of lost opportunities?

He made no answer, either because I had touched him on a sensitive spot, or because he wanted to give me time to develop my thought further. His silence made me bold. I assured him that once youth is over we are pursued until the day of our death by the thought of all the chances of happiness which we have neglected or squandered in the days of our abundance. The glance which we may have refused to interpret as it should have been interpreted may never come our way again. Some of us spend all the rest of our lives looking for it. Only the madness of youth believes that happiness can be put off to some future date, that it will always be there for the plucking.

He seemed to be quite unmoved by my words. It was I who started to cry. He looked at me in silence.

'We have wandered from the path,' I stammered; 'I can't see a thing.'

I began to stumble on the grass. He took my hand and led me back to the path. But no sooner had we reached it than he withdrew his own, which I had been pressing slightly.

I could contain myself no longer.

'Say something – anything! ...'

'What can I say? You don't yet know what *love*, what *happiness*, means. ...'

'And you think you can teach me? ... my poor child!'

'Age has nothing to do with it,' he said very quietly. 'There are some who always know it: some who learn the truth when they are twenty: some only after years of suffering. Most people find it only in the radiance of death.'

'Just talk! ...' I murmured.

'You,' he went on, as though he had not heard, 'have everything to learn. All is before you, and you do not know it.'

I told him, on a note of challenge, that I had had my share of experience: that if I chose to tell him one small part of it he would stop his ears.

'My poor boy! I carry with me what, in your world (and I

know all about that world; I was born in it), is called a "guilty past". .... If you doubt that ...'

He said that, however guilty my past, a few tears, a hand raised in absolution above my head, would make me once more as a little child. ...

'So great is that love ...'

His last words were scarcely audible.

I said again:

'Just talk!'

But as we moved within range of the light that came from the hotel windows I saw how red his face was. A sort of relentless passion seemed to dominate this young man: or rather (how can I express what I felt?) it was as though there were some presence within him that filled him to overflowing. It burned me up. Almost in spite of myself, I said in a low voice:

'I detest you!'

Very distinctly, but in scarcely more than a whisper, he replied:

'And I – love you.'

The word that I had longed – so ridiculously – to hear had come at last. It was the selfsame word I had desired, and yet it was not. I was quite clear about that.

'Poor little idiot!' I replied.

To the best of my recollection, he talked to me of this mad thing that he wanted me to feel, this thing that he would pray each day might be given to me.

'I don't want your pity! However dearly I may have paid for my life, I have, at least, had it. ... I have had my life.'

I repeated the words a third time: 'I have had my life!' but there was a sob in my voice. It was a lie. I had not had it. Everything was at an end for me before it had even begun. I could hope for nothing now from love. I was as ignorant of love at that moment as I had been in the days of my youth. I know nothing of love save that it is the constant object of my desire, a desire that possesses me and blinds me, setting my feet on the ways of the waste land, dashing me against the walls, forcing me into bogs and quagmires, stretching me exhausted in the muddy ditches of life.

He was no longer there. Once more I plunged into the garden, crying as I sometimes do when urgent tears come without effort to my eyes, streaming down my face while my face shows no sign or grimace of grief. I waited long for this storm to cease: waited until the night wind had brought comfort to my burning eyes.

THE END OF THE NIGHT

*

PREFACE

The End of the Night *is not intended to be a sequel to* Thérèse Desqueyroux. *It is the portrait of a woman in her decline whom I have already painted in the days of her criminal youth. It is quite unnecessary to have known the earlier Thérèse in order to take an interest in the woman whose last love I here narrate.*

Wearied by ten long years of life within my brain, she craved for death. But I wanted her end to be a Christian one. Before ever this book was written I had decided to call it The End of the Night, *though I had no idea how this particular night would end. Now that the story is finished, it has, to some extent, disappointed the hopes I had when I decided on its title.*

The reader who demands – and quite rightly – that every literary work should mark a step forward in a spiritual pilgrimage may, perhaps, feel some surprise at finding himself once more dragged down to hell. Him I would ask to remember that the heroine of this novel belongs to a period of my life now long past, and that she bears witness to a phase of intellectual restlessness which I have at last outgrown.

Though my only purpose in writing these pages has been to set the suffering figure of Thérèse in the full light of day, I have come to realize what it was that she meant to me. She took form in my mind as an example of that power, granted to all human beings – no matter how much they may seem to be the slaves of a hostile fate – of saying 'No' to the law which beats them down. When Thérèse with reluctant hand pushes back the hair from her ravaged brow in order that the young man she has fascinated may see her as an object of horror and run from her, she gives to the book, by that single gesture, its whole intention. Again and again, in her contacts with other people, she repeats it, never ceasing, in spite of her wretchedness, to react against the power she exercises to poison and corrupt the lives around her. But she belongs to that class of human beings (and it is a huge family!) for whom night can end only when life itself ends. All that is asked of them is that they should not resign themselves to night's darkness.

Why, someone may say, do I break off this story before it has reached the point at which Thérèse might have found pardon and the peace of God? Let me make a confession. The pages dealing with that ultimate consolation were in fact written, but I destroyed them. I could not see the priest who would have possessed the qualifications necessary if he was to hear her confession with understanding. Since then I have found him – in Rome, and I know now (some day, perhaps, I may tell the story) just how Thérèse entered into the eternal radiance of death.

ROME: *Feast of the Epiphany,* 1935

The End of the Night

I

'ARE you going out this evening, Anna?'

Thérèse took a good look at her maid. The tailor-made suit which she had given her was too tight for the young body and ripening contours.

Anna remained standing in front of her mistress.

'You hear how it's raining? What are you going to do with yourself if you go out?'

She would have liked to keep her with her in the flat; to hear the familiar sound of handled plates, and that incomprehensible song the refrain of which this girl from Alsace was never sick of singing over and over again. On other evenings she always knew that, until ten o'clock, she could rely on the companionship of youth and life. She could hear her at her work, and the sound brought with it a sense of comfort and security. During the first few months of her tenancy of this flat Anna had occupied one of its small, empty rooms. Her mistress had often, in the darkness, overheard sighs, muttered words as of a dreaming child, a sort of animal grunting. Even when the girl was sleeping quietly Thérèse could feel her presence. It was as though she caught the very throb of blood in the body that was lying so close at hand on the other side of the wall. She knew that she was not alone. The beating of her own heart no longer frightened her.

Saturday was the girl's evening out, and Thérèse would lie awake in the blackness, her eyes wide open, conscious that she would not sleep until her maid came home – which sometimes she did not do till dawn. Then, one day, though no questions had been asked, Anna collected her belongings and moved to the floor where the other servants lived – 'so as to be freer in her comings and goings, you mark my words', the concierge had said.

Thérèse was forced to rest content with the short period of comfort on which she could rely up to ten o'clock. When the girl came to wish her good night and to take her orders for next day her mistress did everything she could to prolong their conversation. She would ask her about her family. Had she heard from her mother recently? – but, as a rule, she got only the briefest of answers, such answers as a child might have given who wants to play and is bored by the grown-ups. Not that Anna showed any signs of hostility. At times, indeed, she would indulge in little outbursts of affection, but the marked feature of these interchanges was that complete indifference which a young person is apt to display when she arouses interest in older people whom she cannot love.

Thérèse moved within the confines of a closed world, her only companion a country girl whom she treasured like a piece of bread in her prison cell, powerless to choose, since there was no one else to whom she might have turned. As a rule she did not press her attentions, and, when Anna had duly said 'Good night, ma'am. Are you quite sure there is nothing further?' she would withdraw into her corner waiting for the throb of her heart which always came to her at the sound of the front-door slamming.

But on this particular Saturday Anna seemed to be preparing to leave even before nine had struck. She stood there on her high heels, her rather fat feet forced into shoes of imitation lizard-skin.

'Aren't you afraid of the rain?'

'Oh, it isn't far to the Metro.'

'You'll get your suit wet.'

'We shan't hang about in the street. We're going to the pictures.'

'Who's "we"?'

Rather sullenly the girl answered, 'Just friends,' and made for the door. Thérèse called her back.

'Suppose I asked you to stay at home this evening, Anna – I'm not feeling very well.'

She was amazed at the sound of her own words. Was it really she who had spoken them?

'Oh, in that case ...' The reply came with an ill grace. But already Thérèse had shaken herself free from her mood.

'On second thoughts I believe I'm rather better. ... Run along, child, and enjoy yourself.'

'Would you like me to warm up some milk, ma'am?'

'No, no: I don't want anything. Off with you, now!'

'Shall I put a match to the fire?'

Thérèse said that she would light it herself should she feel cold. She had to resist a desire to take the girl by the shoulders and push her out of the flat. This time the sound of the door, so far from making her feel ill, gave her a sensation of deliverance. She looked at herself in the glass, and said out loud: 'What's the matter with you, Thérèse?' Why should she feel more humiliated this evening then ever before? Faced by the prospect of an empty evening and a lonely night, she had, as always, clung for comfort to the first creature who came her way. Anything was better than that feeling of being abandoned. She longed for somebody with whom she could talk, for the sound of a young life breathing within reach. That was all she asked, but now even that was impossible. ... As always, a wave of hatred rose from the depths of her being. 'The little fool will come to no good. She'll end on the streets. ...'

Ashamed of the direction which her thoughts were taking, she shook her head. She would light the fire – not that the October evening was cold, but a fire is, as the saying goes, companionable. She would settle down with a book. ... Why hadn't she thought of getting a detective novel this afternoon? They were the only things she could read. As a young woman she had been for ever striving to find herself in books, underlining favourite passages in pencil. But she no longer expected to find her own image in the characters of fiction. They vanished, all of them, and melted into nothingness when subjected to the heat of her own aura.

All the same, this evening she did, with a rather hesitating hand, open the glass-fronted bookcase – the same bookcase which used to stand in the room which she had occupied as a girl at Argelouse in the days of her innocence, though it had seen her, too, as a young matron when the state of her husband's health made it necessary for them to have separate rooms. She remembered how, in those days, she had hidden her packet of drugs for whole days together behind the many volumes of *The History of the Consulate and the Empire.* ... The good old honest piece of furniture had harboured poison, had been the accomplice and the witness of her crime. ... What a long road it was that led from the farm at Argelouse to this third-floor flat in an old house in the rue du Bac! After hesitating a moment or two, she chose a volume, then put it back again, closed the bookcase, and once more began to study herself in the glass.

She was losing her hair, just like a man! Yes, that bald forehead of hers might have belonged to an elderly man. 'The brow of a thinker,' she said in a low voice. 'But that's my only sign of age. When I'm wearing a hat I look precisely as I always did. Even twenty years ago people used to say that it was impossible to tell how old I was. ...'

The lines which led downwards from her rather too short nose were no more deeply etched now than they had been in those days of long ago. Why shouldn't *she* go to the pictures? ... No, that would mean spending too much money, because she wouldn't be able to resist the temptation to look in at various bars for a drink. ... She was beginning to pile up a number of small debts. Things were going from bad to worse on the estate. For the first time the expenses of running the place had almost exceeded the income from her trees. Her husband had written her four pages on the subject. It was no longer possible to sell pit-props. The English wouldn't buy. But the undergrowth had got to be cleared out, because the pines were beginning to suffer. In the old days the job would have brought in money, but now it represented a considerable outlay. The price of resin had never been so low. ... He was trying to get rid of some of the trees, but the offers made by the timber merchants were quite ridiculous. ...

Nevertheless, she still retained her old expensive habits. She couldn't go out in Paris without spending money like water. It was the only way she knew of filling the emptiness of her life, the only way in which she could achieve, not happiness, perhaps, but, at least, a sort of drugged, besotted state of contentment. Besides, she no longer felt strong enough to wander the streets alone. The 'pictures' had never been any help to her. Seated there in the semi-darkness, she felt defenceless against the great waves of boredom that engulfed her. The most trivial human creature whose movements she might watch in a café interested her far more than the shadows on a screen. But she no longer dared to give herself the amusement of spying on others, because, wherever she went, she inevitably drew attention to herself. Useless to dress in neutral colours, to choose retired corners. Something in her appearance, she did not know what, caused all eyes to fasten on her. Or was that just her imagination? Perhaps the trouble lay in her worried expression, her pursed lips?

She thought that her way of dressing was correct, even sober, but there was something about it of that vague untidiness, that quality of the *outré*, which marks the ageing woman who has no one to advise her. As a child she had often laughed at her Aunt Clara, because the old spinster could never resist picking to pieces the hats that were bought for her and remaking them according to her own ideas. But nowadays she, too, was apt to give way to the same mania, with the result that all her clothes, though she did not realize it, had a look of oddity. Perhaps in days to come she would turn into one of those old eccentrics in feathered hats who sit on benches in the public parks, for ever tying up parcels of old rags and talking to themselves.

She may not have realized how odd she looked, but she did know that she had lost the power, so necessary for those who live alone, of imitating the insects and assuming the protective colouring of leaf and bark. For years she had been accustomed to sit in cafés and restaurants spying on people who took no notice of her. What had happened to her ring of invisibility? Whenever she went out now all eyes were turned on her. She felt like an animal who has got into the wrong herd.

But here, at least, within these four walls, in this room with its sagging floor and a ceiling so low that she could touch it if she raised her arm, she could be assured of shelter. But it needed strength of mind to stay within such narrow limits. Tonight the idea of remaining there alone was intolerable.

The very thought drove her to a little movement of panic. She went over to the fireplace again and, looking at herself in the mirror, drew her fingers down her cheeks with a familiar gesture. There was nothing in her life at this moment but what had always been there. Nothing new had happened, absolutely nothing. Yet it was borne in on her with complete certainty that she had reached some sort of limit – as when a tramp realizes that the path he is on leads nowhere and loses itself in the sand. Every sound from the street seemed utterly cut off from life, seemed somehow to have acquired an absolute value – the honk of a car, a woman's laugh, the screech of a brake.

She went to the window and opened it. Rain was falling. The chemist's shop-front was still bright. The red and green of an advertisement shone in the light of a street lamp. She leaned out and measured with her eye the distance from the pavement. It was as though she were sounding the empty space without. She had not even the little courage needed to throw herself down! But perhaps mere giddiness would serve. ... She summoned giddiness to her aid, only to fight against it. Hurriedly she closed the window, muttering 'Coward!' It is a horrible thing to have plotted death for another and yet to fear it for oneself. The day before had marked the fifteenth anniversary of that moment in her past when, escorted by her Counsel, she had left the Provincial Court-house and crossed the empty little square, saying again and again in a low voice, 'Case dismissed! – Case dismissed!' Free at last – or so she had thought at the time ... as though it were in the power of human beings to decide that a crime has not been committed – when it has! No hint had come to her then that she was about to enter a prison worse than the narrowest of graves, the prison built around her by her act: a prison from which there would be no escape – ever!

'If only I had set at naught my own life as well as another's!' ... Since that one occasion at Argelouse when she had attempted suicide the instinct of self-preservation, even at moments of despair, had been active, had been strong, in her. During the worst periods of sickness which had afflicted her throughout the intervening fifteen years she had followed a certain routine of health, always coddling and cosseting her ailing heart. She had never yielded to the lure of self-destruction, to that indifference in the face of imminent death which is shown by drug-addicts – not for any noble reason, but simply because she was terrified of dying. The doctor had found no difficulty in persuading her to give up smoking because of her heart. It would have been impossible, once he had expressed his opinion, to find so much as a single cigarette in the house.

She felt cold, and struck a kitchen match on the sole of her shoe. A flame began to lick the inferior wood for which one pays such a high price in Paris. But the crackling and the smell of smoke brought back to this child of the heath-country memories of her innocent youth, of the time *before* she had done – what she had done. ... She drew up her chair as near as possible to the hearth and, closing her eyes, began to stroke her legs, just as she used to see Aunt Clara do in the old days. This fragrance of the first fire of winter carried within it so many others – the smell of mist on the melancholy pavements of Bordeaux and along the lanes of the countryside – a smell always associated in her mind with the beginning of term. Faces rose for a brief moment before her inner eye, rose and then faded: faces that had played a part in her life before the die had been cast and the wager staked, when it was still possible for things to have turned out differently. But now all had been accomplished. Impossible to change one detail in the total of her acts. Her destiny had assumed the form which would remain with it to all eternity. That was what 'outliving oneself' meant – the certainty that one could no longer undo the past.

She heard nine o'clock strike. She must still find some way of killing time, for it was too early as yet to swallow the cachet which would assure her a few hours of sleep. As a rule, though all hope was dead in her, she was too proud to have recourse to drugs. But tonight she could not resist their promise of help. In the daytime it is always easier to be brave. What, at all costs, she must avoid was waking up in the middle of the night. She dreaded sleeplessness more than anything else, that awful lying in bed in the dark, powerless against the horrors of imagination, a prey to all the temptations of the mind. In order to escape from the agony of knowing herself for what she was, to avoid becoming the victim of that crowd of silent presences, among whom she recognized the sickly, heavy jowled face of Bernard, her husband and her victim, and Marie's too, her daughter's, tanned by the sun – all the many faces of those whom she had threatened with destruction, who had fled from her – that she might not be overwhelmed by this surge of ghosts, she had but one recourse in the long nights when sleep would not come – namely, to choose from among them, to get on terms of comradeship with, just *one*, one who did not really matter, and so relive in imagination some brief experience of happiness that would perish with the moment. Only what had counted for little in her life, what had occupied the tiniest place in her experience, held now the promise of a mite of joy – friendships had come to nothing, love which had not had time to grow corrupt. During her periods of insomnia she would wander in thought about the battlefield of memories, turning over the corpses, seeking some face that still was recognizable. How many were there now of whom she could think without bitterness? It had needed no long time for most of those who once had loved her to discover the power she wielded for destruction. Those only could bring her aid to whom she had vouchsafed but a glimpse of herself, who had moved only on the outer circumference of her existence. From them alone she could draw comfort – strangers met some night and never seen again. But, as a rule, even these casual acquaintances slipped from her hold as she thought of them. They melted away, and suddenly she noticed that they were no longer there, that her thoughts were wandering far from them. Even in the land of reverie they refused to be her friends, but left her alone to struggle against the surging onset of others. How she longed to escape from the presence of those others! They woke in her a sense of shame and humiliation. Almost always there had been a moment in their wretched histories when she

realized that the familiar friend was out after his own ends. ...
Always had come that moment of the insidious word and the
outstretched hand. The exploitation of friendship had taken
many forms, from the loan openly requested to the 'promising
investment' in which it was hoped to enlist her interest. All
through the hours of deepest quiet, when the silence of the
countryside descends on Paris, she would think, over and
over again, of all the money she had lent or that had been
wormed out of her by dishonest means. Now that she was
herself reduced to the bare necessities of life, it annoyed and
exasperated her to set the total of her losses against the figure
of her debts. She had surrendered utterly to that 'dread of
being in want' to which the elder members of her family had
always been a prey.

No, tonight she would not run the risk of such torment.
There were ways of laying a compelling hand on sleep. But
she must still wait an hour – a whole hour! She was at the end
of her tether. ... She got up and went over to the table on
which the gramophone stood. She shuddered at the idea of
the din it was within her power to let loose. It was as though
the music waiting there to be released could overturn the
very walls and bury her in their ruins. Then she went back to
her chair and sat staring once more into the flames.

It was at this precise moment, just as she was thinking,
'How can I bear to go on living for another moment? – and
yet nothing's going to happen, because nothing ever does,
because there's nothing that can happen to me any more' –
it was this moment that she heard the bell of the front door
ring. There was something threatening in the short, sharp
sound. But she laughed away her fear even as she was aware
of it. It could only be Anna, who had doubtless had a twinge
of remorse, and was frightened lest her mistress might *really*
be ill. No, probably, on second thoughts, *not* Anna. More
likely to be the concierge, who had probably undertaken to
keep an eye on things in case the old lady wanted attention
during the evening. Yes, that was it. It must be the concierge
(though she didn't, as a rule, ring the bell like that). ...

2

THÉRÈSE switched on the light in the hall and stood for a moment, listening. Somebody on the other side of the door was breathing.

'Who is it?'

A young voice answered:

'It's me – Marie!'

'Marie? – What Marie?'

'Me, Mother!'

Thérèse looked at the tall young woman who was standing on the threshold, her body slightly bent to one side under the weight of the suitcase which she was holding in her right hand. This dazzling vision could not, surely, be the child whom she had last seen three years ago? ... But the voice, the laugh, the brown eyes, all were familiar.

'How well that make-up suits you, dear. ...' Those were the first words that Thérèse spoke – the words of one woman to another.

'Do you think so? It's not the general opinion in the family. ... Oh, how lovely – a fire!'

She had thrown her overcoat and a knitted scarf on to the suitcase. A hideous yellow jumper showed off to advantage the physical contours of a child just growing into womanhood. Her arms were sunburnt, and the back of her rather coarse neck.

'First of all, a cigarette. ... What, have you given up smoking, Mother? ... I've got some in my bag. I'll tell you about myself in a moment ... and it'll take some telling!'

She walked about the low-ceilinged room, filling it with her smell. Then she lit a cigarette and crouched down in front of the fire.

'Where is your father?'

'At Argelouse, of course – duck-shooting. What else should he be doing on 11 October? Now that he gets rheumatism, he's had a hut built with a dining-room, proper floors, and a heating system. ... He spends all his time there. The world might go to ruin for all he'd care. ... Nothing matters to him but the duck. ...'

'Have you his permission to come to see me like this?'

'I took it for granted.'

Thérèse sat bolt upright, breathing deeply. What happiness! She knew what her daughter was going to say before she opened her lips – that she didn't get on with her father, that she couldn't stand being with him a moment longer, that she had come to *her* for help and shelter. Why hadn't she foreseen this? The girl, after all, was *her* child. 'There's nothing of her mother about her,' the Desqueyroux were fond of saying. But there was! She had the same prominent cheek-bones, the same voice, the same laugh. Still, from the day when Marie was born, Thérèse herself had always denied, with a kind of hard anger, that there was the slightest resemblance between them. And now it hit her in the face. How was it likely that a modern girl could stand the sort of people among whom she, Thérèse, had felt stifled twenty years before?

'Tell me about yourself, darling.'

'Give me something to eat first – I'm simply starving.'

She had not had enough money to go into the restaurant-car. She had given away her last franc as a tip. ... She stumbled over her words a little, left the sentences unfinished ... peppered her conversation with exclamations: 'It's such a *bore*! – really *too* frightful!' She blew smoke down her nostrils, spat out little scraps of tobacco.

'I'm afraid there's nothing left to eat here. We shall have to go out.'

Already Thérèse was imagining what it would be like to enter a restaurant with the girl in tow. She felt a little spasm of uneasiness. Though she had said that there was nothing to eat in the flat, she set out to explore the larder.

Anna's alarm-clock was ticking away in the tiny kitchen which was so bright and tidy in all its details. The casseroles stood in a shining row. While she routed out ham and eggs and butter and biscuits, she remembered the bottles of Champagne which she had always kept in the refrigerator.

'There was still one left, which she had been reserving for ... She decided not to open it. But Marie was already at her side.

'Champagne! How gorgeous!'

She added that she was quite famous for her omelettes. 'I always make them when we have a shooting party. ... What, no fat? I hate using butter. ... Never mind; we must have the eggs boiled.'

In the bright light of this small, enclosed space, she saw her mother almost for the first time. Till then she had taken no notice of her looks.

'Oh, poor mum, are you ill?'

Thérèse shook her head. Her heart, she explained, wasn't behaving as it should ... and she wasn't so young as she had been.

'At my age three years makes a lot of difference.'

The girl had already lit the gas, and was standing with her back to her mother.

'I suppose you've left a message for your father?'

'No.'

'But he'll be in a frightful state!'

'You don't know him! ... What a silly thing to say! – of course you do! Surely you remember that he never gets into a state except over himself? I don't believe he so much as *sees* other people. ... I'm not sure that he even acknowledges their existence!'

Without turning round, she added in a voice which had suddenly become serious:

'I understand you *so* well now, Mother.'

Thérèse made no reply. The girl went on:

'I feel so awful about the way I misjudged you all these years!'

Worried, perhaps, by her mother's silence, she broke off and pretended to be concentrating her attention on the eggs. A moment later she spoke again:

'But I'm not really to blame. How could a child be expected to imagine what your life with Papa and Grandmamma must have been like?'

She swung round suddenly, and a rough note came into her voice:

'Why don't you say something? I realize you've got a grudge against me. ... Why, how pale you are!'

Thérèse murmured:

'It's nothing: come and help me lay the table.'

She left Marie to set their meal in front of the fire and arrange the plates. She stood motionless in the dark entry, leaning against the wall. Marie moved from room to room, humming a tune, while her mother followed her with her eyes. All feeling of happiness had gone. Who was this woman whom she addressed as Marie? Why did she talk familiarly to her? For the past three years Bernard had found all sorts of excuses to prevent them from meeting, as they had been in the habit of doing for one week in every year. Nor had Thérèse complained. 'Am I what is popularly called an "unnatural mother"? ...'

Had she, if it came to that, ever given a moment's genuine thought to her child? As a young mother she had, as it were, been dazzled by her own splendour to the extent of never really seeing the child at all. But there had never been any question of outrageous indifference. Later, she had deliberately kept herself in the background. It was better for the girl that she should. Yes, she had stifled that voice within her which had called out for Marie. But though she had always felt that she had been deprived of her rights as a mother, she had never made any effort to fight against the verdict. It would have been easy enough for her to get round Bernard Desqueyroux's rules and regulations, but against the sentence which she had passed on herself there was no appeal. And now something had happened which she had never imagined could happen. ... The whole discussion was being reopened, here, this evening, and it was the girl herself who was taking the initiative! – the girl who was no longer a child. ... She had felt the same constricting weight that her mother had endured; had suffocated in the same dungeon ... so that now she felt a wave of sympathy for the woman who had run away. Without knowing the reason for that act, she accepted everything that had happened. She not only found it all excusable – she actually approved!

Thérèse had not reckoned on that, had not even wanted it. She had always taken comfort in the thought that her daughter resembled her in nothing, that she was every inch a Desqueyroux. She had resigned herself to being judged and condemned by this Desqueyroux in miniature. How much did Marie really know? It was not likely that she had ever been told the details of what had occurred, though it was impossible to believe that she had not learned enough to realize that something frightful had taken place shortly after her birth, in a room at Argelouse. Thérèse had once and for all accepted the fact that what she had done had set a great gulf between Marie and herself. ... And yet ... here was Marie standing before the mirror, one arm raised, her dark head leaning on her hand – for all the world like a young girl in her mother's room. This marvellous creature was *her* daughter. In a low voice she said, 'My child,' and though the sound of the words was barely audible, it seemed to echo in the very depths of her being. She moved away from the wall against which she had found support in the entry, and exclaimed, this time loudly: 'My own little daughter! ...'

Marie turned and smiled, noticing nothing strange in the expression of her mother's face. How well Thérèse knew them, these thaws and sudden bursts of spring! But this time it was no mere thrill of the body, no restless movement of the blood or miracle of desire. Sitting there opposite Marie, who was eating with the voracious appetite of a schoolgirl, she was conscious of a deep happiness. To what should she compare it? – perhaps to the sudden flood of daylight when a train emerges from an interminable tunnel, to the feel of fresh air upon the face, to the smell of leaves and growing grass. ... But she turned away her eyes so as not to see the girl, and busied herself with the business of uncorking the Champagne.

'Just watch – it won't make any noise at all. ...'

Thérèse had learned from others, from one other in particular, the trick of keeping the cork from flying out. ... Marie would have to be sent away. All the more reason, then, for making the most of these few moments. Certainly she could not be permitted to stay long in the flat with her. Thérèse felt free to indulge herself with the pleasure of this one evening, this single night. She would give herself a treat and then return the girl to her father. She looked across at her daughter. Here, for once, was someone she could love, someone who was not a bird of prey. Marie was talking, losing herself in an endless tale of complaint against her father and her grandmother, a puzzling tangle of complications.

'I liked being at the convent much better, but they said that it was too expensive. You've no idea the state of panic they've been in ever since the price of resin dropped. ... They're terrified of being reduced to beggary. I went to only one ball all last year, a wretched affair at the Courzons'. We refused the invitation at first on the ground that I was too young, and that it wasn't the thing to do to go to dances in Lent. But the real reason was that they grudged the price of a new dress for me. It *was* ... Don't contradict me, Mother. You know them even better than I do. Can't you hear Grandmamma saying, "One doesn't accept hospitality which one can't return"? – Ah! I've got a laugh out of you. I'm not a bad mimic, am I?'

'But she *is* your grandmother, Marie.'

'Now, don't *you* start preaching at me! I'm not criticizing her. I hate her because I'm dependent on her. Here, with you, I can put her out of my mind, and Papa too. It will be quite easy not to hate them when I've no longer got them on my back the whole time.'

'You mustn't talk like that, Marie; really, you mustn't.'

She had fled to her, had preferred her to all the rest of them! What a revenge! But did she know all the details of her mother's trial? How far, precisely, did her information go? Almost certainly Bernard must have told her enough to frighten her. During their hurried meetings in the past, Thérèse had noticed little quick movements of panic ... and yet, here she was ...

'No, darling, your father had his faults, but meanness was never one of them.'

'You don't know what he's become. If you couldn't stand him fifteen years ago, what would you feel now? It's impossible to imagine what it's like. ... You'd have to hear him and Grandmamma talking to get any idea ... "No one can save nowadays. Anything one puts by is as good as lost, and the rest goes in taxes. You'll have to work for your living, my girl. That's what it's come to – you'll have to get a job." You ought to see their faces when I answer: "All right, I'll work, then: that doesn't frighten me!" They'd like me to groan and grumble as they do. They can't grasp the fact that I am willing to accept the conditions into which I have been born.'

'That,' thought Thérèse, 'is not a young girl's reaction. She's repeating something she's heard one of her older friends say – or some young man.'

'Marie, look at me.'

The girl put down her glass and smiled.

'I realize from what you've been telling me that it's natural for you to be rubbed the wrong way, and perhaps even seriously irritated by life at home ... but such small causes of friction are not enough to set you against them, or to bring you running to me.'

She spoke the last words almost in a whisper.

'There must be something else. ... If there is, you ought to tell me.'

The girl showed no signs of embarrassment. Only by a just perceptible flutter of the eyelids, by a sudden flush, did she give any indication that the thrust had gone home.

'You've been keeping something back, Marie.'

'You haven't given me much time. ... You're too observant, Mamma. ... It's impossible to hide anything from you.'

'Is he a nice young man?'

'Nice? – no: he's the very reverse of nice. That's one of the words he loathes. He's got a mind of his own. ...'

She had lit a cigarette and was leaning forward on her elbows – no longer a girl, but a woman: a rather heavily-built woman.

'Tell me all about it, my dear.'

'Don't you think that's precisely why I came here – to tell you?'

'I'd already gathered that that is what brought you.'

'Naturally!'

Once more, the old familiar pain. Thérèse, this time, had really believed that she had reached the haven of the blessed, where the beloved is powerless to harm because nothing is expected. But a wholly disinterested love does not exist. We always expect something, no matter how little, in return for what we give. Thérèse believed that she had foreseen every possible step of the journey. She had armed herself in readiness for what was to come, had gathered her strength for the task of detaching the child from herself and giving her back to her father. And now, suddenly, it was borne in on her that this process of detachment would be useless, because there was nothing to detach her *from*. 'She's not bothering about me. I might have died without ever setting eyes on her again, if it hadn't so happened that she needed my help. She remembered my existence only when she found that she was up against her father and would have to fight for her right to love.'

Thérèse recognized the old bitter taste of gall. At the heart of her feeling for her daughter, as deep within every human relationship she had ever known, lay the ancient jealousy, the resentment of the fact that the beloved could burn with a passion for someone else. It had always been her fate to be sought and courted only when she could be of help in furthering this passion, not her own. Always she had been marked out as the go-between, the helper, the one of whom others make use.

Marie looked at her anxiously, noticing how completely the expression of her face had changed. It never occurred to her, in her innocence, that the cruel and crafty mask, the pinched lips, the cold eyes, were all that most people had ever seen of Thérèse, that for many this was the real woman. The over-gentle voice frightened her.

'Why should you want to involve me in your affairs?'

'You are our last hope. ...'

'I might have died, Marie. It's only because you happened to need me ...'

She started to laugh, but broke off suddenly. The younger woman felt hurt. She stared at her mother.

'But, *dear* Mamma, it wasn't *I* who left *you*. ...'

Thérèse turned away and put her hand over her eyes. Marie got up and came round the table, meaning to give her a kiss, but the other avoided her advances.

'Time to clear away. ...'

When Marie came back from the kitchen her mother was standing by the fire, one arm resting on the mantelpiece. Without a glance at her. she said:

'I *left* no one, as you put it, Marie. From the day I was born I've always been the one who was left. That is something you can't understand.'

Quite obviously she did not, but the outburst had shaken her, and once again she made as though to embrace her mother – only to be kept, gently, at arm's length.

'I love you, Mamma. Don't you believe me? No, I see you don't. Why don't you want me to give you a kiss?'

'You know perfectly well. ...'

'*I* know?'

Thérèse nodded.

'Let's not discuss it ... I'm waiting for you to go on with your story, darling.'

Marie did not need to be asked twice. She drew Thérèse after her into all the intricacies of the wretched dispute which she was carrying on with her father and her grandmother over Georges Filhot, with whom she was in love. Their attitude was that they would not even discuss the possibility of so humiliating a match. Thérèse was amazed to find that, impoverished and almost ruined though they were, they could still attach so much importance to social position.

She had a perfectly clear memory of the Filhot family. For the last hundred years it had been settled on one of the farms belonging to the Desqueyroux estate. Old man Filhot had been a familiar sight to her in her childhood, busy with his knitting as he watched his sheep. The son and grandson had dabbled in real estate and made an enormous fortune during the war. But most of this, according to Marie, they had since lost. At one moment Bernard Desqueyroux had shown signs of yielding, only to become more obstinate than ever when the Filhots pretended that they were violently opposed to the marriage. Marie believed that this attitude of his was dictated solely by reasons of family pride.

'Don't forget that they are still very rich, even though they have suffered from the slump. Auguste Filhot (Georges' father) brought off a very big deal involving more than fifty thousand acres. He reckoned, as always to get back his money from felling the timber, so that, actually, the land would have cost him nothing. But he was caught by the fall in prices. Still, even so, they are a great deal better off than we are. ... The family, I admit, is quite awful, but Georges himself is very distinguished. He's got a terribly good mind, and is reading for a degree in Political Science.'

Thérèse thought: 'She's talking out of character – just repeating what she has heard other people saying. I was no less foolish when I was her age. Members of a large family take the colour of their companions. Whether we like it or no, we have to swim in brackish water – or drown!'

What did it matter to her now? She knew why the girl had taken the train to Paris. Georges Filhot was reading Political Science in the Capital, and she did not want to be separated from him.

'I could have borne our being parted, could have faced that bravely enough – if only I had been sure of him. But he's young ... whether there are many men like him I don't know. He loves me – I am sure he does – but only when we are together. I wouldn't admit that to everybody, but I can to you. He often says the most horrible things; for instance: "When you're not there the whole thing just doesn't seem real. My mind is full of other interests, of the people whom I see every day. ..." I am convinced that he likes me better than anyone else, but when I am away from him I don't weigh very heavily in the balance. He's like that. You do realize, don't you, what this separation means? ...'

'Yes, I do. So that is why you came? But hasn't it occurred to you, my dear' – Thérèse hesitated for a moment – 'hasn't it occurred to you that I am a compromising ally?'

Marie flushed and uttered a rather weak protest.

'What nonsense you do talk, Mamma!'

'People have forgotten about me. The passing years have buried me. No one now realizes that you've even got a mother. And you must needs come along and dig me up. Not content with dragging me out of my grave, you go to the extent of identifying yourself with me, of putting yourself and your love affair under my protection ... under the protection of ...'

In a voice so low that Marie could scarcely hear it, she spoke her full name.

'Just think what effect *that* must have on people's minds....'

'Nothing that need make me ashamed, Mamma.'

The girl's reply was calm and steady.

'You must be insane, Marie.'

But the other rose without reply, crossed to her mother, and put her arms round her. Thérèse pushed her away.

'You must be insane,' she repeated: 'you know ...'

'Yes, I know: but what difference does it make?'

'Since you *do* know ...'

'I know ... or, rather, I've guessed – if you'd rather I put it that way.'

'And knowing, you can still kiss me?'

'Darling Mamma ... I don't set myself up as your judge – and if I did ...'

They were both on their feet, facing one another. Thérèse made as though to lay her hand upon her daughter's lips.

'You would forgive me?'

'Forgive you? – but you've done nothing ...'

'What I did weighs very heavily on you, because you are my child. ...'

'Was it as serious as all that?'

'It could scarcely be more serious.'

'But – Mother ...'

Thérèse stared at her in amazement:

'Surely you must have had it all dinned into you?'

'They realized, of course, that I wouldn't stand for hearing you blackguarded – not that they ever said anything definite. ...'

'Not even when they wanted to explain why it was that I never came home?'

'They were always pretty vague about what actually happended. Once or twice in my hearing Papa has spoken about incompatibility of temperament. Whatever the truth of the matter may be, I think that fundamentally he's probably right and that it all comes back to that – incompatibility of temperament. ... I know what that means all right!'

Thérèse had lowered her eyes, but now she straightened herself and looked at Marie. How could the girl be so little affected by the suspicion that a crime had been committed? She was astounded at the news that her husband, her mother-in-law, had said nothing. She must, at least, give them credit for that amount of charity. It was so very unexpected. Not that they had maintained silence out of any feeling for *her*. It was only because the honour of the family was involved, and because they did not want to give Marie a shock. Still, whatever their motives, it must be admitted that they had said nothing which might lower her in her daughter's eyes. But ...

'Why are you looking at me like that, Mother?'

'I was thinking ... that it was rather fine of your father not to blacken my reputation.'

'Blacken your reputation? But I love you all the more for what you did!'

Thérèse got up and went over to the bookshelf. Standing there, with her back to her daughter, she fiddled with the books, setting them straight.

'You *can't* know. ... If you did ...'

'What *are* you talking about? You were in love with somebody else, I suppose: you ran away. ... It's pretty easy to guess that. But why should I mind?'

So that was what the girl believed – the sum total of her suspicions! Her eyes had got to be opened. But Thérèse felt that she could not possibly make a full confession. To be quite so frank as that was altogether beyond her power. Besides, what good would it do? All that was needed was that she should say enough to frighten the girl away.

'Come over here – no, not on the arm of my chair. I don't want you to put your arm round me. Sit down quietly on this little low stool which came from Argelouse. Aunt Clara used to call it a "chauffeuse". Now listen to what I am going to tell you. ... It's nice to hear that they have been so discreet about me ... yes, it is, very nice. They might so easily ...'

'But, Mother dear, don't you see that I think all the more highly of you for not being able to stand that sort of life?'

'And what do the Filhots think about it all?' Marie showed signs of embarrassment. Obviously, they must often have made reference to matters of which the girl knew nothing. They had hinted that if any concessions were due, it was the Desqueyroux who, by rights, should have made them. But Marie was not interested in the attitude taken up by the people of Saint-Clair and Argelouse.

'Come closer, and listen. ... I should feel so much easier if we were sitting in the dark! ... Go back to Argelouse, darling ... now, at once ... and don't ask me any questions.'

Almost in a whisper she added: 'I am not worthy' ... and then, because Marie had not caught the words, repeated them:

'I am not worthy. ...'

'A mother is always worthy. ...'

'No, Marie.'

'Do you know what I have just discovered? – that you are much more typical of your generation than I ever thought you would be! Darling Mamma, you are every bit as hard on yourself as the people of Saint-Clair and Argelouse. You condemn yourself by precisely the same standards. You are making a mountain out of what, to someone of my age, is the tiniest of molehills. You believe that love is something wicked.'

'No ... I don't believe that *your* love is wicked. ...'

'But, Mamma, love is always love. Just because you happened to be married ...'

'So religious precept no longer means anything to you, my child?'

Marie shook her head and replied complacently:

'Georges has helped me to get over that phase. Why are you laughing, Mamma?'

The laugh was deliberate. A single word, the tone in which it is uttered, can give the key to vulgarity of mind. It hurt her to hear Marie talking like that of 'phases'. The girl had drawn the stool closer, and their knees were touching. She clasped her hands round her own and looked at Thérèse with that concentrated, eager expression which is common to young girls when they indulge in confidences and unbosom themselves.

'I want you to understand me ... but I don't want to be compelled to say more than I feel I can. ... Of course love is not necessarily wicked ... but wickedness is an awful thing when it does not wear the mask of love.'

She added a few words almost in a whisper. Marie questioned her: 'What's that you said?'

'Oh, nothing.'

Both of them relapsed into silence. With what wide eyes Marie was gazing at her mother! She had drawn away a little, and sat there, with her hands crossed in her lap, her body bolt upright. Thérèse had picked up the tongs, and was arranging the fire.

'Don't try to understand. I am not a good woman. ... Imagine anything you like.'

'I am not a good woman.' She said it again, and heard the sound of the low stool scraping on the floor. Marie was increasing the distance between them. Thérèse raised her hands and pressed them to her eyes. What was wrong with her to-night? As a rule, she never cried. She mustn't let the girl see. But the tears ran between her fingers, hotter, more urgent than in the days of her childhood. And, as in those days, a lump rose in her throat. The stool had been moved closer again. Eager hands were grasping her wrists, forcing her to disclose her face.

Marie dried her mother's cheeks with her handkerchief.

Then she put her arms round her and kissed the forehead from which the scanty hair had receded. But Thérèse wrenched herself from the embrace with a single quick movement, and stood up. There was something very like anger in her face.

'Go away. ... I had said all that needed to be said, and now, because of these tears, I've got to begin all over again! ... What a fool I am! ... Don't ask me any more, Marie. ... Believe me when I say that you must go!'

She spoke slowly, stressing each syllable:

'I am not the sort of woman with whom you can stay. *Now*, do you understand?'

Marie shook her head.

'No, I don't. You have lived your life. Whatever it may have been that forced you to leave Argelouse, you had every excuse.'

But Thérèse could carry her confession no farther. No one in the world had the right to demand that of her. But when she repeated, 'It is impossible for you to stay here, utterly impossible!' Marie broke in:

'Now I understand! You're not free – is that it? I hadn't thought of that. There is no place for me in your present life. I had imagined that everything was over and done with. ...'

'Naturally. ... How should you suppose that an old woman ...'

Must she let her go away believing that? Of course she must, even at the risk of disgusting her. Would the truth be any better? ... Yes, it would. The sight of her daughter rising from the stool, arranging her hair in front of the glass, taking her béret, broke down her resistance.

'No, no, Marie ... There is no one in my life: I lied. ...'

The young woman took a deep breath and looked at her mother with a smile:

'I thought as much.'

'I am utterly alone. I have never been more alone. ...'

'From now on you will have someone. ...'

Thérèse watched the girl pitch her béret on to a chair and sit down again facing her, trying to force her eyes to look back into her own. Why, thought Thérèse, had she been such a coward? Everything could have been settled so nicely. She would have walked back with Marie to the Quai d'Orsay and, first thing in the morning, would have sent a wire to Bernard Desqueyroux. ... But now – now – the whole exhausting struggle was to begin over again.

She begged Marie to be sensible, to take her word for it that she would be better away. She had behaved abominably to her husband, and he, in spite of everything, had acted with generosity, far more so than she had ever expected. He had done nothing to blacken her in her daughter's eyes, had never attempted to paint her as a hateful character. ...

'If that is what's stopping you ...' Marie hesitated for a moment; then, drawing closer, perched herself on the arm of her chair.

'Listen to me. It's much better that I should know everything. ... No one has ever said anything to me – that I freely admit. ... Presumably, they had some religious scruple about talking, but you can take my word for it that goodness of heart had nothing whatever to do with their silence. Their attitude was determined by outside influences. ... Whenever I dared mention your name in conversation they used to blush scarlet and look away. ... I don't give them the chance now. Even Georges (you do want me to be perfectly frank, don't you?) – and if there is anyone in the world with whom I can talk freely, it's Georges – even he won't discuss you with me. I am sure that there is something in his mind, but God knows what it is! I wanted to put him right about you, but it was just no use. Whenever I opened the subject, he just took his hat. Don't run away with the idea that they've been gentle with you. You needn't feel any gratitude to *them*. In fact, they must have pitched it pretty strong, I think, so far as the Filhots are concerned, otherwise why should they be so lukewarm about a match which ought to overjoy them? Pretty foul, isn't it? Just because my mother wouldn't spend the rest of her life suffocating to death at Argelouse. ... Mother, you're not angry with me, are you?'

Thérèse pushed her away, and sat rigid in her chair. When

next she spoke it was as though she had been running, so out of breath did she seem to be. She said:

'Don't you realize now that I'm doing you irreparable damage? ... I may even ruin this marriage of yours altogether. Does Georges Filhot know that you are with me here?'

Marie shook her head. She seemed to be labouring under some embarrassment.

'You've concealed that from him?'

The girl replied that she had wanted to surprise him.

'I thought that the joy of knowing that I was in Paris would blind him ...'

'To the fact of *my* presence? ... Well, it won't. Go. Don't lose a moment. Your whole future may be at stake. Please don't force me to say anything more!'

She was bending once more over the fire. This time Marie seemed to be perturbed. She moved back a few feet and looked at her mother.

'What on earth *is* it all about? You're not a leper, are you?'

Thérèse murmured, 'You speak more truly than you know,' and heaved a deep sigh. At last this interview was drawing to its close. Marie glanced about her, collecting her belongings.

'I'll take you along to the Palais d'Orsay in a taxi, and to-morrow morning I'll be at the station to see you off. ... The train goes at either seven-fifty or eight-ten, I don't remember exactly which. They'll tell us at the hotel.'

Thérèse could not keep back her tears. It was no use pretending any longer. She was miserable: but there was something very like happiness in her misery. She had done what she had had to do, but, at the same time, had managed to avoid revealing the horrible truth. But all of a sudden Marie came close to her, and, with a hard look in her eyes, said that she would not go until she had learned what it was that had been kept from her all these years.

'It's not a question of me or of you, but of Georges. I *must* know what has kept us apart for so long. If it is what you seem to hint ...'

The girl's threatening tone had the effect of calming her mother, who turned now and faced her.

'I've said quite enough. You are free to imagine what you like. Now that you have your suspicions it will be easy for you to get people to talk. It is odd, though, that none of your little friends at the Convent ever made any allusion to it. You've never had an anonymous letter, have you? Well, then, all I can say is that for once people have behaved a great deal better than I had any right to expect. ... But I mustn't talk like that. I shall be putting ideas into your head. ...'

She looked at Marie's frowning face and brooding eyes. ... It was only too true. Often and often the girl had felt that her coming into a room had interrupted something somebody was saying, that suddenly the whole class was looking at her as though words let fall by the mistress had contained some allusion of which she alone was ignorant. But what, at the moment, was occupying her whole attention was the memory of an incident which had occurred the year before – an incident that had had to do with Anais, the little girl from the farm who had been given to her as her personal maid. ... At first she had seemed devotedly attached to her new mistress; but it was seldom Marie's way to show any particular tenderness to those who loved her but whom she did not love in return. But what made matters worse was that the swarthy little creature was actually antipathetic to her, an object almost of disgust with her untidy clothes and sour smell. She had not always been careful to spare her feelings. All this the little thing bore well enough until the day came when in common with the whole village, she got to know that young Filhot was 'keeping company' with her 'lady'. It came out later that most of the tittle-tattle which was going the rounds at that time had its origins in her (she had, for instance, more or less said, in so many words, that Marie was in the habit of receiving the young man in her bedroom), and she was discharged. There was a violent scene with her parents, as a result of which they had to leave the farm. Two or three months later there reached Marie through the post an envelope containing part of an article clipped from a Paris paper, referring to a criminal trial which had been the talk of the town for a few days. Marie was not in the habit of reading the papers, and had no knowledge of what was going on in the world. Nevertheless, she carefully perused the lines which some unknown hand had taken the trouble to cut out for her benefit. So far as she could make out, it was part of a speech for the prosecution, but the editorial comment, which might have furnished the explanation she needed, was missing.

She had hunted in vain through the back files of the *Petite Gironde* and *La Liberté du Sud-Ouest*, but without coming on any echo of the drama in question. The clipping which had been sent her was, obviously, some weeks old. She could have quoted it from memory, word for word, without making a single mistake: '*Gentlemen of the Jury: in a few moments, my honourable friend who is appearing for the defence will appeal to your feelings as fathers of families. He will paint a harrowing picture of the fate which awaits the children of the accused. Well, in the name of Justice and of an outraged society, I too will ask you to give a thought to these poor young creatures. They are the chief victims of this unnatural woman. Because of what she has done, men will point at them for the rest of their natural lives. They will never be allowed to forget. Wherever they go they will hear the same terrible words, always the same terrible words: "Look at those children: their mother was a poisoner!"* …'

For the space of a second the eyes of mother and daughter met. It was the young girl who first averted hers. Never once had she associated the mysterious adventure of Thérèse Desqueyroux with crime – at least, not consciously. But, for all that, she had been careful not to show the cutting from the Paris paper to her father, but had burned it, without breathing to anyone a word of what had happened – perhaps from apathy, from laziness, from indifference, or from a horror of complications. Even now she told herself that she was mad. No member of her family had ever been murdered: no member of her family had ever been condemned on a criminal charge. As far back as she could remember, her mother had enjoyed complete freedom.

Thérèse could see that she was suffering, but the knowledge left her quite unmoved, wholly without interest. She seemed to have no feelings left. She merely waited for the verdict.

Very likely she would be called upon to say nothing. One or two questions would be asked: she would answer them, and everything would be over.

'What deaths have there been in the family?' Marie was asking herself. Aunt Clara? She had no recollection of the old spinster: but this business could not possibly refer to her. She had been an object of genuine affection to her mother, who still mourned her passing. ... The victim must be somebody who had no connexion with the family.

Now and again a raindrop splashed upon the balcony more loudly than its fellows. Marie prepared to interrogate her mother. ... Thérèse made up her mind that she would answer with a simple Yes or No. She sat there waiting for the blow to fall. Suddenly the silence was broken:

'Swear to me that nobody has died as a result of anything that you have ever done.'

'I do swear that, Marie. There has been no one.'

The girl breathed more easily.

'You have never had sentence passed on you, Mother ... in a court of law, I mean?'

'Never.'

'It's your fault that I'm asking these things: you've always been so reticent. You will forgive me, won't you?'

Thérèse inclined her head.

'Since you've never been involved in a lawsuit, then ...'

'I did not say that, my dear. You misunderstood me. All I said was that I had never had sentence passed on me. ...'

'Now you're quibbling!'

'It's all really perfectly simple. I *was* once involved in a lawsuit, but the trial was cut short. My case was dismissed. ... That is the whole truth. Please don't ask me any more.'

'But if your case was dismissed ...'

Thérèse got up, took her daughter's hat and coat, and tried to push her towards the door. But the girl remained leaning against the bookshelf and refused to move.

'Spare me, Marie!'

'You said that you had never killed anyone. ...'

'That was true.'

'In other words, you were innocent?'

'No.'

Thérèse sat down again, this time on the low stool, her elbows on her knees, her whole body tense.

'One more question: tell me the name of the victim, and then I'll go. I swear I will. Was it a stranger?'

Thérèse made a negative movement with her head.

'One of the family, then?'

She nodded.

'Not Aunt Clara? ... Not Papa?'

It was as though she were back in her childhood, playing some guessing game. The accused woman did not raise her eyes, nor did she unclasp her hands. Not so much as a muscle of her face moved, and yet Marie felt sure that she had guessed correctly. Her mother remained sitting there like a woman turned to stone, while the young girl buttoned up her coat. She had no intention of asking any further questions. She did not want to know any more. Whatever it was that might lie behind this silence, it did not concern her. She was not curious about other people – not even about her own mother. It was quite enough for her to realize now how impossible it was that she should ever marry Georges Filhot. Perhaps she could give herself to him ... if, of course, he were willing to take her. ...

'There's an umbrella in my bedroom. ... Don't go for a minute or two. ... My heart's come on again – but the attack will pass. I must go with you as far as the hotel.'

Marie replied that that was wholly unnecessary. All she wanted was a small loan so that she could pay for her room and her railway ticket. She would send a postal order from Saint-Clair.

Quite obviously she did not want to be any further indebted to her mother. But it was past midnight. She couldn't be allowed to go off like this, alone, thought Thérèse, although the Hôtel d'Orsay was only a few steps away.

She said again: 'You can't go out alone in the middle of the night.'

'I can't be any worse off than I am here.'

'Wait until the rain has slackened.'

'I shall wait until you give me the money, and not a moment longer.'

How well Thérèse knew that particular phrase! It was only too familiar. If it had not been for the fear of starting up the pain in her left shoulder, she would have laughed. She said:

'Help me up.'

But she must have spoken in too low a voice, for Marie seemed not to have heard. She took a firm grasp of the mantelpiece, and pulled herself to her feet, stifling a groan. Then she went into the next room. Marie could hear the sound of a key turning in a lock. She was thinking, not of her mother, but of Georges. He had been in Paris for several days. Must she leave without even seeing him? There could be no question, after all, of releasing him from his promise, because he must have known all about this wretched business for a long time past. ... No, nothing was lost. The wisest course would be for her to go back as quickly as possible to Saint-Clair, without telling him anything about her ill-fated trip. Georges! Georges! The thought of him at this moment filled Marie's mind to the exclusion of all else. Her mother had come back now and had sunk down again on to the low seat, but what she might be feeling had no sort of bearing on the matter in hand. She had ceased altogether to be real. In any case, from now on, Marie could tell her family that any idea of the daughter of Thérèse Desqueyroux marrying Georges was quite out of the question. ... So far as that went, she held all the trumps. No, any danger there might be would come from the Filhots. ... But if they had really been opposed to the match, they would have put up a stronger show of hostility. The great thing was that Georges should not weaken. Everything depended on Georges. ...

At this point Marie began to look at the other side of the question. Not once, but again and again, Georges had gone out of his way to impress on her that nobody was really necessary to him. ... What a horrible thought! ... Why had she ever deluded herself? So long as they were together, breathing the same air, she had felt a lightness about her heart.

But now that Georges was settled in Paris a host of dangers threatened her happiness – and she could not even go to see him. ... But why on earth not? Why had she yielded to that first reaction of horror? Hadn't it always been an understood thing that she should spend some days in each year with her mother? It would seem perfectly natural to Georges – and also that she should prolong her stay for his sake.

On second thoughts, what a fool she had been! How could something that had happened fifteen years ago possibly concern her? As though a girl of her age could be held responsible for the actions of an hysterical old woman who, in any case, was probably embroidering something much more simple, much less dramatic. If the charge had been shelved, didn't that mean that she had been a great deal less guilty than she wanted to make out? ... Anyhow, guilty or not guilty, why should this forgotten scandal fill the life of a young girl with echoes? She sat down again opposite the low stool, and gently touched her mother's hand. Thérèse trembled and looked up. She could not believe her eyes. Marie was smiling! There was something forced, no doubt about the smile, and the corners of her mouth were none too steady – but she was no longer an enemy armed and threatening. She said:

'Mamma, dear, I want to beg your pardon.'

'*You* beg *my* pardon? – you must be mad!'

'I lost my head, and acted without thinking. I pretended to feel what one is supposed to feel when one hears that sort of thing for the first time. ... But I don't really feel like that at all. Do you believe me?'

'I believe you are sorry for me and want to comfort me.'

'I'll prove that what I say is true, Mamma. ...' Had she ever read Maupassant's *Pierre et Jean*? Marie had once taken it out from the 'Panbiblion' Library. Georges had thought it terribly old-fashioned of her. He regarded all the novelists of that period as superficial ... and, of course, *Pierre et Jean* was a bit ... The main theme of the story was the discovery by a young man that he is illegitimate, and his reaction to the realization that his mother has had an intrigue. ... Well, she really couldn't find words to express how ridiculous she thought it that children should presume to sit in judgement on those who had brought them into the world; that they should pry into their parents' sentimental pasts and wax indignant or despairing over what they might happen to find there. ...

'I know it's not quite the same in your case ... but the general argument holds good. Far from condemning you, I feel that all this is going to make me feel on much easier terms with you. So long as I was ignorant of it, it was only natural that I should see something of the family in you, that I should believe that you shared some of their views. ... But you can't pull the wool over my eyes any longer. ...'

Thérèse looked at her. That, then, was what the child was after! She thought that her mother, now that all her defences were down, would become her accomplice. ... She might even expect her to give her blessing to stolen meetings with Georges. ...

'Listen to me, Marie. ...'

She tried to find the right words for what she wanted to say. ... When, oh when, would this exhausting discussion come to an end?

'Listen to me. You are quite right in not wanting to sit in judgement on me. But don't you realize that that is precisely what you *are* doing if you think me capable of ...?'

'What on earth have you got into your head? I'm asking nothing of you that any mother might not do for any daughter.'

All pretence of tenderness had gone. There was a sharp edge to her voice now. Thérèse broke in:

'You must see how important it is that I should not give your father any reason to complain of my conduct.'

'How terribly proper you're being, Mamma. If the people at home could hear you now they wouldn't believe their ears!'

'Marie!'

All the girl's pent-up emotions burst out in a spate of words:

'*You've* been in love: *you* know what it means. I may be only a beginner, but I feel that there is nothing left for me to learn.

I've told you once, and I tell you again, that I'm *sure* of Georges, *provided* I can see him every day. If we are separated I shall lose him. This Paris interlude is going to be a terrible testing time. ... I won't insist on living with you – we're agreed on that – but what more natural, after all, than that I should pay you short visits from time to time?'

'I shall do precisely as your father wishes me to do.'

'I can hardly believe that it's you speaking, that it's you who are uttering these respectable, middle-class sentiments! ...'

Thérèse cut her short:

'For Heaven's sake don't let us start that all over again! Can't you see that I have had as much as I can stand? Here, take the key, get yourself some sheets from the cupboard in the dining-room, and make up the bed in the little back room. I shall send a wire to your father as soon as the post office is open. ... No, don't say another word!'

She held out the key, without looking at Marie. When next she raised her head the girl had vanished. She heard the key turn in the lock of the linen cupboard at the other end of the flat, and then the noise of furniture being moved. This went on for a considerable time. A little later, when she went into the hall and listened, the sound of regular breathing came to her ears. Now at last, she could go to bed! That she would sleep was in the highest degree unlikely, but it would be a relief merely to lie flat and ape the immobility of death. Contrary, however, to her expectation, she sank into unconsciousness as soon as she had turned out the light and closed her eyes. She plunged headlong into the deepest depths of sleep, and no part of what had occurred that evening revisited her in dreams, no word that had been spoken drifted back to the surface of her consciousness. Nature took its toll of her as of an exhausted animal. In the room next door a single log still glowed. The thin light of dawn picked out the disorder of the furniture: the low stool on which she had endured such agonies, and the bottle of Champagne standing forgotten upon the side-table.

3

SHE was awakened by the noise of the vacuum-cleaner. Her first thought was: 'Too late to warn Anna ...' She must already have gone into the girl's room. Wrapping herself in an old flannel dressing-gown, she went to look for the maid. As soon as she saw her she realized that she was in one of her bad moods.

'Have you been into the spare room?'

'Yes, and a pretty mess it's in!'

'Did you wake her?'

'There was no one there. Whoever's been there has gone.'

Thérèse went through the dining-room and opened the door. The little spare room was indeed empty. The suit-case had disappeared.

Marie might have taken the train back to Bordeaux: but she might, equally well, have gone to her young man.

'Shall I bring the coffee?'

Thérèse caught a hint of knowing familiarity in Anna's tone. She began to explain.

'My daughter turned up unexpectedly last night – after you had gone out. I'm surprised that she has left without saying good-bye to me. I suppose she didn't want to wake me. ...'

'I expect your visitor did you good, ma'am. You don't feel so bad now, do you?'

Thérèse pretended not to understand the crude irony of the question. She still, she said, felt tired. Anna took the forgotten bottle of Champagne from the side-table.

'I've no doubt this did you a lot of good, ma'am' (a mocking smile accompanied the words). 'When I was in hospital they gave me some after my operation. It put me on top of the world in two shakes!'

Thérèse shrugged her shoulders. She felt too tired, too indifferent, to bother about trying to convince her maid. As she dressed she thought: 'What does it matter what she thinks? But the little incident filled her mind to the exclusion even of Marie. The respect, the timid and, at times, almost tender deference with which she inspired Anna was something on which she had grown to rely. The girl must have been listening to a lot of gossip for her belief in her mistress to crumble so quickly at the first hint of suspicion. ... Anna ... so even *that* loyalty was to be taken from her! ... Well, there was no time to worry about it now. She had got all the rest of her life in which to brood. There were more important things claiming her attention. First of all, she must telegraph to Bernard, must *shift the responsibility*. Marie was right: all the dreary old for- mulae, the commonplaces of the Desqueyroux clan, rose almost automatically to her lips: *shift the responsibility*.

On leaving the post office in the rue de Grenelle she had a moment's hesitation. Should she go back to the flat and face the look of contempt in Anna's eyes? No, that was more than she could manage. She had given no order about meals. Well, so much the worse for Anna: she could just wait. The autumn morning was bright. There was a nip in the air. The street looked tempting. She would sit about in front of one or two cafés: she would drop in to a cinema. The seats, too, in the public gardens might be pleasant while the sun was out, and there were always the churches, where, huddled in the shadows among the kneeling figures, she always felt as though she were intruding on some secret rite, were listening at an in- visible door. The great thing was not to return to the rue du Bac, not to feel upon her head the weight of those walls and ceilings which were, somehow, saturated with her misery – above all, not to see that new, that brazen, look in Anna's face – and not, oh not, to live once more through the horrors of last evening! 'I accused myself, bared the secret of my heart – and all, it seems, for nothing if Marie has really gone off to see that man ... I have lost my daughter's love for nothing. ... No,' she went on, talking to herself (some passing schoolboys turned to stare), 'this morning it doesn't mean anything at all to me. The pain of it seems to have gone. ...'

Odd that the problem of her daughter should leave her so completely unmoved. Anna's opinion of her conduct seemed much more important. ... 'But, then, life is like that.' The hope of recovering with Marie the ground that she had lost had not had time to take root in her heart, while Anna, Anna's respect and affection, was the daily bread and water of her lonely existence ... and now *they* had been taken from her. ... She had nothing left. But though she repeated the word 'Nothing, nothing!' she felt no pang as she sauntered along the pavement of the Boulevard Saint-Germain with the misty sunlight of the October morning on her face, and in her nostrils the smell of asphalt and rotting leaves. Rather was she conscious of a sense of lightness. She seemed to have been freed by some *operation* of she knew not what. It was as though she were no longer walking in a circle, but moving straight ahead towards a goal. Had she, during the struggle of the night just past, unconsciously uttered the words, made the gesture, needed to break the spell? What had she said or done that was different from what she ordinarily said or did? Whatever the answer, the fact remained that her mind felt clearer. She was marching now in a perfectly definite direction.

But for a certain sense of frustration, a feeling of breathlessness, the presence, as it were, of death in her heart, she would have been almost happy. How beautiful the deep vistas of the sky about Saint-Germain des Prés! How suddenly moved by love she felt for the tired young faces which looked at her and smiled! She did not want to die, no longer craved annihilation.

Seated outside the Deux Magots, she forced herself to swallow an anis, just in order to get a little bit drunk. 'I must kill,' she thought, 'those moments of remorse that pride grows fat upon. Pride can turn all things to account. I was disappointed last night when Marie did not press her questions. I didn't astonish her so much as I hoped I should. ... In the background of my life there is a crime which came to nothing. ... There are other things in the many lives that swarm upon these sidewalks and in this café. ... If only people would realize that their crimes, their vices, their blots and blemishes have no manner of importance – or, if it comes to that, what they are pleased to call their virtues, either – not even the giving of themselves – for it is a gift of next to nothing ... I loathe and detest that little feeling of complacent self-satisfaction that comes over me when I think that I seemed, last night, to be sacrificing myself for Marie.' Wretched, miserable self-satisfaction – much better twist its neck! ... A complete, an informed, contempt of self – that was the goal at which she must aim. She made a sudden movement and overturned her glass. It fell to the ground and broke. A young man sitting at the next table got up, swept the fragments together and, doffing his hat, offered them with every sign of ceremonious politeness to her, while his companions guffawed. She looked at him with bright eyes, but said nothing. He seemed abashed, set down the fragments of glass in front of her, and said very seriously:

'Please excuse us, Madame: we are very young.'

She nodded her head and smiled. 'He doesn't know that I have no feelings left,' she thought.

She turned into the rue de Rennes, walked along the rue de la Gaieté as far as the avenue du Maine, realized that she had lost her way in a maze of squalid streets, and had to stop for a moment in order to get her breath. Opposite her was the open display window of a horse-meat butcher. A woman who might have been any age, obviously pregnant, her bare feet stuck into felt slippers, was keeping a watchful eye on the proprietor, who was weighing up a small piece of bluish meat. Thérèse decided that she would hail the next passing taxi and tell the man to take her to a good restaurant. People who live sheltered lives, she thought, don't know what real suffering means. She had always led a sheltered life herself.

'La Coupole,' she said, getting into the taxi. She thought of herself as ruined, but the amount of money at her disposal would have seemed like fabulous wealth to the woman who was now moving off with the scrap of bluish meat wrapped in a piece of yellow paper. So long as one can chew the cud of one's suffering, free from all external constraint, one is not really suffering. Luxury has become part of ourselves. Our very misery is a luxury. The fact that we can lock ourselves in a room and cry – that we can always lay our hand upon a sum of money when we need it ... So went Thérèse's thoughts. But when the wine-waiter came she said:

'Have you a good still Champagne? I'll have some, please – chilled.'

She got home late. While she was hunting in her bag for the latch-key she heard Anna's voice.

'I think that's Madame now. Yes, it is ... Mademoiselle has been waiting ever since six o'clock. ... Yes, I gave her some dinner ... but she didn't eat much.'

Thérèse's first feeling was one of sheer pleasure· at the thought that Anna no longer suspected her of having lied. She must know now that it really was Marie who had spent the night in the flat.

She went into the drawing-room, still wearing her hat and her shabby coat. Marie got up from a chair. She had lost her earlier look of hard brilliance. Her complexion was muddy, her lips looked swollen. She had become definitely plain. She told her mother at once that she had sent a wire to Saint-Clair to say that she would be home next day.

'You wanted to see me again before you went?'

'Yes: can you let me have the price of my ticket? I had to spend some of what you gave me yesterday.'

She stopped speaking. It was as though she were anticipating a question. But Thérèse looked at her in silence. The girl seemed to make up her mind quite suddenly.

'I've seen Georges. We had lunch together.'

'Well?'

She could not answer. The tears welled in her eyes. She took a damp handkerchief from her bag.

'But I don't see, my dear, what new fact ...'

'The new fact is that I told him I had found out the truth about ... about your past. That made it possible for him to talk freely to me. His parents have become more and more opposed to the marriage ever since they learned ... It's not so much what happened once, as the way you've been living these past few years. ... I can't help it: you've got to know. It's all your fault, it's all because of what *you've* done!

It seemed to Thérèse at that moment as though the whole of the day had been a dream, as though she were just waking from a long sleep to find herself in the same low chair, facing the same angry, exasperated judge. She voiced a protest:

'But, Marie ... this "way I've been living," even assuming it to be all that you seem to think it is – and, I must say, I should like to know what, exactly, they accuse me of – this "way of living" was perfectly well known to the Filhots at the time when they appeared to be perfectly happy about the match – or so I gathered from you.'

Marie embarked on a long, confused explanation. At the time in question old Filhot had probably thought that the Desqueyroux were sufficiently rich to justify him in shutting his eyes to uncomfortable facts. As things stood now, both families were more or less ruined. The Filhots needed capital.

'The gist of what his father says seems to be, "Marry whom you like, but not a girl from this part of the world!" and, you must admit, we've given him a pretty good case! ... Georges himself is above such sordid calculations, but he has got no job. He must work for his Law degree, and there are so many things besides me to occupy his mind, so many things that interest him more than I do!'

She was crying now, her face pressed against the quilted back of the arm-chair. Thérèse asked her what she meant to do. ... She would go back to Saint-Clair, would take up again the life which she had already felt to be intolerable, even when she had hopes ...

'But now it will be just death! ...'

She sat there, her head hidden in her arms. She muttered something which Thérèse only half heard.

'Say that again – if you dare!'

The girl turned on her a hard, defiant look.

'I said, you're not going to ruin *my* life.'

'You do hit the bull's-eye every time, don't you? – just like the rest of them.'

She began to walk up and down, rubbing her hands together. She remembered Marie's radiant entry into this very room twenty-four hours earlier, and how she had seemed to expand and blossom. Now it had come to this! She glanced at the small face which sleeplessness and despair and hatred had made ugly. She supposed she had deserved such hatred. She wasn't going to be so hypocritical as to accuse Fate. Even if she had never committed an irreparable act, even if she had remained all her life just Madame Bernard Desqueyroux, sitting from December to July at the window of the little drawing-room which gave on to the main square at Saint-Clair, and, for the rest of the year, in the house at Argelouse, her daughter would never have meant anything to her. There was nothing of the mother in her. For some unexplained reason she was wholly without that instinct which makes it possible for other women to live again in the children whom they have brought into the world. Yes, even if her existence had been one long, smooth course, unbroken by any shock, she felt sure that, sooner or later, she would have experienced the same sort of astounded surprise that had come to her yesterday evening at the sight of a full-grown woman who had turned out to be her own daughter. After years spent under the same roof with her, she would suddenly have been brought to realize Marie as a complete stranger, with tastes and antipathies of her own, the result of a slow and secret development, and completely without interest for her – an object of utter indifference. 'To have spent my life like that would have altered nothing.' Yet, faced now by an enemy who had come with the sole intention of calling her to account, she was ready to admit her own guilt, without pleading any extenuating circumstance. The one real crime for which she had been responsible, the crime from which all else had flowed, had, of course, been to marry at all, to bear a child, to submit herself to the common law of mankind, when she ought to have known that she had no part or parcel in such things.

But no! she still wasn't being truthful with herself. If there was nothing of the mother in her, why, had she felt that little shock of pleasure when Marie had come into the flat yesterday evening? Was it just that she had been overjoyed at such a chance of taking vengeance on the family? Perhaps ... But if that were so, why had the spectacle of the girl's misery seemed so horrible to her? Why had she been conscious of so strong a desire to make up for the past? She would gladly have given her life – but if that had been all, it would have been too easy. ... No one really needs another's life. We can buy nothing at the price of our blood, and, anyhow, she ought to have killed herself ages ago for it to do any good, and even so her shadow would have lain like a blight over Marie's sad and trivial destiny. Why should there be this awful communion between two people? 'Even dead I should have spread poison. What can I give you now – money?'

Suddenly she stopped walking up and down and stood perfectly still, her gaze fixed on the younger woman.

'Marie, I've got an idea!'

The girl did not so much as raise her head. With her elbows on her knees, she was swaying gently from side to side.

'Listen, something has occurred to me.'

She spoke quickly. She must say what she had to say before she stopped to think: must go straight ahead, burn her boats. She began:

'If I've understood you rightly ...'

What she had to say wasn't very pretty. It all came back – as things usually do in life – to a question of self-interest. The young man was fond of Marie, but his present circumstances made it impossible for him to go against his father's wishes. That was the long and short of the matter, wasn't it? (Marie nodded. She seemed now to be following her mother's words with deep attention.) Furthermore, old Filhot, needing capital as he did, wanted to marry his son to someone who didn't come from their part of the world? Marie indicated that this was a very fair description of the position.

'Suppose I made over all my Larroque money to you?' It was all, of course, in local land – about seven thousand acres, most of which had been stripped bare of trees by her father – which explained why, for the moment, her income was so much reduced. All the same, it represented a very handsome investment for the future. In fifteen years the newly planted trees would be fully matured. They would be worth, even taking the slump into account, several millions. If the Filhots wanted money now, there was nothing to prevent them from mortgaging the property. ... She could not give actual figures, though she was expecting them any day now, because, having no liquid capital, she had instructed her man of affairs – unknown to her husband – to send her a full statement. In any case, there was very good reason to assume that the Filhots would be able to raise on her land the capital of which they stood in need. It was not likely, things being as they were, that Georges Filhot would find anywhere else the kind of pair of shoes he was looking for – 'as your grandmother used to say'.

She brought out the phrase almost gaily, so successfully did this suggestion that she should give up the whole of her personal fortune lighten the burden on her spirit. But Marie only shrugged. It was an impossible proposition. Her mother couldn't strip herself bare like that. She must keep something on which to live. She had yielded to an impulse. She'd only got to think about it calmly for ten minutes to change her mind.

Thérèse protested that the matter had been in her head for a long time. She would be happier than she had ever hoped to be if only she could make up, in however small a degree, for the wrong she had done. She could manage on a very small income – just enough to enable her to finish her days in some inexpensive Home for the Aged. (She had invented this solution on the spur of the moment: she was quite determined to die of cold in a hovel rather than set foot in one of those institutions!) She added that she had been depriving herself for a long time now of most of the comforts of existence, that, sooner or later, her heart would 'go back on her' (the doctor had made that perfectly clear), and that all she wanted was a corner where she might die in peace.

Marie swore – but not this time, quite so vigorously – that she would never accept such a sacrifice. In any case, her father would have to agree, and, last but not least, the Filhots induced to withdraw their opposition in return for this concession. But Thérèse had an answer to everything. She had had her own dowry when she married, and what she did with her own was no concern of her husband. Of course, he would be a bit surprised at first, when he heard of her decision, but there was no reason whatever why he should disapprove. ... As to the Filhots ...

'Marie would you like me to see this Georges of yours, and explain the whole scheme to him?'

'Oh no, no! He mustn't see you: you must keep out of his way. ... I'm sorry if I'm hurting you, but ...'

Thérèse shook her head. It wasn't a question of her being hurt, because she was no longer capable of feeling anything. But if the young man had such fantastic ideas about her, wasn't that all the more reason for arranging for him to see her in the flesh?

'I believe I am the only person who might persuade him. My plan has the double advantage of overcoming both the objections put forward by his father: it gives him the capital he needs, and it gets rid' (she hesitated for a moment) 'of Thérèse Desqueyroux. You do see that, don't you? I shall just fade out of the picture, disappear completely, and my death will pass unnoticed.'

'No,' protested Marie: 'that's not the point. I don't mind admitting that I should like you to have a talk with Georges – if only that you might be able to give me your impression of his state of mind ... though, of course, he would be on the defensive, and wouldn't, for a moment, give himself away. ... You've had so much experience ... You do see what I mean, don't you? ... What's the matter, Mamma? Are you ill?'

Thérèse opened her eyes and gave a sickly smile.

'It's nothing. I've been on my feet all day. There's nothing to worry about. I shall feel better when I've had some food. Anna will bring me something. You ought to rest, too. ... Think over what I've been saying.'

'It's so kind of you, Anna, to help me undress ... and you've put a hot-water bottle in the bed! How lovely it is to lie down! Raise the pillow a little, will you? ... That's better ... and now tilt the lampshade so that the light doesn't shine in my eyes. Has the soup gone all cold?'

Anna held out the cup.

'I hope it's to your liking, ma'am. ... The young lady has already gone to bed.'

'Whatever you do, don't make any noise in the kitchen. It's not quite ten yet. Shall you be going out this evening?'

Anna shook her head. She was going to do some work on her trousseau.

'In that case ... I wonder whether ... would you very much mind ... just for a quarter of an hour, bringing your work in here? ... We needn't talk. But I should so like to feel that you were near me. It would help me to sleep.'

'Of course I will, if it would give you any pleasure, ma'am. ...'

The circle of light made by the lamp on the ceiling reminded her of the illnesses of her childhood, when, as now, she had lain and watched the worn hands of humble folk stitching away at coarse calico. One secret, at least, had been revealed to her, that beneath the thick crust of our actions the heart of the child remains unchanged, for the heart is not subject to the effects of time. At forty-five she had become once more a little girl who was afraid of the dark and could be comforted by the presence of her nurse.

'Anna, you had something on your mind this morning; what was it?'

The maid was shaken by a fit of trembling.

'This morning?'

'Yes, when you saw the tumbled bed, the disordered room, the bottle of Champagne. ...'

'It didn't mean a thing to me, ma'am.'

'People have been telling you things, bad things, about me, haven't they? ... the concierge, the butcher? ...'

'Not the butcher, ma'am ... and, anyhow, I know it's all a lot of lies. ... I'm the one who should do the talking, as I always say; aren't I, ma'am?'

Thérèse made no reply. She felt that tears were dangerously near, and held her breath. Anna mustn't see her crying. But how can one cry without choking and sobbing? (Whether one be ten or fifty, one's tears are always the tears of a child.)

'Oh, ma'am, what *is* the matter?'

'It's nothing, Anna.'

'Has the young lady been making you unhappy?'

'All over now. I'm going to sleep. Please stay where you are just a few minutes longer.'

She closed her eyes and, after a brief pause, told the maid that she could go. Anna folded up her work, rose, and said:

'Good night, ma'am.'

Thérèse called her back.

'I wonder ... would you give me a kiss?'

'Gladly, ma'am.'

Anna rubbed her mouth on the back of her hand.

4

'But really, my dear, I'm not a fool. Of course he won't think I've come to ask him a favour. The question won't even arise. It's simply that if you two are going to get married he ought to know what I plan to do with my property. ... I don't suppose our meeting will last for more than five minutes. ...'

'All the same, I wish you'd made him talk – if you can. Try to find out ...'

It was with a certain amount of astonishment that Marie watched her mother standing in front of the mirror which hung over the mantelpiece, tying a short veil over her eyes. She had dabbed the merest touch of rouge on lips and cheeks ... but it wasn't really that that made the difference. No, all of a sudden she had become a totally different woman. It was as though this expedition on which she was about to embark had revived her social sense. She was about to play a role which once had been familiar to her. All the long-forgotten gestures were responding to the call of memory, as they do when an actress returns to the stage after a long absence. Marie, too, had recovered her earlier brilliance. Sleep had given a look of freshness to her face, and her eyes were bright with hope.

'He may not be in ... but of course he will; I was forgetting: he always lunches at the hotel, because he has an *en pension* arrangement. If he isn't back, just wait. ...'

'Naturally I shall wait. ... Now, don't worry, dear.'

There was the same sunlight, the same mist, in the streets as yesterday. Thérèse walked to Georges Filhot's hotel in the Boulevard Montparnasse, near the station. She made no attempt to rehearse what she would say. She felt free, now, to watch the men working on an excavation in the road, a child pulling a cart which was too heavy for him, even the woman leaning against the wall who did not hold out a hand to her as she passed. She had made up her mind to strip herself of all her worldly wealth. She could taste already something of the happiness which the act would bring her. So far the thought had given her nothing but pleasure. She could not imagine what life would be like when she had only just enough money to keep her from starving. But she faced the future unafraid. 'You'll feel very differently when it's an accomplished fact,' she kept telling herself. But even so, she could not get within measurable distance of genuine fear. Perhaps she did not really believe that she would be called upon to keep her word. It was far from certain that the marriage would ever come off, and even if it did, even if the family acquiesced in her determination to surrender her fortune, Bernard Desqueyroux would always see to it that she had more than a bare livelihood. Still, she would have to draw in her horns. She tried to imagine certain definite privations which she might have to endure, but without in any way lessening the pleasure which she felt at the prospect of her sacrifice.

She walked up the rue Vaugirard as far as the Boulevard Montparnasse, turned into the latter, and kept to the left-hand pavement, taking the general direction of the station. She studied carefully the dingy fronts of the old houses and the signs upon them – Hôtel de Nantes, Hôtel du chemin de fer de l'Ouest – for Marie had been unable to give her a number.

Behind the glass door some men were standing round a table at which the manageress was sitting. After a moment's hesitation, Thérèse entered and moved towards the stairs. A waiter, his shirt-sleeves rolled up, and looking quite remarkably grubby, put down a box full of blacking brushes on one of the treads, and turned his puffy face to her.

'Monsieur Filhot? – Fourth floor – room 83,' he said, when she asked him to let Monsieur Filhot know that a lady wanted to have a word with him, adding:

'He's probably in: you'd better go up and see.' But she insisted, and slipped a coin into his hand. He stared at her with a hideous grin.

'No name? Just – "a lady"?'

She climbed the stairs very slowly behind him. They were steep, and the higher they went the darker they became. The smell of cooking which had been noticeable on the ground floor gave place, as they mounted, to a pervading odour of slops and drains.

A voice exclaimed:

'Why, of course: ask her to come up.'

Somebody leaned over the banisters, and she heard the voice again: 'What a lot of fuss!' Obviously the tall young man standing on the fourth-floor landing was expecting an entirely different lady. ... His features suddenly froze.

'*I* am Georges Filhot, Madame.'

The open door of his room did something to dissipate the gloom of the landing, but he was standing against the light. All she could see was that he was tall and stooped slightly; that he had a low forehead and black, tousled hair; that he was in his shirt-sleeves and wore a knitted pullover. The collar of his blue shirt was open. Thérèse assured him that she would not trespass on more than two minutes of his time. There was something she wanted to tell him. She entered the room with a firm step and turned to face him. He had deliberately left the door open. She told him who she was.

Long years had taught her what to expect to see on the faces of people at Saint-Clair or Argelouse when her name was mentioned – a look of hungry curiosity; and it was a precisely similar expression that showed now on the exaggeratedly long and bony countenance bending above her. She saw in it, too, a hint of anxiety and mistrust. This she set herself at once to dispel.

'There's nothing to worry about. I've not come here to meddle in matters that don't concern me. I've merely called on you,' she continued hastily, 'to say that should you and Marie have to make a decision, it is well that you should know ...'

She spoke perfectly calmly, with something of her old ease of manner. Although she made her meaning perfectly plain, she had a feeling that her words had failed to have any effect on the young man, and she set herself, while she was speaking, to discover what it was that was so odd about him. She noticed that he had a slight cast in one eye, and that this blemish gave to what otherwise would have been a perfectly ordinary face a certain charm, the sort of muzziness that goes with intoxication. Without the slightest hint of false humility, but also without in any way seeming to give him a lesson in manners, she asked whether she might sit down. He apologized awkwardly, and pushed an arm-chair towards her, first clearing it of an overcoat, a dirty shirt, and several gramophone records. Then he passed his hand several times over his cheeks and chin, remarking with some show of embarrassment that he had not shaved. He shut the window.

'One can't hear oneself speak,' he said.

'It must be awful living so near the station.'

'Oh, noise doesn't bother me.'

He sat down on the bed, facing her, and listened attentively to what she had to say.

'I want you to realize that I have not come to ask your intentions, or anything like that. ... My husband has told me nothing of any plans he may have for Marie, and I live too far removed from my daughter to have any views of my own on the matter. ...'

She was aware of a certain quality in her voice quite unlike its usual tone, something that had nothing to do with her own deliberate choice – a breathlessness, a hoarseness in the lower register. She heard herself say:

'This making over of my property to Marie will mean that I shall go out of her life completely.'

She uttered the phrase quite simply, and stressed it with a movement of the hand. She was not trying to make an effect, nor yet to pose as a victim. Georges Filhot assured her that he was 'not the sort of man to worry about such material details'. In a tone that was a curious mixture of insolence and timidity, he added:

'We are not like our parents, who thought of nothing but dowries and wills and legacies. The slump has blown all that sort of thing sky-high. It doesn't interest us any longer.'

'I can quite believe that. But your father has a right to know what I mean to do with my money. I give you full liberty to pass on to him what I have just told you – if you think it necessary to do so.'

'Is Marie with you?'

He looked at her rather uncertainly. Now that the window was closed, the room smelt of old clothes, tobacco, and soap. The sun had gone behind a cloud and suddenly the place took on a sordid look. Thérèse knew that the moment had come to make an effort on Marie's behalf.

'She is going back this evening: have you any message for her?'

'Madame, I want you to understand ...'

At once she collected all her faculties. She looked at him with an expression which she knew well how to assume at will. It combined complete detachment from any personal concern with an air of passionate interest in what her interlocutor might wish to confide in her. He told her that he was twenty-two, and that the idea of marriage terrified him. If he had got to marry, her daughter was the woman he would choose. ...

'Ah!' Thérèse broke in; 'have I your authority to repeat what you have said, to her? You aren't, of course, in any way committed. ...'

It wasn't, he said, evasion on his part. His feelings for Marie were of the tenderest. She formed part of all his memories of childhood and youth. Had it not been for her, his holidays at Saint-Clair would have been intolerable. ...

'I love that part of the country, and hate it too. Can you understand that?'

'Oh, I ...'

He blushed, remembering who this woman was, and what the mere mention of Saint-Clair must mean to her. But somehow he could not identify with Thérèse Desqueyroux the woman who was sitting there looking at him so thoughtfully from behind her short veil.

'I'm not saying that I shall never marry,' he went on after a pause; 'only that just at this moment the whole idea seems impossible! In the first place, there's Law School and all the endless examinations. ...'

'That wouldn't make any difference,' broke in Thérèse – 'just the reverse, in fact. Marriage has a settling influence: it keeps a man at home. But I can quite understand that at your age you hesitate.'

'It *is* natural, isn't it, Madame? You see, I am only twenty-two.'

She kept her gaze fixed steadily on the long, thin face. Though the features were prominent, they had an odd, sketchy look. The dark brown eyes, with their faint suspicion of a cast, seemed curiously unfocused. The lips alone were strongly and boldly marked.

'It would be more accurate to say that you are *already* twenty-two.'

Almost as though he were suffering physical pain, he said: 'You mean that I'm no longer so very young?'

'Scarcely that ... but somehow, once one has started on a journey, it is as though one had already reached the end ... don't you feel that?'

Yes, he most certainly did.

'You'll hardly believe it, but, do you know, the day I turned twenty I actually cried!'

'You had good reason to do so,' said Thérèse very simply.

He listened to her with deep attention. She said that youth, so far from being the beginning of things, is nothing but a time of misery. ...

'But,' she went on, holding one of the records close to her eyes in an attempt to read the title, 'you, who love music, must know that it can express that truth as nothing else can ... Schumann, for instance. ...'

'That, I think, is what I chiefly demand of music. Do you think that many young people suffer in just this way?'

When Thérèse replied that he ought to be better able than she to answer that question, 'I had a friend,' he suddenly said, 'who killed himself last July. There was no apparent reason for him to do so, or none of the reasons that are usually given to explain suicide. We were very intimate. There was no woman in his life: he had no vices. ...'

'Did he take drugs?'

'No – but I think (the idea came to me while you were speaking just now) that he had some such feeling as the one you were describing ... He wanted to precipitate the end of something. He wanted to have done with everything once and for all. It is not a feeling that I, personally, have ever had. ...'

Thérèse got up.

'Marie is waiting for me, and I am keeping you. ...'

In quite a different tone – a tone of brisk common sense, she added:

'I realize that what frightens you at the moment is the thought of marriage in general. May I tell her that? – and may I add that your feelings towards her are unchanged?'

He did not answer her question; instead: 'It's odd, isn't it?' he remarked; 'I had completely forgotten who you are. I had never imagined ... Marie never gave me the slightest idea. ... She's a poor hand at describing people. ...'

For a few moments neither of them said anything. Then, to break the silence, he asked whether he might say good-bye to Marie before she left. He supposed she was taking the ten o'clock train?

'Why don't you dine with us?' She made this suggestion on the spur of the moment, and almost without thinking what she was saying. 'Afterwards, you can see her to the station.'

He showed no surprise, and accepted with enthusiasm. It was understood that he would turn up about six.

At this moment a servant pushed open the door, which had been left ajar.

'Madame Garcin's asking for you. I said you had somebody with you. ... She's waiting downstairs.'

Georges Filhot turned towards Thérèse and said, with a rather complacent air:

'Madame Octave Garcin, you know. The Garcins of Laburthe. ... Aren't they some sort of relations of yours? They're living in Paris now.'

'I knew her mother-in-law very well,' said Thérèse. 'You mustn't keep her waiting – though I expect she's used to it.'

He protested with a somewhat fatuous air: 'No, no ... really, I shouldn't like you to think ...'

A tall young woman was standing in the hall when Thérèse reached it. She glanced hurriedly at her in passing. It was almost one o'clock. She walked home full of the thought of how happy she was going to make Marie. How impatient the poor darling must be getting! ... She mustn't raise her hopes too high. ... But, despite her good resolutions, she couldn't, when she saw her daughter waiting for her on the landing, help exclaiming:

'Guess who's dining with us tonight?'

Marie smiled, but did not trust herself to utter the name.

'He'll be here round about six – and, later on, he'll take you to the station. ...'

Marie drew her mother into the drawing-room, and, without giving her time to take off her hat, flung her arms round her neck.

'How good you are! – and what a little beast I've been!'

Thérèse freed herself with a faint movement of impatience.

'You mustn't say things like that. I'm not good.'

She led the way into the dining-room.

'Tell me everything that happened – everything! What you said and what he answered. ... What did you think of him?'

'You mustn't get too excited!'

The feeling of happiness which had been with Thérèse all the way home, the thought that she was going to give her daughter pleasure, vanished suddenly into thin air. She mustn't, she kept on saying to herself, paint the future in too rosy a light. There might be a harsh awakening in store for Marie.

'Yes, he's going to dine with us, that's all settled. ... But ... he doesn't want to feel that he's tied. ... It's as well that you should realize that once and for all. He made a great point of it.'

'Ah!'

Marie's gaze was fixed on her mother. She went on pouring water into her glass although it was already full.

'You're soaking the tablecloth, dear. Whatever you do, don't worry. It's the thought of marriage that frightens him. He can't, at the moment, face the idea. After all, it's only natural at twenty-two. But there is no doubt whatever in my mind that he is very fond of you.'

For a few moments neither said anything more. Marie dabbed at the water she had spilled. She pushed her plate away.

'I can't eat a thing. So he told you that his feelings for me ... he did really say "feelings"?'

Thérèse was sure that he had, though she was equally convinced that he had not used the word *love*. The corners of Marie's mouth began to tremble in a way she knew of old. Hastily she added that 'feelings' was only another way of saying 'love'. Marie pressed her with questions. What else had he said? He must have said a good deal considering the time they had spent together.

'Oh, I don't know – something about your being all mixed up in his mind with memories of his holidays, about your being a part of his life. ...'

'And after that?'

Sitting there with her elbows on the table and her chin resting on her linked fingers, Marie never once took her eyes from her mother's face.

'I really don't remember. ...'

'But you were almost half an hour with him. ...'

'I think we talked about music. ...' Marie's face assumed a long-suffering expression. 'He's crazy about music,' she muttered.

'And you hate it ... all the Desqueyroux do ... what bad luck!'

The girl protested that there was no point nowadays in being able to play the piano.

'However well I might play, Georges says, my interpretation would never come up to his records.'

Thérèse made it clear that, all the same, she did think it unfortunate.

'Why?' insisted Marie; 'he can have all the music he wants.'

'I know that, darling. Still, it's delightful for a musically minded man if his wife can play at sight. ... But that's not the point. What's really serious, if you want my opinion, is the fundamental lack of sympathy implied by that difference between you. When a woman hates music and her husband can't do without it, there is bound to be something of a barrier between them.'

She was speaking in a low voice: there was a look of anxious melancholy on her face.

'I'll learn to love everything he loves,' Marie broke in passionately. 'I'm not worrying my head about that. It *is* possible, don't you think? ... If he insists. ...'

Thérèse shook her head.

'You can be easy on that score ... he won't. After all, if you are really going to live together, it may be no bad thing that he should have that way of escape open to him. ... He will be able to wander whenever he likes in a country into which you cannot follow him. Music is often a blessed compensation for too great a propinquity. ... Sometimes it's the man it helps, sometimes the woman ... which is all as it should be. Even when husband and wife are both devoted to music it sometimes happens that the very pleasure they share becomes an instrument of separation. Music unites those only who love one another with the same *kind* of love operating at the same moment of time.'

'But we do love one another, Mamma. He spoke of his love – you said he did – or, at least, of his feelings.'

Thérèse had got up, and now hurried into the drawing-room, followed by Marie, who could not let the subject alone.

'Time and time again he has said that I am the only woman in his life. ... What are you smiling at?'

Thérèse compressed her lips. 'I won't tell her about that Garcin creature,' she kept saying to herself, and replied that she wasn't smiling, but merely making a face – she'd had a sudden twinge of neuralgia. ... She was going to lie down for a bit in a darkened room. Marie had better set about making arrangements for dinner. She mustn't forget the Champagne, and she must order an ice-pudding. She knew what Georges liked.

'It'll give you something to think about, dear.'

Lying stretched on her bed, Thérèse listened to the clink and clatter of china. The afternoon was overcast. The furniture feebly reflected back the dull light. The day was pursuing its usual course. The noise of cars and lorries reached her ears, the screech of brakes and the shrill cries of children at play – an audible reminder that humanity was still busy reproducing itself. The chair-mender came round, sounding his little horn. 'Marie must not pitch her hopes too high ... but I must be careful not to strike a mortal blow at her happiness. Do I want to strike a mortal blow at her happiness? It would be a worse crime than the one I committed years ago. I had some excuse then. I was buried alive, and I lifted the stone which was keeping me from the air. What *is* this essential *me* to which I'm for ever harking back? I really do mean most awfully well!' (She laughed quietly to herself, alone there in the dark.) 'When I embarked on that confession the other evening it was only because I wanted to make Marie go back to her father. ... I rose above myself, and I rejoiced in my ability to do so, even though my suffering was perfectly genuine. ... But what really gave me pleasure was that decision I made yesterday to surrender my fortune. When I did that I felt as though I were floating at an incredible height above my ordinary everyday self. I climb and climb and climb – and then suddenly I slip back into this frozen nastiness of malevolence – which is my true self when I'm not making an effort, the self to which I keep on returning. ...'

She shifted her pillow, making it higher. 'No, I'm not really as horrible as all that. The trouble is that I demand clarity of vision in others. What irritates me about Marie is the way she has of living in a world of illusions. I've always had a passion for tearing the bandages from other people's eyes. I've always insisted that those round me should see things as they are. I suppose it is that I need companionship in despair. I can't understand *not* despairing. Is it mere viciousness on my part that makes me want to shout at Marie, "You *must* know that he doesn't love you, that he never will love you, or, at any rate, not with the same sort of love that *you* feel"? I want to make her see what a vast difference there is between a woman who will inevitably turn into an old Argelouse gossip and a young man who is for ever tormented with curiosity and anguish. What impudence it is to think that one can snatch at a man and his destiny and make him one's own private property! I'll tell her that. I'll tell her that even if she does marry him she'll never be able to climb to the level on which he lives. ... She might, of course, in the long run, manage to knock him off his perch, but if she does that, then he'll fall dead at her feet – quite dead. No,' she whispered to herself, 'I'll tell her no such thing.'

The afternoon wore itself out. Cars hooted at one another at the street-crossings. She could hear the trams on the Boulevard Saint-Germain. In a moment of sudden quiet a bird shrilled and fell silent. She would remain shut away here in this room, making scarcely a movement, as though her simplest gesture had the power to wound Marie. She must keep a careful watch on her tongue, say only the most ordinary things.

When Marie came and knocked at the door of her mother's room, Thérèse called back that she felt much better, that she would be all right by dinner-time, but would rest until then.

Just after six o'clock she heard the front-door bell, and then a man's voice, followed by Marie's nervous laugh. At moments they both spoke together in low tones. 'They're probably talking about me,' thought Thérèse. Silence returned, and she might well have assumed that there was no one in the drawing-room. They had, at least, *that* between them. Their bodies could take pity on hearts estranged, uniting above the sundering gulf in an effort to hide it from their eyes, to pretend it was not. No doubt he was resting his head on her shoulder. For the moment all their problems were resolved, and the questions waiting for an answer might be left, for the time being, in suspense.

With deliberate intent they moved a chair, spoke some indifferent phrase in loud voices, coughed. A smell of cooking came from the kitchen. Thérèse switched on the light, got up, and put cold cream on her face. He had never seen her without her hat. She knew a way of doing her hair which made her forehead look less bald. While the tongs were heating she put on a dress of black marocain, and a blue scarf which hid her throat. She did not want him to see her face as it really was, did not wish to be known by him. Her appearance should lie no less than her words. She would speak as little as possible, would efface herself. It might not be easy. There are those with whom one finds oneself talking whether one means to or not. This morning their conversation might have gone on indefinitely. But this evening Marie would be there. But immediately after dinner the young people would leave her. The train went at ten. The play would be over. In all, it had lasted but two days – her confession to her daughter, her offer of her fortune, her mission to the young man. She had played a noble role, and had been pleased at the way she had interpreted it. To-night she would once more see things as they were, would enter again upon her state of nothingness.

5

SHE realized, as soon as she joined them, that she had interrupted a conversation about herself. There was an awkward silence which, somehow or other, she must manage to fill. During dinner she fell back, with a sense of relief, on recollections of Saint-Clair and Argelouse. She talked about people whose sons were known to Georges Filhot. He never – he and she – seemed to be speaking of the same generation: 'Yes, I suppose her son *would* be about your age. ...' – 'No, the Deguilheim I mean must be your friend's uncle. ...'

'What makes Argelouse so melancholy,' said Georges, 'is that the trees are scarcely longer-lived than the human inhabitants. Their generations pass away as quickly as those of the men and women who are their neighbours. The landscape is for ever changing. You would hardly know Argelouse today. It is a very different place from the one you knew as a child. The older trees are all cut down. There are wide open vistas where once the view was obscured by woodland. ...'

'In my day,' replied Thérèse, 'the landowners were proud of their pines. Rather than fell them, they would let them rot where they stood.' A moment later she added: 'I shall never go back there.'

Neither Marie nor Georges said anything. They sat there, watching her drink.

'But if I did,' she went on, 'I should recognize the sandy soil, the rocky outcrops, the swift-flowing, ice-cold streams, the smell of resin and of bog, the sound of pattering hooves as the sheep come to the shepherd's call.'

'Anyone hearing you talk would think that you had loved Argelouse.'

'Loved? – not exactly. But I endured such suffering there that it comes to very much the same thing.'

He did not know what to answer. As the moment of leave-taking drew near, Marie kept her eyes glued to his face. It was as though she were drinking her fill, knowing the thirst that lay in wait for her. He asked whether he might smoke.

'I suppose you'll be going home some time between Christmas and the New Year?' said Thérèse; 'in less than three months you'll be seeing one another again.'

'Three months!' exclaimed Marie.

She bent her head above her plate so that her hair fell forward and left visible an ear which was not one of her best features. She kept twisting a ring that she wore on her right hand, smiling at Georges the while. Thérèse noted that she had rather an 'unkempt' look. The stuff she put on her hair had failed to subdue it completely, and the loose, short strands sticking out from her head gave her the appearance of a young crow. Now and then Thérèse caught her stealing a sidelong glance in her direction, but it was quickly averted. Georges was eating slowly, and continued long after his companions

had finished. He refused nothing, and dawdled over his cheese
and his dessert as though there had been no sweet course. He
gulped down the Champagne almost as soon as his glass was
filled.

'You ought to be off now, darling,' said Thérèse: 'Monsieur
Filhot will take your bag down for you.'

When the moment came to say good-bye, Marie clasped
her mother in a warm embrace. Thérèse freed herself rather
too quickly.

'Now, be sensible young people,' she said. Once more she
was left alone. She was conscious of a state of mental agitation,
of a restlessness which was definitely pleasurable. She took up
a book, but could not settle down to read. 'I have not broken
up their relationship,' she told herself: 'I have spoiled nothing
for them. All things considered, I have been rather a help than
otherwise to Marie, and if the marriage does come off ...' She
thought again about her decision to make over her fortune,
but this time without any feeling of satisfaction. She was
beginning, indeed, to be somewhat uneasy on that score. The
magnificence of the gesture no longer had power to satisfy her
vanity. She saw now what a difference so great a sacrifice
would make to her own life. She tried to calm her new-born
anxiety. 'They'll never consent ... or, at any rate, they'll see
that I get an adequate allowance, and that will be a great deal
better than my present condition of uncertainty. ... I may, in
the long run, be better off than I am now.' She uttered a little
laugh. 'A generous impulse is never thrown away.' She had
put on very little make-up and, was surprised to see in the
mirror how high her colour was. She had taken a small amount
of Champagne: it must be that. When the tight bands of despair
loosen it is usually because of some tiny, some purely physical
cause – a good night's sleep, a glass of wine. ... The sense of
misery seems gone for good, though actually it has withdrawn
only a short distance. We know that it will return, but for the
moment it is no longer with us. The world is a good place,
after all – perhaps we have still a long life before us. No loneliness short of death is irreparable. Who knows what meeting
may come our way this evening, tomorrow? So many paths

cross our own. At any moment a spark may kindle, a current of sympathy be set up. Tonight, Thérèse would give free play to her sense of happiness. Her heart was no longer troubling her. 'Perhaps I'm not going to die after all,' she thought: 'perhaps I'm going to live.'

She opened the window and leaned out above the ill-lit and still noisy street. The iron blinds were being pulled down in front of the shop-windows with much rattling and banging. Sleek black limousines were gliding over the roadway, baying briefly with their horns at the crossings. The screech of brakes on a motor-bus drowned every sound but one – which she sensed rather than heard on the landing outside her own front-door. It was followed by voices – Anna's and a man's – in the entry; the one was asking a question, the other answering. Thérèse closed the window, and saw Georges Filhot standing bareheaded before her. He was still wearing his overcoat. She was suddenly conscious once again of her ailing heart. Her jaws contracted; the hard look which came into her eyes with the onset of pain made the young man think that she was angry with him for coming back.

'Did you forget something?'

He stammered out that he merely wanted to tell her about Marie. Everything had gone off all right. He had managed to get her a corner seat.

Thérèse had dropped into a chair, and was leaning slightly forward in an effort to get the pain under control. She was quite motionless, like one of those small reptiles that simulate death when attacked. She begged him, rather gaspingly, to take the other chair. He realized then that she was not so much vexed, perhaps, as suffering.

'Just a little queasiness ... it's better already ... in a few seconds I shall be all right."

They were conscious now of no sounds save the ticking of the clock and of a wireless in one of the neighbouring flats. He forced himself not to look at the corpse-like face before him, but his eyes kept on wandering back to the great dome-like forehead on which scarcely a line was visible. He could not help taking note of the lowered lids, of the dark circles round the eyes, of the lips which were not so much closed as forcibly clenched. Suddenly he realized that she too was watching him from beneath her lashes. He flushed and turned away his head. She sat up straighter.

'I'm better now. Tell me about Marie. Did she go off in a happy frame of mind?'

He thought so.

'What did she say to you?'

He did not dare to say in reply, 'Most of what we said was about you ...' and yet, wasn't this the moment for him to get her to clear up the point that was worrying him? As he had said more than once to Marie, it wasn't that her mother had felt the need to regain her freedom at any cost – *that* didn't surprise him. What he found really incredible was the version of the affair put about by the people of Saint-Clair. How was it possible to believe that the woman whose tormented face he now saw turned towards him had been able, day after day, week after week, to administer poison in tiny doses and keep a man in a condition of long-drawn-out agony? Marie had agreed with him that the whole thing was utterly inconceivable. Truth to tell, by diminishing her mother's responsibility she was serving the interests of her own love, and that was the one thing she cared about. But she had not known what answer to make when Georges had voiced his surprise at her not pushing her inquiries further. 'Your mother was perfectly willing that you should question her, yet you wouldn't take advantage of the opportunity!' No doubt it was all very painful, but any-thing would be better than uncertainty. 'Had I been in your place, I couldn't have gone on living. ...' To that her reply had been that he was now on sufficiently familiar terms with Thérèse Desqueyroux to ask her himself. This goaded him to a protest: 'It doesn't matter to *me* except on your account.' His words had caused her intense happiness, and she was, no doubt, at this very moment, brooding over them in the train. She did not know that he had been lying, that Thérèse's mystery thrilled him apart from any bearing it might have on her. It was not of her he had been thinking as he climbed these stairs and rang at this door. But when Thérèse pressed her former question with a 'Won't you tell me what you talked about?' he kept his true thoughts hidden. 'What *does* one talk about to a young girl?' he said with a touch of contempt in his voice. Thérèse smiled. All that mattered, she said, was that her daughter should have gone off happy. He expressed a fear that he might have given her too much hope. He was terrified lest one day she might be disappointed. ... He was watching Thérèse closely, and saw that her face displayed no sign of irritation.

'Marie does not expect an immediate decision. The great thing is to have gained a little time. Whatever you make up your mind eventually to do, you won't feel that you have been rushed. She will be free this summer to see you every day. She must take her chance.'

He was pleased to find that she could view the problem from so detached a point of view. She really was a mother in a thousand. There was nothing she did not understand.

'In my heart of hearts,' she went on, 'I feel that her chance is, on the whole, pretty good.'

He smiled, not knowing what to answer, and slightly raised one shoulder.

'What do you do with yourselves in summer-time at Saint-Clair? In my young days ...'

'Young people today have always one thing they can fall back on – the mill-stream. We bathe in it every day, and when we come out of the water we lie in the sun.'

'What!' she exclaimed, 'even at Saint-Clair?' He thought she sounded worried and shocked, and hastened to reassure her.

'We are terribly well behaved. ...'

She interrupted him: 'You don't think I'm worrying about *that*, do you?' – and remembered suddenly that they were discussing her daughter. There was something rather fatuous in the smile he turned on her as he proceeded with a somewhat succulent deliberation to describe the bathing expeditions, which were so like, yet so unlike, the sort of thing that went on at the seaside ... the cold, still water above the mill-dam through which their bodies were so clearly visible, and later, when they were lying on the dry grass of the bank, the speckled light falling through leaves on human flesh, making it so much more a living thing than it could ever look on treeless shores.

'Marie and I get on wonderfully together. We just lie there, side by side, for hours at a time, saying nothing. Occasionally we take a dip, but one can't swim for very long; the water is too cold and there are too many weeds. So we climb out and lie down again. The crickets and the grasshoppers stop chirping and then start up again, quite close to our ears, as though we were dead. Our eyes grow used to seeing only the life of the tree-tops – squirrels, jays ...'

'Marie's neck and arms are still sunburnt – I noticed that.'

'She never looks so pretty as at the end of the holidays.'

'You *are* in love with her, you know!'

'I'm not sure,' he replied. He seemed to be in a softened mood and smiled vaguely. He got up, lit a cigarette, and, as Thérèse began, 'We must ...' and then broke off, went and leaned against the bookcase.

'What? What must we do?'

'... See to it that the life of the human creature whom we have chosen, or who has chosen us, remains a long siesta in the sun, an endless lassitude in which the body can enjoy an almost animal surrender. We must never forget that the person lying there at our side, within reach of our hand, is at peace with the world, fulfilled and acquiescent – that both of us would rather be where they are than anywhere else. The day must be so hot and still, the mind so torpid, that treachery, even in thought, becomes impossible. ...'

'It is true that as soon as it gets a bit cool our minds begin to wander, and we feel the need to wander off somewhere else. Marie asks me suddenly, "What are you thinking about?" '

'And you reply, "About nothing, dearest," because it would be too complicated a task to make her free of the world whose threshold you have just crossed, where there is no room for a woman. ...'

'That is what Mondoux always says.'

Thérèse asked, 'And who is Mondoux?' though she knew in advance precisely who he was: the wonderful object of hero-worship who is almost always present in the lives of men of Georges' age, the friend who has read everything, can play any piece of music, and follows a mysterious star of his own: the marvellous person whom you simply *must* meet – and whom every woman knows that she will hate. 'It's not easy to get on intimate terms with him, of course – but if he takes a liking to you ...' As a rule, the prodigy in question is chiefly remarkable for his spots and his Adam's apple. Usually he is desperately shy, frantically proud, and very jealous. ... The influence of the Mondoux of this world is always considerable. ... 'But why should I worry?' thought Thérèse: 'Marie has no reason to be afraid of Mondoux. ...'

'I must bring you two together: he'll interest you. But are you sure I'm not keeping you up? It's eleven o'clock already.'

'Oh, sleep and I ...'

All the same, she got up and said nothing more that might have the effect of keeping him from going. He asked to be allowed to see her again. Marie had told him that he need not be afraid of making a nuisance of himself. He watched eagerly for a sign of assent. Thérèse gave no answer to his question, but – 'Poor Marie!' she sighed.

'Why "poor Marie"?'

'Because when you go down for the New Year there won't be any bathing or lying in the sun.'

'But we shall see one another. She doesn't often come to our house, nor do I go to hers. But she's a good horse-woman, although you may not know it, and we go riding in all weathers. We usually meet at Silhet, the derelict farm. ...'

'It was derelict even when I was young. ...' She could still see in imagination the obscene drawing traced on the wall in charcoal, and the heap of turves in the corner where sometimes a shepherd would spend the night.

'We tether our horses in the sheep-pen. We build a big fire.'

For a moment or two they neither of them said anything more. It was Thérèse who broke the silence.

'Perhaps my husband will be more willing now to receive you. It would be a good deal more comfortable for both of you ... and you could have some music.'

He looked at her with a grin.

'That shows how little you know Marie: she loathes music.'

Thérèse shrugged her shoulders and smiled, as though saying in so many words, 'What can I have been thinking about?'

'Oh, well,' she remarked, 'it really doesn't matter these days. There's always the gramophone.'

He pulled a face, and seemed to be choking back a word of protest. She was suddenly conscious of a deep sense of happiness, and felt ashamed.

'You'll write to her, won't you?' she asked with precipitate eagerness.

And when he promised to send her a letter soon –

'Not soon,' she insisted, 'but *now*, at once. Think how awful these first days of separation will be for her.'

'I hate writing letters,' he said, 'except, of course to Mondoux. I've made a regular collection of "Thoughts", you know, from the ones he's sent me, arranged under three headings – *Politics, Philosophy, Religion*. I'll lend it you one of these days. It really is remarkable. ... Why are you smiling? Are you laughing at me?'

She shook her head. 'How idiotic men are at that age,' she was thinking: 'how aggressively stupid one can be at twenty.'

All the same, Georges promised to write to Marie, and asked whether he might pay Thérèse another call.

'What for?' she asked, and, seeing that she had put him out of countenance, added brightly: 'To talk to me about Marie? Come as often as you like ... though I am scarcely ever at home.'

There was something sad and preoccupied about the way in which he thanked her, remarking, as though quite casually that he and Mondoux 'met most days for lunch at the Deux Magots'.

She followed him into the entry. His hand hesitated on the door-knob, and he turned to her.

'I should so much like to know ...' he began, not without embarrassment ... 'But no,' he finished; 'that can wait until another day.'

Only on the second attempt did he succeed in shutting the door behind him. Thérèse listened to the sound of his footsteps growing less and less distinct as he descended the stairs. Then she went back into the drawing-room, where confusion reigned in a fog of tobacco smoke. The padded arm-chairs and the low fireside seat had changed places. Life had come back to these waifs and strays from Argelouse. She could guess pretty accurately what it was that he wanted to know, but he would never get more out of her than she might decide to tell. She felt herself, to a really miraculous degree complete mistress of her past actions. 'It's all a question of lighting,' she thought, standing in front of the glass and studying the face she saw reflected there – the face, not of the real Thérèse, but of a stranger, the face that had been reflected in his own childlike gaze. She need only, with a single gesture, have swept back her hair, leaving uncovered her brow and temples. Yes, with her own two hands she could, in the space of a second, have effaced that lying image of herself. But now she touched her mouth with lipstick, put powder on her cheeks. As though replying to the comment of some unseen adversary, she said out loud: 'After all, he *is* going to write to her: I made him promise to send a letter. Marie will be happy. ...'

She couldn't *not* have realized the lie she was acting, but now she nestled into it, seeking rest. She felt thirsty and went into the kitchen.

'Not gone to bed yet?'

The room was clean and neat. The copper saucepans, which were never used, shone brightly. She saw Anna sitting there, her elbows on the table, her head between her two clenched fists. Her greasy hair, badly cut and left too long, half hid a face puffy with tears. What was wrong with the girl? Had her boy friend left her in the lurch? Was she ill? Was she, perhaps, in the family way? This was the moment for which Thérèse once had longed when suffering should breach the wall which separated her from Anna, making it possible for her at last to find a way into that squalid little destiny. ... But tonight she averted her gaze, took a glass, swallowed its contents at a single gulp, and left the kitchen without so much as making a single sign of friendship.

On her way through the dining-room she felt suddenly that she had got to stand still for a moment. ... Till now she had forgotten all about her heart, but it was beginning to force itself on her attention. Moving very slowly, leaning on the furniture and against the wall, she reached the drawing-room and sat down, her body held slightly forward. She had forgotten the feel of that terrible hand which seemed to grip her left shoulder, of the pain that spread right through her body, thrusting deep into her breast. In the silence of the night she could hear her own breathing. Her eyes wandered over the walls of her prison. Life had come into it again this evening and still hung poised among the disordered chairs and the smell of tobacco smoke. Life had come back. She did not want to die. The doctor has assured her that if she took only a little ordinary care of herself and avoided all imprudence. ... She repeated to herself what the specialist had said when last she consulted him. The X-ray photographs had not been very distinct – impossible to tell from them what precisely the trouble was. She was seriously ill, of that there could be no doubt. 'But,' he had added, 'one never knows in heart cases.' After all, living the life she did, it ought to be easy for her to take the necessary precautions. But from now on she must not run any risks. The pain began to grow less intense. She wouldn't lie down, but would spend the night sitting in her chair. Marie was still in the train. She must be beyond Orléans by this time. Maybe she was thinking that she had all his love. Well, let her think! It was better so. Thérèse would do everything in her power to make that illusion a reality. Why should she pity Marie? – Marie, who was only seventeen and bursting with health. Seventeen! ... life stretching before her as far as eye could see. ... 'While here am I, already standing at the door of the slaughter-house! ...'

The hour of one sounded from many clocks. The pain had grown dull now; but it was still there. The hand had just perceptibly loosened its hold. She was no longer thinking of Marie, of Georges, of anyone. Her whole attention was concentrated on herself, on the trouble deep-seated there at the very centre of her being, as though by staring it out of countenance she could keep the undisciplined organ within bounds, could still its frantic beating, could check the head-long race, and bring it to a halt upon the very brink of nothingness.

6

ABOUT eleven o'clock one morning, a week after Georges' visit, Thérèse was walking slowly along the street intent on any signs of flats to let. Though the stairs in the old house where at present she was living were far from steep, they called for an effort on her part which could not but be dangerous. The specialist, to whom she had paid a second visit, had expressed it as his opinion that she ought to be somewhere where a lift was available, unless, of course, she could find ground-floor accommodation. That she should be ready to give serious consideration to such a view was, in itself, a considerable step forward. A week ago she would never have entertained the idea of moving.

She was not particularly worried by Georges' silence. Had anyone told her that he wrote her long letters each evening, which he as regularly tore up each morning on rising, she would doubtless have replied: 'That is no news to me.'

In front of the Deux Magots she bought a paper. As she turned round, she saw a face smiling at her, a hand raised in welcome. It was mere foolishness that her heart should beat so, mere foolishness that she should be so much affected by such a casual meeting – especially when, as now, she had been expecting it. She was perfectly well aware why it was that, instead of pursuing her course towards the river, she had turned to the right by Saint-Germain-des-Prés. She threaded her way between the tables. Georges had got up at her approach and, looking, as usual, slightly washed-out, introduced a young man whom she had not at first noticed. 'This is Mondoux, René Mondoux.' Her first impression of his companion was that he was not the figure of fun she had been expecting. True, he was narrow-shouldered and carried himself with a slight stoop, but the eyes which looked out from his childlike face had about them a frankness which made it difficult for her not to avert her own. The effect of them was to make her forget entirely the ready-made suit and the heavy laced boots with their brass 'hooks'. At all costs, she felt, she must make him like her.

From a brief-case stuffed with books he took a magazine the title of which set her mind working hard. She placed him at once as one of those 'high-principled' youths who had often been drawn to her in the past because she had so much the look of being a castaway. But Mondoux replied to her advances with non-committal statements, behaving like a rather crude undergraduate who prides himself on not taking women seriously. Thérèse, by this time thoroughly ill at ease, beat aimlessly about the bush, and found it quite impossible to behave naturally. While Georges was giving signs of that sort of nervous excitement which we most of us show when we have brought two of our best friends together, without any real conviction that they will get on, she began to trot out the kind of remarks which had always, in the past, earned her a reputation for brilliance, only to see them quite blatantly swept aside by Mondoux. Convinced that she had to do with a young man of religious scruples, she touched on the problem of evil and the theory of predestination, subjects with which the most ignorant of women, given a certain degree of cleverness, can embarrass even the elect. 'I hope,' she said, breaking off in the middle of one of her remarks, 'that I am not hurting your feelings?' But scarcely had she put the question than something which Georges let drop made it clear that she was on the wrong track altogether, and that Mondoux's attitude was very different from what she had supposed it to be. She at once retreated from her previous position, assumed a more humble tone, and instinctively sought to win him over by such well-tried tactics as the solemn gaze and the special voice. Since, however, these seemed to have no effect on him, she redoubled her efforts until she was within measurable distance of making a thorough fool of herself. Suddenly she was aware that Georges Filhot was staring fixedly at her. The happiness which had been accumulating in her heart for the past three days burst like a thunder-clap.

Marvels of marvels – he was actually suffering! Only too well did she know the outward symptoms of jealousy. A single glance sufficed to make her aware of them. How many years was it now since she had last been given those unmistakable proofs of a man's love – the pursed lips, the look of anger and reproach in brooding eyes? To answer that question she would have had to take her mind back to the first months of her life in Paris. That this happiness could be hers again was a staggering revelation. The discovery that it was so brought on a slight heart attack. She kept her pale face raised to Mondoux's – either because she wanted to make Georges suffer still more, or in an attempt to master her irregular breathing and check the pain which had begun to spread through the whole of her left side. She looked like an animal sitting there with ears pricked. And a sound it was that had caught her attention, the sound of steps, remorseless steps, deep within her. Death, though by definition a state of nothingness, seemed lodged within her ailing body; and its presence there gave added stature to the joy which, so unexpectedly, had welled from deep privacies: and from that joy it took an additional meed of strength. It was as though, after all these years, love had come to her only to hasten the dissolution of her flesh. No, her exhausted heart could not withstand so heady a draught. Beneath the pressure of this monstrous happiness it would break in pieces.

She turned to Georges.

'Would you mind calling a taxi for me? I am not feeling very well. Please don't dream of coming with me.'

'May I come and see you this evening?'

'Not this evening: tomorrow.'

'I'll just drop in to see how you are.'

She forbade him to do any such thing. She did not want him to see her in the degradation of physical suffering ... and his presence would merely have the effect of making her worse. She must have time in which to pull herself together. It was the suddenness, the surprise, that had got the better of her. By the following evening she would be ready, would have her heart under control. In the taxi she kept on saying to herself, '*I mustn't* die! ...' But was the fact that the boy was capable of jealousy any proof that he loved her? Even supposing that he did, wasn't it more than likely that he had succumbed to one of those illusions of passion which so often afflict the young? It was highly improbable that he would suffer for long because of a worn-out woman who was already more than halfway to the grave. Struggling for breath, she realized the price she would have to pay for the least little strain of excitement imposed upon her heart.

For a short moment, on the landing, she stood quite still. She felt for her key. He might come to see her this evening. Most certainly he would come tomorrow. But would she still be alive tomorrow? She was powerless to keep his face from haunting her. Tomorrow evening he would hang his coat on one of this row of hooks. There was a letter for her on the hall-table. She recognized Marie's handwriting. For the last two hours she had not once thought of Marie. She gazed with a hostile eye at the silly scribble. The elongated envelope, too, was silly; so was the lilac paper, the red ink. The whole thing breathed an air of foolishness. While Anna was taking off her hat and her boots so as to spare her all unnecessary movement, she began to feel ashamed of herself. She did not want any luncheon. She would just sit on the low chair by the fire until the pain had gone. Leaning slightly forward, she remained there, quite alone, holding the envelope in her two hands. Marie's happiness ... Marie was her daughter. ... But what does the tie of blood matter? They were just two women who barely knew one another. It was up to each of them to take her chance. Marie was seventeen and pretty. ... They used to bathe together in the mill-stream, and lie side by side on the parched grass in a world filled with the scraping of grasshoppers – while she, Thérèse, already half-way to dissolution ... Had Marie shown any pity for her mother on that evening when she had forced her to confess her past? Perhaps worst of all had been her utter lack of interest. She had demanded no detail, had made no effort to inquire into the circumstances of what had happened. ... Georges would be more pressing. Thérèse knew full well the meaning of that half-expressed question which he had all but put to her when, just as he was leaving, he had sighed and said, 'I should so much like to know ...' It was in order that he should know that he was coming back. O God! would his visit turn into a cross-examination? Was she to go through all that a third time?

She had deluded herself with the belief that she had actually suffered on that endless evening when her daughter had forced from her lips those broken bits and pieces of admission; that she had sacrificed herself in order that Marie should go back to her father. But the truth of the matter was that she had never truly loved her child. 'I renounced something that was never mine, sacrificed what I did not possess. ...' But how very different it would be if, tomorrow evening, she were to be exposed to another attack, this time from Georges! ... Ah! if that happened, she would lie right enough! ... yet, somehow, it wouldn't be lying, because the Thérèse who, fifteen years back, had deliberately, for week after week, worked out a carefully prepared plan, finding each day the strength to do what she had plotted to do – to commit murder by inches, seemed now an utter stranger, seemed to be some-one who had no connexion whatever with her present self. What was there in common between that crazy creature of the distant past who had made up her mind *not* to count the num-ber of drops of arsenic in her husband's glass and the Thérèse of the here and now? ... what slightest resemblance could those two women have to one another?

How awful it was to be so clear-sighted! If only she could deceive herself. She could see only too plainly that she had done nothing during these past days but poison Marie's happiness! And this time what excuse had she? Of what crime had the girl been guilty save that of running to her for help and seeking comfort in her arms?

The chirping of birds in the ivy of the garden, the cries of children at play during the four o'clock recess, the clip-clop of horses drawing the Bon Marché delivery vans, the hooting and braking of cars slowing to a halt – all the complex of familiar sounds. Death meant no longer hearing that confused rumble, life, sitting here with ears attuned to its long monotony. With one brief act she could achieve the sacrifice of herself, with one brief act she could find atonement, could pronounce sentence on herself, could *crush the reptile*. ... She tore open the envelope, telling herself that she would be guided by what the contents of this unread missive might suggest. Should it convey an order, then she would submit – of that she was determined, no matter how severe it might be.

Papa and granny were nicer than I had expected them to be. They had agreed not to make a hullabaloo about my running away, so as not to get on my nerves. I told them at once about you, and about what you mean to do with your money in the event of my marrying. They didn't say much, but I could feel that they were very favourably impressed. Papa said: 'That, of course, would make things a great deal easier ...' And granny, going out of her way to be beastly, added: 'With such a dowry it would be a shame to marry the grandson of a mere tenant-farmer.'

I didn't say a thing ... I had every reason to be patient. The post had just brought me a letter from Georges. I hadn't expected one so soon, because he hates writing. ... I know whom I ought to thank for *that*. This, mother dear, is where I come to the point, but I don't know how to express what I want to say. ... I'm a stupid creature, and I find myself wondering how you come to have such a little fool for a daughter. It's true, of course, that I'm a Desqueyroux – so that, I suppose, is the explanation! I want to beg your pardon ... but I should hate you to think that I am acting the hypocrite when I say that, or that I'm trying to produce an effect. I've thought a great deal about what passed between us, and I know now that you are a good woman ... that I have never, until now, realized what true goodness meant. I think that we both of us agree with Georges that what happened years ago has been wrongly interpreted. Georges says that you alone have the knowledge which can lead to a genuine understanding of the situation (those are his exact words in the letter he wrote me). How could I possibly doubt you after the way you treated me in spite of my having shown so little understanding and so little compassion ? Thanks to you, I know now what rendering back good for evil means. But my chief feeling for you is admiration. I should admire you, even if Georges didn't, but, as a matter of fact, you made the most extraordinary impression on him – and he is by no means a fool! My happiness is entirely in your hands. That is so patently obvious that you might be excused for thinking that I am writing all this out of sheer self-interest. I only wish you could realize how absolutely sincere I am! After my time with you, I find my surroundings here, both things and people, too utterly *dim*. I just manage to keep myself going by thinking what life will be like with you and Georges. If *they* write about the arrangements you have decided to make in my favour, please say that they depend entirely on my marriage. Granny is perfectly capable of engineering a match more in keeping with her own tastes. She had resigned herself to the Filhots, though she despises them, because we're in such a bad way. But this possible increase in my dowry has revived her ambitions. It must be clearly understood that you are making this sacrifice only that I may be in a position to marry the man of my choice. ...

Thérèse saw again in imagination her daughter as she had looked as she stood on the landing, leaning slightly to one side because of the weight of her suit-case. It was her child who had written this letter which was so overflowing with affection, her child who was dreaming of a life in which all three of them should be together. It was no mirage. The happiness to which she was looking forward was perfectly possible: it, and no other, must be made a reality – for no other was attainable. To what wicked madness had she surrendered during these past few days? She had always believed that the crimes and vices of mankind are due to the undisciplined power which leads people to imagine the impossible, to create a chimera which they feel impelled, at all costs, to embrace. But, this time, she was going to see things 'in their true light'. The phrase had been a favourite one with

Bernard Desqueyroux. In their early days together he had never grown tired of repeating, 'You don't see things in their true light.' She would find the necessary strength to sacrifice the other possibility. But what other possibility, in fact, was there? It has no solid reality at all. She had read an absurd significance into George's irritability when she had pretended to be lost in admiration of Mondoux. If it came to that, was *she* really in love with *him*? She had never definitely asked herself the question. 'Actually, I was in love with his feeling for me.'

To such, much calmer, thoughts did Thérèse give herself as she sat motionless on her low chair through the sunless afternoon, with the pain at her heart already less intense. She conjured up a vision of Georges Filhot as she had seen him for the first time, unshaven, with a cast in his eye, wearing a grubby pullover. She forced herself to see how ordinary he was. It was utterly ridiculous to risk a heart attack for someone who was so much like everybody else! The magnifying and distorting glass which she had so often held between herself and others had suddenly vanished, and she saw him as he really was (and not as he appeared to Marie, to Mondoux, and to Madame Garcin), a thin, overgrown boy, a country lout with a cast in his eye. She felt ashamed, felt annoyed to think that she had attached such value to anyone so hopelessly second-rate. She was on the point of sending off an express-letter telling him not to come. But, on second thoughts, she decided that she must see him for Marie's sake.

At five o'clock Anna closed the shutters and lit the fire. In spite of her new mood, Thérèse could not resist a feeling of happiness at the thought that she would not spend the next evening in loneliness. The knowledge that she was to have a visitor banished all threat of boredom from those long hours of calm reflection. The fever had left her, and the pain. Not now would she tremble in every limb, or lose control of herself at the first sight of a stranger. At last, perhaps, she would creep from her hiding-place and die, not lonely and forlorn, but in Marie's arms.

And so these two days passed in newly won peace of mind.

When, at the appointed hour, she heard Anna open the front-door, her heart was beating no more quickly than usual.

7

HER very first sight of Georges brought a wave of happiness, because he really was the ordinary young man she had been visualizing ever since the evening before. He looked, standing there, as though he were entangled in his overcoat (he always forgot to take it off before coming into the drawing-room), and she noticed once again the mania he had for puffing and mopping his brow in an attempt at once to give himself courage and to show what hard work it was for him to be so punctual.

She had permitted only one lamp to be lit, and it stood on the table behind her. It was, therefore, with the eyes of faith rather than of the body that he now saw the face at which, for hours, he had been longing to gaze. Rather too quickly, in rather too perfunctory a manner, she began at once to talk of Marie. She thanked him for having written to her so promptly.

'I wrote because you asked me to.'

She pretended not to understand, and held out the letter which Marie had sent her. He took it, glanced it over casually, and then raised his eyes to her face. Without paying any attention to his look, she exclaimed:

'What a sensitive creature she is! How keenly she feels things! I can admit now that I never used to credit her with much intelligence. We judge and condemn our children, as a rule, rather crudely, rather too simply, from the things they say, which don't, as often as not, express their thoughts at all. But Marie is very, *very* intelligent. ...' She stressed the repeated *very*.

All the time she was speaking she could feel, beyond any shadow of a doubt, that her words were making him more and more irritated with Marie. How often, in the course of her life, had she put up a show of indifference with the sole intention of persuading the man she loved that she was not thinking of him at all! Not that the manoeuvre had ever done her the slightest good. Her passion had always given itself away, even in the effort she made to conceal it. Today she was behaving like a gambler who increases his stake tenfold at each throw. Realizing this, she broke off in the middle of a sentence (for she was acting in entire good faith) to say:

'I liked your friend Mondoux a lot.'

This she said at random, simply in order to change the subject. Once again she saw that, without meaning to, she had scored a bull's-eye.

'I gathered that you found him sympathetic. But' – he added with a show of annoyance – 'I can't say that your feeling was reciprocated. He didn't begin to understand you.'

'There was nothing *for* him to understand. He saw at once the kind of woman I am – or, rather, the kind of woman I am *not*!'

'That is where you had the advantage of him. You summed him up accurately at first sight, whereas he entirely missed your real, your unique, quality.'

'My unique quality ...'

She left the phrase unfinished, realizing, even as she spoke, that she was giving Georges precisely the opportunity for which he had been waiting, to question her about what had happened at Argelouse fifteen years before, in the gloomy house buried in dark pines. Terrified, she hunted for something to say that would neutralize the effect of her words, but she could find nothing. She felt mentally lucid but completely paralysed. Leaning to the fire in order to avoid his gaze, she knew that, inevitably, the fatal question would come. Once again she was to be subjected to a *cross-examination*. What should she do? Should she say just enough to alienate his sympathy, without, at the same time, giving him any excuse to leave Marie in the lurch? ...

'You most certainly are unique,' he said; 'you are like no one else. That is why I believe you capable ...'

This time she raised her eyes to his and, without any apparent effort, asked a question in her turn:

'Capable, you mean, of anything?'

Georges Filhot blushed furiously:

'You don't know what I was going to say. I believe that you are capable of anything – in a big way. For instance, it would never occur to you to defend yourself against a terrible accusation which you had done nothing to deserve.'

She got up, took a few steps about the room, then came to a standstill, leaning against the wall behind Georges' chair. He did not dare turn his head. In a hard voice she replied that he was free to believe anything he liked. Tremblingly he asked:

'Don't you mind, then, what I think of you?'

'You know perfectly well that it matters to me above all things.'

With an air of nervous hopefulness, he changed his position. He knelt on the seat of the chair and raised his eyes to hers.

'Primarily,' she went on, 'because of Marie.'

He heaved a sigh: 'That I find very surprising' – and added a few words in a tone so low that she could not hear what they were, though they might have been, 'I don't give *that* for Marie!' – though worded, probably, in cruder terms. At that she faced him, summoning up her courage to look him straight in the face. All that she had valued in life, all that had been granted to her by a niggardly fate in a few brief moments of her youth, and was now, she felt, gone for ever – the anguish which she alone could allay, the pain which she alone had caused – all this she saw suddenly revealed in the rather weary eyes now turned to hers. She felt the dread approach of a terrible word which her ailing heart could surely not endure. She longed to stave it off. She forced herself to smile. She said:

'I am not an interesting woman ... you are quite wrong about me. ...'

But even before she had completed the sentence she heard, as it were, the voice of a stranger:

'You are the only person in the world who interests *me*. ...'

She made a movement like someone ducking to avoid a repeated blow. 'That is just silly,' she murmured. 'Why should I interest you?' And then, at last, the anticipated word struck straight to her heart, although she scarcely heard it:

'Because I love you.'

Yes, straight to her heart, so that for a moment she was aware of nothing but sheer physical agony. A spasm passed across her face, which Georges read as an expression of fury.

But she no longer had sufficient strength even to stretch out her hands towards his frightened face. She had no words now in which to protest against the foolish humility of his childish cry:

'You're laughing at me! ... I know that I am repulsive to you!'

She tried to make a movement of denial. Slightly raising her right hand, she touched his tousled hair, pushing it back as she might have done, had he been her son, before kissing him good night. He closed his eyes. He was still kneeling on the chair, his elbows resting on its back. Thérèse's heart was beating less violently now. She drew a deep breath. He spoke again:

'You're ... you're *sorry* for me. ...'

She made no answer, because her voice had failed her, and this involuntary silence served her better than any protest would have done. 'Well, *be* sorry for me, then,' the child before her said. She could do no more than press his head against her shoulder with a gesture that he interpreted as one of pity. And, because the pain had gone, although her position was uncomfortable, she remained quite motionless, conscious that his hair smelt of cheap brilliantine. But in a moment she must free her arms, because the attitude was painful. There, now ... it was over.

Very firmly, she asked Georges to sit down on the low stool. She herself took the arm-chair opposite, though she was careful not to lean back. She had to watch every movement now. She said:

'You know, you're only a child. ...'

'I realize that you will never take me seriously. I had to choose between being despised and being hated. I'm not sure that I shouldn't have preferred ...'

It was Thérèse's gentle smile that made the boy believe that she despised him. But she was thinking of those moments in

her life when she had been ready and eager to hear the words
'I love you', all but seeing them form themselves on another's
lips, only to be withheld at the last moment in obedience to the
prompting of a shabby knowingness. How often, too, had she
not held her own mouth tightly shut in an effort to keep back
the declaration which would have spelled defeat. For the
whole squalid game had consisted in just such mean trickery,
had been controlled by her terror lest the other win back his
presence of mind and grow indifferent. This precocious
schoolboy had, as the saying goes, 'let his heart speak'. 'But,'
thought Thérèse, 'his vision will grow clear and, in a moment,
he will see me as I really am. ...' She got up and took a hurried
glance at the face she saw reflected in the glass above the
chimney-piece. ... A little colour, which owed nothing to
rouge, stained her cheeks. Her eyes were shining. Her fine
brow was unwrinkled. The deeply etched lines from nose to
mouth made her look not old so much as implacable. She saw
herself, in that moment, transfigured by the passion of which
she was the object. What gazed back at her from the depths of
the mirror was her ideal self reflected in the humble look of
this lunatic youth.

She was conscious of a profound sense of calm. There was
something delicious in being able, from so safe a vantage-
point, to taste her triumph. She was about to show herself
defenceless, to give herself away, to stammer those words of
amazement, of gratitude which spring to the lips of women
no longer young when they know themselves to be beloved.
She was on the point of opening this boy's eyes with her own
hands, of being herself the instrument of his disenchantment,
of giving him the sudden spectacle of an ageing, pitiable
woman. But as she stood there, resting her burning hands on
the cool marble, she felt beneath her fingers a few loose sheets
of paper. They were part of Marie's letter which Georges,
after the first hurried glance, had left but partly read.

She closed her eyes and clenched her teeth. She bent above
the sheets covered with foolish scribbling. Marie? Would she
never leave her mother alone? Each must take her chance as it
came. Hadn't Marie herself given this young man into her

hands? She thought Thérèse harmless, and never dreamed that danger could come from *her*. Stupidity of youth that thinks itself alone provocative of love! But love probes deep beneath the covering flesh, feeling for a secrecy of passion, of knowledge and of cunning, for something that may belong even to those who have already lived their lives. At this very moment, perhaps, Marie was lying awake in the great room at Argelouse listening to the ceaseless murmuring of the pines that hedged it in. She was feeling wholly safe, no doubt, because, from now on, Thérèse would be privy to her passion and her life. It was the same room that Thérèse once had occupied, just underneath the one in which Bernard had moaned and groaned. She had lain there listening eagerly to the sounds of his sickness. ... She could murder people now without being near them! Hers was the gift of killing at long range.

She took the sheets one by one in her trembling hands, laid them in order, and slipped them into their envelope. She raised her arms, pressed the palms of her hands against her eyes, turned sharply to where the young man still sat hunched on the low stool which had witnessed her own agony, and said in a low voice through clenched teeth:

'Go away!'

He got up and looked at her with the eyes of a beaten cur. His lips moved. He ought, he supposed, to apologize. She pushed him towards the entry, gave him his overcoat, opened the door. He walked through it backwards, his eyes still fixed on her. The stairs were dark and evil-smelling. The switch was out of order. She said:

'Be careful to hold on to the banisters.' He went down the stairs four at a time, and had already reached the ground-floor when he heard his name called: 'Georges!' It was her voice summoning him back.

He joined her on the landing. She could hear him panting. He walked towards the door, but:

'No,' she said, 'don't come in. I only wanted to say ... it's all true!' The words came with an effort (she was speaking in a hurried whisper). 'I don't know what you may have heard about me, but I want you to realize that I am the sort of person who *cannot be slandered*. ... Won't you say something? Do, at least, make some sign so that I may know you understand.'

But he stood there motionless, leaning against the banisters. Their eyes had grown accustomed to the dark, though neither could make out the features or expression of the other's face. They could see only the body's mass, could hear only a sound of breathing. She recognized the smell of cheap brilliantine, was conscious of the presence there of someone young and warm and alive.

'I had to tell you that,' she whispered; 'now you know.'

The sound came up to them of the street-door opening and then slamming shut. Somebody mentioned a name to the concierge. A flicker of light showed for a brief moment at the foot of the stairs. One of the tenants was striking wax matches to an accompaniment of grumbles, in an effort to light his way up. Thérèse and Georges hurriedly slipped back into the entry. The light was still on in the drawing-room. They blinked, but neither dared look at the other.

'Did you understand what I meant?' she asked.

He shook his head. 'I don't believe you. You are accusing youself simply in order to get rid of me. It's all because of Marie. Well,' he went on in a sudden burst of anger, 'you may as well know that your manoeuvre won't do you the slightest good. I'm not going to marry her. Do you hear what I say? I shall never marry her. ... That's spoiled the effect of your little scene, hasn't it?'

Thérèse, leaning against the bookcase, half closed her eyes and turned away her head, prey to a terrible delight which she did her best to stifle. He was not going to be Marie's husband. Whatever happened now, the girl would never have him. Georges would never belong to her. Thérèse's joy filled her with horror. She longed to fall dead, now, at this moment; longed for the pain that was crushing her breast to be the last before the final pang of dissolution. But nothing in the world could prevent her from feeling the marvellous happiness that wept with the knowledge that it was her he wanted. As soon as she was sufficiently composed to look at him with hard, expressionless eyes, she turned slowly. He was standing in the middle of the floor, his arms hanging, his head bent, his eyes fixed on the ground. He had the furtive look of a dog that has misbehaved.

'That is a matter of regret to me,' she said harshly. 'I hope that you will change your mind, but there is nothing more that I can do. In this matter, at least, I am conscious of being wholly innocent. There is nothing further to be said between us.'

She opened the door and stood back against the wall to let him pass. But he did not move, did not take his eyes from her face. At last he spoke:

'You'd better know ... you'd better realize ... that I can't live without you!'

'Mere words. ...'

She spoke lightly, pretending to attach no importance to his 'I can't live without you!' But, actually, she had understood him well enough. She had knocked about the world too long to be deceived: too long not to recognize the accents of hopeless despair when she heard them. She knew that he meant what he said. His type was familiar to her. She went up to him very gently and, as she had earlier in the evening, drew his head down upon her shoulder. He let the whole weight of it fall on her forearm, so that, in order to see his face, she had to bend her elbow as might a woman looking at her nursling. He did not smile. His eyes were open: the look in them was all but wild. It surprised her to see so many signs of exhaustion in so young a face. The only marks on it were those that told of rough boyhood games, scars, and scratches. The brow was already deeply seamed. But when he closed his eyes the smooth unsullied lids were those of a child.

With sudden energy she freed herself from the brooding fit, made him sit down in the arm-chair, pulled up the low stool, and forced herself to speak sensibly to him. She was, she said, an old woman with nothing to offer him. The best proof of affection that she could give was to turn him from so sad a piece of human wreckage as herself, from a creature for whom the future held no hope.

All the time that she was speaking she was deliberately

pushing back the hair which she wore low over her exaggeratedly high forehead, leaving her ears exposed. This she did with a careless air, though only at the cost of an heroic effort. It surprised her to find that the effect upon him was not immediately noticeable – so hard is it for us to understand that love often takes no account of appearances, that the white hairs which we are at such pains to hide from the lover's gaze would not displease, but might move him to a show of tenderness, were he to see them. But he never does see them. The woman whom Georges was devouring with his eyes was no worn and broken creature, but someone invisible to all but himself, to be glimpsed in a moment's look, heard in that rather hoarse voice of hers, each word of which had for him a quite extraordinary value and importance. In vain did she display before his young and ardent gaze her high, denuded brow. It was his privilege to see her freed from time's tyranny, liberated from the prison of her flesh. No matter how guilty our passion, it always sees through to the spirit's mystery. A life may have been dragged in the filth of the gutter but not for a single moment can that fact lessen the splendour which is seen by the eyes of love.

And so it was that Thérèse, try as she might to break down his poor defences, was amazed to find that the passion in the eyes that would not leave her face showed no signs of growing less intense. Had he the faintest realization of how much effort each word this woman spoke had cost her? She longed by every means in her power to mask the gulf of age between them, to hide her own sure knowledge that, whatever happened, this love of theirs was condemned to die – and that almost at once. Yet it was on those very facts of age and death that she forced her mind to dwell, striving to make him realize the truth. 'You are twenty,' she kept on saying, 'and I am over forty' (even now she could not bring herself to mention her exact age). 'What can you possibly hope of me? One night would be enough to dissipate the fantasy you have created. ...'

He protested that he was no longer twenty: 'I am twenty-two. Besides, have you forgotten what you said that day you came to see me in my room? It was *you* who came to *me*, don't forget that, not I who sought you out. ... You said' – he shut his eyes the better to draw up from his memory the exact words she had used on that occasion – 'don't you remember? ... I was stupidly boasting that I was *only* twenty-two, and you replied: "It would be truer to say you are *already* twenty-two." And then you added a terrible phrase, terrible for me, because it suddenly made me see clearly something from which I had been vaguely suffering ever since I first began to grow up: "As soon as one starts on a journey, it is as though one had reached its end." ...'

'What a memory you have! ...'

Thérèse was laughing. But what would she not have given never to have spoken those words! Georges shook his head:

'I have a memory only for what concerns you. But that is so keen and so retentive that in the horrible boredom to which I have become a prey ever since I first set eyes on you my only real distraction has been to recapture and chew over everything, no matter how trivial, that I have heard you say. I can think indefinitely about any one of your sentences. Between the moment when it came new-minted to my ears, and that when it seems to lose all meaning for me, whole hours, whole days, may pass. ... But that particular phrase has never ceased to take on greater precision in my mind ... to start on a journey is to reach its end. Why, then, set my age against yours? What is the difference between two people like ourselves who have started on their pilgrimage together? ... My youth – so much water flowing through my fingers, so much sand I am incapable of grasping. ... It is only a seeming source of strength, a false freshness, to which the few people who claim to love me have attached importance. ... For the real me, for the only part of me that will remain in a few years' time, they don't care a rap – not even Mondoux, who, as a matter of fact, thinks me a bit of a fool. He says: "The animal is the only part of you that I find really interesting." ...'

Thérèse laid a hand on the boy's knee. She was trying to find the necessary word in which to answer him, as though somewhere there existed an antidote to the poison of what he had remembered. She said the first things that came into her mind – that youth, as he realized, was, in itself, nothing at all: that the only thing that mattered was to find some reason for continuing to live. All men, be they noble or degraded, have some private reason of their own. Among his own friends there must be some who were fervent for God, for the King, for the working class, for this, that, and the other – or, quite simply, for sport. How many young men and women today found occupation for their minds in the culture of their bodies. ...

She spoke eagerly, while Georges shrugged his shoulders and shook his head.

'No, the really necessary thing – you said it yourself one evening ...' And, as Thérèse, with a sigh, muttered, 'Is there something *else* I said?' he added: 'Don't you remember, that evening when I first got to know you properly? ... after I'd taken Marie to the station and plucked up courage to come back here. You were wonderful. You said' (and he gave her back her statement almost word for word) 'that what is really necessary is that life with the person one loves should be one long siesta in the sun, an endless state of relaxation – an animal quietude – with the certain knowledge that *someone* is there within touching distance, accepting life and fulfilled, sharing with us the feeling that we want to be just there and nowhere else in the world. And all about us there must be such heat that the mind is drugged, so that all thought of treachery becomes impossible. ...'

'Those were just empty words, my poor boy; the sort of thing one says to fill an awkward gap. You must realize that sentiments like that have no relation to reality. Love is not the whole of life ... not for men, at least. ...'

She developed the theme at length. But had she talked on until dawn the sound good sense which she preached, from a feeling of duty and not without effort, would have made no impression whatever on his mind. Probably he did not even hear it, but retained only so much of what she said as would nourish his despair. She could furnish him with matter for despair, and with nothing else. That was why, almost without meaning to, she led her discourse into just those paths he craved. As she enumerated all the reasons which might lead a young man of twenty to be in love with life, her voice, by degrees, took on the tones of irony. Hearing her speak thus, he paid attention, showing her a face at once hungry and sad. His teeth flashed between half-parted lips. 'There are always politics ...' she said, and went on to say that the essential thing was not to be the kind of person who was for ever occupied in watching the movements of his own sensibility. Such people, more often than not, were ashamed of their weakness. They pretended to take an interest in what stimulated those among whom they lived. They hid, as though it were some shameful scar, the panic terror and despairing tenderness which the thought of one, sole human creature rouse in them – despairing, because for them all possession must be an illusion, must slip through their fingers at the very moment of fruition. Not a minute could pass but they tormented themselves with wondering whether they were still beloved, whether the passion they inspired had not already shown signs of weakening.

Of all this she spoke as though the person she were really trying to persuade was herself.

'It is a bad thing, isn't it, to re-read old letters? Much better tear them up without looking at them again, because they prove only that what once existed exists no longer. Even when all goes well, he who maintains that he loved us can always, in the long run, do without our company, because he is absorbed in other interests, in business or in family affairs. ... The most we can hope for is a little charity. We can expect no more than the drop of water which the rich man in hell once asked of Lazarus. And not even that, for almost always it is the beloved who is the poor man, caught up in glory, maybe, but stripped of all possessions, having nothing to give even though we may be burning in the flame of our desire. ... Oh, Georges, I am talking a lot of nonsense! My words are without meaning, or what meaning they have is for me alone ... Don't look at me so wildly!'

She got up and moved behind the low stool on which he was

sitting, and covered his eyes with her two hands. He seized and held them in his own. The thought came to her – how old her hands were, and worn, marked with faint blotches. He was seeing them so, now at this moment. But, doubtless, seeing them, he loved them as he loved everything that was a part of her. He pressed his lips to the palms, to the wrists. She made no effort to withdraw them, but thought of the words she had not been able to keep herself from uttering, the words that he would con over endlessly in his heart. In a low voice she said:

'I am poisoning you.'

Scarcely had she spoken the words than she felt her cheeks flame. He did not move, but continued to hold her small, stained hands against his mouth. But a faint tremor told her that the sentence had gone home. That way, she told herself, safety might lie. She must press on along that road in the hope that he, at least, might find salvation. Marie was lost because of what she, Thérèse, had done: but Georges might still be saved. Without consideration she said again:

'Yes, I am poisoning you ... as I have poisoned others.'

'I understood what you meant, Thérèse,' he replied in tones of mockery (using her Christian name for the first time, investing it with a shy tenderness) – 'I understood ... you needn't insist.'

More passionately than before he pressed his lips against the hands he still held prisoner. They could hear Anna busying herself in the bedroom. Then came the sound of the kitchen door being closed, and they knew that they were alone in the flat. The house was wrapped in sleep: the noises of the street had dwindled. A flicker of flame was reflected from the glass-fronted bookcase which she had brought from Argelouse. On the marble of the mantelpiece the violet envelope showed clear, on which, in scarlet ink, Marie had written – *Madame Desqueyroux, rue du Bac*. She could not take her eyes from it. Like a swimmer who, in order to recover his breath, lies face upward on the water, she floated motionless, feeling his mouth against her hands. She neither stirred nor gave the faintest sign of acquiescence.

'Don't you believe me?' she asked in a voice that revealed her irritation.

Without any show of violence, she freed her arms, which he was trying hard to keep imprisoned, and moved away from him. They were, both of them, on their feet now, taking each other's measure with their eyes. His smile, at once incredulous and fearful, exasperated her. When he said, 'Deep in your heart you hate me ...' she replied:

'I hate you because you don't want to believe me. You are like all the other fools at Argelouse: you think of my crime as they did. Your imagination will not face the fact that I could commit so dark a deed. You can't understand that it ranks as small compared to what I have been accomplishing here, before your eyes, ever since I came into your life. You are the true son of those country folk who think themselves innocent so long as they have not actually compassed the death of another human being. You have got to realize that all through one winter I dropped arsenic regularly into the cup of a man whose captive I was more completely than if I had been locked into a cell with stone walls. ... But that is an old story. Today it is Marie, it is you, who are my victims – though you believe you love me. ...' She had looked away while she was speaking, but now turned her eyes to him again before continuing: '... or, rather, did believe so for a few short days. ... But that is all over now, isn't it?'

Seeing him shrug his shoulders:

'What does that mean?' she asked in accents of annoyance. 'What are you trying to imply? – that I did not do what I say I did! It was evil, but nothing like so evil as my later crimes. They were more cowardly and more secret. With them I took no risks. I ask you once again, haven't you seen what I've been trying to say ever since we first met? You shake your head. Does that signify that you don't know what I mean?'

He was leaning against the wall, staring at her.

'Georges, why are you looking at me like that? ... I am not a monster. You, too, have been guilty ... you would realize it if you took the trouble to search your conscience – and you would not have to search for long. ... I don't mean that you ever gave anyone an overdose of medicine in an attempt to get rid of them ... but there are other ways so many other ways, of pushing people aside!' Then, in something like a whisper: 'How many have you thrown neck and crop out of your life?'

The boy's lips moved, but no words came. She had moved close to him and he could not avoid her approach.

'I am not thinking only of women ... but of those secret episodes ... such as we all have in our lives ... episodes which date back sometimes to the days of childhood.'

'How did you know that?' he asked.

She laughed happily: she was satisfied. In a gentler voice she said, 'Tell me about it,' but he shook his head.

'I can't.'

'There is nothing you can't tell me. ...'

'It isn't that you make me feel ashamed ... it is only that it's all too difficult to explain – can't *be* explained. ... It never entered my mind to tell anyone, because they would have laughed in my face. The whole thing was so frightfully unimportant, actually.'

Still looking at him, she pressed her point: 'All the same, try. If you break down – well, it can't be helped ... I'm here; I'll do what I can to make it easier. ... Come along, now. ...'

They were still standing, facing one another, Georges leaning, as before, against the wall.

'It was when I was at school,' he began in a low voice: 'I was fourteen, and in the third form. One of my companions was a boy who came from a town some distance off, a boarder who never left the school grounds, a grubby, ill-kempt little fellow, though he was what we used to call a "good-looker". He had a sort of passion for me. At that time I was an extremely sensitive kid, and generally held to be very good-natured, though, in fact, my temperament was fundamentally arid. I did nothing to keep him at arm's length. I allowed him to play a prominent part in my school life – not out of friendship, but from sheer indifference. So far as I was concerned, he was just one intimate among many, though rather more of a sticker than most. Finally, he got permission from

his parents and from the Superior to spend his half-holidays
with me (my people had a *pied-à-terre* in Bordeaux where they
lived for the greater part of each year while I was at school).
I never thought that a boy who kept himself so remote from
the rough and tumble of every day would succeed in persuading the authorities to make the necessary concession, and
I think he brought it off only because he was so good, so
clean-minded, and so pious. It was believed that he might
have a salutary effect on me – because I was already suspected
of holding unsound views. Though I had backed him up
when he applied for leave, I was secretly rather disappointed
when I saw him running towards me one morning, grinning
all over his face, with news of his victory. I pretended to share
his pleasure, but from that day on he had to put up with a
good deal from my black moods. What I couldn't forgive
was the fact that he had trespassed on that world of "home"
which I regarded as sacred. Besides, I found his affection
excessive, absurd, embarrassing. I made him realize that I
resented it. I think his unhappiest moments were on those
Thursdays and Sundays when, after the midday meal, we
drove him back to school in the car through the gloomy,
stifling, dusty streets. ...'

Georges broke off, passed his hand over his eyes, and looked
at Thérèse.

'You see, it's really all about nothing, as I told you it would
be.'

'I don't agree; go on.'

'You'll realize in a moment,' he continued hastily, 'how
utterly trivial the whole story is. You're in for a big disappointment. Just after the Easter holidays he told me that, the
following October, he was going to a school near London.
It must have been perfectly obvious to him that I felt no
emotion whatever at his news. "Perhaps we shall never meet
again," he said. I really daren't tell you what I answered ...
and that, I think, is about all,' he finished up, after a brief
silence.

'No,' said Thérèse, 'that is not all.'

With complete docility he continued:

'The sadder I felt him to be, the more irritable and unsympathetic did I become, and so things went on until Prize Day. That was our last chance of saying good-bye, and when the ceremony was over he seemed very anxious that his mother should come and thank mine. What feeling was it that urged me to act as I did? I didn't *want* the two mothers to meet. Our friendship was a closed chapter. There was no point in opening the book again. I can see myself now, dragging my mother away at top speed. The crowd had scattered through the park. The grass beneath our feet was bruised and bent. The orchestra was playing underneath the trees, and the July morning was already very hot. I could hear behind me a breathless shout – "Georges! Georges!" Because he was with *his* mother, he couldn't run after us, or hadn't sufficient courage to make the attempt (he knew well enough that I had seen them), and he must have known that I had heard his cry of "Georges! Georges!" ...'

'And the cry still echoes in your ears – is that it?' said Thérèse.

He looked at her without replying, and there was distress in his eyes. She asked:

'Did he ever write to you?'

He nodded his head.

'And did you answer his letters?'

In a low voice he said, 'No' – after which they were both of them silent until Thérèse put a further question.

'What happened to him?' And then, seeing that the boy lowered his eyes: 'Is he dead?'

'Yes,' he answered, and the words came quickly. 'He died in Morocco. He had enlisted. ... It is no use my saying that his action had nothing whatever to do with my behaviour. I have found out since that after he got back from England he led a terrible existence. ... I don't know why I have told you all this. ...'

He stood there without moving, staring into space. What he heard was not the sound of cars in the rainy Paris evening, but a childish voice crying to him beneath the trees of a park, as it had been doing all these years.

Thérèse seemed suddenly to come awake, as though the pain which she had brought to the surface had struck at her as well as at him.

'My dear boy, what you have recalled is, in itself, nothing, less than nothing.' And then (as he shook his head): 'You said so yourself, Georges – nothing at all.'

He groaned: 'You've made me feel awful!' She stretched out her arms, tried to draw him to her, but he broke violently from her touch. It was then she realized that she had lost him.

She had sat down again on the low stool, and now, with a mechanical gesture, pushed back the hair from the forehead that was so much too high, disclosing her large, pale ears. But this time the action was not deliberate, which may have been why Georges saw her at last as she really was – a woman whose face was terrible, a woman with old hands which, fifteen years before, had tried to dole out death, and, but a brief moment ago, had held him tight. But even now he could not believe his eyes. He rejected the apparent in an attempt to find the unknown truth of her who had laid this spell on him. This was she – the same now as she had ever been – and yet, not she, but a woman to whose self-exculpatory words he was so stupidly listening. No, she had never willingly done him harm, nor ever would. She had struggled, she said, and would go on struggling until her latest breath. As often as had been necessary, as often as would be, she had climbed and still would climb the steep slope, only to fall once more to the bottom, as though she had nothing else left in all the world to do; would drag herself out of the depths and then slip again to the bottom, and so on indefinitely, caught in the same weary process. For years she had not realized that this was to be the rhythm of her destiny, but now she had come through the dark night and could see her way clearly.

She sat there, her hands clasped about her knees. She did not look up. She heard him say:

'I wish there was something I could do for you.'

That, she thought, might be just a conventional phrase, something said before he took to his heels and ran. But he repeated it, and there was a note of passion in his voice.

'I wish there was something I could do for you.'

He felt sure that she would reply, 'There is nothing you can do.' He would be free then to escape from this room, from this nightmare: his life would once more be as it had been before they met. ... He would be back in his own little room, and it would be too late to put a record on the gramophone because of the neighbours. ... What would there be to think about when he could no longer think of her? ...

Tonight, all of a sudden, she had become somebody quite different from the woman who had exercised such fascination on him from the first moment of their meeting. She had become like the woman they talked about at Argelouse, and her evil spell had, but a while back, been laid on him. He remembered something she had said – as he remembered every word that she had uttered in his presence – to the effect that one can make the most contrary judgements about the same person, and yet be right – that it is all a question of the way the light falls, and that no one form of lighting is more revealing than another. ... But was it the real Thérèse, this sinister being who had taken sudden shape before his eyes like an illustration in some anthropometric textbook?

He said, a third time: 'I am tormented by the thought that I can do nothing for you.' But the truth was that he was thinking only of escape, of finding himself back in his little room where he would undress without turning on the light (because, when his shutters were open, the electric sign over the front-door provided illumination enough). He let the curtain fall upon her face. It could not be hers, nor hers the frightened voice which broke so suddenly upon the silence.

'There is something you *can* do for me ... something very easy, something which is well within your power. But you won't do it.'

He protested with a passion that was not make-believe. He stood before her while she, still on the low seat, mechanically pushed back the hair from her forehead. He turned away his eyes. No, she went on, she would say no more. What was the use of talking? With a supreme effort he flung himself on his knees, so that their eyes met on the same level. He saw her now at close range, could examine, as through a magnifying-glass, the flesh which time had scored and wasted. Her gaze was as lovely as he had ever known it, but round the eyes that had so often set him dreaming he now could see a world of ruin which he had never previously suspected – the burned-up environs of a dead sea.

'If you really want ... yes, it concerns Marie,' she went on hesitatingly. 'Don't be frightened: I am not asking you to commit yourself, but only to wait, to do nothing that might compromise the future, to let time do its work. You know me well enough by this time. I am not one of those mothers who long to see their daughters "settled", nor even the sort of woman who humbles herself so that her child's happiness may be assured – for what likelihood is there that you will ever make her happy? No, it is for myself now that I beg and pray ... not for Marie.'

Eagerly, burningly, she pressed her point. He was the only person who could vanquish that power in her which made for destruction, that gift which found expression without any conscious willing on her part, the terrible virtue which proceeded from her. He saw that her eyes were full of tears; he heard the muted murmur of her voice. 'Yes, I *do* understand,' he stammered ... 'and I will promise. ...' If there was one person in all the world whom, at this moment, he fiercely wished never to see again, it was her daughter, Thérèse's daughter! ... the incarnation of everything he most desired to flee from. But he said again: 'Don't worry about Marie.' How could he have resisted a supplication so formed, so uttered?

'It ties you to nothing. ... But I still feel that if only you have patience ... What really matters to you (I know you so well my poor boy) is not loving but being loved. You need some woman to take you in her charge: yes, to cherish you at those moments – and they will be many – when passion for another will set you beside yourself. ... You see, I am not even suggesting that you should be faithful. ... Do you think that Marie is not ready to take whatever blows you may shower on her, even before they come? That is not what matters. What matters is that you should be part of her life and that you should stay in it for ever.'

She was too close to him. He could feel her breath on his face as she spoke. When she seized his hands he made a gesture of assent. He was on his feet now, head bent, eager to be gone, it seemed. And now it was Thérèse who, at pains to thank him, and longing for renewed assurances, kept him back upon the very threshold. When next she spoke it was to say (and her words sounded like an order and a prayer):

'You will forget that silly schoolboy story, won't you?'

'D'you think that likely?' he retorted, and smiled a mysterious smile. He put his hand on the door-knob, but she called him back again:

'Choose some book from my shelves – any book you like – and keep it.'

'Oh, books!'

He shrugged, still smiling. Now, at this moment, Thérèse was too far gone in exhaustion to feel for him anything that resembled love or even tenderness. Waves of pain began to spread all through her left side, killing remorse. She was going to pay dearly for this evening which had come hard on the heels of so many others! 'What a poor, mad creature I am!' What a good thing that incidents of this kind worked themselves out with no one by to witness them. At least, there would be no one to talk about them. But she had accomplished what she had set out to do. ... And yet, was she so sure of that? Once more she took his two hands in her and gazed into his eyes. 'You won't go out of Marie's life – you'll stay there, won't you? ... remember, you've promised. ...' She urged her case with passion.

'Until death ...'

Her mind at rest, Thérèse closed the door, went back to the drawing-room, stood for a moment motionless; then, on a sudden impulse, opened the window and leaned out into the dank darkness. But the balconies of the floors beneath hid the pavement. She could not see Georges Filhot. She heard the sound of steps receding which might be his.

8

SHE must not dream of lying down. She remained sitting in a chair, her head supported by cushions, her eyes wide open in the darkness, her whole attention concentrated on getting her breath. It was the quietest hour of all the night. The tiniest sigh, she thought, of pain or joy would make itself heard, would suffice to trouble the silence of the world. Gradually she recovered her breath, like a dancer leaning against the scenery in the entr'acte. A pause had come in the drama: never again would she be caught up in the action of the stage.

How impossible to imagine that this silence of the night-time was composed of a thousand agonies and embraces! She believed herself to be at peace, when, actually, she was but standing aside from the game of life. But the game was going on elsewhere, though she might not know it. He whose steps she had heard moving away down the deserted street was now, perhaps, like her, courting sleep. On the other hand, he might have gone somewhere else for comfort. She did not ask herself the question, though it was of him only that she thought.

How had he been dressed this evening? He had no taste in clothes. She tried to remember the colour of his tie (it was never pulled tight enough round his low collar). She saw again in memory the expression on his face when he had sat there supporting his head on her arm. To look at him she had bent her elbow as a mother does who smiles down at her baby. He had not smiled back at her, but had stared at her with a dark fixity. She had noticed then that his left eye was 'a bit askew', as they said at Argelouse. Why was she reminded of the beard which had already begun to show like a smudge upon his chin? ... She had it now – it had made her think of a photograph in *L'Illustration* of the corpse of a young Spanish anarchist shot by carabineers. ... She thought how even now Georges might have been here at her side, without risk, without guilt. Her pain was too acute. Her ailing heart would have spared her the necessity of going through the trivial ritual of love. He could have slept like a child beside her.

When children have bad dreams their mothers often take them in their arms. And she, protected by the torment of her body, with the threat of death for ever in her breast, could have fed in peace upon the sense of a human presence, and none to see. Even he, with her eyes upon him, would not really have been there at all, for sleep is a kind of absence. One last vigil, one last joy ... a strange joy, which none but she could have understood. ... Why had she been in such a hurry to cast him forth into the night? The circumstances which might have made that joy a moment possible might never occur again ... never!

The physical anguish was growing less. She could breathe now more easily, and began to slip further and further into a world which was filled with the things and people of an earlier day. But Georges Filhot had no place in it. She saw herself dining with her husband in the flat on the Île Saint-Louis where she had lived for several years, into which, in strict fact, he had never penetrated. Marie was seated between them, grown already into a young woman. Thérèse wanted to leave the table unnoticed by either Bernard or Marie, but Anna, coming round with the wine, made a sign to her not to move. All the same, there was something urgent – though what it was she did not know – that she had to do: she must go out. ....

She woke with a start. She thought it was the morning, but had scarcely switched on her lamp when she saw that she had been asleep for less than an hour. Once again she plunged the room into darkness. The knowledge that she would not sleep had no power to frighten her. It would be marvellous just to lie there thinking of Georges. There, at least, in the secret kingdom of her imagination, adorned with its patient inventions, she was wronging no one, poisoning no one. 'But he belongs to me no longer,' she thought; 'he belongs to Marie ...!' From now on she forced herself not to separate them in her thoughts, but to evoke them as a constant couple. She struggled hard against an obscure sense of shame.

With bitter joy, with the pleasure that comes of biting on an aching tooth, she concentrated her mind upon their merged and wedded images. No night could ever be too long for her to live in imagination their sweet and simple days of married life, seeing the children they would have, the sorrows they would share till death should come, into which one must be the first to enter so that the other need not fear to follow into the eternal sleep. Thérèse had always had the faculty of conjuring up with exactitude a life that never would be hers. She believed that the sublime splendour of ordinary existence was hidden from those who lived embedded in it, that for them the bread of every day must lose its savour. Only hearts like hers, fated to bear an infinite frustration, could feed on its intolerable absence.

'Not merely for an hour or for a day, but each night of one's life,' she thought, 'to lean one's head on a responsive shoulder, to sleep within the arms of love, not on the fading meeting-ground of dreams, but night after night till death draws near – is not that the happy destiny of most created beings? Marie will know that happiness, and Georges will know it too. I shall have given to them what I have never had myself, set on their heads a crown which it has never been for me to wear. What matters whether it be in Paris or at Argelouse? I will tell Georges ... I will tell him. ... But he is not in love with Marie' – she spoke the words in a half-whisper – 'he is merely resigned. ... But why is he resigned? Not now because of love, not even because he pities me. ... To keep his word, perhaps? ... So many men are like that. They think that at all costs they must keep their word....'

Sitting there, her eyes wide open, she trembled at the thought that once again she had done all that was needful to ensure for Georges and for Marie a lifetime of extreme unhappiness. Her instinct was always sure when it was a matter of sending others to hell! She tried to find excuses for herself. 'It's not really as bad as that. For Marie I have no fears. She will have the one thing without which her life would cease to mean anything at all – Georges' presence ... even though he may cause her abominable torments. Women, when they have been left forlorn, always remember with delight the pain that they have suffered. Evil for them is one thing only, the loved one's absence, absence unlit by any hope of eventual return – that is the one horror for which there is no cure. ...' But what of Georges? ... Georges forced by her into a path the mere thought of which filled him with loathing?

Her eyes had grown accustomed to the dark. She could see the shape of the wardrobe, the solid bulk of the arm-chair, and that vague glimmer on discarded clothes which seeped through the slats of the Venetian blind but was not the dawn. It would be a long time yet before the rumble of traffic would begin. 'Georges ... Georges ...!' she said over and over to herself, and the pain of the word struck deep. ... But surely, surely ... Marie would be necessary to Georges. She felt certain of it, knowing him as she did. Could she have known him better if she had borne him in her womb, brought him into the world, nursed him at her breast, and seen his slow waking to the consciousness of life? ... He was one of those boys who forever crave attention with a sickly urgency, who cannot for a single moment be forgetful of themselves. ... It was only necessary to see the way he was for ever touching his nose, his lips, his cheeks – one of those whose gaze is ever inwards, who watch themselves growing older minute by minute and ripening for death. No, there could be nothing for him, no other hope, but Marie's love. An evil it might be, but the least of many evils. Actually, he had put up the weakest of struggles. Quite suddenly he had surrendered – too quickly to please Thérèse, who would have found resistance sweet in him! But no, he had promised, without apparent effort, to stay true to Marie. There had been something almost unbelievable in his docility. On the very threshold of the door he had renewed his promise. How had he phrased it? She tried to remember, but at first could not, though she was certain that the words would come back to her, so striking had she found them. 'He said – ah yes, I've got it now – he said (and it was more simply worded, far less solemnly than I should have expected) ... he said, "*As long as I live. ...*" '

Nothing very strange in those words when one came to think of it. Why, then, had they impressed themselves with such vividness upon her that they were now deeply etched into the very fabric of her mind? She could almost hear his voice, the particular note that it had sounded as he spoke them: *As long as I live*. ... Obviously, when he had ceased to live ... How ridiculous to have parted on a phrase like that! He had flung it at her with no other intention than to give added weight to his promise. He had meant that nothing short of death should ever release him from it. 'No!' she groaned. 'No! No!' She was saying 'No' to the thought that *would* come, the thought she fain would drive away, the senseless fear which was born of her flesh, an agony as yet dull and not fully formed, but which would grow, she felt sure of that, would invade her being, possess her utterly. No, there *could* be no threat in that one short sentence: those five little words could have no other hidden meaning. There was nothing for her to discover behind their immediate message: *as long as I live*. ... Leave well alone, then: so long as he was alive Marie would not be abandoned. So long as he was alive Thérèse's mind could be at rest about her daughter's destiny. ... Must she go on all night repeating that *so long as I live*, turning it over and over in her mind till she went mad? She tried to calm her fears. 'Suppose, taking things at their worst, that he *did* mean the words to convey a hidden threat – I need only drop him a line this morning telling him not to consider himself engaged ... or, no, better still, I'll go to see him.'

She got up, shivering, opened the window, and pushed back the shutters. It was raining. The thin dawn light was reflected back from the roofs. A footstep echoed in the empty street, as Georges' had done last night. ... Why had she not run after him? Too early as yet to get up for good, to go to his hotel. They would think she was mad. Impossible to call there before eight o'clock. Two hours to wait. She wrapped herself in a dressing-gown, went into the drawing-room, and switched on the light. The room sprang suddenly into existence, looking just as Georges had left it. She stared at the arm-chair in which he had knelt, closed her eyes, and seemed to recapture, mixed with the reek of stale tobacco, the smell of cheap brilliantine. No, she would not open the window or throw back the shutters. She wanted to breathe in every scrap and atom of that smell. She was afraid to disturb the spectacle of untidy muddle. It was a proof, or so she felt, that Georges was still alive. The fire to which he had stretched out his legs was still smouldering. Yes, he was alive. Everything might have happened for her as for another woman. She might have found herself at this same hour, in this same place, having got up cautiously so as not to wake him; might have heard his breathing through the half-open door. But she had willed to send him to his doom: had destroyed him beyond recall. In a short while now she would see him again at his hotel, but it would be beyond his power to recreate the mirage. Never again would she be in his eyes the woman whom, for a few short days, he had needed as a bastion against death. He knew her now, knew the genuine Thérèse. She threw her mind forward, seeing in imagination just how he would look when she entered his hotel bedroom. ... Ah, but, at least, it would be the look of a living man! That he should be alive was all that mattered! What had she thought? What had she been rash enough to think? What idiocy? No, she would not any longer yield to such temptation.

She threw the window wide open, sat down in the armchair on which, a few hours earlier, Georges had knelt, and, wrapping herself in a blanket, put her bare feet on the low stool. That *so long as I live* seemed now quite harmless to her. She was amazed to think that she could ever have suspected it of concealing the least little threat. A damp gust set the cigarette ash on the table swirling.

She was awakened by Anna, who asked no questions.

'I couldn't sleep lying down,' said Thérèse nervously.

The maid's face was a blank. That girl was a bit of a problem, too! ... Nine o'clock already! – perhaps by this time Georges would have gone out – better not run any risk of meeting him. She would merely knock at his door, and then, when there was no answer, open it just long enough to see the unmade bed. Or perhaps she had better leave a note on the table, telling him not to consider himself engaged, telling him that he was a free man. She scribbled it there and then, and dressed in a hurry, feeling a wreck, but forcing herself to get the better of her weakness. Time enough to die of exhaustion when she should have found out that Georges was still alive. She told the taxi-driver to take her to the Hôtel du chemin de fer de l'Ouest. Once there, her fears would be set at rest. Nevertheless, she deliberately imagined the worst simply to prevent the worst from happening. She conjured up a picture of the hotel in an uproar. 'Want to see Monsieur Filhot? Don't you know what occurred last night? ... The people in the next room heard a dull bang ... didn't realize what it was. ...' She could distinctly hear the manageress saying: 'Would you like to see him? ... You wouldn't notice any change. ...' Or perhaps they might say: 'He went out at seven o'clock ... Said good morning just as he always did. ... We never dreamed he'd be brought back ...' Thérèse shook her head and drew a deep breath. From now on she could be at peace. What she had just imagined in such detail had no real existence. She had no gift of prophecy, and the ways of destiny are always unexpected.

The hotel seemed quiet. Georges' window was open, but the shutters were closed. There was no one in the passage, no one on the stairs. She climbed them quickly. She would pay dearly for the effort later on. Someone was humming behind the closed door. ... It must be he! No, the sound was coming from the next room. All the same, she thought that she could hear him breathing. She knocked, then listened, and knocked again. The room was empty: the bed had not been slept in. There was a stale smell as though the place had not been aired since the previous day, the kind of smell that one always finds in hotels of that class – a mixture of dirty sheets and dirty clothes. She closed the door. Why get into a state? He had probably gone out early, and they had 'done' his room already. She could easily find that out at the desk. Even if they told her that he had not come back at all last night, what was there so unusual in that?

Seated on the bed, and leaning slightly forward, she followed with her eyes the pattern of the artificial linoleum. Here he had lived and suffered: here each morning he had set his bare feet. On the bed-table lay some stencilled law-notes.

Above the bed was the picture of a young girl with a plump face, cut from a Movie magazine. Another one of the same girl in a swim-suit. What a large part cinema stars play in the lives of the young men of the present day ... women who give themselves to their adorers by camera-proxy only! ... She straightened her back. There on the wall, like a black target, she could see a gramophone record still hanging. There were a few cheap books on a row of shelves.

(How contemptuously, last night, he had exclaimed, 'Oh, books!') And then, suddenly, she became aware of an oblong of white paper, laid on the table where it could be easily seen. She took it in trembling fingers and held it close to her face. The handwriting was neat and very legible, but she found great difficulty in reading it.

I waited for you in vain this morning at the Deux Magots. They tell me here you haven't been back since yesterday evening. ... You dirty old dog! When you *do* return, come over to the Capoulade. I shall be there till two.

She understood: it was Mondoux. ... No use inquiring at the desk. Georges had been out all night. But Mondoux did not seem to be particularly surprised. She breathed again. Yes, to Mondoux his friend's absence was, apparently, perfectly natural. At any moment now Georges might turn up. She would wait. ... 'As though it were the easiest thing in the world!' ... she murmured with a sigh.

The morning stream of cabs and buses was setting in towards the station. She went over to the window. It had stopped raining. Some workmen were buried to the waist in an excavation at the bottom of which a black drain-pipe had been disinterred. The mechanism of daily life was working at full speed under the watchful eye of a traffic policeman. No use trying to check it. One could kill only oneself. But one could drive others to suicide. ... 'If Georges has killed himself, it's I who should be arrested and put in prison. ... I'm going mad!' She shut the window, went back to the bed, and sat down again, acutely conscious of the sound of steps, voices, bells. If only it were he! A door slammed on the floor below, somebody stopped humming on the other side of the wall. She could hear the strange noises which come from drainpipes, as though somewhere a hidden orchestra were playing. ... This time she was not deceived. Someone was coming quickly up the stairs, was stopping just outside the room. She could hear him panting, getting his breath. No, it was not he.

At first she did not recognize Mondoux.

He, too, had heard someone in the room, had thought for a moment that Georges had returned. But it was only that woman! He had just come, as it happened, from her flat. Only that woman. And she was thinking, 'It's only Mondoux!' Mutually indifferent, they glared at one another angrily. Mondoux asked in a hard voice:

'When did you last see him?'

She replied that he had left her just before midnight. Mondoux muttered something and looked away. The only other time she had seen him he had been seated in front of a café. Standing here, he seemed enormous. His features were finely chiselled. He had a clean-cut look. His eyes were frank, but his neck was very short, and his body just a bag of bones.

'What did you talk about? Did you part on good terms?'

Yet another judge – there had been so many of them! She had no intention of putting up a defence. Perhaps she was being watched? She told him, with an air of docility, that they had talked of her daughter, that they had been perfectly open with one another, that they had said good night as friends.

She did not want to lie. It was not her fault if the truth could not be expressed. It is impossible to put into a few words the story of two people at desperate odds. What was it that had really occurred between them? She found it quite beyond her power to explain. Even at bay in the witness-box she would have remained silent. But why should Mondoux be so worried? She dared not ask the question, yet could not but see that he was half out of his mind with anxiety. What she had been fearing became, on a sudden horribly real. She stammered:

'What reason have you for being so frightened? Is it so odd that he shouldn't have come back last night?'

He interrupted her almost roughly. Why was she playing with him? he asked. She knew perfectly well what it was he feared.

'No, really I don't. I hardly know him ... and he's such an old friend of yours. ... It's for you to tell me. ...'

He made a gesture of denial, a victim, no doubt, of the same powerlessness which had prevented her from giving him the full story of her last hours with Georges yesterday evening. Standing there, facing one another, in the tiny room, it was as though their absent friend were a barrier between them, as though each saw the other across a sundering sea. They had nothing in common but their pain.

'I half thought of going to the police-station: but they'd have laughed in my face. Not been seen since last night, eh? They'd have told me to wait and not get worked up over nothing. Assuming that the worst has happened, there couldn't be anything in the morning papers. We must wait for the noon editions.'

Thérèse murmured, 'You're mad!' He shrugged. She sat down on the bed. Confronted by the Great Power, which was, perhaps, after all, not really blind, she was without defence; faced by the nameless Will – in which she did not believe (she had not really believed, just now, that by anticipating the worst she could side-track fate: yet she had behaved as though she did believe it) ... a mad prayer rose to her lips from the dark abyss of nothingness in which her spirit lay crushed. She pretended to believe that a child, still living though on the point of death, might be saved by the sheer exercise of a mother's will. She could scarcely have been more breathless had she in very truth been pulling on a rope, dragging a heavy body to the bank. But even now she had flashes of sanity. 'What nonsense!' she said; and again, 'What nonsense!' – but, at the same time, as though to win forgiveness for her lack of faith, forced herself to make a supreme effort. Struggling violently against she knew not whom, she set herself with an almost furious fervour to beg and pray. Mondoux had opened the window and was leaning on the bar. She asked him when he would begin to *do* something. He could not hear her through the noise of the street, and she remained seated on the bed, all strength drained from her, ashamed of having voiced her weakness in a prayer ... as though she had ever believed that prayers could have the slightest effect upon what was done with and finished! Nothing now but to wait. ... If the worst had already happened – well, she must get used to the thought, must blunt its fangs – the thought with which it would be so hard to live: 'He would not have died if he had never known me.' Intolerable thought – yet she would grow accustomed to it, as she had always grown accustomed in the past. Already she was preparing her defence, beginning once again those endless pleadings. It was she, perhaps, who must be the first, the innocent, victim of her acts. But her innocence no longer mattered to anyone. The only thing that mattered was that somewhere a boy was lying with a bullet in his brain. She was impatient to have the thing discovered, his parents told ... and Marie! Oh, Heavens! – this death would settle nothing. Marie! It would be the beginning, not the end. Mondoux, leaning out above the street, did not hear the groan with which she uttered the name 'Marie!' She was resolved no longer to make the least movement to help the girl. She would ignore her utterly, since, no matter what she might do, she could deal her only a death-blow. She would have nothing more to do with Marie. When, finally, the bomb should burst, she would keep her eyes tight shut, she would stop her ears, as she used to do as a child when she was awakened in the middle of the night by a storm. She would not stir a finger, would say not a word, no matter how violently she might be abused – would say nothing, but would let the drama move to its predestined end, the drama that was already potentially present in Georges Filhot's body lying stretched she knew not where. Would not human justice at long last have its way with her? No one escapes twice in a lifetime from the police. ...

She heard Mondoux's voice. He was speaking to somebody in the street. Thérèse sat up, but dared not go to the window.

Mondoux turned round, and, in the most ordinary way in the world, said:

'Here he is!'

She repeated the word: 'Here?' She was beyond feeling anything. Her hands were icy. Already she could recognize his footstep on the stairs – the step of a child brought back to life. She felt as weak as though the life now given back to Georges had been suddenly drained from her own body. She must not faint. He was alive. Again she said:

'It's he?'

Mondoux had left the room. In a moment Georges would appear in the black emptiness of the doorway. He would not be swathed in bandages. There would be no blood trickling down his face.

There, at last, he was, a dazed look in his eyes, a dark smudge of unshaved beard on his cheeks, his shoes thick with mud. There was no time for her to catch his eye. No sooner had he seen her that he backed on to the landing, slamming the door behind him. She heard at first a sound of whispering, then a sudden loud exclamation from Georges: 'No, no; I want to be left in peace!' It was the voice of a sick, ill-tempered man. Mondoux came back. He said that Georges had gone to have a bath. He hated to be seen in such a state – 'after walking about all night, as he often does. ...' Thérèse tidied her hat in front of the glass, and, with her hand on the door-knob, said:

'He's alive.'

She felt weak, but calm and at peace, conscious only of a sensation of happiness.

'You had got yourself thoroughly worked up. ... I was a bit annoyed – I don't mind admitting it – but it's a far cry from that to believing him dead. ...'

Thérèse smiled. 'Tell him that I came here only to leave a letter for him. There it is, on the table.'

She turned once more, and, rather hesitatingly, 'It's about my daughter,' she said. 'Would you be so very kind as to read it? I will take your advice as to whether he should see it. ... You're a better judge ...'

From now on he would be suspicious of her most trivial actions.

Mondoux glanced through the letter.

'I'll give it him at once,' he said dryly.

Yes, it was essential that Georges should feel that he was free. He was by nature inclined to think that he had certain obligations, to shoulder burdens which were beyond his strength.

He added that after the kind of crisis his friend had been through peace and quiet was absolutely necessary. Thérèse broke in on his words:

'You never said anything about a crisis. ...'

He became confused, and protested, like a naughty school-boy, that there was nothing *to* tell her. In a vain effort to calm him, she forced herself to speak in the hoarse tones which she knew could be so effective. In vain she fluttered her eye-lids. Mondoux remained unresponsive. He even showed signs of anger when she complained (though very gently) that he had given her no word of warning.

'By what right have you come into his life?'

The fury which he had been holding in for the last hour burst into sudden flame. Thérèse, after a moment's hesitation, said in a low voice:

'It was about my daughter ...' as though she had to explain her actions to this unknown young man.

'A fat lot you care about your daughter!'

She looked at him in amazement, and made a movement expressive of weariness. What did this angry youth matter to her? She tried not to hear his nasty voice.

'Don't think I didn't see through your little game! It's pretty low to work on a fellow when he's worried, when his imagination's sick. I suppose you thought he was in love with you?'

She ought to have left him then with a shrug. But she, who thought that nothing mattered to her any longer, found his laughter, his irony, intolerable. She could not stop herself from exclaiming:

'If I'd wanted ...'

'Oh, of course, if you'd wanted ...'

Why was she staying? Why was she being so stubborn? Her own voice sounded strange to her. Were those whining tones hers? It was as though she were listening to some other woman stammering:

'He swore he loved me.'

'He's sworn the same thing to a great many others! Oh, you bowled him over all right, I grant you that! ... He thought you were a kind of genius ... but it didn't last long.'

The same voice, this voice of a stranger, of an idiot, which was not Thérèse's voice, protested:

'It lasted as long as I wanted it to.' And in the same cringing tone she repeated: 'If I'd wanted ...' If she had wanted, if she had opened her arms wide to him, if ...

'So what? ... You did yourself out of your treat. ... Why? ... from a sense of virtue?'

She threw him an indignant look, and asked in a trembling voice:

'What have I done to you?'

'It couldn't be, I suppose, that you wanted to make him quarrel with me?'

'I?'

'Yes: you wanted to make him jealous. You hadn't time to tell him that I had been making a pass at you. We had only met once, and he wouldn't have believed it. But you'd have tried it on, all the same, pretty soon. ... It's a hackneyed trick, but it works. All women use it. Meanwhile, you just pretended that I was your type. ... After you'd left us the other day at the Deux Magots, he made the hell of a scene!'

'You enjoy humiliating women, don't you? It makes you feel good. How right you are! It's the only pleasure that you are likely to get from them! But it's not a very satisfactory sort of pleasure, because you never succeed in really hurting us. Only those we love can hurt us. Men are to be feared only when they are loved. It's curious to think that anyone can be so ill-mannered as you have been to me and yet remain so wholly inoffensive. ...'

'Don't think I care a damn what you say!' Mondoux spluttered. 'Not a damn!' he repeated. But he opened the door and pushed Thérèse towards the stairs, turning away his face, which had become distorted and unrecognizable. For one moment she looked straight into his eyes ... and saw that they were but the eyes of a child. ... Why had her anger so suddenly subsided? She had been swimming on a great tide of hatred, and now it had ebbed. How had she ever been brave enough to say what she had said?

'You mustn't believe what I said. ...'

He pushed her out, but she clung to the frame of the doorway.

'You mustn't believe what I said,' she murmured in a low voice.

'It doesn't matter to me what you say!'

Georges might come back at any moment. He wouldn't want to find her in his room.

' "For God's sake get her out of here!" ' – that's what he said to me. "I don't want to see her again – ever!" ...'

Thérèse braced herself motionless against the door. Mondoux could not endure the frozen gaze she turned on him. Quite gently she had freed her arm from his grasp. On the landing she straightened her small head.

'I wanted to hurt you ... I didn't care what I invented. ...'

Almost in a whisper, he replied:

'No, you didn't care. ...'

In a sudden panic she asked:

'What are you going to do to get your own back? ... Are you going to report me to the police?'

In amazement he watched her going down the stairs, waited until she had passed from his sight. Then he went back into the room, sat down at his friend's table, put his elbows on it, and stayed there, his chin resting on his clenched fists.

9

IT was of him that Thérèse was thinking as she walked along the street, past the houses. Georges Filhot no longer occupied her mind for the moment, nor did Marie. Only in Mondoux, her latest victim, was she interested. Not that she could have done him a great deal of harm, but the blow which she had delivered with so sure a hand had helped her to measure the extent of her power and take cognizance of her mission. It was not surprising that people turned to look as she passed. An animal can be detected by its smell even before it is seen. She felt that she was being stared at, and began to walk faster in her impatience to reach her lair and go to ground. Henceforward she must live the life of a recluse. Only so could she be sure of doing no further damage, only so could she escape reprisals, because, sooner or later, all those whom she had harmed would join forces. ... She was such a good target. True, her case had been dismissed, but with a past like hers slander would find food to feed on. ... What slander? She was beyond the power of slander to touch. Had she not committed more crimes than could possibly be imputed to her? But no one was bringing a charge against her, no one. Why was she imagining things?

Feeling slightly giddy, she leaned against the gate of a carriage entrance. She closed her eyes for a few seconds and then remembered that she had eaten nothing. How hungry she was! It occurred to her that she had had no breakfast. She was not going mad – she was sure of that, but she must be careful to take nourishment regularly. She went into a confectioner's shop and drank a cup of tea. Order came back into her mind. Everything, once more, seemed simple. Georges Filhot was alive. From now on she would banish Marie entirely from her mind, would confine her own existence to the space between chair and table, would go out only at nightfall. Never again would she venture into the street in broad daylight. Never again would she expose herself to the curious eyes which she could feel boring into the back of her neck.

Here she was, home at last! If only the concierge was not hanging about the staircase. No, there she was, in front of her lodge, busy gossiping with Anna. Why did they look at her in that embarrassing way? The concierge had got her mouth open, was in the middle of a sentence:

'Someone's been asking for you this morning ... a big man ... asked me a whole lot of questions. ...'

'What sort of questions?'

'Oh, I don't rightly remember. ... Did you go out last night? Did anyone come to see you? ...'

'And what answer did you give him?'

'Said I didn't know ... that it wasn't my job to spy on the tenants. ...'

Thérèse did not dare to ask, 'Who do you think it was?' She did not even demand a description of her unknown visitor. The old woman would doubtless have replied, 'A young, lanky fellow ...' and perhaps Thérèse would have recognized Mondoux, who, as a matter of fact, *had* turned up in the rue du Bac just about the time she was getting out of her cab at the Hôtel du chemin de fer de l'Ouest.

She climbed the stairs, a prey to profound uneasiness. She paid no attention to her heart. She bolted the door and, without even taking off her hat, sank into an arm-chair. Her chest was hurting, but the idea that she might die alone and unfriended no longer made her feel afraid. She wanted assurance on one point only, that no one would come near her. ... Anna must have entered by the service stairs. She must get rid of Anna. She had always believed her to be on bad terms with the concierge. Seemingly they had made it up. ... Probably *she* had been the peace-offering. ... But if she gave her notice, that would mean making a mortal enemy of her. ... How find the weak spot in her armour by working on which she could induce her to go of her own accord? 'If there are those who set store by her staying on with me, nothing on earth will budge her: she'll stick like a leech. ...'

She dragged herself as far as the bedroom, a victim once again of fears and torments. 'But this is ridiculous,' she thought: 'I'm in no danger. I may be guilty, but my guilt is not of the kind that the law can touch. But there are those who would like to pull me down ... and it's always possible to cook up some sort of case. It is child's play to compromise a woman who's been within an ace of being condemned in a court of law. ...' In vain she said again to herself, 'But there is absolutely nothing!' She could feel a running noose about her neck. No amount of reasoning could prevail against this sense of certainty. The very silence of the flat seemed equivocal. It was a long time now since Anna had given up singing her Alsatian songs. She was for ever listening, and it was not likely that she had missed much of what had gone on when first Marie, and then Georges, had been in the drawing-room. To each of them Thérèse had admitted her guilt. What an ally her enemies would have in her servant! No, she didn't sing now, didn't make a clatter with the dishes. All she did was to try to pick up the compromising words that fell from her mistress's lips!

Thérèse went to the window, parted the curtains, and noticed a man on the pavement, looking up. He was making a pretence of waiting for the bus, standing by the stop, but never taking his eyes off the flat. 'You know perfectly well that he is waiting for the bus. ...' She uttered this denial of her fears out loud, as though to prove to her own satisfaction that she was still sane. She told herself that since leaving her room she had *not* heard anyone breathing outside the front-door. But, for all that, she was convinced ... To clear her mind on the point, she went to open it, and almost bumped into the concierge, who had 'forgotten to give Madame her post. ...' Thérèse saw at close range the flat, grey-coloured face with its bright pig's – no, rat's – eyes. What a hideously *greedy* look the woman had!

'Why are you staring at me?'

'You don't look well, ma'am. ...'

'I feel just as I always do. ...'

'But what I said, ma'am ...'

'Did the man who came here yesterday ask whether I was ill? He didn't? ... But, really, this kind of gossip doesn't interest me. ...'

She slammed the door and shot the bolt. The concierge, taken by surprise, started to grumble: 'That's a nice way to behave, I must say!' Instead of going downstairs, she opened the door of the flat opposite, which was empty, and joined Anna in her kitchen by way of the service entrance.

Thérèse sat motionless on the low stool, leaning forward as she was used to do when her heart troubled her, alive to the slightest sound, all her awareness concentrated into her sense of hearing, like a fox listening for the hounds. Anna was carrying on a solitary monologue ... no, someone was answering her. A whispered conversation was going on in the kitchen. Somebody was there plotting with Anna.

Thérèse dragged herself as far as the dining-room, put her ear to the keyhole, and recognized the concierge's voice. The woman couldn't have had time to go down by the main staircase and come up again by the service flight. The mystery demanded careful thought and a cool head. The immediately important thing was not to lose a single word of what was being said. The concierge was advising her friend to keep a close watch on Thérèse. It was *her* opinion that the family ought to be told. ... Anna said that she knew the address. ... How did she know it? Thérèse wondered. She'd got it from Marie, of course. ... They were carrying on a correspondence behind her back. ... Anna heard a sound, opened the door, and started back at the sight of her mistress's white face.

'I came to see whether luncheon would be ready soon ...' and (to the concierge) 'so *you're* back, are you?'

The old woman stammered something about passing the time of day with Anna, and disappeared down the service stairs. Anna, busying herself at the oven, was conscious of a terrible pair of eyes watching her, but dared not turn her head.

Thérèse returned to her low stool. She had felt with her fingers the mesh about her neck. She would never breathe freely again. The chief thing was not to leave the flat. True, *they* were watching her, but they couldn't do much more than that. A woman's home is her castle. ... Unless, of course, a specific charge were laid. But there was no ground for that. The admissions heard by Anna could not be used against her now. But if she went out she would fall into the trap which had been so carefully set. It was general knowledge that she was guilty and deserved a heavy sentence ... all that was needed was some sort of legal pretext. ... The police have always got more than one trump up their sleeves when they've made up their minds to do someone down. Here, in the flat, she might be under hostile eyes, but nothing much could happen to her because *they* were certain that sooner or later she would go out.

Anna came into the room.

'Luncheon's ready, ma'am.'

There was something unusual about her voice, and her eyes never left Thérèse's face.

'Aren't you going to eat something, ma'am?'

How annoyed she looked because Thérèse didn't want to eat! Madame must make an effort.

Instinctively, Thérèse stiffened her will in order to resist her adversary's. If *they* were so keen for her to eat, it was specially important that she should refuse all nourishment.

When Anna brought in the coffee she found her mistress sitting facing the door. Her eyes never left it. Later, when she came back for the tray, the coffee-pot was still full. Thérèse had not moved from her former position. ... Not that she didn't feel a strong desire to run out and disarrange her enemies' scheme by the sheer audacity of the move. *They* would be taken by surprise, and wouldn't dare try anything. She would be able to see what they were up to.

When, at four o'clock, she refused to touch the tea which Anna had poured out for her, the maid tried sipping it in front of her, smacking her lips, and saying, 'Oh, *that's* good!' just as she might have done if her little sister had refused to drink her broth. Thérèse immediately took the cup from her and drank the contents greedily. But there was something terrifying in the way she still stared at Anna.

'Is your heart troubling you, ma'am?'

'No, Anna ... or, rather, yes. ... But that's not why I'm feeling bad. ...'

She seized the girl's wrists and held them tightly.

'You won't tell *them* anything? ... Pretend to be on their side, but don't tell them anything!'

'I don't know what you mean, ma'am.'

'It's no use trying to deceive me. ... They've got me.'

'I'll warm the bed, ma'am; then you'll be able to sleep.'

'Why are you so anxious that I should sleep?' Thérèse asked with sudden violence. 'Don't reckon on that: I shall never sleep again.'

'But no one wishes you any harm, you poor dear.'

'Sit down, Anna. It may be foolish of me, but I'm going to tell you everything. Draw up your chair. They've got you to go in with them, but they haven't told you what it's all about. I'm someone who's got to be made to disappear. But it's not easy to make a person disappear legally – not even when that person is a criminal. You don't seem to understand, yet it's all so simple, really, if you only knew! I committed a crime for which I might have been sent to penal servitude – but the case was dismissed. ... My other actions don't come within the reach of the law: they are not, strictly speaking, crimes at all – from the legal point of view. But having regard to what I did once – even though the case *was* dismissed – they'll manage to get through my defences somehow. ...'

Anna, by now thoroughly terrified, took her mistress's hands and tried to catch her restless eyes.

'Oh, ma'am, you *must* get some sleep: really you must: your poor mind's wandering. ...'

'No, I'm not mad, but they'll try to make you believe I am – because that's all part of their plan to get me put away. Out of sight, out of mind. I'm perfectly sane, Anna. How can I persuade you that all I've been telling you is strictly true? I know it's hard to believe, but it's true all the same. No one will listen to me, no one will believe me any more. I've talked about suffering all my life, but only now have I found out what suffering means. ... Why are you undressing me?'

But she let herself be undressed without a struggle. Anna pushed her gently towards the bed.

'The bottle's not too hot, is it, ma'am?'

'No ... I'm all right.'

Thérèse felt for a moment that the sense of tension had lessened. She clung to the large, moist hand and would not let it go.

'Do you remember, Anna, how sometimes you used to bring your work in here, and sit by me till I dropped off?

Those were good times! How happy I was! I didn't realize it at the time, and now it's all over. No, don't go and fetch your work, don't leave me alone, don't let go of my hand!'

She stopped speaking, and, shortly afterwards, seemed to have fallen into a doze. Anna tried very gently to free herself from her mistress's grasp, but as soon as she began to do so the despairing voice was raised again in protest.

'I'm not asleep ... I've got an idea, Anna. How would it be if I went to the police-station? Where is the nearest one? ... Isn't that a splendid idea? I'll tell them everything, from the beginning – the whole story in detail. That'll cut the ground from under their feet! But where shall I begin? They won't have sufficient patience to listen to me. They won't believe me, Anna. There's no difficulty about slander – people will always believe that! ... but the truth ... the truth's a world of its own. They'll never be patient enough – they won't believe me. But if only they'd arrest me my mind would be at peace. The worst would have happened. I shouldn't have to go on living in this perpetual state of watchfulness. ... Please give me my clothes: I must get dressed.'

Anna took her in her arms, and said the first things that came into her mind: that they'd go out in the morning: that the police-stations were too full of people at this time of night. Now that she'd made up her mind what she was going to do, she'd much better have a good night's rest.

'That's true ... I can go to sleep now ... I've nothing to fear.'

But no sooner had Anna got up, thinking that she had dropped off, than she was recalled before she had even got her hand on the door-knob. Patiently, she returned to her chair. But she *must* go at a quarter to nine. The chauffeur from the second-floor flat would be waiting for her at nine. She had agreed, for the first time, to let him come to her room. He had promised that he would not overstep their usual freedoms. Anna closed her eyes and breathed deeply. Why should she worry? Nothing was going to prevent her from being on the watch behind her half-opened door at nine. ... The old lady would fall asleep all right in the long run ...

and if she didn't ... well, she'd go just the same, even if it meant trampling the poor old thing underfoot. ... There'd be plenty to think about while she waited ... not much chance of her being bored while she sat in the glow of the lamp. For the long-dreamed-of moment had come at last ... the night that was to bring her happiness! ... The old lady seemed calmer now. She consented to drink a bowl of soup. 'Yes,' she said, 'I think I shall sleep now. ...' But at eight o'clock, and again at half past, when Anna tried to creep away, she was called back in tones of terror, and from then on Thérèse lay with eyes wide open.

At nine o'clock Anna said: 'This time ...' Thérèse did not protest, but she started to cry. The childlike sobbing had more effect on the maid than any supplication. She stayed on, though nine had struck, seeing, in imagination, the man standing there outside her room, whispering her name, listening at her door, trying to open it. Thérèse's breathing had by this time become regular. Now and again she uttered a confused jumble of words, started to complain, cried out 'No! no!' turned over on her left side away from the night-light.

Anna heard a faint ring at the back-door bell. It must be he! She got up, without producing so much as a sigh from Thérèse, crossed the hall on tip-toe, reached the kitchen without being called back, drew the bolt, saw the great burly figure filling the whole doorway, and drew him into the tiny kitchen.

'No,' she said in a whisper: 'don't switch on the light.'

In a low voice she explained what had happened. He made no reply, but put his hand over her mouth.

They heard the sound of a chair being overturned in the dining-room. When the kitchen door was opened their eyes had grown sufficiently used to the dark to allow them to see the thin, ghost-like figure standing there motionless. Thérèse heard a voice, and knew it for a man's.

'You're sure she's not armed?'

She wanted to cry out, 'Don't kill me!' but she could utter no sound, and slid to the floor in a faint.

When she came to she was sitting up in bed, supported by pillows. She put no questions to Anna and made no reference to the man whom she had surprised in the kitchen, who must have helped to carry her to her room. Anna realized that her mistress now regarded her as someone 'on the other side', as someone who had gone over to the enemy. She could extract from her but the shortest of answers to her inquiries, and then only with difficulty. 'Yes, I feel better.' 'I think I shall go to sleep now.' 'You can stay on the couch. ...'

The sick woman was wearing herself out in a painful effort to stay awake. The least sound aroused her suspicions. Tomorrow she would get up with the lark, and go straight to the police-station. The light was not long enough for her to get the story she would tell all tidied up in her mind. No one would believe her. ... The sense of impotence was intolerable! She had always lived alone without ever really knowing what solitude meant. People talk a great deal about solitude, but they haven't the least idea what it actually is. What chance was there that her statement would ever reach the ears of the Police Commissioner? She would see her words tumbling to the ground like dead birds before they even reached their goal. There was nothing for it but to lie low. It was by way of the service stairs that the enemy would force an entrance. That was the spot on which she must keep a particularly watchful eye.

She was convinced that she was the centre of a vast and secret plot. ... Of that she had no doubt whatever. How could she have known that there was not at this moment, in the whole world, one single thought which had her as its object? – that through the whole length of this night no human creature was the least little bit concerned about Thérèse Desqueyroux? Nothing, anywhere, bore on her case ... nothing – except a letter which had been written at five a.m., posted in the rue de Rennes, and was now on its way to Bordeaux: a letter addressed to her daughter – *Mademoiselle Marie Desqueyroux, Saint-Clair, Gironde.*

The envelope had been inscribed in a more than usually firm hand. Georges Filhot had crossed the *t* of Saint-Clair, and

underlined *Gironde*. He had dropped the letter into the box
with feelings of happiness and relief. Each sentence of it had
been gone through and corrected by Mondoux. There was
nothing now for Georges to do save stop his ears against the
sound of Marie's cry. In this sort of complication there could
be nothing worse than pity. As Mondoux said, kind-hearted
executioners are the cruellest of all. In the name of compassion
they give twelve blows where one would have sufficed.
Looked at from that point of view, the closing phrase –
composed entirely by Mondoux – seemed to Georges Filhot
to be quite perfect of its kind: 'I beg you not to answer this
letter. I have quite made up my mind. For your sake, I have
decided that nothing shall make me break my vow of silence –
no prayer, no threat. Once more – don't accuse me of ruth-
lessness. The only time I really behaved like a cad was when
I kept alive in your heart a hope which I could not satisfy.
For that I ask your forgiveness. Forget me. I enclose a note
from your mother, from which you will see that she no longer
regards me as being engaged to you.'

10

ABOUT one o'clock next day this letter arrived at Saint-
Clair, and was delivered to Marie. She was alone at the time,
sitting in the dining-room, wrapped in a shawl. At sight of the
beloved handwriting she thought she would faint from sheer
joy. There was no longer any need to pretend. Bernard
Desqueyroux had gone over to his old mother at Argelouse
to superintend the killing of a pig.

She devoured the envelope with her eyes. She would open
it later, in her own room, behind locked doors. The November day was suffused with warm sunlight: the town was full
of noises. The sawmills were singing their song to the east
wind, which bore upon its wings the scent of resin and stripped
bark. That was a sign of good weather. She could hear the
little local train jolting over the narrow-gauge track. Life was
full of happiness.

She turned the key in the lock, and, conscious that she was
alone, kissed the envelope which Georges had touched. Then
she tore it open, saw her mother's writing, and was immediately seized with feelings of dire foreboding. At first she
glanced hurriedly through the note, then read Georges' letter
from end to end – so quickly that when she had finished it
she could still hear, in the mild afternoon air, the bumping
of the dilapidated freight cars. 'I enclose a note from your
mother, from which you will see that she no longer regards
me as being engaged to you. ...'

Not for one single moment did Marie stop to consider the
reasons which might have led Georges to bring about this
rupture. A childish impulse led her at once to simplify, to
seek first the guilty party, to concentrate her hatred on one
person, and one person only – though refusing to admit that
the individual in question might turn out to be the man she
loved. 'She has betrayed me. ... To think that I ever trusted
that wretched woman! ... What a fool I have been! ...'
Suspicions formed straightway in her mind. What mightn't
her mother have said to Georges? But why? Jealousy?
Vengeance? But she had reckoned without Marie! If the
young woman still stood there, alive and kicking, her cheeks
blazing; if the blow had not struck her to the ground, the
reason was that she did not believe in this disaster which had
overtaken her. She would do what was necessary. There
were ways and means of getting a young man back. She knew
how to recapture Georges. It wouldn't be the first time, nor
yet the last. ... The bus to Bordeaux was due to start in ten
minutes. The Paris train left at five. It would land her at the
Quai d'Orsay at midnight. She would send a telegram to her
father from the station. To do nothing would have been more
than she could bear. But she had only just time to pack a bag.

The servants did not see her go out. The bus was almost
empty. She felt far from despairing. The whole force of her
passion was concentrated in a great surge of hatred. Later on
she would imagine the coming scene with Georges, would
decide what to say. For the moment her mind was busy with
the thought of how she would burst into the rue du Bac this

evening, of how she would surprise her guilty mother in her first moments of sleep. It would be impossible to go at that late hour to the Hôtel du chemin de fer de L'Ouest. She would hurry there first thing in the morning, and wake Georges. The whole thing would be child's play. ... She wanted to be sure of the power which she exercised over him. The night would be long, but her mother would help to make the time pass quickly. She turned against Thérèse the same furious rage which she had inherited from her, though in her case it was balanced by no compensating gift of self-criticism. Still, she thought, she must remain calm, must set about pumping her mother – might, perhaps, have to compel her to write another letter to Georges taking back what she had said in the first. ... All that remained to be seen.

Thus it was that while Thérèse, sitting up in bed where she had remained in the same position all night, was pretending to be calm in order to get rid of Anna, whose presence now filled her with fear and horror, this storm was driving down on her from the land of heath and pine. No matter how suspicious the wretched woman had become, she was inclined to think that, for this day, at least, the moment had passed when she might look for an enemy offensive or a sudden attack. Up in her room on the seventh floor, Anna was probably entertaining the unknown man of last evening. The flat was empty: every door was bolted. Assured of a sort of armistice by the hours of darkness, she could forget her persecutor for a few short moments. She broke through the invisible cordon of the besieging army, and came to grips once more with her humble sufferings of an earlier phase. She remembered the last blow she had received before discovering the appalling plot. ... Georges' words, repeated by Mondoux, came back to her: 'Tell her to go away! Tell her I don't want to see her again – ever!' *He* had said that, in the same voice which, a few hours earlier, had spoken such tender words. ... All the same, she blessed him for those few brief instants of blinding happiness and certainty! Even now she could taste again that cooling draught of water, could make once more the gesture of drawing her hands away from his lips. When all was said, they had done nothing wrong. Her thoughts of him were innocent enough. She dreamed only that she was leaning her poor, distracted head on his young shoulder. ... Ah! it hadn't taken the enemy long to profit by those few seconds of inattention! The bell rang with shattering loudness. Thinking that she had been dreaming, she clapped her hands to her head. There came a second ringing, this time insistent, furious.

Thérèse got up and switched on the hall-light. For a moment she leaned against the wall (she had taken nothing but tea and biscuits).

'Who's there?'

'It's I ... Marie!'

Marie! So she would be the one to strike the first blow! Thérèse could not move from the wall. Painfully, she worked her way to the door, remembering that earlier decision she had made to let herself be taken without uttering a word, without making the slightest movement in her own defence.

'Come in, Marie ... Come in, my child!'

She was standing beneath the ceiling-light. Marie stopped dead at sight of the ghost-like figure. Her mouth fell open.

'Come into the drawing-room, darling. I can't stand for long.'

Marie had recovered herself. 'What a sight for sore eyes!' she said to herself. Her mother had rung the changes so often in the last few days. It was all part of her cunning. But, this time, she should see!

'What a time to turn up!'

'I came on the midnight train.'

She expected to be asked some questions, but her mother looked at her without uttering another word, ready for the blow she knew would come. The fixity of her gaze was intolerable. This was just another of her tricks – this way of staring at people.

'You know what has brought me?'

Thérèse bowed her head.

'I act quickly – as you see: luckily! But why did you do this to me?'

Thérèse sighed:

'I have done so many things: to which, in particular, are you referring?'

'Can't you guess? No? What about that letter you wrote to Georges two days ago? Ah! that's touched you on the raw! You didn't think I should get the proof of your treachery quite so soon! ...'

'Nothing astonishes me. I know that they have powerful forces at their command. They've done more difficult things than that – as you'll very soon see.'

She spoke calmly, with an air of detachment which had its effect on Marie, try though she might to keep her fury at boiling-point. 'All the same,' she thought, 'what an actress!'

'What task, what mission, have you been given, my child? You had much better lay your cards on the table in dealing with me. I shall not resist: I will do just as you wish; only, act quickly. I'll say precisely what you want me to say. I'll sign any statement they like. There's no point in your being so mysterious about it.'

Marie, in a fury, broke in upon her words: 'You've always thought me an idiot, but I'm not quite so stupid as you gave me credit for being! First explain why you wrote that letter!'

'Really, my dear, I'd much better give an account of myself to the Police Commissioner or the Magistrate.'

'You're just making a fool of me! ...'

But Marie broke off short in the middle of her sentence. This couldn't be play-acting, this terrible fit of trembling which shook her mother from head to foot, nor that single tear which was trickling down her nose – which she made no attempt to wipe away – nor yet the look of terror, nor her general air as of a beaten, cornered animal.

'You could never understand, never believe what I know, and what nobody else knows. You are a mere instrument in the hands of others. You obey forces of which you know nothing. They wanted Georges to kill himself, so that they might lay his suicide at my door. But, all unaided, I stopped the murder from taking place. I had been charged with the responsibility of committing it. He was to die because he had known me. But I threw their plans out. That must be made perfectly clear when the moment comes to settle accounts. Oh, I'll pay: I shall make no attempt to defend myself. But so far from murdering him, as I had been commissioned to do, I saved him, though no one will believe it. What purpose is served by crying aloud in this desert? To whom can I call from the depths of this tomb? You are there, standing before me, yet you are really thousands of miles away. ...'

She uttered a groan and turned her face to the wall. What pain was this which seemed to have her in its grip?

Marie was no longer conscious of her own wound. She would have liked to do something definite, could almost have wished that the bed were on fire that she might have wrapped her mother in blankets and put out the flames. ... 'It was I who prevented that suicide!' she had said. Suppose she had been telling the truth? Often and often Marie had found herself leaning out above that abyss of melancholy from which Georges rose so rarely to her level.

In the silence which filled the flat she could hear her mother crying, her face turned to the wall, her head buried in the crook of her arm, not crying, like a grown-up person, but rather, snivelling like a little girl who has been punished for some misdemeanour. And, indeed, it was as she would have dealt with a little girl that Marie now lifted her and laid her on the bed. She said to her: 'No one wishes you harm, Mamma. I have come from Saint-Clair to look after you. Nothing can hurt you so long as I am here.'

'You don't know what I know. A man came here yesterday evening. He asked whether I was armed, and spent the night hidden in Anna's room. He was some sort of policeman. They are in no hurry: they'll get me in the end. They know that there is no other way out for me.'

'Nothing's going to happen tonight. I'm watching over you. ... Go to sleep now. See, I'll keep my hand on your forehead.'

'So they've told you to win my confidence, have they? I know all about it: I'm not taken in. But it's nice to have you here, all the same.'

How differently this night was turning out from what the girl had expected! When her hand went numb and she moved it, her mother uttered a groan, and she had to put it back as it was before. She was cold. This was Paris again, with the melancholy street sounds coming to her through the autumn darkness, the distant puffing of a locomotive somewhere over near the Central Markets. And somewhere, too, Georges was sleeping, behind the indifferent, inaccessible façade of one of these houses. She had never meant anything to him, though she had pretended to believe that she did. It was him she wanted, him and no other, a great, hulking creature with a cast in his eye. Him and no other. She held nothing against him. She had made the surrender of herself without the slightest vestige of a hope. 'You may abandon me if you like, but you can't alter the fact that I belong to you.' She wept, but her tears betokened neither anger nor despair. Lying there, fully dressed, at her mother's side, she could hear the elder woman's breathing, and the muttering of incoherent words. But, because she was eighteen, she slept.

It was not without a deep sense of happiness that Thérèse felt the other's physical proximity. Although she believed that Marie was hand in glove with her enemies (an instrument rather than an active plotter), she let herself be carried away on a wave of sleep. The sound of a voice woke her. It was full day already. Marie was no longer beside her. She and Anna were whispering together in the drawing-room. Ah! that other woman had lost no time in getting her hooks on her! Thérèse strained her ears to catch what was being said.

'It's impossible to get the doctor to her. She thinks he's in the pay of the police and has been sent to lock her up. She threatens to throw herself out of the window if he comes into the room. But she trusts you, Miss. You mustn't leave her. Put off going out ...'

'Not for the world ... but perhaps I shan't be long gone. I shall be back before the end of the morning. ... It's no use your talking. ...'

Was her mother the only person in the world? Whom was it she was going to see? Who was it who was waiting for her?

That was the question Thérèse asked herself as she lay there listening. 'Someone she's frightened of, of course: someone who's got a hold on her. But she won't be able to take me in. ... As soon as you get back, my girl, I shall see what you've been up to.' She heard the door slam, and the sound of Marie's footsteps growing fainter on the stairs. When Anna came in she pretended to be asleep.

Marie walked so quickly to the Boulevard Montparnasse that, in spite of the cold fog, she was perspiring freely by the time she arrived. Hastily she touched up her face in the shelter of a doorway. There was as yet no one behind the hotel desk. A waiter was washing down the entrance hall. He disarranged Marie's plan of action. She had made up her mind to go straight to Georges' bedroom and surprise him when he woke.

'Hey! – Young lady!'

Marie, already half-way up the stairs, cried down that she was expected.

'And by whom, may I ask? By Monsieur Filhot? Oh, dear me, no. He's finished with you, has Monsieur Filhot!'

Marie, leaning over the banisters, saw two mocking eyes rimmed with red looking at her.

'I know that ... because he settled his bill yesterday noon, and went off without leaving an address. He said to send on any letters care of Monsieur Mondoux.'

The man would have been more niggardly with his information had not the expression on Marie's face struck him as comic. The way she'd look in the next few seconds would be well worth any little effort on his part.

'Yes, fetched by a lady he was, in a car and all. Took off to the village wot she comes from near Paris. ... Madame Garcin ... not the first time she's been here, not by a long chalk. Didn't mind waiting, either. ... Mean ter say you don't know *her*? Very handsome she is, and a very free-handed lady!'

Marie knew Madame Garcin by name. She knew that she played a part in Georges' life, and had often pulled his leg about her. 'You have my permission when in Paris to play around with Madame Garcin.' It was understood between them that Georges was not in love with her. All the same, to

have gone with that woman after writing as he had done to
Marie, breaking off their engagement! Looking at the charming morning visitor, the hotel waiter felt less inclined now to
find her expression comic. She seemed to have shrunk under
his eyes: her face had grown visibly more pinched: she was
clinging to the banisters. There'd be a scene in a second or
two. He went up the first few steps and took her by the arm.
She made no effort to prevent him, but stood there staring
straight in front of her. If he hadn't had so much to do, now
would have been the moment to carry the joke through ... as
a matter of fact, it wouldn't take so very long. 'If you want a
bit of fun, there's a nice little room on the sixth floor. ...'

He came quite close and gave her a meaning look. She had
no idea what he was after. She pushed him aside – not roughly,
gained the street, and hailed a taxi.

'It's fine that you've been so quick,' said Anna as she opened
the door to her.

In the darkness of the hall she could not see the look of
misery on the girl's face. Marie threw her béret and her coat
on to the low stool, and went into the bedroom where her
mother was pretending to be asleep, though actually she was
keeping a shrewd eye on Marie from behind half-closed lids.
Whom had she been to see? What task had the poor child
been given that should make her look so awful? Thérèse
could not long keep up the pretence of sleep, because she was
trembling in every limb. In vain she clenched her teeth.

'Are you cold, Mamma?'

Marie, seated on the edge of the bed, had taken her in her
arms, and was trying to smile.

'I'm not cold – I'm frightened.'

When the girl asked gently, 'What, frightened of me?'
Thérèse replied that she ought to be on her guard against her
just as much as against the others.

'But I can't help it. ... I just can't believe that you mean me
harm. ... What is it, darling? You're crying!'

Without a moment's warning, Marie had surrendered to
an onrush of tears, and by so doing had, all unwittingly,

helped her mother by diverting her attention from her own misery. It was the sick woman now who was playing the part of comforter.

'Have a good cry,' she said, and began to rock Marie as she lay against her shoulder. It was, probably the first time since her daughter was a baby that she had found vent for her maternal instinct.

'Mamma, what have we done that we should suffer so?'

'You have done nothing, but I ...'

'He has gone away, Mamma, without leaving an address ... with another woman. ... It's all over!'

She submitted to having her head stroked: she wiped her eyes on the pillow.

'No, my child, no. ...'

'Why do you say "no"?'

'He'll come back; you haven't lost him.'

As though she had read her daughter's thoughts, she replied, in her usual voice, to everything that she saw passing through Marie's mind.

'No, I'm not mad: I was never less mad than I am at this moment. When you are happy again you will remember all I am saying to you now. You will remember this dismal morning.'

It needs but little encouragement to bring renewed hope to a young heart. It was all nonsense, of course: still, Marie stopped crying and clung closer to her mother. They sat there together for a long while.

Marie offered to make some coffee and toast. When they had eaten, Thérèse consented to have a bath. She did not hear the back-door bell, nor know that a telegram had just been delivered for Marie. Her father ordered her to return that same evening. *Insist you come back first available train.* He was obviously beside himself with anger. The girl joined her mother in the drawing-room, where she found her in a state of trembling collapse. She had thought, she said, that rescue had arrived. She could never now summon up enough courage to face being given over to Anna's tender mercies. Anna was the mistress of a police officer. She and the concierge were being well paid. Ever since Marie's arrival they had been pretending. Marie had frightened them. So long as Marie was there nothing could happen. She had put a spoke in their wheel. They were trying to make use of her, but had not dared to show themselves in their true colours. And now she was talking of going away and leaving her to her fate!

She began to whimper. It was as much as Marie could do to prevent her from falling on her knees. She had become the prey to a fit of despair which, at times, was like a child's unreasoning impulse. She did not want Marie to go. She wouldn't *let* her go. Marie promised to come back, but said that she must go to Saint-Clair in order to explain what was happening.

'But they know much better than you do what has been happening, my poor dear. No, you shan't go!'

'But I must, Mamma darling.'

'All right, then!' Thérèse exclaimed suddenly (a phrase which she must often have used as a child came to her lips from out of the distant past). 'All right, but I'll follow you wherever you go!'

'Oh, Mamma, you can't do that!'

But Thérèse was walking up and down the room, saying with childish insistence: 'I'll follow you wherever you go – to Saint-Clair if necessary. Why not? I should feel in much less danger there than here, because I should be with you. Besides, at Saint-Clair I am Madame Bernard Desqueyroux. I'd like to see the local police breaking into the Desqueyroux house! Our family has no truck with the police. We made that pretty plain fifteen years ago.' She lowered her voice, and, in urgent, mysterious tones, added: 'If I go, all Anna's plans will fall to the ground. Your father won't be able to say a thing. He can't throw me out in my present state.'

She spoke the last words in a perfectly normal voice. It was as though, for the space of a few seconds, she had seen herself objectively and had passed judgement on what she saw.

Marie said again: 'But you *can't* do that.'

She took her mother's face between her two hands and shook it gently as though to wake her from a dream.

'How can you go back to that house after all these years, Mamma? - go back of your own accord to the place where you almost died of suffocation - from which you escaped?' In a whisper she added - 'and at what a price!'

'At what a price?' said Thérèse with a wild look (and there was no laughter in her voice as she went on): 'I've nothing against your father now, you know. He won't get on my nerves any more. It's such a big house, too, with so many empty rooms. I can stay hidden away in one of them, and be quite forgotten. And then, when they've got sick of trying to track me down, I can go away again. I shan't feel that it's a prison now.'

Marie began to see the plan as less mad than she had thought it. She had been dreading the reception she would get from her father after this second flight of hers, but her mother's presence would provide an adequate excuse. Already she was beginning to plan the general line of her defence. She had heard by letter of her mother's illness (she would say), had taken the first available train to Paris and now, having been summoned back to Saint-Clair, had brought the sick woman with her, because she could not possibly leave her unattended. It was for the family to decide what had better be done.

'Would you really like to come with me, Mamma?'

'This evening? But no one must know. Anna must just knock at my door tomorrow morning and find me flown!'

Thérèse laughed: then, with a sudden return to seriousness, looked beseechingly at Marie. She could scarcely believe in the feasibility of her plan, but plucked up courage when she heard the girl dictating a telegram to Saint-Clair over the telephone.

'Not so loud!' she begged: 'Anna will hear you!'

Marie had the greatest difficulty in warning the servant without her mother being aware of what she was doing. When the last bag was strapped, the sick woman showed renewed signs of agitation. She was afraid that she might be arrested as they left the house.

In the train, with her mother dozing in the seat opposite, Marie began to think once more about Georges. She would write to him tomorrow. The great thing was to establish a bridge, to make quite certain that all was not over between them. His mind was never the same for two days together. ... Had she been able to see him again, she could have reasserted her hold on him. If only he had been in this morning, had woke up to find her arms about him. ... She cried in the ill-lit carriage. No need to hide her tears there. Suddenly she felt her mother's hand on her face. Thérèse's voice rose on a note of impatience:

'I've told you he'll come back, my dear'; and then, with her old familiar laugh: 'You'll have quite enough of him before you're done. You'll find out that he's just like any other man – just a great, coarse male!'

II

TIME, which always spells defeat for love, treats hate more slowly – but the end, in either case, is the same. On the platform of Saint-Clair station Thérèse failed to return the salute of the bald gentleman who was waiting for the train's arrival. It was Bernard, her husband. Had she seen him casually in a Paris street, she would probably not have recognized him. He was less fat than she remembered him. A plum-coloured pull-over fitted tightly round his stomach and the little bulge which was the product of too many 'nips'. He still could not tie a stock properly. There was boredom as well as timidity in the expression with which he contemplated this mad creature for whom he had got to make himself respons-ible: but no other course was open to him – of that he felt sure. Bad luck is bad luck, and that's all there is to it. But, as his mother was fond of saying, 'however much one may condemn divorce ...' It really was a bit hard that after all these years of separation this woman should be unloaded on him. Still, it was a matter of principle ... besides, the law is the law.

'You must be very careful, Papa,' said Marie. 'Give her your arm as far as the car.'

Seated at the wheel, Bernard took comfort in the thought that it had not been necessary to say anything. The effort of explaining, even of expressing himself, had become, with the years, more and more terrifying to him. Whether from laziness or from inability to find the right words, he had developed almost a passion for silence. He would think nothing of driving thirty miles to avoid getting home before any visitors who might be there had gone. The dread of meeting the curé or the schoolmaster in the public square entirely regulated his walks abroad. He was perfectly content to have Thérèse there at his side, so long as he needn't make conversation.

The sick woman was kept waiting in the small drawing-room. Her own room was not yet ready. She could hear a murmur of voices next door, but the sound did not worry her. Exhaustion had got the better of her mental anguish. There was nothing for her to do but await their verdict. She would obey any instructions they might give her, and they could hardly be other than to go to bed and shut her eyes. All she could do now was to surrender herself blindly to the will which had been strong enough to get her back, after fifteen years, to this little drawing-room in which she had planned her crime. The colour of the wall-paper and the curtains had been changed, the furniture was upholstered differently: but the darkness made by the enormous plane-tree outside the window was just as she remembered it. She found the same frightful objects in the old familiar places, silent witnesses of her former hatred.

They got her up to the west room, which had always been kept for guests. She had never lived in it. Nothing there reminded her of any moments in her past life – except of one afternoon ... and how vividly that came back! The family had been at Argelouse, but on the day in question she had had good reason to fear that they knew of her presence at Saint-Clair. She could see herself now, hiding in the shadows, while a servant busied herself with putting away sheets in the linen-cupboard next door.

On the evening of her arrival she had a crisis, and lay in

Marie's arms, fighting for breath. But an injection gave her
relief. Then, during the night, she had a second, more violent
one, and nearly died. From then on everything became simple,
both for her and for the Desqueyroux. She was certain now
that she had nothing more to fear. The figure of death stood
between her exhausted frame and the hue and cry which had
haunted her imagination. So far as the Desqueyroux were
concerned, the chief obstacle had been overcome by reason
of her desperate condition. Her mother-in-law, who had
sought sanctuary at Argelouse, and had told Bernard that she
would not set foot in the Saint-Clair house 'so long as that
monster is there', had failed to put in an appearance, though
she had gone so far as to lay down her arms. 'We must leave
her,' she had written to Bernard – 'to the mercy of God.' She
had also said: 'Our little Marie is being quite wonderful.'

The girl had undertaken the whole duty of looking after
Thérèse. As little use as possible was made of the servants, in
order to avoid gossip. 'She's done us enough harm as it is. ...'
The sick woman surrendered herself entirely to her daughter's
ministrations with a show of confidence which lasted until
close on Christmas, though as that festival approached she
became rather more restive. Marie had completely changed.
She no longer sat sewing in a sort of frenzy of activity, but
wandered up and down the room, pressing her face to the
windows. Beyond looking after her mother's bodily needs,
she paid no attention to her. 'She has received her orders,'
thought Thérèse: 'she is fighting against some influence. Our
hiding-place has been discovered. All the same, she scarcely
ever goes out. ... But there are all sorts of ways in which
they can get messages to her in code. They're working on her
from outside. But whatever they do, they won't poison me.
Still, just because she's my daughter, they've got an idea into
their heads.' Such was the meaning of the words which she
muttered to herself.

One dismal morning, when the rain was lashing the windows, she felt perfectly convinced that she had been betrayed,
because Marie, buttoned up in a blue oilskin, told her that
she was going out, and asked whether there was anything she

wanted. Oh, whirligig of time! The same question which, in her loneliness, she used to put to Anna on the evenings when the little maid used to appear in her best tailored suit and imitation lizard shoes found words now: 'Going out, dear? Aren't you afraid of getting wet? ...' But it was addressed this time to Marie, with the same certainty that nothing in the world would stop her from going to meet whomever it was who might be waiting for her. And, indeed, in spite of the reassuring words which the girl spoke (she needed exercise ... one always went out in Paris no matter what the weather, so why not in the country, especially here, where the sandy soil absorbed the rain?) there was a fierce look in her eyes which said as plainly as any words: 'If need be, I'd trample you underfoot. ...'

Two evenings ago the Christmas holidays had brought Georges Filhot back to Saint-Clair. The Filhot's cook had passed the news on to the butcher, and Marie could not resist the temptation to send him a note: 'Can't we say good-bye? I'll be at Silhet, the empty farmhouse, about ten o'clock tomorrow. ...'

He wouldn't come. She kept on telling herself that he wouldn't come. At the door she turned to blow a kiss to her mother, who, propped against her pillows, was following her every movement with tormented eyes. But one gets accustomed to the sufferings of invalids when one has been nursing them for a long time.

As she crossed the little square she repeated the words of Georges' terrible undertaking: 'I have sworn that nothing shall make me break my silence; no prayer, no threat.' Even should he risk coming to the tryst, what likelihood, was there that she would find any happiness in the meeting? All the same, she was filled with hope – the hope which her mother daily encouraged. More than once Thérèse had made reference to the grandchildren whom she would never see. Only last evening she had said:

'You are learning how to be a nurse. You are learning patience. You will have to be very patient with him.'

Though Marie realized that those had been the words of a

mad woman, she remembered them now as she left the Argelouse road, rutted by farm waggons, and turned into a sandy
track where the dust had been barely laid by the rain. The
leaves were still on the oaks: the air was mild. Winter, in this
heath country of the south-west, seemed like an indefinite
prolongation of autumn. The rain created about her a sort
of stuffy hothouse world which was filled with the smell of
rotting wood and dead bracken. She could see through the
pine-stems that the sheep-byres, where in the old days they had
tethered their horses, were now open to the sky. The farmhouse chimney was smoking. Someone had kindled a fire of
shavings and pine-cones. Perhaps it was the shepherd. Better
for her if it had been ...

She entered the house. The smoke made her eyes smart.
Georges was seated on a pile of twigs, his legs stretched to the
blaze. At sight of her he jumped to his feet. She noticed that
he had grown thinner, and that, as always when he was tired,
the cast in his eye was more marked than ever. He had put
on the spectacles which formerly she had forbidden him to
wear when he was with her. She maintained that they made him
look ugly. He had not even taken the trouble to shave. He
was, as he had always been to her, a great, overgrown boy,
at once passionate and weak, and she, her face wet from the
rain and whipped to a high colour, her eyes shining, was
conscious of her own heightened vitality. ... She was wearing,
with her tweed suit, a pair of shiny boots which reached half-
way up her calves. She thanked him for coming. He told her
to get close to the fire, and made room for her.

The scrawls, the initials, and the drawings executed in
charcoal on the walls were as clear as they had been a year ago.
Had she wished to recapture him, how easy it would have been.
She had but to take his hand. But, realizing why he had come,
she got up.

'I'm not cold,' she said. 'No, stay where you are. That letter
of yours wasn't the end. I didn't want to go away without
saying good-bye, but once that is done, I promise to leave you
in peace.'

He assured her that he did not want to be left in peace. But his protestation brought her no sense of joy. He looked, she noticed, as he had always done at such moments. A hint of local brogue had crept into his voice: his breath came in short pants: his coarse lower lip showed with too bright a red. All this she took in quite coldly. She felt nothing of her former pain, was even aware of a certain sense of repulsion. Yet it was not he who loved her, but she whom passion had caught by the throat, so that she longed to die. He realized that he was 'making a mess of things', and did not insist (he never did). He told himself that he was a fool for coming, and started to whistle, his eyes on the fire. 'I've got some new records,' he said: 'absolutely top-hole ones. But, of course, I'd forgotten ... you don't care about music. ...'

Without bothering any more about her, he proceeded to indulge in a private concert – 'la, li, la, la'. She thought of her mother lying in the room which looked to the west, its windows streaming with rain, a terrified expression on her face. She asked a question at random to put an end to the whistling.

'How is your friend Mondoux?'

'Would you believe it ... but, of course, you don't really know him. If you did, you'd realize how very oddly he's behaving. He's suddenly discovered the existence of women! He says it's a marvellous experience – that it's brought him everything he wants. Poor Mondoux! the thing's become a perfect mania with him. ... If only you knew him. ... But ... Why are you crying, Marie? I'd hoped that you had learned common sense. ...' She stammered through her tears (and the words were a lie):

'I'm not crying about you.'

'You mean it's not I who am causing you pain now? I thought as much.'

He laughed rather self-consciously.

'I've become terribly attached to her,' said Marie, wiping her eyes, 'though there was a time when I used to detest her. At moments her poor brain is completely wandering. But the odd thing is that her personality remains as strong as ever. It can't go on for long – not for more than a few months, probably. One of her crises might prove fatal at any moment.'

Georges said:

'Of whom are you speaking?'

She looked at him with amazement. She could not imagine how it was possible for him to have been at Saint-Clair for twenty-four hours without knowing all about Thérèse Desqueyroux's arrival and hearing what was wrong with her. She could only suppose that the Filhots had deliberately refrained from mentioning her name in his hearing.

'I had to bring my mother back with me,' she said. 'It's not just her nerves – it's something much worse. She's had two crises since we got here. It's all up with her,' she added with a sob.

But it was no more 'up with' her mother today than it had been on any of the preceding days, when Marie had been dry-eyed, had eaten her meals with a keen appetite, had read her paper, and had wondered what would happen to her once Thérèse was dead. She dabbed at her cheeks. She must not bore Georges, who, no doubt from a sense of fitness, had left off whistling. 'I beg your pardon,' she said. He had drawn near to the fire again, and was holding out his two hands like a screen. Without looking at her, he asked:

'Do you think she would recognize me?'

'I'm sure she would! She's got all sorts of odd whimsies in her head – imagines that the police are after her. But apart from that she is perfectly sensible, and, provided she doesn't think you are one of her enemies ...'

'Incredible!' he said in a low voice. 'A woman of such intelligence! ... But it doesn't matter now, since you say there's no hope?' He spoke the last words on a note of interrogation. He seemed to be suffering.

Marie looked at him, and he turned his attention once more to the fire.

'The doctor thinks that the next crisis will carry her off.'

'Thérèse!' he exclaimed in scarcely more than a whisper. Marie could not see his face. She noticed that he passed the back of his hand several times across his eyes. She asked:

'Were you two so deeply attached? ... I hadn't realized.'

'I don't suppose I saw her more than three or four times in all, but once would have been enough.'

He relapsed into silence. A little later Marie heard him murmur:

'The world without her ...'

The rain dripped from the roof and gathered in puddles between the broken floor-tiles. The moaning of the pines around the abandoned farmstead filled the air with the sound of an infinite lamentation. She had never seen him suffer emotionally for anyone but himself. This look of passion in his face was new to her. With her he always seemed like a dead man, had the look of a dead man. It was a commonplace among the neighbours to say, 'He seems so *dead*' ... and now, for the first time, he was showing signs of animation, was coming alive. Yet her mind did not check suddenly at the thought that her mother might conceivably have played the traitor. Marie was seventeen: how could she have imagined that this young man could feel a sentimental interest for an old, distraught woman? Because distraught was, in fact, what she had always been. ... Suddenly the girl spoke her thought in a hard little voice:

'She has always been mad. We have always known it. She is mentally unbalanced – and dangerous, as we have learned to our cost. As a matter of fact, that is what makes her so interesting to you, isn't it?'

He answered her with an air of weariness:

'You don't understand me ... you never have understood me. ... You are incapable of realizing that I am the kind of man who can never *not* be conscious of himself. ...'

'Oh, but I *do* understand you,' she broke in with a laugh; 'indeed I do!'

'No' – he pressed his point with a note of scorn in his voice – 'you don't understand me. You don't know what it is like never, for a single moment, to be sure of one's own identity. ... That sort of talk seems idiotic, mad, to you. But it's not my fault if I am aware, all the time, of this mental disintegration in myself. ... The very first time I set eyes on Thérèse I realized ...'

'Thérèse? – so you call her that?'

She began to laugh again.

'I realized – oh, how can I explain? – that she would drive me along the track of my own tormented consciousness. Yes, that was clear to me from the very first words she spoke. She read me with quite extraordinary clarity: she explained me to myself. For the first time I took on form and substance *to myself*. So long as she was there, I *existed*. Even when we were apart I had only to think of her. But now ...'

In a whisper he uttered the words, 'Thérèse – dead!' – and covered his face with his hands. Marie was aware of a mixed emotion, part irritation, part jealousy. It was with her as when he put on a record which she found boring, when she would so much have preferred that he should talk or make love to her. But there was something in her present mood the significance of which she did not yet realize, something that took the form of a vast and confused sense of misery.

'Still,' she said, in the same hard little voice, 'don't forget – though God knows *I've* forgiven her – that she *did* commit ...'

And when Georges, with a shrug, said irritably, 'Surely you're not going to go over all that old ground?' she replied with a sudden spurt of anger:

'I seem to remember that you didn't find it so unimportant once! I suppose *you* don't remember how indignant you were that I had failed to get her to tell me *why* she did – what she did do?'

'Oh yes, I do ... I don't think I realized at the time why I was so interested in that business about the poison. I thought then' (he hesitated, searching for the right word, and shot a glance at Marie) 'that it was because I had such a high respect for her, and that made me anxious to get my mind clear on the point. I couldn't bear to suspect so remarkable a woman of such a horrible crime. At least, that is what I believed my motive to be at the time. But I find it so hard to be sure what I really did feel. As soon as I can give a clear definition to my feelings, they cease to be genuine. It is only afterwards that I realize precisely how my mind was working. I protested my faith in your mother's innocence, and pretended to believe that she could not have been guilty of such a thing, simply and solely because I wanted to get out of her the answer for which I was longing. And I did get it – straight between the eyes. She told me that that crime had been one only among many that she had committed every day, that we all of us commit. Yes, Marie, you too. The world recognizes as crimes only what the law can take hold of, violence that is tangible and capable of proof. ... It wasn't long before she made me dig up from the darkness of my past a mean little act of which I had been guilty, a tiny scorpion chosen from among a thousand similar ...'

'What do you mean, a "scorpion"?'

'If I told you about that schoolboy foolishness you would say, "Is that all? – just a little thing like that?" Where is the use in me trying to make you understand what I *know*, what your mother knows, too?'

'Oh, I realize that I'm just a poor little fool!' Marie grumbled. 'I know that tone of yours when you say, "What an idiot the girl is!" and it's no use your denying it. ...'

It was pointless for her to suggest that he should. He showed no anxiety to disclaim her charge, but all too readily agreed with her. She *was* a little idiot, for ever shut out from the world of his sufferings, the world into which she could never follow him. But, at least, she had something that her mother had not got. There was some comfort, she thought, in being seventeen, in being able to bury her face in the shoulder of the man she loved. ... She sat down on the pile of turves and began fondling Georges' forehead and temples and ill-shaved cheeks. He was probably thinking that she was just a girl avid for sensation, but he was wrong. That was not really what she wanted, but what else was there left for her to want? She would have given everything she had to be able to walk with him in that world to which her mother had found the key without any difficulty at all. ... Besides, does being held in a man's arms preclude one from understanding him? Perhaps her mother ... She shook her head in an access of horror. That mad woman? ... Mad? She had not been mad in

those Paris days when Georges had first got to know her. ...
Poor Marie, on what food was her imagination to feed? She
hid her face in the hollow of his shoulder, her arms tight
about him, and stayed thus for a long time. Rest, at last! It
was as though, after so much hostility, he was ready, now, to
accept the gift of herself. She could feel the measured rhythm
of his breathing.

'Do you think,' he asked, 'that she would let me go to see
her?'

There was violence in the gesture with which she broke
away from him. She got up, and he made no effort to prevent
her. She went to the open door, took several deep breaths of
the mild and rain-drenched mist, then turned to him.

'We can go at once, now, if you want to,' she said, quite
calmly.

'No, no – not now.'

'Any afternoon, then ... I'm always there, and I'll tell her
you've come.'

'It might, perhaps, be as well if we weren't seen together,'
he said, after a moment's pause. 'You'd better go first, since
you're walking.'

He had to look her straight in the eyes as he spoke. What did
he read in her expression that he should feel suddenly frightened? Hastily, he added:

'She loved you: you do realize that, don't you? You occupied her mind to the exclusion of all else. Care for your
happiness was an obsession with her. It is just as well you
should know that I existed for her only because of you. That
is true – I swear it is! But you knew it already, didn't you?
You do believe me, Marie?'

'What's so odd,' she said with a laugh, 'is that you should
think it necessary to reassure me. Doesn't that strike you as
funny?'

She waved her hand. He watched the wall of rain close
about her, then went back and sat down once more against
the pile of turves.

MARIE hung her dripping 'oily' in the dressing-room. Thérèse followed her with her eyes. She knew already, from certain almost imperceptible signs, that the woman who had come into the room was her enemy – her mortal enemy. A rainy silence pressed about the house. None of the bells were working. Bernard Desqueyroux had gone back to his mother at Argelouse.

'You didn't get too wet, darling?' she queried, but the question remained unanswered.

'Did you meet anybody?'

'No one of the slightest interest. ... Time for your medicine.'

The sound of the saucer on the marble top of the wash-stand, of a cork being drawn from a bottle, of a spoon being stirred in a cup – from out of the dim past these little tinklings came rushing back into the consciousness of the woman lying there in a frenzy of terror. Just so had she heard them in the close heat of a long-dead time of siesta, when hurriedly she had emptied the last drop of poison into a cup, so that peace and quiet might be restored to her, and muted death complete its task without breaking the silence which lay within the room and on the world.

It was Marie now who came towards her, cup in hand, stirring the liquid with a spoon. She was close to the bed, her back to the light. It was difficult to see the expression of her face as she bent above the concoction. ... There was nothing of her mother in her appearance, but, seen in silhouette against the window, she might have been her mother's ghost. This was Thérèse drawing close to Thérèse.

'No! Marie ... No!'

She pushed away the cup with a little gesture of panic, looking up at her daughter with supplicating eyes. Suddenly Marie understood. It would have been easy for her to take, as she so often did, a sip: no more than that was needed to set the sick woman's fears at rest. Perhaps the idea did cross her mind. Why, then, did she not make the effort?

Whatever the reason, she did not. Instead, she said harshly: 'You must drink it.'

Seeing that her mother had fallen into one of those trembling fits of which she had been free since coming to Saint-Clair, she asked with an assumption of innocence:

'Surely you're not frightened of me, are you?'

Now at last, Thérèse stood upon the terrible summit. She must stop for breath. She could go no farther. She had reached the term, not of human suffering, but of her own ordeal, the limit of her endurance. The moment had come for her to pay her debt. She could not now refuse. She was trembling no longer, but, looking at Marie, took the cup in her two hands and drained it at a single gulp, her gaze still fixed upon the shadowed face. Marie took back the cup, as she, herself, had taken another cup from Bernard fifteen years before, and went to rinse it in the dressing-room, as she, too, had done. She buried her face in the pillows. Nothing to do now but wait for the moment when she should say to Someone, 'Here is thy creature, worn by unending struggles with herself. Thy will be done.' She had turned her head a little sideways, and her eyes sought the plaster crucifix which hung upon the wall. With deliberate care she crossed her left foot over her right, and slowly spread her arms and opened her hands.

Because she had reached the summit she was already on the reverse slope. She knew now that the cup had contained no poison, that Marie was innocent of crime. 'I must have been mad to believe such a thing.' But what of all the rest, of the vast nightmare through which she had been moving? The mist shredded away from before her eyes, revealing the real world.

'Marie!'

girl got up from the arm-chair into which she had

'd you meet this morning? No, don't turn your
dow. Come where I can see your face.'

ow whom I met? A man who had arranged

to meet me, a man who was waiting for me in a lonely spot ...'

'Why do you want to frighten me, my child?'

'I don't want to frighten you. The man who spoke to me a while ago at Silhet is not one of your enemies. ... The very reverse, in fact. ... He is coming here to see you, quite soon.'

'In all the world there is nobody who loves me!'

'Oh yes, there is – somebody who was waiting for me at a deserted farm. ... Surely I need not tell you his name. You can guess, can't you?'

'You saw him? He was waiting for you? Look in my eyes. Do I seem to show regret for him? Don't you remember, Marie, all that I have done with him on your behalf? Didn't I foretell ...?'

The girl shook her head with a sullen air. 'Don't you know what it is I long for?'

Yes, perhaps she did ... but all that she remembered now was Georges in the kitchen at Silhet ... his tears.

'*You* may have longed ... but he! ... Don't you realize what you are to him?'

'You little fool!' said Thérèse. 'An old woman who is ready to listen to the story of men's lives and pretends to understand always enjoys a certain prestige. She is admired, loved, and mourned when she is dead. Young people have no one to whom they can talk. It is so rare, at twenty, to find anyone who will listen and understand. ... But that is quite different, dear child, from ... that has nothing to do with ... love. I feel quite ashamed to use the word. Coming from me it is a matter for laughter.'

'If only you could have seen how he was suffering. ...'

'Of course he was suffering. ... In a sort of way he clings to me. He will miss me for a few days. ... but after that, you'll see! You'll have your fill, later, of his talk about himself. You'll say, "If only poor mamma were here, she'd take him off my hands for a bit!" ...'

She laughed as she talked of these things, and her laughter now was natural. She looked younger, but, for all that, there was something terrible about her bared gums. Yes, thought Marie, it *was* something quite different from love. Why should she be anxious? When all was said, Georges had been at Silhet before her, had been eagerly awaiting her arrival, had been longing for just that show of tenderness which she had withheld. She knew from experience that in those moods of disappointment he became hostile and indifferent. What her mother was saying was true:

'When you are seventeen you can't hope to see far into a man's mind. Your empire over him will grow as year follows year. ... You see if it doesn't. ...'

The rain had stopped. The plane-trees on the Square were dripping.

'You ought to take advantage of the sun. ... Go for a stroll in the South Walk.'

'But what about you, Mamma?'

'I'll have a little sleep. Don't worry about me. You can leave me alone now, I'm not afraid any longer.'

Marie kissed her. 'You really are cured?'

Thérèse nodded and smiled. She listened to her daughter's steps receding. Now, at last, she could feast upon what she had discovered. Georges had suffered, had wept to hear that she was dying. No, she must put that happiness from her, that monstrous happiness. When the heart torments us at the very gates of death it is as though the long arrears of passion can break our backs even on the threshold of nothingness. ... He would come, and Marie would be there. She must make herself ready for that confrontation, that she might show no overt sign either of her pain or of her love.

13

THE first evening that he came a single lamp was burning on the table. Thérèse explained by signs that she could not speak. He saw her hands, like those of a skeleton, stained with purplish patches, lying spread upon the sheet. Only by degrees could he make out what was left of the face that he had known – the root of the nose, the bony structure of the forehead and the jaw. But what vitality there still was in the gaze whose fixity he found it hard to endure! She took his hand as he stood close beside the bed. Marie, a few paces behind, looked at them.

'Come close, Marie.'

The girl took a few steps forward. Thérèse grasped her wrist and forced herself to join their hands within her own. Marie made as though to withdraw hers, but Georges held it hard until she gave up the struggle. They dared not draw apart because Thérèse had closed her fingers about their linked palms.

Gradually her grasp relaxed. They thought she was asleep, and reached the door, walking on tip-toe. Then Thérèse opened her eyes. She was fighting for breath. What a long time Marie was taking! She must have gone with him to the front-door. Perhaps, standing there, with mud and rotting leaves about their feet, they were plighting their troth with a kiss. ... The frightful pain which gripped her chest eased when, at last, the girl returned and sat down at the other end of the room, as far as possible from the bed.

Thérèse could read nothing on the averted face. She did not know that her daughter was thinking: 'In the whole of my life I shall never go half as far as this old woman has gone in the last few days. ... It is because of her that he has accepted me, has raised me from the ground – for her sake, in memory of her. ...'

Thérèse was far from imagining that Marie could entertain such bitter thoughts. Had she known, would the knowledge have caused her pain – or joy? She could not herself have said what answer she hoped would come when suddenly she asked:

'Are you happy, Marie?'

The girl dropped her hand from before her eyes.

'I thought you were asleep.'

Once more a note of supplication came into the elder woman's voice:

'Swear to me that you are happy.'

Marie went over to the table, saying, 'Time for your medicine,' and once again Thérèse listened carefully to the sound of the bottle being uncorked, to the tinkle of the spoon against the cup.

About midnight the dying woman had a crisis. When she came round from her syncope, the first thing she saw was Marie's watching face.

'What terrible pain you must have been through, Mamma!'

'No, I felt nothing, except the prick when you used the hypodermic. ...'

But that rattling in the throat and that congested face? Is it possible that human beings can go through such a hell of agony, yet keep no memory of it?

The doctor arrived, still half-asleep, with puffy eyes and his hair tousled. He had put on a top-coat over his nightshirt. After listening to Thérèse's heart, he followed Marie into the passage. Their whispering was interspersed with bursts of louder talk. 'But of course you must get them. It's not far to Argelouse. Tomorrow morning, then, first thing ... not later.'

Was this the end? As it happened, Thérèse was not feeling particularly ill. She found it impossible to believe that she was going to die. When next she woke she saw Bernard Desquey-roux, still wearing his goatskin coat, and Marie, both standing in the room looking at her. She assured them with a smile that she felt better. Bernard left the room with much squeaking of shoe-leather, while the girl, after performing a few small services for the patient, settled herself in an arm-chair. A little later she joined her father on the landing. This time Thérèse could not overhear what was being said, though she could recognize her mother-in-law's high-pitched tones. The whole family was waiting on the event. All normal life was in a state of suspense. ... But they were wrong, thought Thérèse: she was not going to die yet.

Bernard came back into the room. He had taken off the goatskin.

'I've come to relieve Marie. ... The poor young people must have a chance to see one another.'

She realized then that the engagement had been officially announced. Bernard sat down at some distance from the bed, and took a newspaper from his pocket. Was he going to stay there all day? Just before luncheon he left her, but came back in the afternoon, and remained at his post until Marie arrived to close the shutters. During the next few days he observed the same routine. Never a word did he speak. The paper crackled a little in his fingers, and whenever he turned or folded back a page there was a great noise of rumpling which got on Thérèse's nerves.

His last visit of the day took place when the doctor turned up, always rather late, at the end of his round. This particular doctor gave off a smell of pipe-tobacco. His beard, sparkling with raindrops, caused Thérèse no feeling of disgust. He listened perfunctorily to her heart and said: 'We're coming along nicely.' They must be beginning to realize that she was not going to die after all. ... Why was Georges Filhot prolonging his stay at Saint-Clair? What was *he* waiting for? 'He can read for his exam without going to lectures,' Marie said. Perhaps, too, he had decided to remain with his father, who needed him. ... Paris no longer attracted him. One day the girl remarked:

'Don't you remember, it was after he'd seen you that you had your heart attack? He'll come again when you're better. The doctor won't allow any visitors except the members of the family. ... What was that you said?'

Without opening her eyes, Thérèse answered: 'But I've not the least desire, dear, to see him.'

Bernard, whom she had so completely forgotten, had once more become a part of her life. As once before, so now, he was solidly established in her days – thinner than he had been, more careless in his dress, his head drooping forward so that she could see the back of his neck, silent, with that bloodshot look which comes into the eyes of a man who habitually takes too many 'nips', and has probably had a slight stroke. It was no longer matter for wonder to her that she had done what she had done. Now that the same man was there before her, weighing down her whole existence with his sheer bodily bulk, nothing seemed to her more natural than to want to get rid of him, to free herself for ever of his presence. ... She had failed in her attempt, and he was still there. It was she, this time, who was going to die, he who would do the watching, who would feel that same impatient desire to get it all over and done with that had been hers fifteen years ago. He crumpled the paper, cleared his throat, and twisted his little finger violently in his ear. Whenever he came back from the Café Lacoste, where his own particular table was always reserved for him, he had frequently to put his hand before his mouth with a muttered apology. Thérèse pretended that she wanted to sleep. When that happened, he went into the room next door, being careful to leave the door open. Although she could no longer see him, she was conscious of him as a living entity. 'No, no,' she said to herself, 'I don't really want him not to be ...' but beneath the deposits which the receding tide of life had left behind that one desire was ever present, as young, as fresh as ever, eternally indestructible.

Thérèse could not make up her mind to die. As a matter of fact she was noticeably improving. Her appetite had returned, and she was no longer oppressed by terrors. Of course, her heart might 'let her down' at any moment.

'We quite understand that, Doctor,' said her mother-in law; 'but meanwhile it does nothing of the sort.' Marie was at the end of her strength, and could watch beside the invalid no longer. Bernard, when it was fine, went out shooting. Someone else would have to be found.

One morning Marie asked her mother whether she still distrusted Anna, and when Thérèse, with a shrug, replied, 'You know perfectly well that I wasn't right in my head ... poor little Anna,' went on, '... because she'll be here this evening. She's bringing your clean linen. ... It'll only be for two months. She is engaged to a chauffeur who is touring with his employers. But in two months' time ...'

'In two months' time?'

Marie blushed and said:

'You'll be up and about, Mamma.'

Anna's presence brought a great change into her life. Marie

and her father put in only short appearances now, in the morning and in the evening. Thérèse had once more become as a child who finds comfort in the proximity of its nurse. She need fear nothing so long as Anna was there. The little maid seemed to take pleasure in rendering her the most squalid services. She never appeared to be bored.

'I have all my trousseau to make, and you know what that means!' She had grown thinner, and pretended to be in no hurry to see her fiancé. Still, she would have to leave very soon now. The chauffeur might arrive at any moment. He was looking for a place ... and wasn't very keen on staying in Paris. ... Thérèse, listening to her humble prattle, thought, 'By that time I shall be dead.' She could no longer contemplate life without Anna.

Suddenly, up from the dark recesses of the house there came a spurt of music: piano, violin, and cello filled the gloomy afternoon.

'The gramophone,' said Anna. 'They've come back.'

On fine days, when the betrothed pair went out riding, she could hear, in the morning, the stamping of horses in the paved yard. Their return was heralded afar off by the sound of the eight hooves on the frozen road. But when it was foggy or raining the noise of the gramophone was the only sign that Georges was present in the house. At such times Thérèse lay there imagining that the music set a great sea of sound between the young man and his Marie which the girl could not cross. Thérèse was the only one who could walk on that watery surface, and so draw near to the lost mortal on the farther shore. ... But before that could be they must let him come, just once more, to the room in which she lay. She had something to say to him, something urgent. It had nothing to do with love. ... But who could be sure that it was not of her that he was thinking when he put on those records of the *Archduke Trio*, which, she remembered, they had discussed one evening.

'No!' exclaimed Thérèse. 'No!'

'Who are you saying "No" to? You're dreaming, you poor dear!'

The maid approached the bed. Thérèse took the large coarse hand and held it until she felt it grow damp in hers.

'How long, Anna, before your young man returns?'

'A fortnight, ma'am.'

'A fortnight! Nonsense! ... I shall still be alive in a fortnight!'

'Quite enough alive to do without me!'

Towards dusk, Bernard came into the room. Thérèse said:

'I have one last favour to ask of you. ... Don't look like that: it's all right; it won't cost you much.'

He assumed a worried air.

'You know how bad times are ... what with resin ... everything's going from bad to worse. Have you seen today's market prices?'

'Just one final whim of mine. ... I should so much like it if, for the little time that remains, you would engage a chauffeur ... Anna's young man.'

'A chauffeur! You must be mad! I got rid of the one I had eighteen months ago. A chauffeur, indeed, with resin ...'

'Yes, so that Anna can stay on here. It won't be for long.'

'One can never be sure with heart trouble. ... You've got the doctor thoroughly puzzled. ... A chauffeur! What should we do with him all day? That's the last sort of suggestion I should have expected. You've chosen a fine time, I must say! ...'

Usually so silent, he stunned her now with words. Indignation made him loquacious. She did not feel strong enough to argue. There was nothing she could do about it. Here she was, on the point of death, and he refused her the one thing above all others for which she really longed – Anna's continued presence ... and just for the sake of a few banknotes! Hadn't she been ready to give up the whole of her fortune?

She said with a sigh:

'I'm ready to surrender everything. ...'

'Oh, now ...'

He broke off, but it was too late. Thérèse knew what he had been about to say – now that they would come into the money anyhow. ... She gave him a look which must have stirred his memories, even after fifteen years.

'Go on talking, my dears ... I don't seem to hear you saying anything. ...'

'But we *were* talking ... Grandmamma. ...'

'I thought she'd gone to bed,' Marie whispered, snuggling up to Georges. 'When you shut your eyes like that, darling, you look as though you were dead. ... You know, don't you, that Mamma wants you to pay her one more visit? Ah! that's woke you up! She's promised she won't have a heart attack this time. ... I think there's something important she wants to tell you.'

'I'll go tomorrow if the doctor will let me.'

'Oh, she's seen to that. ... I wonder what it is she wants to talk about. ... You will tell me, won't you?'

He made no answer. The public clock began to strike: the sound continued for a long time. The old lady's voice exclaimed from the back drawing-room:

'Eleven! ... It's time I turned you out, Georges. ...'

He did not know that almost every night, when he took his departure, he woke Thérèse, and she followed as long as possible the sound of his footsteps through the sleeping village, where the dogs started a sudden frenzy of barking. A little snow had fallen during the last three days, but had melted almost as soon as it reached the ground. It shone faintly on the roof-tiles. Tomorrow he would see her once again. She must not vanish from this world until he had confided to her what, for so many days, he had been turning over and over in his mind. 'I will say to her ...' He raised his eyes towards the winter stars. What would he say to her? That she could sleep now undisturbed by any anxiety on his account; that she had done him no harm; that she had done nobody any harm; that it was her mission to force an entry into half-dead hearts and there turn up the soil; that with her sharp stare she cut deep into the waste stuff of men's souls, making them, at long last, fruitful. ... What did Marie matter to him ... or any other woman? What Saint-Clair or Paris, the family timber-yards and sawmills or the School of Law? ... It was from the spring which Thérèse had made to gush deep within him that he must draw new life ... from this pain, this yearning, always frustrated for a passion that should know no end. Never more would he be satisfied with himself, never, never know contentment. He would learn to find those limits of his nature beyond which stretched the leagues of an infinite passion. ... Obscure and terrifying little acts, accomplished in loneliness and deep security, mark out our limitations more surely than great crimes. ...

Thus Georges pondered, as his footsteps echoed between the walls of the deserted village.

'I'll stay out here on the landing,' said Marie dryly. 'Mind, now, only five minutes. When they're up I shall come in.'

He was aware that he hated the voice of this woman at whose side he must, from now on, live and die. He pushed open the door. Thérèse was seated beside a blazing fire. At first sight he thought that she looked fatter. Her cheeks were rounded (though that may have been the effect of a slight swelling). Her eyes seemed smaller. Beside her, on a low table, stood a bell, several bottles, and a half-full cup. The blinds were not yet lowered, and the window-panes looked black.

She gave him a sidelong glance, but almost immediately turned away her eyes. ... He kissed her hand and smiled. But she seemed worried about something, and moved her lips as though the right words would not come. He said nothing, thinking it was she who ought to begin their talk.

'Well ... but first of all, promise me ... it's about ... I hardly dare ...'

She looked at him anxiously.

'It all depends on you. ... Your father has lorries, hasn't he?'

He thought she must be delirious.

'What have lorries to do with it?'

'Because ... he's had experience in driving heavy vehicles ... Anna's young man, I mean. ... If your father could take him on ... He has first-rate references. ... In that case, you see, I shouldn't lose the girl. ... But I hardly dare hope. It would be too wonderful!'

Hungrily she tried to interpret his expression. He did not seem very happy. Why was he frowning?

'If what I've said annoys you ...'

He protested that of course it didn't. He would mention the matter to his father. He didn't think there was a vacancy just at present ... but they could certainly find something for the man to do until one occurred. ... She sighed happily, and looked at him. His head was bent forward, and he had that same look of a naughty dog which she had noticed on a certain night in the rue du Bac. ... From very far off, thickened by distance, she heard a voice. 'It's he,' it said: 'he, and for the last time ... the dearly loved youth ...' Yes, it was Georges. In what way had she hurt him now that he should turn on her that suffering gaze? He saw the trouble in her eyes. Now was the moment to fling at her what he had made up his mind to say, what she was no longer capable of understanding. He began:

'No, you never harmed me. ...'

He had forgotten all the rest that he had prepared so carefully. He asked her a question, at random:

'Do you want to go to sleep?'

Marie opened the door and called to him that the five minutes were up. Leaning against the frame, she could see Georges standing there, bent slightly forward above Thérèse's chair, which, for her, was out of sight. He seemed not to have heard her voice, and repeated the question he had put:

'Do you want to go to sleep?'

The sick woman shook her head. She scarcely ever slept now, because of the difficulty she found in breathing. The nights seemed endless.

'Would you like a book?'

No, she could not read now. 'I just do nothing. I hear the clocks strike, I wait for the end. ...'

'The end of the night, you mean?'

Suddenly she seized his hands. Only for a few seconds could he bear upon his face the fire of desperate tenderness that flamed in her eyes.

'Yes, my dear: the end of life, the end of the night.'